TAKING THE WORLD

PART THREE OF THE STARCHILD SERIES

BOBBIE FALIN

Taking the World

The Starchild Series, Volume 3

Bobbie Falin

Published by High Flying Press, 2022.

This is a work of fiction. Similarities to real people, places, or events are entirely coincidental.

TAKING THE WORLD

First edition. September 28, 2022.

ISBN: 978-1736642252

Written by Bobbie Falin.

Table of Contents

to Sam, forever

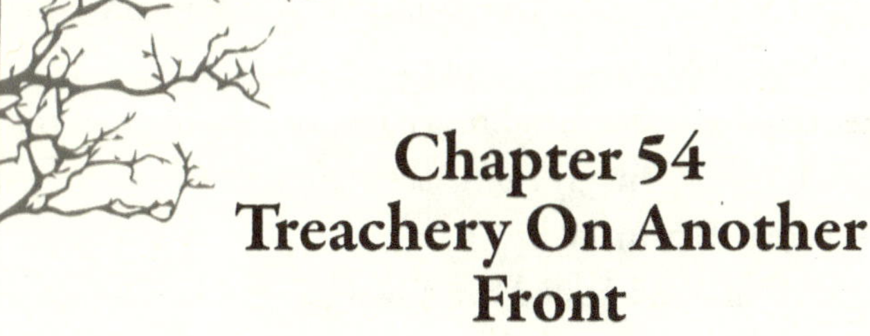

Chapter 54
Treachery On Another Front

The moonlight dimmed, then brightened again.

"Oh, Kep!" A wave of shock and confusion boiled up from the warriors around Kaphri. Connecting hands broke grips as they scattered.

Before she could react, everything changed.

She was on her back in darkness, her clothes soaking wet, the air around her heavy with cold damp. A shrill scream of rage replaced the sound of Geffitzi dismay. Something large and powerfully heavy struck the ground near her head, sending a cold spray of mud and leaves against the side of her face.

Hredroth! She was under attack! But, from what? Where was she?

A savage sense of loss and fear wrenched her gut. Something had happened. The Geffitzi warriors...

There was a distant flicker of light above her, a sense of movement—she rolled sideways instinctively, barely avoiding a blow that sliced the air above her head. In that same instant, everything shifted again.

The silence was a thunderclap to her senses. She was standing. The air felt clean and cool. She—

All the muscles in her body went rigid as the long-absent geas crashed in to the spaces the Wyxa had held empty in the Palenquemas.

"*I said get down!*" A hand caught her arm. She felt the impact of her body hitting a rough stone surface, but there was no pain. There was no room for pain inside the torment of the geas.

Danger! Her mind screamed, fighting back. Something had gone wrong! A heartbeat ago, normally calm, calculating Geffitzi warriors had panicked—were still panicked.

But a Geffitz warrior had pulled her down beside him. A Geffitz warrior still had some control even if she did not. She rolled onto her side, burrowing against the hard body beside her—drew her knees up tight and curled into a ball.

Such pain!

"*We can't sit here.*" Tobin's mental hiss sliced through her agony. "*We have to find cover.*"

"*Damn it, Kitahn, where? There's nothing but open plaza in every direction.*"

"*Kep, I don't believe this. Of all the... Uri! The gate's open. Grab her and get inside! Tobin, take the lead.*"

What was going on? The flood of shock, panic, and, from Frax, outrage, tore at her. She fought her way back to the surface of conscious thought, but what she received from the Geffitzi minds around her only added to her confusion and mounting terror. The danger was real. Imminent. She managed to force the geas away from her senses long enough to see that it was still nighttime around them before it wrapped her in its grip again.

Remotely, she felt Uri snatch her up.

"*Damn it, Priestess, uncurl!*" A hard thumb found a pressure point.

She gasped with fresh physical pain, her limbs loosening. Then he was running.

"*The rest of you. Go! Go!*"

In a mad scurry they plunged through an opening into the deeper darkness of an enclosed space.

"*Get your feet under you.*" Uri thrust her against a stone wall and slammed into place beside her. Beyond the havoc the geas was wreaking on her perceptions, she could hear heavy breathing and knew the others had followed close behind them.

Her legs, half-bent, refused to support her. She felt a distant scrape of rough stone against her spine as her body slid slowly down the wall; it was nothing compared to the pain wracking her body. Hredroth! The agony! She tried to raise a hand to her forehead and realized that Uri had his fingers clasped tightly around her wrist.

Too much was happening. It was pushing her into a sensory overload. Defensively, she began to retreat into a mental darkness.

"*How could this happen?*" Frax's sending was a furious snarl. She felt him mentally grappling about for her. "*How could you know...? No! Uri, don't let her shut down. We need answers.*"

"*This was all a trap! You treacherous bastards...*"

"*Shut up, Velacy.*"

"*Come on, Willow.*" Uri's sending felt tight with concern and fear as his big hands chafed her wrists. "*We need you.*"

They were under some sort of attack; she knew that. From a distance she could hear her companions and feel the panic and outrage in them, but the geas was gripping her with such an intensity that she had to struggle to concentrate outside it. It was a terrible, all-engulfing need that would devour her if she did not regain control of it.

Desperately, she began to fight back against it.

But—what could be more important than succumbing to its demand? The geas ate through her thoughts, seeking to eliminate anything that would conflict with its purpose. Nothing must delay her any longer. Nothing must stop her from answering that call. Not even...

"Gemma!" she gasped.

The image of her tiny companion disintegrating into a stream of golden dust was finally enough to break the grasp of the geas and force it back into perspective. She drew another ragged breath and caught Uri's hand to let him know that she was regaining control. His fingers closed about her wrist again.

The sudden easing of the geas left her even more disoriented. She groped out telepathically, trying to distinguish something of their surroundings. They were in a large, stone, square-walled space, enveloped in darkness. She located Frax, Velacy and Seuliac pressed close against the wall beyond Uri. Past them, Tobin lie, belly to the floor, peering out the tall, narrow opening through which they had plunged. The tension that hung over them was nearly physical.

"*Where's Gemma?*" She would have surged away from the wall but Uri held her in place. She didn't notice. Instead, she searched about the space frantically with her mind.

"*What are you talking about?*"

"*I saw her. Where is she?*"

She didn't need the answering silence of five warriors to tell her the little dragon was not with them.

She'd seen her precious companion appear inside the fog-ringed circle. She'd seen her distort into a stream of gold and flow through the air toward the Swampfather's hands and the crystal that he held. The crystal that now hung around her neck.

The Ankar Mekt had locked her friend inside a talisman that could no longer serve the purpose for which they had created it and she had no idea how to free her. The realization, after her wild surge of hope, left her suddenly shattered. A tear slipped down her cheek.

It ratcheted into a shaking torrent of loss in a few short breaths.

A slap stung her cheek.

Stunned back into the present, she raised her free hand to her face.

"*All right now?*"

She gave Uri a brush of acknowledgement but his grip stayed tight about her other wrist as he broadened his sending.

"*Frax. She's back with us.*"

"*How could you bring us here? How could you know?*" The commander's questions were a blaze of anger and suspicion in her head.

"*I...*" Now that she had regained a grip on her immediate reality, it was obvious from the reactions around her that they were not at Windmer Hold. Using the crystal to teleport them out of the Wyxan swamp had been a risk. She'd thought she knew what to do, but it was not a part of her Power. It had been the only way she'd seen to stop the Ankar Mekt from sending the Geffitzi warriors to their death in the Black Temple.

But, if they were not at Windmer, where were they? "*I pictured Windmer—*"

"*This is not Windmer!*"

In the tense silence that followed, she searched her memory, frantically replaying what she remembered. The jump had been a new thing, but she'd known how to do it. There'd been no doubt. The image had been clear, the others' minds attuned to hers. Everything had been right. Everything had been...

"*Something else, outside our image. It tried to take control.*"

The warriors' curses went unheard as she took up the crystal in her free hand. In the darkness the clear droplet with the tiny fleck of gold at its center felt firm and comforting beneath her fingers. Twice it had saved her. She could not believe it had betrayed her now. Especially if Gemma—

Her hand shook so hard she had to let the crystal go.

"*So something or someone overrode the image in your mind,*" Uri said quietly.

"*Why?*" Seuliac demanded. "*What purpose would bringing us here serve?*"

Where were they? The warriors obviously knew. Their reactions were full of shock and the fearful expectation of danger, even though the feel of the structure was distinctly Geffitzi. Before she could form the question, she felt the swift edge of Frax's anger and concern inside her head again.

"*Who would want to send us here?*"

"*I don't know,*" she replied slowly. "*There was just...*" It had been too swift for her to get a clear impression, but she knew what it had not been: it was not anything of Araxis or the evil force in the Black Temple. That eliminated two very dangerous sources.

The image of the Swampfather crept into her mind. He had been there, calm despite the drastic disruption to the Wyxa's plans her retaking of the crystal had caused, as if he had anticipated it all along. He had even wished them godspeed.

There was a quick sense of Frax's measured evaluation within her outer mind.

"*Klandar Bayne.*" He shifted his attention. "*Uri? Could that Wyxan have done this?*"

"*It's possible. After so many years of Kitahni trespass they are sure to know this place from your peoples' mind-images.*" Uri's fingers relaxed from around her wrist at last. "*But why?*"

"*How do we know this isn't some plan you worked up with those creatures, Kitahn?*" Velacy snapped. "*You were the one they talked to. Maybe this is your plot...*"

"*To bring us here?*" Tobin cut in angrily. "*Are you out of your mind? Do you know what—?*"

"*Not now, Tobin!*" Frax cut him off. He turned his attentin back to Kaphri. "*Is there anyone in this place with us?*"

She responded instinctively to his question, reaching out and up. And up. Hredroth, they were on the ground floor of a large tower! If they were not at Windmer, they were somewhere very similar.

"*No,*" she said.

"Keep in mind, Priestess, these might be Geffitzi warriors."

Geffitzi warriors, here? Was that what was causing this reaction of fear in them? Where were they, that thoughts of their own people would strike such a panic? But his warning was a sobering reminder of how she had missed their presence on her first encounter with Geffitzi in Omurda.

She was quite familiar with that subtle mental essence now, however. She searched out again, concentrating heavily. *"Nothing."*

An almost tangible tension seemed to flow out of the others.

"By the Goddess!" Frax sagged against the wall with a shaky sigh of relief. "Finding myself suddenly at the land gate of Rhynog couldn't be any worse than these last few moments."

Uri gave a fervent snort of agreement beside her.

"You can have no idea." Seuliac's voice, heavy with irony, came softly out of the darkness.

There was a startled silence, then Tobin gave a sudden, hysteria-edged hoot of laughter. Uri chuckled softly beside her as low sounds of amusement rippled from the others.

Their reaction deepened Kaphri's confusion. She understood Frax's reference to Rhynog, the Aedec's main holdhall, but not their sudden relaxation of what, only moments before, had been intense fear. And shrill screams and damp forest scent were still fresh in her memory. What had that been? There had been no reaction from her companions to that. Why?

All those questions faded to insignificance in comparison to the memory of that flicker of gold she had seen in the Palenquemas. It had been Gemma, rushing in to help her. She was sure of it.

Then she was suddenly gone.

Kaphri reached out beyond the walls of the tower, sensing for any trace of her tiny golden companion.

Nothing.

This whole situation was wrong. This was not Windmer Hold. The Geffitzi weren't telling her anything and they weren't making any sense. "*But Gemma.*" she broke in. "*Did you see—.*"

"*Control your imagination and focus on what's happening now,*" Frax ordered her shortly.

Perhaps she had no experience in carrying herself or others across the face of a world in the blink of an eye, but she knew one thing for sure: whatever had happened during that last few seconds in the Palenquemas and the first few moments here had not been part of her imagination! Maybe she hadn't controlled their escape from the Palenquemas as well as she should have, but she knew—she knew—some other will had intruded into hers. She had felt it at the last moment, taking control, pushing her and the warriors' image aside. Was it whatever had attacked her moments after her arrival here, pulling her into its wet, dark realm?

Everything had happened so fast. She hadn't seen anything in the darkness.

Other things had pulled her in before... She shivered. Whatever had threatened her this time had been a physical presence with a solidity that could have killed. And those shrills of fury...

It was not a threat now, however. The Geffitz commander was right: she should focus on their immediate situation. There would be time for other concerns later.

Her companions were stirring about in the darkness. Uri and Seuliac had moved out into the center of the dark space and Frax was issuing orders.

"...stow the packs against the wall behind the right gate. Seuliac, you still have a canna disk? You hold the gate. Tobin, you, Uri and Velacy secure the tower and post a watch up top. All of you: watch out for Balandra. She can't sense their mental presence. And remember, even if they aren't here right now, they could be at any moment.

"*Priestess...*" his attention focused on her in the darkness. "*I need you with me. We're checking out the serpentine and the upper gates. There are a lot of dark, enclosed places along the way. If you sense anything, you tell me immediately.*"

She gave a mental nod.

"*What if she's wrong? What if we run into some of our own?*" Tobin demanded.

Kaphri understood Frax's hesitation when he paused: the likelihood of encountering another Geffitz in this place seemed slim based on the accuracy of her sensing, but if they did, it would be a dangerous situation.

"*Try not to take the first action, and if you have to do anything, wound or render unconscious,*" he answered at last. "*Rifkin once told me that there was a pass-phrase, 'see you in hell'. If they answer 'even the devil has some standards', say 'the devil recognizes his own'. That might identify you to any of Kitahn. Beyond that I can only say be careful.*"

She could sense Tobin's dissatisfaction with his brother's response, but he did not persist.

Frax mentally sought out for her. "*Let's go.*"

The other warriors had already moved off, Tobin, Uri and Velacy gone into the blackness while Seuliac took up a position near the gate through which they'd entered.

Although she didn't sense any physical threat around them, the warriors' continued caution kept her on edge. She stayed close on Frax's heels as she followed him deeper into the darkness of the tower.

They passed through a wide, arched opening into another large, enclosed space, then ducked beneath a half-lowered metal portcullis. A wide, walled way shimmered in moonlight and black shadow beyond. Across the cobbled pavement, she could see yet another, smaller tower with its gate open onto more blackness.

Frax paused in the shadows. "*Check it out, Priestess. Don't miss the sidewalls that parallel the road: they have passages inside them that run from this tower to the next one.*"

She knew from Windmer that the long slots in the walls boxing the road were not solely for light and air.

"*Please, where are we?*" she finally asked.

Frax seemed surprised by her question. "*Caer Cadarn.*" He looked down at her in the dim light. "*And in a potentially deadly situation. My people don't have a reputation for hospitality to strangers at the best of times. If any of Cadarn still survive here, Priestess, I don't want to come upon them unaware. For your own sake, especially, don't make a mistake.*"

With that warning, he was gone, slipping across to the opposite side of the gate in order to view the roadway from another angle.

Caer Cadarn! For a moment, Kaphri was too stunned to move. They had transported to the stronghold of the Kitahn family. Small wonder her companions had been so shocked to discover their destination. But how was that possible? She definitely had not done this! Why, in Hredroth's name, would Klandar Bayne—or anyone else—want to send them here?

A hard, impatient mental nudge brought her back to her task. Frax was waiting for her scan.

His warning fresh in her mind, she searched out with renewed care. There was no sense of life in the shadows before them or the walls beyond.

Moving into the open was a true test of faith in her sensing abilities. If she had made a mistake, she might feel the sting of a missile in her back at any moment. Her heart drummed in her ears as they slipped into the darkness of the second tower and she searched upward. Its structure was similar to the first, with two outer and one inner gate, but it was shorter than the first tower, with only three levels above them. No living presence answered her touch.

As she stepped forward her foot struck something in the darkness. It rattled loudly, echoing off bare walls.

They froze.

"*Stay still,*" Frax commanded.

There was the familiar blue glow of canna nut and they stared down at the pile of metal, rags and bones that had lain in the darkness of the guard tower, undisturbed, for over twenty-two years. The red and green of Cadarn were still visible, the red muddied to the look of dried blood in the blue light. A sword lay beyond the finger bones of the outflung arm, the weapon obviously dropped when the guard had fallen in death.

Kaphri took a quick, instinctive step backward, Frax's anger at the dead in Windmer all too vivid in her memory. How much stronger might his response be as he viewed Araxis' handiwork within his own home?

He stared at the tattered remains for a long moment before he bent to brush at the dust on the decaying cloth of the tabard. "Fallen on duty," he murmured.

She eased the breath out of her lungs in relief as he straightened and stared into the darkness ahead. "*Is the hold truly empty, then? No one of Cadarn would leave a fallen comrade like this unless they could not bury him. Or unless they wished others to believe that was so.*" He exhaled through his nostrils. "*No. Not yet. We proceed with full caution for now.*"

As he started to slip the disc back into his beltpouch his gaze fell on her bare feet in the dim glow. He swore softly. "*Kep, Priestess. I didn't know your feet were bare. Can you walk?*"

"*I'll manage. But it may not be a bone that I step on next time.*" She pointed a toe at the fallen man's weapon.

"*Stay behind me for now. We'll remedy the boots as we can, later.*"

Beyond the second tower came a thing Frax called the serpentine, a long stretch of roadway that ran upward, then cut sharply right and down to run back, paralleling the first section for a short stretch before turning another sharp corner and running upward again to another tower. Along the whole way, the walls stood silent, deadly vigil on both sides, past the next tower, again with triple gates, and beyond the next stretch of open roadway, right up to the massive structure Frax called the Grand Gate. Along the way they found the remains of more guards, clad in the red and green of Cadarn, all lying where they had fallen from the deadly effects of Araxis' plague. It left her cold and silent, and fearful of another explosion of rage from her companion.

Frax, however, had hardened his reaction to what they were seeing. He pushed forward purposefully and cautiously, and, Kaphri could sense, with a growing perplexity.

All of gates they encountered stood open, a fact that plainly baffled him. As near as she could understand, it was his feeling that no Kitahn would have ever allowed such a thing—to leave the great hold so vulnerable. Yet, every gate yawned wide, even the immense bronze doors of the main gate at the top of the long labyrinth. Frax stood in inside that yawning way, frowning, then motioned her forward and they passed through that massive portal.

Dawn was just beginning to rosy the sky as they paused to look at the fortress that was Caer Cadarn.

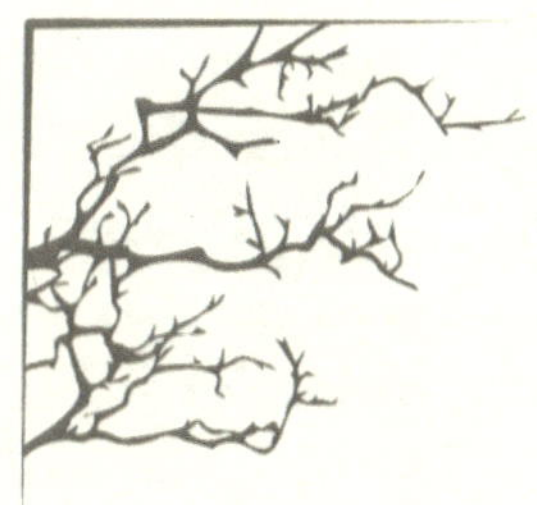

Chapter 55
The Keep

A gray stone plain stretched before them and away on both sides to the caer's towering outer walls. Inlaid into the surface, a broad road of blood-red paving stones cut a straight line across to an immense fortress at the plateau's center. The rising sun cast the building into shadow, making it a featureless, ominous hulk in the stark, cold space. The outer walls of the caer continued beyond it, off into the distance.

"Hredroth!" she breathed.

Apparently, the awe in her reaction satisfied Frax. "*This is Cadarn, the most ancient of the four original Geffitzi caers. Only it and Rhynog survive today. This area is the original structure,*" his arm swept the bare expanse before them. "*Long ago, the massive earthquake that completely destroyed two of the other caers severely damaged the outer walls of Cadarn. They say that seven sections, each more than the length of ten men, sheared off the plateau. The inner hold,*" he gestured toward the hulking dark shadow, "*was reduced to rubble. But the stone of the plateau did not crack. Scholars insist that's amazing, considering the forces that struck it. It took many years to rebuild the outer walls and raise the new fortress.*

"*This place has a strong defense. The plateau is perfectly squared and sheer-sided below the walls, thanks to the work of my forefathers' hapless subjects. Even if the enemy successfully stormed the outer wall—Kep forbid!—there is no protection or shelter for the attackers within our lady's gray embrace. They would find themselves at the mercy of the defenders in the caer fortress, without any cover to mount an assault on that second set of walls.*" He pointed toward the fortress again. The rising sun limned its top edges in rose light. "*Don't let the outer starkness fool you. Out here, it's bare. Bleak. It's a place for warriors to work and train. But inside there it's different. The buildings and furnishings are exquisite, and a deep layer of soil supports plants and trees in gardens renowned for their beauty.*" She caught a fleeting image of green lawns and quiet shade, but it was as quickly gone when he shrugged. "*The main holdhall lies within those walls. It's another veritable fortress in itself.*"

"*Surely no one could succeed in getting that far,*" she protested.

"*We would hope not.*" He gave her a grim smile. "*We've had many generations to perfect our defenses, Priestess.*"

Yet, all those years and all those defenses had not been enough to keep Araxis out. She had to look away for fear Frax might read her thoughts in her eyes.

His attention, however, had shifted. "*The gate to the inner fortress appears closed.*" He started forward again, out of the shelter of the gatehouse.

He stopped. "Oh, Kep!"

Kaphri's heart froze at the sound of horror and outrage in his exclamation.

He was moving again, around the left corner of the tower, staring back to where it met the defense wall.

She felt his mindshields flick up.Slowly, dreading what she would see, she followed.

Her knees nearly gave way in shock.

So many bodies! Piled twice her companion's height, the mound lay bleaching in the elements. Many more bones were scattered about that corner of the yard; the remains of Geffitzi, fallen as they went about the horrific task of removing the dead of Cadarn.

Frax leaned his head against the tower's stone. "There is no one here," he whispered hollowly. "No one of Cadarn would leave our dead this way if they could bury or burn their remains. Cadarn is empty."

Empty, except for her and the warriors—unwilling visitors to an unexpected and unexplained destination.

All this carnage and, possibly, a great deal more to come if they didn't exert their efforts in the right direction—if they lost their way in this twisting mess of steadily growing manipulation.

There was nothing to say.

Frax straightened. He turned his back on the horrifying mound of death, his eyes bleak as they met hers. "*Time is passing and the risk of pursuit increases with every second we delay. Let's get back to the others.*"

They had no time for ceremonies or burials. Someday. But not this day. Other things must happen first.

The way back was tense and silent. Kaphri hurried along, struggling to keep up with Frax's long stride. She scanned the way back even though he did not order it, but there was little need: death had held Caer Cadarn in its grasp for over twenty years.

They picked up Seuliac at the base of the first tower and made the climb to the watch room in silence. The others met them in the growing light on the top floor. One look at their faces told Kaphri the results of those searches were the same as theirs. Still, Tobin started forward at the sight of Frax, his expression a mixture of guarded eagerness and concern.

Frax shook his head.

She caught a sensation of mental exchange between the brothers, then Tobin turned away. Kaphri saw his fists clench and unclench at his sides as he withdrew a few steps to stare out the watch windows. His young face was hard in the dawn light.

Uri stood to one side, regarding his friend closely. "*You didn't really expect to find anything, did you?*"

"*No,*" Frax answered wearily. "*But we had to check. Riftkin and the Circles would expect it. It wasn't easy, but the task is done. Now let's move on to more immediate things.*" His attitude became abruptly crisper. He motioned the other closer but left Tobin at the window. "*Tell us, Priestess; how did we get here?*"

She was suddenly facing a wall of somber-faced warriors. Uri studied her calmly, while the gleam of intense interest in Seuliac's eyes disturbed her the way it always did when she caught him watching her. Velacy's expression was openly hostile. And she knew Frax was trying to read and analyze every aspect of her response.

"*I told you, I don't know.*" She left her mind open, unresisting to any who wanted to examine the truth in her sending. "*I've never seen this place before. I focused on the image of Windmer—the image of the hold gates. The same one as all of you! But when I drew on the crystal to move us, something pressed another destination—this destination—over ours.*"

"*You said she had control of that damned thing,*" Velacy snapped. "She doesn't. *Take it away from her.*"

"No." Frax glanced over at Tobin's back. "Tobin, how far would you say the Moonplain of the Ankar Mekt is from Cadarn?"

The younger Geffitz drew a deep breath before he turned around. "*Flying?*" He scowled. "*At their swiftest, the Balandra can probably fly it in five days. At worst, six. Why?*"

"*Because they're coming after us.*"

"*Only if they know where we are.*" Tobin looked out the window, then back at the rest of them. His expression was irritated. "*We're hundreds of miles to the south and east now. How would they know that?*"

"*They found us in that damned swamp!*"

"*Yes, Velacy, they did.*" Frax nodded. "*And the Evil One probably has a force headed this way, too. There aren't many viable destinations for us on the western side of the Yerebetan Ridge—just the Palenquemas, the Sighing Road in the Llowlech, and Cadarn.*"

"*So, the night he tried to snatch her away....*" Velacy interrupted with a glare at Kaphri.

"*He knew we headed this direction and started after us,*" Seuliac finished for him. "*But he couldn't anticipate that the Wyxa would pull us into the Palenquemas. Yet, somehow, he found that out, too. Why else would they go so far out of their way to engage their old enemies, except to capture her?*"

"*But how did they know she was there? They couldn't search the rest of the south that fast.*"

"*Let's hope not,*" Seuliac murmured.

Kaphri understood and agreed: the numbers and speed the task would require were intimidating.

"*The crystal,*" Uri said.

The others looked at him.

"*The crystal.*" The conviction in his sending rose. "*It's the only way.*"

Kaphri moved to grasp the talisman.

He shook his head. "*Leave it on. It protects you while you wear it. I've been thinking... And I've had plenty of time to think while some of you recuperated from your injuries. I believe the crystal acts to shield your location.*

"*While you wore it, you complained of a headache, caused, I think, by the Evil One's frustrated efforts to work his will on you.*" Kaphri felt a twinge of guilt at the memory of how she had tried to downplay those headaches with him. "*It was only after you took it off at Windmer that things really began working on you. You started having the dream that you couldn't remember.*"

"*Yes, the dream of being pulled back to the barrier. You all felt it when he finally succeeded in pulling me there.*" The others had been reluctant participants at the edge of Araxis' action when he snatched her back to the barrier. Something held them frozen and helpless, thwarting their attempts to defend their world—to kill her—while her evil uncle had used up the last Ly Kai survivors to force her to open a way for his forces to invade the south.

Something had protected her from the warriors' gut reaction that night. Had it been Gemma or the crystal serving the role?

Uri continued. "*When he located you that night, perhaps he realized you were moving toward the Palenquemas and the Balandras' ancient enemy. Araxis might not have encountered the Wyxa previously, but the winged ones have. They knew what a disaster it would mean for them if the Wyxa captured you.*" He frowned. "*What I don't understand is how they found us in the swamp so accurately. The Wyxa exert potent protections over their land. I would expect them to block your presence, whether you wore the crystal or not.*"

Kaphri swallowed hard, recalling the terrible emptiness when she reached out for the stars in the swamp. "*That's true: they suppressed the geas and all power from the stars. But I was wearing the crystal in the swamp. I tried to use it against them when they captured me,. I had to do something! Frax was injured, and they refused to listen. They attacked me.*"

Comprehension lit Uri's face. "*You used it! That would explain things.*"

Frax considered her. "*The Wyxa told you the amulet's role in the Black Temple. They told you what it is?*"

"*They said it was blocking the re-entry of the thing Uri called Bithzielp and his forces into this world.*"

"*The Balandra might be sensitive to the presence of that thing after its long use against them,*" Uri observed.

"So they felt me use it on the Wyxa, and Araxis sent them after me." As power went, that made perfect sense to her.

"There's no need to blame yourself," Uri said. *"If, as the Wyxa believe, this is all predestined, you can't prevent any of this from happening, anyway."*

"Predestined?" Kaphri gave a mental frown. *"What—?"*

"The Wyxa think one of their own, the Winisp, foresaw the return of the Balandra to our world," Frax said shortly. *"That's not where we want to go right now."*

The quick, reassuring smile Uri flashed her did not hide the fact that he shielded.

"Seven days. It took the Wyxa seven days to capture the Priestess and me. Seven days..." Frax looked to Uri.

"We were held five additional days while you recovered from your wounds," Uri added. *"Then three more, to bring us up to last night. So, fifteen days."*

"It would take roughly six days, in a straight line, for the Balandra to fly from the place they came through the barrier to where the Wyxa pulled us into the Palenquemas," Tobin stated flatly.

"Six." Frax was rapidly calculating. *"The Priestess used the crystal on day seven. They would have been around the edge of the Palenquemas, searching. At least some of them must have started down toward the Llowlech. Did they recall that force when she revealed her presence in the Palenquemas? Why divide your strength when you have a sure fix on your prey—especially if you anticipate a powerful opposition? Let's say three days to gather and re-group forces?"*

Seuliac nodded. *"Entering that swamp took preparation. A force that size could never cross it without catching the attention of the Wyxa unless they moved very fast. They would make one long, hard drive."* His quiet observation made her shiver with the memory of the screeching horde descending upon them. *"They would need to rest and hunt in preparation for such a prolonged flight, and, even if they carefully sat down in small groups to rest once they began, their first wave would not be in top battle form when they attacked the Wyxa. I would send a second wave as a backup. Of course, there would be no reason for the second wave to continue inward once they discovered we were no longer there. They'd turn back."*

Velacy frowned, puzzled. "*Why? They wanted to fight the Wyxa.*"

"*They didn't fly all the way into the swamp to fight the Wyxa, Velacy,*" Uri said. "*The Evil One wanted her before the Wyxa did something to her. The Balandra will come here as fast as they can fly.*"

"*How can they know? We could be anywhere!*"

"*She used the crystal to bring us here,*" Seuliac said grimly.

"*Meaning, we just moved halfway across the continent in what may have been a long blaze of glory.*" Frax finished the thought.

Kaphri sighed. "*I made a very serious mistake in using it.*"

"*Do you think you had a choice?*" Uri asked.

"*No.*"

"*Well, then.*" He shrugged.

"*So, what would you say? Our time is shortened to four days?*" Frax glanced over at Tobin.

"*No,*" Seuliac spoke up. "*Even these Balandra have physical limits. After this last big push into the Palenquemas and back out again—not to mention the battle with the Wyxa—they must rest. If any of them survived. I think we may safely allow ourselves seven days. If Tobin Kitahn's distances are correct.*"

Tobin gave him a dark glare.

Frax considered the warlord's words, then nodded. "*I'm willing to agree with a seven-day headstart on them, but they'll be on our trail fast. It's too much to hope the Wyxa destroyed them. They might still have a scouting party around here, too.*"

"*I want to see the caer.*" Tobin stepped away from the window.

"*Of course,*" Frax nodded. His brother was a mere babe in their mother's arms when he left Caer Cadarn. "*But don't enter the hold. Anyone else who wants can go with you.*"

"*Anyone?*" Tobin looked chagrined at the idea of the Aedecs joining him.

"*There's safety in numbers.*" Frax had no fear of Seuliac unearthing any secrets that night endanger Cadarn. But, even deserted, the place would leave an impression of Cadarnian strength for the Rhynogians to carry with them. "*I do warn you; it's the same as Windmer—strewn with the remains of the dead. Watch for anything out of the ordinary. Just because we haven't found anything wrong doesn't mean this place is safe. And lock down what you can of the labyrinth on your way back out. I want to check a few things here in the tower. The Priestess needs shoes. And clothes.*"

Kaphri drew a sharp breath. "*But—*"

"*You come out of those Wyxan things.*" He glared down her protest. "*You're on lookout. You know what to watch for as well as any of us. If you see anything, tell me. We'll meet back here in an hour. Let's move!*"

FRAX FROWNED AS HE followed the other warriors down the tower stairs. So, the Winisp, after two thousand years, had triumphed, at least in some small measure, and he and his company had moved on. To what? What did someone or something intend by sending them here?

He should be happy they'd escaped almost certain death at the machinations of the Ankar Mekt. They had left the swampdwellers behind, but it couldn't be that easy to slip their influence. The creatures felt too strongly about the crystal and the threat to their world to simply let them go.

Unless—his heart quickened—there was another force at work. This was Cadarn. There were things here...

Kep. Their situation hadn't gotten any better with their coming here if that was the case. Tobin knew it—that's why he'd protested earlier—and Uri. Of the other two, Seuliac, at least, would suspect.

There was no question about which direction they must go now. He had some tough decisions to make, and not everyone would be pleased with them.

He drew a deep breath, taking in a sense if the stone of the walls that surrounded him.

This was Cadarn!

The sheer impact of the thought almost overwhelmed him. This was the home of his ancestors, torn away from him, that he'd so often imagined reclaiming. And now he was here.

He closed his eyes and drew another deep breath, forcing his muscles to relax as he absorbed the essence of the structure around him. So ancient the stone. Did Tobin feel it...the pride, the power, the struggles of the countless generations that had gone before? It was all here. In the stone. The spirit of Cadarn.

Kep, he wanted it back! He wanted his people here again. Home again. The pain of desire twisted inside him, tightening until he clenched his teeth to keep from roaring out in frustration and despair. To be here and to know the clans in the north were fighting the invading Balandra for their lives! It was a terrible, bitter thing to fear there might not be anyone left to return here if—no, not if, but when—when they triumphed.

Resolve hardened inside him, wrapping a cold shell around the other feelings—the doubt, frustration, and fear that raged inside him—sealing them away. The girl had gotten them this far. Whatever was happening, whatever the hand that pushed at their back, they were in the south again, something he would not have believed possible a few weeks ago. They had a chance to regain everything.

If they were smart enough, brave enough, and capable of seeing and seizing the opportunity, they had a chance.

The Priestess had done it. They could, too.

Nothing, he vowed, would stop them.

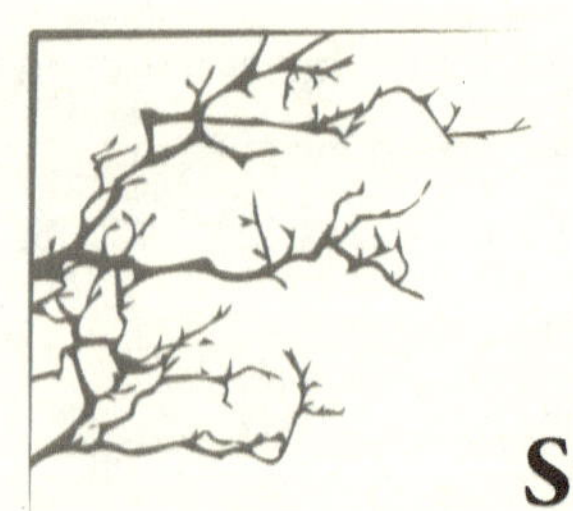

Chapter 56
Stealthy Attack

Kaphri was aware of Frax's approach long before his hand touched the door. She did not turn away from the window when he entered the guard chamber: her attention was riveted on the dark line of forest that lay beyond the grassy plain below her.

Something lurked out there. She could sense its cold, calculating regard. The feel of it was ancient, almost like... She frowned. What? Was it good? Evil? She could not tell. But it was a presence of some reckoning; it knew they were in the tower, and it was watching.

Waiting.

Was it her imagination, or had there been movement at the edge of the forbidding darkness? She leaned forward, keeping close to the wall to shield herself from those unseen eyes.

"*What's wrong?*" Frax asked, instantly wary.

She tore her attention away from the timberline to look at him. "*What is that place? The wood. What is in there?*" Her questions were low and swift with intensity. "*Is that what concerned Tobin earlier?*"

"*Yes and no.Here, take this.*" He thrust the bundle he carried into her hands as he moved up beside her to gaze out the window. "*That, Priestess, is the Grimmenwood.*"

"*What?*"

"*The Grimmenwood. The first line of defense for Caer Cadarn. A force from an earlier age of this world dwells there. You see the road?*" He pointed out a ribbon of stone that ran across the plain to lose itself in the dark tangle. "*That's the only breach in the woods for hundreds of miles. By an ancient agreement with the Lords of Kitahn, that force guards Cadarn."*

She drew a quick breath. Yes. Old. Like the Wyxa. "*And what is that ancient force?*"

"*A demon, if the enemies of Cadarn are to be believed.*" He straightened away from the window with a shrug, but something darkened in his eyes as he continued to study the shadowed boundary.

"*Do they speak true, these enemies of Cadarn?*"

"*Whatever it is, the Grimmen has protected Cadarn and its bloodline since the beginnings of our time. It's bound to us by an ancient pact. Legend says the first lord bargained with it, mixing life to secure this land for himself and his heirs.*"

Mixing life? Despite mindspeak, she still found times when the warriors' concepts were difficult or confusing to interpret. Mixing life. Mixing lifeblood? Life force? Breeding! A Geffitz Lord had bred with what lurked out there? She looked up at him, unable to disguise the shock in her eyes.

"*It would have been countless generations ago, Priestess.*" As he met her eyes, the faintest hint of a bitter smile turned up one corner of his mouth. "*Perhaps it's true; perhaps it's only a thing of legend.*"

Did these Geffitzi honestly believe such a thing? Kaphri recalled Velacy's hate-filled expression as he snarled "demon breed" at Tobin in the forest near Windmer.

The young Aedec warrior obviously did.

Frax believed it too. There was something unmistakable in the way he said it—an undeniable light of defiance in his gray eyes as he watched her.

And her reaction? To another ancient, powerful force that might try to manipulate her?

She turned away, suddenly unwilling to meet his gaze.

ONCE AGAIN, IT FELL to him to snatch away a bit of her innocence—to widen the breach between them. But earlier, in the gate passage below, Tobin started to say something about it, and, with the Aedecs in their company, it was only a matter of time before the subject came up again, possibly in a much uglier tone. Better for him to tell her while he controlled the reveal.

"*Demon or not, one thing is sure, Priestess,*" he said. "*To enter the Grimmenwood without one of Kitahni blood for a companion is certain death.*"

He studied her, noting the tiny lines of tension around her eyes for the first time. She was beginning to think, to listen, and evaluate what he said about their situation. To question things with reason rather than reactive defiance. She was no longer the innocent or the prisoner to be ordered about. Klandar Bayne was right: to succeed, she had to discover the strength inside of her.

She wasn't entirely ready yet, however. He was the commander of this little group, and he intended to remain in control.

He followed her when she turned and walked to the huge table that dominated the center of the room.

The windows to the north, south, and west on the top floor of Cadarn's primary guard tower gave way to breathtaking views of the countryside around the caer, while the ones to the east overlooked the twisting serpentine as it climbed to the main gate high above it.

The caer's most renowned view, however, occupied that table.

The surface was a massive map, sculpted in miniature relief, of the countryside for miles around Cadarn. It was rendered with such intricate detail that its beauty was reputed to snatch a viewer's breath away. A master craftsman—many—had worked countless hours to create it.

Kaphri's finger traced the thin silver thread of road winding away from a tiny caer set upon a base of gray stone. She stopped short of touching the dark edge of the green forest that closed about the line. "*Then this Grimmenwood encircles the caer?*"

"*Completely. Caer Cadarn and a portion of our lands are an island set inside its embrace.*" Extensive as it was, the map covered only a small detail of the lands held by his Clan.

"*The Palenquemas is to our north.*" The gray of the swamp, marked with vague details, edged the outer corner of the map on her right. "*And the Great Water is to our west.*" She found the seaside village situated down the tiny slope to the west of the caer in front of her. She had seen the roofs of buildings in the distance from the western windows of the tower. "*And to the south...?*"

"*A mountain chain,*" Frax supplied quietly.

She studied those little ridges of stone before her for a long time. Tiny as the mountains were, the artists had still managed to imbue them with a sense of difficulty and steepness.

"*And to the east?*" she asked.

"*The Grimmenwood. Clear to Pterfellen. Then more mountains.*"

"*Is there a plateau on one of those mountains?*" The map did not extend that far eastward.

"Yes." He spoke aloud, softly. He did not need to touch her mind to feel the tension building inside her. She was beginning to understand their situation—how treacherous the move to this place was. "*The geas is drawing you there, isn't it*?" he asked.

She gave a heavy sigh. "*How long have you known?*"

"*Suspected. Since we first studied Tobin's maps of the south. Your interest kept returning to that area.*"

"*What is the place?*"

"*Sacred Ground. Only a few holy men ever traveled there.*" A sudden shaft of ice slid down his spine. "*Kep! That's where Araxis built his city!*" Stupid! Stupid and thoughtless! How long before he sent the deadly plague down on the Geffitzi had the Evil One exercised free hand in this world?

A surge of bitter anger followed his shock. What difference did it make? What could his people have done, if the Goddess Kep didn't even step in to defend her own holy ground?

He mastered his emotions, forcing reason. No use lamenting the situation. He would better serve his people by recovering their lost lands.

"*They never gave me the slightest hint where it lay, beyond forbidding the general direction of the south, but something tells me you're right.*" The Ly Kai had been so terrified of the south that they defaced the southern marker on the tower where they took refuge and forbade anyone to look in that direction.

"*We worship our Goddess from afar,*" he said bitterly. "*Her place is sacred, and we respect her solitude. By its nature, the area is very isolated.*"

"*A place where he was able to act, undisturbed,*" she murmured.

And they were suddenly so much closer to it. Which left the question hanging unanswered: who had manipulated their jump so they arrived here instead of in Windmer?

But was it a bad thing that they had moved several hundred miles toward the geas destination in the blink of an eye? It had gotten them cleanly away from the swamp, away from Balandra and Wyxa on the verge of a battle, in what appeared the right direction.

Some might look upon it as a godsend. Frax did not. He asked no favors and expected none.Anonymous benefactors were unsolicited and, in this situation especially, unappreciated.

He realized Kaphri had turned and was watching him, studying his face for insight into his thoughts.

That was another thing he felt a sudden urge to question. She could read his mind, so why didn't she? Because he threatened her with harm in Omurda if she violated his mental sanctity? He realized now that was a stupid bit of ego. Her skill far surpassed any Geffitz telepath.

Why did she refrain? Was it because a particular rigid code of mental ethics bound her?

Based on what he knew of her now? Yes. As poorly thought out and insane as her actions sometimes seemed, she really did try to do the right thing.

In Geffitzi eyes, she was a disaster waiting to happen.

What would it do to her if he told her Klandar Bayne said everything rested on her choices—her ability to see the need and respond? It would tear her to pieces trying to do the right thing. It would immobilize her with fear of making a wrong choice.

He couldn't tell her. Uri knew. But he wouldn't tell the others. They would constantly be second-guessing her every move and arguing whether her choices were the right ones. That was just Geffitzi nature.

What about him? Would he fall into that trap of knowing and doubting?

Only if he believed what Klandar Bayne had told him.

The Swampfather wanted them to believe all this was preordained—that the Winisp had predicted their quest—even though the ancients of the Ankar Mekt, his own people, refused to believe him. They thought only the Wyxa could resolve a situation of such world-shattering magnitude. That some insight made them wiser and better able to manage things than the rest of Kep's Children.

Frax had tried to be reasonable. He had offered an alliance between the Geffitzi and Wyxa. They dismissed it as insignificant, then coldly implemented their plan to send his troop into the heart of the Black Temple with an empty talisman to seal a gate that would continue to leak enemies into their world.

If the Priestess had not reclaimed and used the crystal, they would be dead, their quest ended. So, no. They, not the Wyxa, were in charge of their destinies.

He pulled his thoughts back to the present. Frowned. "*If the Wyxa had not pulled us into the Palenquemas, I planned for us to cut eastward through the Llowlech, along the Sighing Road, and across the plains below Shada.*"

She turned her attention back to the map. "*But now we must go through this demon-wood of yours.*"

His mouth tightened at her phrasing. "*Yes.*" They must enter the woods and move eastward as soon as possible.

And here she stood, the thought ran through his mind, with that cursed mass of flaming hair. And this time, he did not believe he could bully her into cutting it.

He stared at it with sudden, deepening fascination. Her hair was like down. Tiny filaments feathered from the shafts, making them stand upright in a thick, rich fluff. Now he understood why the braid tucked at his belt had never come undone: those filaments wove about each other and held fast.

Her hair must be very soft; his heartbeat quickened with a sudden urge to reach out and touch the wide strip of fire, to lace his fingers in it.

It would be so easy to turn her to him, tilting her small face upward. To part those lips...

The heat of his reaction shook him with its intensity.

Was he insane? Outrage at the betrayal of his thoughts lashed through him. It was madness to think such foolish, dangerous things.

He drew a breath and concentrated on the details of the tower chamber around them until his physical reaction came under control and he could turn his attention back to the girl before him.

When he looked down, however, he found he was still reluctant to pull away from the warm seduction of his earlier thoughts. It had been months since he'd been with a female. Given this brief respite from immediate danger, it was no surprise that with close proximity, even to one of his people's greatest enemies, he might feel a little stir of reaction. Kep knew, they'd been through enough lately! It did not mean he would act on it.

Allowing himself to linger for a moment longer, he savored her proximity, the top of her head just level with his chin, the tumble of her hair tickling his nose.

She was a good height for a female. A comfortable height. His eyes ran over the smooth, bare flesh above her ear, tracing down the side of her head with slow languor. He noticed for the first time how the hair turned into a narrow strip of soft red down that followed the line of her backbone past where the white collar of Wyxan cloth lay against the warm golden tones of her flesh.

"*There must be another way east!*" The desperation in Kaphri's protest jerked him back to the present.

His irritation flashed as his mind resisted the shift back to their immediate discussion. What was the matter with him?

"*Could you go north for a day's travel?*" he asked. If she could, he might be able to salvage something of his original plan and avoid the Grimmenwood. It would be more dangerous. Entering the wood was risky, but the place offered them a dense, unbroken cover the other route did not.

He knew what her reply must be.

"*No.*" The geas would not allow it.

"*Then our way leads through the Grimmenwood, Priestess.*"

"*The mountains...*"

"...are *almost impassable. That direction would slow us down too much.*"

"*The wood...*" She spun away from the table and he had to catch her shoulders to prevent a collision.

The sensation of her warm, curving flesh beneath his hands sent such a pleasant shock wave of heat through Frax that it left him floundering for clear thought.

Alarms sounded in his head. This was all wrong! He had reasoned this out moments ago: this was a reaction he would never allow himself under these circumstances, and definitely not with her!

His mind struggled to break clear of an increasingly heavy blanket of lust that seemed to settle over him. Even as he fought it, another disturbing realization was breaking through his awareness: something was wrong with the girl, too.

Kaphri's muscles were rigid with tension under his grip, but it wasn't lust running through her. It was terror.

Not of him. She appeared oblivious to the passion he was battling as she stared up at him with the eyes of a small, cornered animal. Of what, then? What did she fear?

Frax was struggling to focus on anything beyond the sensation of her flesh beneath his hands, yet he could not will himself to let her go. Whatever was at work here affected them both but in drastically different ways.

"*I can't go in there*!" She made a helpless, distracted gesture with one hand. "*That place ... whatever dwells there... We've only just had one narrow escape. To simply walk into another situation is madness*!"

So—she feared the Grimmenwood. He could cope with that.

"*Priestess, listen to me*." He gave her shoulders a shake that nearly undid him. He wanted to finish the motion, to pull her tight against him. Instead, he forced his focus onto the fear radiating from her. "*Is what you sense from the woods worse—more evil—than what pursues us?*"

He could feel her fighting panic as she made a concentrated effort to focus on his question.

"*No*."

"We have no choice, Priestess. I don't like it either, but if we're going to get to the origin of your geas, our path must be through the woods."

Must. He picked the wrong word to use. He might have chosen better if he hadn't been so desperate to control his thoughts.

Unreasoning terror boiled up in her. *"There is a choice! I can go into the mountains. As long as I wear the crystal, I can hide."*

Her sending snapped his mind into focus. *"I can't let you do that, Kaphri."*

"You can't stop me."

The statement was like a physical blow. Frax stared down at her, stunned by her vehemence.

Panic surged inside him. After what she'd done in the Palenquemas, bringing them here, he knew she was capable of anything—including disappearing before his eyes—if she felt the need.

Whatever was happening here, he had to break through its influence and force her to reason. He couldn't lose her. He had to have—to keep—her with him!

Take her! It was a scream inside his mind, out of nowhere, shaking him with the strength of its passion. Bend her to your will! You are a Lord of Cadarn: she cannot refuse you anything. His fingers tightened spasmodically, sinking into the tender flesh of her shoulders. He barely heard her exclamation of protest and pain as his vision went red.

Of course, it was right. Of course, he should have her. He...

Realization finally broke through his heated thoughts, making his mind go cold and clear.

The Grimmenwood.

He should have known—should have foreseen this. He'd been away from this place for most of his life, but he'd heard the stories about the woods. The Grimmen was a treacherous force to deal with, even for the Kitahns.

Was the cursed thing working to stir these reactions in them now? Why?

He did not put any motive beyond the Grimmen. It was Eldren: the same, no better or worse, than the Wyxa or the Guardian. But why would the force in the woods push for him to bind the Priestess to him with seduction and conquest, while working to drive her away at the same time?

That didn't make sense!

It was as if...

It was as if two forces were at work here, each trying to drive them in a different direction.

His thoughts ran fast and cold now. Kep! Two forces, each seeking to control them in the most basic way possible: through their emotions. The Grimmen would have to act through him. Generations of its blood burned in his veins. But it did not claim any influence over the Priestess. What was working on her?

Icy suspicion sliced his brain. The Wyxa! If they could force her to use the crystal in fear, they might be able to reach in and snatch her back to the Palenquemas before she entered the woods and moved beyond their reach.

The two ancient forces weren't working against Kaphri and him; they were working against each other through them!

How and why were not important. The only thing that mattered was that they did not succeed.

He was back to his senses. Now he had to pull the girl back to reason.

Telling her something was attacking her thoughts would not do. She was in no state of mind to believe him. In her fear, she might suspect him of lying. Then, the Wyxa would gain a stronger hold over her.

Only one thing would work. The thing that had brought her this far. That was so deeply ingrained in her she could not ignore it, even in this state of fear.

"*No. Maybe I can't.*" He released her shoulders, giving her a light shove away from him. "*Run. Abandon us here—trapped on this side of the barrier. We'll fight off the forces who seek you while you run away and hide. That's what your people do, isn't it—create a situation, then run and hide?*" Kep! It wrenched his guts to say that, but he had to do something, and attempting to slap her out of a fear-driven hysteria was not an action he wanted to risk.

He knew his words stung her—that he would think she would abandon them—and yet, it was what she had just said.

"*No! I'll send you back. Not to the Black Temple—but someplace safe. Then you can join the battle to protect your people!*"

Her fingers moved to clasp the crystal.

The Wyxa were maneuvering for a swift, direct attack.

"*No! You can't use that thing!*" His hand flashed out to catch her wrist before she touched it.

"*But I can send you back! I'm trying to help you.*"

"*Priestess, stop! It won't work to send us back.*" Frax's grip tightened as she struggled to wrest her arm from his grasp. He gave up trying any subtle appeal. "*Listen to me! The Ankar Mekt is trying to fulfill their plan by making you think you have no other choice. They want you to use the cursed thing so they can snatch you back to the Palenquemas. Think! For Kep's sake, you know this isn't right.* "

She stared at him in disbelief, but he saw his words slowly taking effect. "*What are you saying?*"

"*I'm saying the Ankar Mekt is still trying to work its will on you. They're trying to drive you to using the crystal. When you do, they'll snatch you back to them.*"

"*That's ridiculous!*"

"Is it? Do you believe the Ankar Mekt would let you take the Guardian Stone and destroy their plan if the Balandra attack hadn't distracted them? They couldn't! Their plan won't allow it. Think, Priestess! Search inside you. Now you're aware of it and in control again, what do you feel? Is the threat you sense really from the woods?"

KAPHRI RELUCTANTLY opened her mind, shuddering as she touched the presence beyond the tower. The steady regard was there, the same as before, but there was no threat in it: only wary watchfulness.

A vision of the screeching black cloud of figures sweeping down upon them in the moonlight passed before her eyes and she mentally recoiled. There had been so many of them! So many foul, screeching fiends.

A wave of hopelessness washed over her. If the Wyxa could not stop Araxis and the Balandra, what possible effect could their small band have against what pursued them? They were being presumptuous in their efforts.

Her breath caught in her throat. That thought had not been hers!

Frax was right: the Ankar Mekt was working to recover what it had lost.

The simple recognition broke the Wyxa's grip on her. The maelstrom of emotions holding her in its grasp released to drain away, leaving her to feel weak and ashamed.

She looked down, unable to meet the Geffitz commander's eyes. "*By all the Gods,*" she barely managed the mental whisper. "*Sometimes, I'm so afraid.*"

"*If you were not afraid, you would be a fool. There are no fools in our company. But, if our path leads through the wood, it's the path we must take. Neither the Wyxa nor anything else can stop us.*"

Ah, simple Geffitz philosophy."*We do what we must do,*" her sending echoed their warrior mantra. Her gaze was clear and even as she looked up at him.

A WASH OF RELIEF RAN over him. The crisis had passed, binding them with words that locked them onto a single, dangerous path.

He was not finished, however. "*And that, after what just happened, is what I came up here to talk to you about. I want you to swear that what happened in the Palenquemas with the Wyxa will not happen again. You can't turn back for us if we are lost. You have to go on. I want you to swear to me that in the future, no matter what happens to the rest of us, you will continue with your task. That you won't turn aside for any reason. Swear you'll not let this—this death and devastation around us—happen again.*"

Her eyes slid to the window behind him, and he knew she was wondering what the value such an oath would hold very shortly. He'd already told her the wood would only allow those in the companionship of Kitahns to pass. If something happened to him and Tobin, the Grimmenwood would surely make short work of the rest of their party.

That could not happen.

"*Listen to me, Priestess.*" His fingers caught her chin, forcing her to look up at him. "*You've got to swear this to me: that you'll destroy the barrier.*" When she tried to turn her head away, his fingers tightened. "*No! Listen to me!*" How could he make her understand?

The sight of tears in her eyes sent a swell of shock running through him.

When he still would not let her turn her head, she closed her eyes, making the silvered droplets tremble on her lashes.

"*Kep, Kaphri, don't cry.*"

His sending only seemed to make the situation worse. Her eyelids fluttered as she tried to keep them closed against his gaze.

A single tear slipped from one corner.

"*Kaphri, don't. Please.*" She had been through some of the most challenging things he'd ever experienced in his warrior existence without a whimper of complaint. She couldn't break down now. He watched, caught between despair and fascination as she fought some inner battle, her lips trembling. So soft. So inviting.

So vulnerable... Before he could stop himself, Frax bent his head and let his lips gently brush hers.

Only a little kiss. For comfort. Only a little...

Again. So lightly, her mouth parting beneath his as she drew a breath in startled but unresisting response.

So sweet. Unmistakably a first kiss. He tasted the tentative response as his lips moved over hers.

Another time he might have played this so well, drawn it into a languid, sweet seduction that would have bound her to him. Another place, and he could have slowly stolen her will to resist anything he would ask. The pressure of his mouth deepened, his lips catching hers more fully now, his fingers fanning out along her jawline to direct her response as his left arm slid around her, drawing her slim form against him.

His blood roared in his ears.

Another time. Another place. But not here. Not now.

Somewhere inside his head, a part of him screamed horrified protest. This was not right!

Too late, he realized whatever force was working on his emotions had merely found a subtler front on which to attack him. He didn't care. His arm tightened as her mouth moved under his, returning his kiss.

"Frax, I—Oh, Kep! Isn't this cozy."

All passion dissolved with the cold fury in that voice.

"Tobin." Frax's response was carefully neutral as he looked up at the younger warrior standing in the doorway across the room. He loosened his arm, allowing Kaphri to slip away, absently noting she shielded tightly as she hastily put several steps between them.

The look in Tobin's eyes was pure venom. "Is this why you let her snatch us away from the Wyxa, Frax? So you could get your hands on her?"

"Tobin..." What could he say to the younger Geffitz? This isn't what you think? This isn't what it looks like? I'm a fool? It would sound so hopelessly ridiculous. Frax cursed himself furiously. There was no acceptable response.

"They were going to send us back, Brother! Back to help our people! And you let her pull us away. Has she bewitched you that much? She's the enemy, Frax. She's of the same blood that stole our lands and now destroys our people. Our people, Frax! The ones who are dying while we're trapped down here, pursuing her interests. Do you think she cares what becomes of our people? That she cares what happens to our world?"

"Tobin! You know better. I know you'd choose to go back if you could—we all would—but the Wyxa only wanted us to replace the damned crystal in the Black Temple. They didn't care what happened to us afterward. We would've been destroyed within seconds if we'd gone back. You know that." Frax reached out, touching his brother's mind, only to discover with dismay that Tobin's emotions were running as hot and wild as his own had been only seconds before.

Tobin wrested away, throwing up a mindshield between them.

"Destroyed? At least we would be fighting for our people! Is that what you were doing here just now?" The gray eyes raked the girl with outraged disgust.

"That's enough, Tobin!"

"Why? Am I upsetting you? Do you think I should remain silent, watching you chase after this enemy bitch like a dog in heat while our people are dying? I will not!"

Frax fought to keep his voice low and calm. "I know you don't agree with the direction we've been forced to take, Tobin, but throwing our lives away on a useless gesture would avail no one. If you will just listen..."

"You listen! I don't care what you do, but I'm leaving here. I'm going back, and I'll get through the cursed barrier, no matter what." The younger Kitahn turned on his heel and stormed out the tower door, slamming it behind him.

Frax stared after him. How could he be so stupid? He should have anticipated Tobin's reaction to their escape from the Palenquemas. With his younger brother's volatile nature, he should have seen, on first review, choosing to pursue this action over returning to aid their people would seem like a betrayal to him. He should have addressed it with Tobin as soon as they cleared their position here. In the younger Kitahn's mind, no consideration for personal safety would be allowed to temper what he considered necessary action.

Of all the stupid, unreasonable, stubborn, reckless... He caught himself. What was happening with these emotional rampages? First himself, then Kaphri, and now Tobin.

His mouth tightened to a hard, bitter line. Gone, any thought of himself or Kaphri. He knew what had caused their outrageous actions.

Tobin didn't realize his emotions were being manipulated.

Now he would have to chase him down, reason with him, and make him see the necessity of their role in this. They would lose valuable time, but they would need his skills more than ever when they entered the Grimmenwood.

The girl hung back, silent and watchful during the exchange, and he appreciated that. There was no anger or reproach in her, only the silent question of what he would do.

"*You're still on watch,*" he told her.

Before he could take a step toward the door, a clear-ringing musical call rose up from outside the tower and time froze around them.

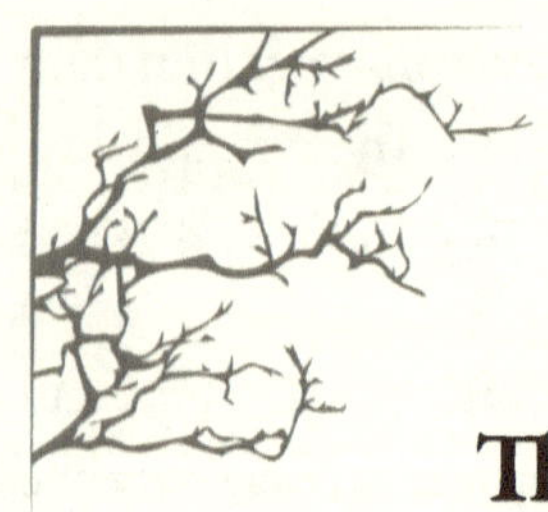

Chapter 57
The Song is Sweet

The call went on and on, rising and falling. As one sound faded another rose to take its place, then another,weaving an intricate spell. It held Kaphri frozen, mesmerizing her with the glorious tones.

After a breathless span of time, she realized the sound was fading. It was leaving! Seized with a terrible dismay at the thought of its loss, she tried to push past the Geffitz commander who blocked her path to the door.

"What?" Even more caught up in the musical spell than she, Frax stared down at her blankly.

"*By the Gods...!*" the sense of horror that shot through his thoughts was enough to stop Kaphri's efforts to get past him. "*How could...? Oh, Kep, not now!*" His expression of confusion deepened as he spun for the door.

"Frax!" The tower door barely missed him as it flew open. Uri stood there, his face pale and distraught as he took in his cousin's expression. "It's not you...?" For a moment, he appeared at a loss, then horrified comprehension passed over his face. "By the Goddess! Of course. It's Tobin!" He was gone, his boots pounding down the steps of the tower as he shouted for Velacy and Seuliac to follow him.

Frax moved as if to go with them then checked himself in mid-step. His mental touch was vague and unfocused as it found her. "*Priestess. My brother. Where is he?*"

Kaphri reached out, extending her search further and further when she failed to find Tobin's mental presence. Nothing! She reached farther.

How could he move so swiftly? She ran to the north windows to stare at the distant figures retreating across the open field separating Cadarn from the woods. Several trails of broken grass traced passages from the caer to the dark line of forest.

She shifted her body as Frax wedged into the space beside her.

"*There.*" Her finger trembled as she pointed to the tree line. "*He is there. On the back of some creature...?*" Her sending tapered off in fearful confusion as she twisted to look up at her companion. "*Frax?*"

His face was ashen, his expression one of numbed shock as he watched the figures vanish into the shadows of the Grimmenwood. Without answering, he slid back inside the room to sag against the nearest wall, his hands raised to press long, sun-browned fingers against his forehead as if he were in pain. His mind was tightly shielded.

Seeing his reaction, Kaphri's fear rose. "*Frax! What is going on?*"

He did not seem to hear her.

She turned back to the window. The figures on the plain had vanished, and she could no longer sense Tobin. But when she reached out the presence in the wood was still there. Observing them. Waiting.

Uri's returning footsteps carried a sound of defeat. His expression was pale and troubled as he entered the watchroom. The Aedecs followed, their faces somber. For once, current events had rendered Velacy silent.

"He's gone," Uri announced. He studied Frax. Kaphri could sense a deep concern in him.

"What happened?" Frax's question was hoarse, as if it took a great deal of effort for him to speak.

"Velacy was the closest to the gate." Uri turned to the younger warrior.

"I don't know," Velacy snapped, his expression sullen and defensive. "We were coming down from the caer when he started acting strangely, sort of distracted, as if he was listening for something, but I couldn't hear anything. When we got back, he came up here. The next thing I knew he was storming down in some kind of black fury. He snatched up his stuff and left. A second later that call came and I couldn't move." He glared defiantly around at the rest of them.

"That's the way it is with the Cyrwin song. It catches you up in its spell." Uri said grimly. "They came for him, Velacy. There was nothing you could do."

Velacy stared at him for a long, wary moment before he seemed to accept that they were not blaming him for what had happened.

"Did you see them?" Seuliac's question sounded mildly intrigued.

Velacy gave a quick shake of his head and looked away.

Frax had not moved during the exchange. Uri walked over to put a hand on his shoulder. "The quicker we give chase, the better."

"What?" Frax blinked as if just becoming aware of the other Geffitz's presence. With a wooden movement, he pulled away from the wall and shrugged Uri's hand off. "Why—no. No. His loss is unfortunate, but there's nothing we can do about it."

His eyes found Kaphri. "*You. Put on the boots and bring the rest of...*" He motioned toward the bundle they had both lain aside, then started for the door.

"Wait a moment!" Uri caught his upper arm in a grip that jerked him around. "Don't you plan to go after him?"

Kaphri could feel the vagueness that held Frax rapidly dissolving into cold, angry purpose now that he had begun to move. His expression was stony as he looked at Uri. "No. He is Kitahn." He said it as if that were all the explanation necessary. "We go to the

Grimmenwood, but Tobin is on his own. Nothing must turn us aside now, Uri. Nothing!" He looked down pointedly at the hand gripping his arm.

Uri released his hold and Frax left the tower room. The Caspani heir stared after him then snarled a low curse under his breath.

Angrily he motioned for the rest of them to follow him as he stomped from the room.

"*Uri, what happened to Tobin? What is this Cyrwin song? What is going on?*" Kaphri had taken the heavy silence for as long as she could bear it. Being confused by her experiences in this place was difficult enough; now another disaster had obviously befallen them and no one was saying anything.

Sunlight streamed in through the open gate they had scrambled through in terror hours earlier. Uri was helping her shrug into a backpack that Frax had supplied for her along with the pair of stiff but tolerable boots.

A short distance away Velacy and Seuliac paused at adjusting their own packs to listen to the exchange.

The big Geffitz grunted as he squatted down beside her to tighten the shoulder straps to fit her slight frame. He'd been as silent and pensive as Frax since leaving the watchroom. "*Well, Willow, it's just a little... There! Is that too tight?...of the Kitahn family heritagecatching up with them. At about the worst damned time possible.*" He gave an unhappy sigh.

"Cursed demon spawn!" Velacy muttered darkly.

Uri was on his feet before Kaphri realized he had moved. A snarl of fury erupted from his throat as he took a step toward the younger Aedec.

Velacy, his expression a mixture of surprise and angry defiance, retreated a quick step. Beside him, Seuliac remained, unmoving, his eyes bright with interest.

"Don't bother, Uri."

Her heart gave a painful lurch as Frax's voice cut through the tension that held them.

The memory of hard arms about her...

This was no time for such thoughts. She fastened her attention on her companions.

The Caspani heir glared at Velacy for a moment longer before turning aside with a snort of disgust. Frax walked past him to stand in front of the two Aedec warriors.

"There is only one way for us to go now: through the Grimmenwood. This situation is not what I planned. All I can do is offer you safe passage over the road to the other side of the forest. From there you can do what you will, but you can be sure, if you try to enter the woods to follow us you'll die."

"Good enough!" Velacy's eyes flashed fire. "We want none of..."

"No," Seuliac said quietly.

Velacy spun, expression dumbfounded, to stare at the other. "What!"

Kaphri heard Uri draw a long, slow breath beside her.

Seuliac regarded Frax steadily. "The battle does not lie that direction."

"Our path leads through the Grimmenwood," Frax re-stated flatly. "I cannot guarantee your safety."

Seuliac shrugged. "Is what would lie along our path in the Grimmenwood any worse than what follows us?" Kaphri's heart gave a sudden twist on hearing Frax's question from the tower room repeated. "Besides, we'll be in the company of a son of Kitahn. From what I've heard, it's all that's necessary."

"The blood of Kitahn doesn't even assure my safety, Warlord. I have no idea how it would react to the presence of Rhynog. The wood could destroy us before we get to the other side."

"Perhaps, but no one will ever say Rhynog walked away from this task. We won't gain anything by dissolving or splitting our forces at this point. You need us."

Frax nodded curtly. "All right. Then take these, for what protection they might offer." He pitched something to each of them.

Velacy twitched as if Frax had thrown him a hot ember when he saw what he gripped, but Seuliac stared down at his thoughtfully. He looked up with a wry smile. "I never thought I'd see a day I'd consider putting on one of these," he murmured.

Shrugging off his pack, he shook out the red tabard and slipped it over his head. Sunlight glinted off the silver flare symbol on his left breast as he tugged the cloth into place.

"I never thought I'd see the day I'd offer one to an Aedec," Frax responded without emotion.

"What's the plan?"

"Through the wood, due east. Down the escarpment and over the Ysgubar."

Did Seuliac tense? Velacy certainly did.

"Pterfellen lies across the Ysgubar," The white-locked Geffitz shot a quick, unreadable look at Kaphri before looking back at Frax.

Frax gave a single, slow nod.

The characteristically cold, hard smile touched Seuliac's lips once more. "To the sacred, then—if we can first successfully pass through the profane."

"The devil will more likely be waiting in Pterfellen." Frax turned and exited the tower to the outer courtyard.

Velacy had not moved. He gripped the tabard, outrage radiating from him.

"Put it on, Velacy," Seuliac said.

"This is madness!" the younger Geffitz hissed in fury. "He's willing to sacrifice his brother to the monsters of this place. He'll leave us to the mercy of the wood and no one will ever know." His fist was white as he raised the cloth before him. "And this! This is treason to our house! To our name!"

"I don't think so." Seuliac's manner seemed mild as he looked over at his companion, but Kaphri could sense the hardness beneath the surface. Velacy's color heightened further, as if the warlord had rebuked him for being a stubborn child. "It's the way the battle lies, Velacy, and what matters is that Rhynog will be there. Put it on and say no more." Seuliac bent to scoop up his pack and followed Frax out the gate.

Velacy snarled a curse at the warlord's disappearing back before he seemed to recall that Uri and Kaphri were still in the tower with him. He shot a quick, uneasy glance at Uri, then angrily slung the cloth over his shoulder and stormed out.

"Huh!" Uri made a sound of bemusement as he stared at the doorway through which the others had disappeared.

"*They are going into the woods with us?*" Kaphri thought Uri was more intrigued with what had just transpired between their companions than disturbed by their destination. But then, she suspected he'd been aware of Frax's decision to offer the tabards. They always exchanged information.

He glanced down at her with a faint frown. "*So it would seem.*"

"*Is that good?*"

"*It's surprising.*"

"*Why?*"

"*Cadarn and Rhynog walking a common path by mutual agreement? A truce is one thing; but for Rhynog to knowingly depend on Cadarn for protection—that is something unbelievable! Many dead lords of both clans are surely turning in their graves right now. I wonder if those three can really set aside their differences. For us to succeed, I fear they must.*" He paused for a moment in thought, then shook his head.

"*Will the colors of Cadarn protect them, Uri?*"

"*We believe it will. You have a tabard, too.*" He reached over to tug the pack off her shoulders. "*Put it on now. I would've given it to you earlier, but it seemed wiser to let those two come to a decision first. The red and green of Cadarn are definitely the most vivid way to mark us for safe passage, but the Grimmen won't be fooled. It's impossible to guess how it'll respond. Frax is right: he's not even totally safe in there.*"

Realizing now what the piece of red fabric was, she pulled it from the bundle Frax had given to her in the watchroom above. The musty smell of age was heavy as she slipped it over her head and brushed it smooth. If fell over the white cloth of her breeches to her knees.

She held her breath for a moment in fear Uri might say something about the Wyxan clothing she still wore. But, like the Geffitz commander, he appeared to be preoccupied with other things as he helped her into the backpack again. She slowly eased the air from her lungs in relief. As much as she feared and desired to be out to Wyxan influence, she felt reluctant to change her clothing, partly in defiance of Frax's command that she do so, and partly because they were the nicest things she'd ever possessed. They were foolish, vain reasons, and she knew she would never dare give voice to them if challenged.

Uri gave her pack one final tug and turned, beckoning her toward the doorway.

Reluctantly she stepped past him. "*Is it truly as dangerous as they are saying?*"

"*The Grimmenwood?*" His hand firmly propelled her out the tower gate. "*Oh yes! Make no mistake about it. The creatures of the wood will kill us in a heartbeat without Frax.*"

"*Do you fear the wood, Uri?*"

He smiled sourly. "*Yes, I fear it. As I told you once, Willow, more than a little blood of Kitahn flows in my veins. But some of the creatures that dwell in the Grimmenwood are what we call the Eldren: Kep's First Children. Like the Wyxa, they are from an earlier age. They view the world much differently than you or I do. It's only her children of the Second Age that the Earthmother has taught the distinction between good and evil. The Eldren judge such things by a different standard. And I'd feel much easier with two of Kitahn at my side.*" He shook his head.

She already knew more about the Eldren than she had ever desired from her experience with the Wyxa. Still, she had to pursue the topic. "*Are the creatures that took Tobin some of these 'Eldren'?*" She realized that the whole time since the call had paralyzed them, she had not received a single image of the creatures from the warriors' mindspeech.

"*The Cyrwins? Yes.*" Uri paused to tug the huge doors of the gate closed. "*We're falling behind, so let's go.*" The other three had already crossed the broad plaza where they had emerged from the Palenquemas. Frax set a swift pace, stalking far ahead of the Aedecs.

"*What are these Cyrwins?*" She turned to look at him. "*I—Oh!*" She recoiled, suffocating terror rushing to engulf her.

It was an illusion—just an illusion—her mind screamed as she fought to tear herself out of sudden terror. She had seen this before, in the moment they had arrived here, and it was not real!

"*Hey! Willow! They're only statues.*" Uri was staring at her with concern.

Statues? They were something else to her. This was the creature from the attack she had experienced on their first arrival in this place.

"*For a moment I thought that they attacked,*" she told him cautiously, hoping he might say something to reveal if the illusion she experienced was part of the things' purpose without having to ask.

"*Nerves,*" he muttered with a shake of his head. "*Where we're going we can't afford the mistake of a fleeting impression, Willow.*"

It was a mild rebuke for her to steady herself, but it also told her what she needed to know: the effect the statues had on her was not something of which he was aware. If she told him what had happened he would pass it on to Frax, which would be pointless. The commander would ask questions she couldn't answer and it wouldn't do anything to alter the path they must take.

She shuddered. "*What are those things?*"

"*Those are the Cyrwins. The guardians of this caer and its ruling family.*"

Cyrwins. The word was like ice water splashed on her flesh. Those were the things that had taken Tobin? As Uri turned away, she remained rooted to the spot, staring up at the two great stone statues that reared, one on each side of the tower gate, their splayed, sharp front hooves slashing the air.

They were similar to images she had seen of Geffitzi work animals—horses, they called them—except these were larger. And, where she had perceived those horses had a thick coat of hair, the sculptor of these creatures had made them smooth-skinned and serpent-like. She could see the pattern of scales on the mighty stone ripples of their flesh. Her eyes traveled almost feverishly over the huge nightmare forms, taking in the long, delicately tapered muzzles, the graceful, elongated necks that flexed so threateningly. Their legs were long and slim, their rearing, twisting bodies lithe and screaming of speed. Long, lashing tails ended in barbs raised to strike a final, deadly blow. Their very appearance shouted cruelty and evil.

"*Demon breed,*" she murmured.

"*What?*" Uri swung about sharply to look at her.

She moved hurriedly to catch up with him, glad to leave the rearing stone monsters behind, but uneasy to have them at her back, even inanimate as they were.

Uri studied her as she fell into stride beside him. Recollection of his angry reaction to Velacy's use of the word prompted her to elaborate on her comment hastily. "Frax spoke of a joining between the first lord of Kitahn and the power that dwells in the Grimmenwood."

Uri grunted and nodded. *"Ah, yes, the blood of the Eldren. Well, now the tale comes back to haunt them. No one knows how much truth is in those stories. There's been so much posturing and arrogance in the old houses for so long that it's difficult to determine truth from fiction. It is true the sons of Kitahn hold a certain power over the wood, but it also holds a certain power over them. The wood allows them within its depths where it allows no others. Of course, that has never been enough for the Lords of Cadarn. It's been one of their favorite pastimes to search out terrible, vicious creatures to loose in the Grimmenwood for sport. It's part of Kitahni heritage. Down through the generations they've ridden its paths, wild and roughshod, spilling blood to feed its soil and savoring the joy of the kill while building the wood's strength and power. But it makes certain demands of them, as well. The Cyrwins are children of the Grimmenwood. They guard this caer and have even gone into battle for Cadarn, though they will only bear the truebloods of Kitahn upon their backs. In exchange, all the sons of Kitahn are lured by the Cyrwin song. You felt it, and you're not even Geffitzi. Imagine what it is like for them. Many believe it's a test of their willpower, and sometimes they fail. Some have succumbed to it, falling into an obsession that grips them like a fever burning away thoughts of anything else. Some have languished and died. Others,"* he shrugged, *"have disappeared into the wood, never to be seen again. They say that on rare occasions the Cyrwins seek out and take heirs into the woods to subject them to a test of worthiness. If they pass the tests, the Cyrwins will accept them as equals and follow their leadership."*

"Is that what they've done in taking Tobin?"

Uri nodded wearily. "*Frax fears so. If it's true, Tobin might be better off dead.*"

"*Uri!*"

"*The song is sweet, the singer is not.*" His expression was bitter when he looked down at her. "*The tests they set are cruel, Willow. To fail is to die a terrible death. Most of the young Kitahns hold a burning hope they'll be fetched to the testing, to ride out of the woods bonded with one of the Cyrwin as warrior and steed. But there are many more dead sons of Kitahn who went into that wood with hope and pride in their hearts than have ever emerged, triumphant, as Cyrwinmasters.*

"*They are magnificent beasts of the hunt and war, Willow. Fleet as the wind. But I can tell you right now, I wouldn't want to encounter one. They're a nasty-natured, bloodthirsty lot, with a wide streak of evil and malice in them. It's said those are the mutual traits that bind the two—the Cyrwins and the Kitahns.*"

She glanced up to meet a gleam of teasing amusement in his eyes. "*Can he succeed, Uri? Does he have a chance of becoming one of those Cyrwinmasters?*"

The big Geffitz sobered. "*Believe me, if anyone ever had the slightest chance of succeeding, it's Tobin Kitahn. There has always been something different, something untamed, about that boy.*"

"*I hope you're right.*"

Uri looked at the woods, a frown creasing his features. "*I do too, Willow.*"

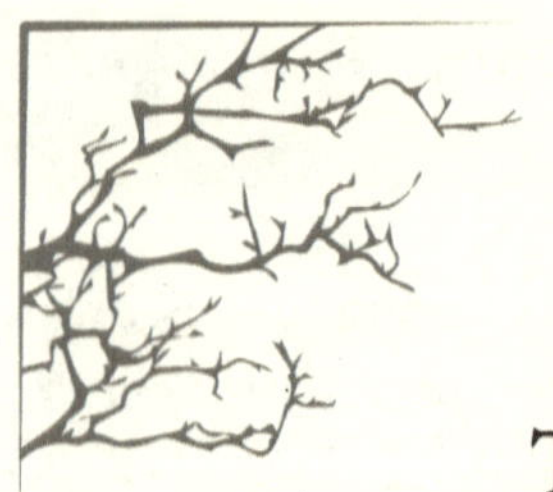

Chapter 58
The East Road

The situation was a complete disaster. Tobin was gone, the Wyxa were still trying to manipulate the Priestess, the Balandra and Araxis knew exactly where they were, three of his companions were the enemy, and their path was leading them through the Grimmenwood.

Before the barrier, their goal was clear. They would take her back before the Circles and let wiser heads decide what to do with her. After the barrier, it became more complicated. Something trapped them in the south, and they had nothing to gain from destroying her. Their goal changed, but it remained clear: helping her move forward with the geas correlated with helping their people regain their lands. Now, he wondered if any of those things still held true.

Kep! His head felt as if it would burst. Frax blinked hard, trying to fight off the muzzy, pre-occupied sensation blanketing his brain. The effects of the Grimmen's twisted workings were slow to fade, making it difficult for him to focus right at the worst time! He had too much to think about and no time for delay.

The Evil One, Araxis, needed the Priestess in order to restore his original power. He had opened a way for the Balandra, long banished by the Wyxa, to re-invade this world and help him resume his reign of terror. Which was a solid reason to eliminate her. But the Guardian, Gemma, claimed the Priestess was the only one who could help the Geffitzi reclaim their stolen lands and defeat the threat to their world. Even the Wyxa did not deny that. Which seemed a good reason to help her. Then there were the forces, including the Wyxa and others, unknown, who wanted to secure their own desired outcomes without consideration for the Geffitzi Clans.

He refused to approach this situation with any thought of a loss: a Geffitz commander who viewed things from that perspective would never make a move. One went into battle with an eye toward success, using every resource available.

It would have helped to be able to define what their success might be in this situation. He would settle for the removal of Araxis and his barrier. And her. The last of the Ly Kai invaders, gone.

What resources did he have? An ignorant girl who might act if she found a way to remove the things working to block her actions. If she mastered and used the right defenses, of which she possessed no knowledge. He couldn't be sure she was able to resolve her own situation, much less solve the greater problem.

Was he acting on what he hoped she could do?

Yes. Hope was all he had.

Hope was not enough.

She had to learn how to react when the challenge came, and not just lift her chin and allow the blade to bite her throat, which appeared to be her natural inclination. But he couldn't teach her, not now, while he led this mixed lot into the Grimmenwood. With Tobin to share the burden, maybe, but not while trying to keep them alive against a truculent, if not outright hostile force. Besides, his skill lay in commanding men already trained to fight.

One among them, however, did it all: supervising every aspect, from induction through the command of warriors on the battlefield. One with a superior reputation for getting things done—to the reluctant admiration of his enemies—and he did have the time to devote to the task.

Frax looked over at the Warlord of Rhynog.

URI AND KAPHRI CAUGHT up with their three companions at the northwest corner of the massive stone plateau that was Caer Cadarn. There the main road curved off to the north, toward the forest, while another, slightly less imposing way forked to the east, along the longer axis of the plateau. When Frax struck off down the narrower route, dismay conflicted with her relief. With the looming threat of Balandra on their trail, she'd feared he would take the shorter path north to the cover of the wood. It would have been the safest choice. But the geas steadily tightened inside her as she walked, and she feared that if they continued northward, its resistance would freeze her to immobility. With the turn to the east, the pain eased. Still, the sheltering trees were a long distance across the grassy field, and the open space around them now set her heart pounding in fear.

The others must have shared her sense of threat: ahead, Seuliac and Frax both scanned the sky.

Velacy, however, kept his eyes locked on the ground, his jaw set in a stubborn line. She saw he had put on the tabard.

A flicker of sympathy ran through her. She understood how he must feel; they were both being swept along against their wills.

Massive stone buildings clung close to the base of the plateau. The structures were multiple levels, their many-windowed faces silent and dark.

Despite the warm morning sun on her skin, she shivered at the sight of them.

"Troop barracks." The buildings finally stirred a reaction in Velacy. His eyes swept the long row of stone fronts and he spat on the roadway.

To Kaphri, the empty structures represented another depressing reminder of the life driven from this land. It was a relief to leave them behind for the sheer, towering stone wall of the plateau once more. Uri had withdrawn into his thoughts beside her, and the walk along the base of the caer began to stretch on endlessly. More than forty paces ahead, she could see Frax and Seuliac locked in some private debate. The warlord shook his head as Frax, with a slight downward motion of a raised hand, persisted in some point.

Velacy had lapsed into his sulk once more.

The way was suddenly not long enough, however, when they reached the easternmost corner of the plateau.

Kaphri's heart drummed in her ears and her palms were moist when she looked across the wide field of tall, lush grasses between them and the dark forest wall. She could sense the mysterious watcher there, waiting, and she shuddered. She was afraid of it, yes, but it was nothing compared to the terror the Wyxa had worked on her in the tower. That had nearly driven her to distraction.

It had pushed her to the point of threatening to abandon her companions.

She blushed miserably at the recall. What must Frax think of her behavior?

But—her breath caught in her throat—he had kissed her! Amidst the burn of confusion and humiliation, her heart gave a little secret flutter of timid joy. After everything that had happened, with Tobin being snatched away, she had resolved not to think about the incident. But she could not stop the secret rush of elation the memory stirred inside her. He had taken her in his arms. He had held her and said her name. He had kissed her.

What did that mean?

What, came back her sobering thought, did she want it to mean? The giddy sensation dissolved, replaced again by fear. Too much was happening, too fast, and she had no idea of the consequences of any of it.

She flexed her cold fingers.

The road curved to the south now, around the eastern face of the caer. Frax had paused at the turn, studying the trees across from him while he waited for the rest of them to catch up. She noticed the grass in front of him was pushed down and aside by the passage of something large. Perhaps a Cyrwin had approached from that direction while coming to lure Tobin away.

"*Single file.*" The commander started forward at a northeastward angle toward the closest line of the woods.

Uri gestured her onto the path ahead of him, then closed in behind her. In front of her, Velacy glanced up at the sky. Kaphri followed his gaze.

Nothing broke the clear blue of the late spring morning.

Halfway across the field, a cool breeze whipped briskly up on their backs from the west. It bowed the grass in waves and carried a strange yet vaguely familiar scent. Seuliac and Velacy's attention snapped to the west, their heads lifting as they inhaled and their steps slowed.

"*Uri?*" She glanced back at the warrior behind her uneasily.

"*It's the smell of the Great Water, Willow. Although they have large inland holdings, the Aedecs have traditionally lived with the sea. The name of their caer is Rhynog, or Seacrown. It's been many days since they've breathed that scent.*"

The Great Water. Yes. It carried the scent of the breeze in the marshlands as it chased the fog away on their first day in the Palenquemas, when she and Frax discovered how far the Wyxa had carried them.

Seacrown. Windhedge. "*Uri,*" sudden curiosity caught her. "*What does Caer Cadarn mean?*"

"*Ah. I wondered when you would ask.*" The sense of amusement had come back into his sending. "*It means Castle Blood.*"

"*Castle Blood?*" She felt her face go pale.

Uri grinned. "*The story goes that a particularly difficult Kitahni lord had stirred up enough trouble to unite several neighboring holds against him. Their armies were approaching with combined numbers so large that it was sure they must be successful, even in breaching the woods. Kitahn's forces were already weakened by repeated battles with these same clans, and it looked as if the caer would, at the very least, undergo a painfully long and costly siege.*

"*Now, there's a certain rare and renowned red fabric dye which comes only from a plant in the mountains behind Cadarn. At the time, it brought a great deal of money into the caer's coffers with its exportation. The arrogant, defiant lord ordered the whole year's supply mixed with water and poured on the outer ramparts to warn the would-be attackers that their blood would stain his walls with the upcoming battle.*

"*It worked even better than he expected. From her high plateau, Cadarn can be seen beyond the Grimmenwood for a great distance from the north. The effect of the reddened walls on the approaching attackers proved so powerful and terrifying that it forced the holderlords to reconsider their battle plans in the face of their men's fears and superstitions. They quietly disbanded their unnerved armies and went home. The name stuck—and the dye fell out of popularity very quickly with the rest of the world.*" He laughed. "*So it became a traditional ceremony. Each time a new Lord takes—took—his place as the master of the caer, they reddened the walls as a warning to any who would test his power. It's the same dye that colors the tabard you wear.*"

Kaphri looked down in dismay. A ray of sun sparked a flare from the silver on her breast. Blood and battle. She gave an inward shudder.

She could not, however, resist one last look back at Caer Cadarn from a distance. Sure enough, the great walls towering above the plain were faded but still stained dull red. The sight of the place in the early sun was enough to cause her to pause. Fear squeezed her heart. Everything around her seemed hugely strange and terrifying.

"*Not everything that has to do with the Geffitzi is blood and battle, Willow.*" Uri's hand caught her pack lightly and propelled her after the others again. "*It's too bad you couldn't see the seaport below the caer. The place is renowned for its beauty. The sea walks in late spring—just about now—are carpeted with the warm pink of tamarin blossoms, and the air is heady with their sweet scent, while oriander hedges bow low under their burden of white blooms. It's an ancient town, and the streets are lined with huge trees that spread their shadows over vined walls and lush gardens.*"

"*Its name, Uri,*" she snatched at the distraction he offered. She needed something to help her fight off the feeling that she was suddenly overwhelmed. "*What is its name?*"

"*Kessimi.*"

The word was pretty but carried no image. "*What does it mean?*" She was almost afraid to ask.

"*A Kitahni lord named it for his ladylove.*"

"*Her story, Uri, what is it?*"

"*Oh-h,*" Kaphri felt his amused hesitation. "*That doesn't quite fit with what I'm trying to do here.*"

"*Tell me.*"

He sighed. "*All right. An early Kitahni lord named Tarlik kidnapped a feudal enemy's daughter and held her hostage. This girl, Kessimi, was a lovely, sweet creature, and while he held her prisoner, he fell under the spell of her innocence. When Tarlik got what he demanded of her father, however, he found himself forced to uphold his part of the bargain, to return Kessimi. He wanted to keep her, but to prove to her that he was an honorable man, he sent her back to her family.*

"*Losing her nearly drove him mad. He named the seaport—the seaport from which she left him—in her name.*

"*The girl was eager to return to her folk, but once there, she found her thoughts were only for the Kitahni captor from whom she had been delivered. Discovering this, her furious father set about arranging a speedy marriage for her with another house. Horrified at the thought of an alliance with any other, the girl fled to the protection of a religious order. Meanwhile, Tarlik, consumed with his thoughts of Kessimi, lost interest in other things and would only sit in his greathall, day after day, staring darkly and silently into nothingness. A younger brother, grown impatient with his Lordship's brooding, finally slipped away to the rival court, hoping to discover a means of firing his lord's interest in life once more—even to stealing Kessimi again. Kessimi's mother's guards swiftly captured and unmasked him as the enemy. The woman, however, loving her daughter and weary of the feud destroying her family and sapping her kingdom's resources, saw a chance in the younger Kitahni Lord to exert some of her influence. She revealed Kessimi's situation to him and gave him secret safe passage out of the kingdom so he could return to tell Tarlik, who instantly came to life with outrage at his love's ill-treatment. He sent a warning to his old opponent that he was coming and that nothing would stop him from retrieving Kessimi from the place where she had taken sanctuary.*

"*He sailed his ship boldly into the harbor and stormed the convent, kicking in doors until he found her and carried her from the place. Meanwhile, her father, persuaded by her mother that a peaceable match would be more beneficial than conflict—that Cadarn would make a better uneasy ally than an outright enemy—refrained from a confrontation. He also thought he could get back what he had originally lost at his daughter's kidnapping. But it was kept as a portion of her dowry.*" Uri paused, arching an eyebrow as he waited for her reaction.

"*Is that true?*" she demanded, caught between chagrin and disbelief.

"*Actually,*" Frax cut in coolly, "*She was with child when she returned to her family, and her furious father turned her out, sending her to the monastery. When word got back to Tarlik, he stormed in to reclaim her, making the breach between the houses even worse. Another house intermediated, eventually achieving a sanctioned binding, but it did not heal the rift between them.*"

"*Really? I heard the bloody bastard kept her! Didn't fulfill his end of the bargain at all.*" Seuliac's sending was dryly amused.

"*Not so!*" Velacy protested. "*He put her on her father's ship and sent her packing, glad to be rid of her. She was so furious at his rejection that she seized the ship and became a scavenging pirate—preying particularly on Tarlik's fleet.*"

There was a moment of hanging silence; then, the four warriors roared with laughter.

Kaphri could only look at them in confusion.

They had reached the edge of the wood.

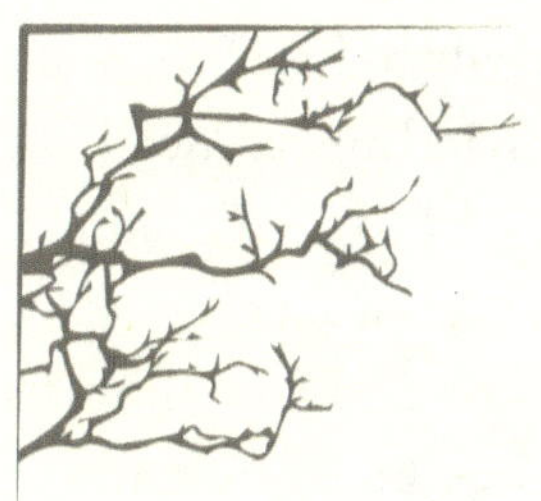

Chapter 59
Betrayal

The laughter relieved some of the stress that had been building in them. Even Velacy lost some of his sulkiness, but it was short-lived as Frax put his hand up, signaling them to remain where they stood at the edge of the field.

They watched in uneasy silence while, head up, back straight with alert tension, he stepped forward to stand just within the shadowed reaches of the forest. After what seemed to Kaphri a breathless eternity, his hand went to his belt, and he drew the long blade that hung there.

"What the hell's he doing?" Velacy muttered.

"Offering first blood," Uri answered softly, his eyes locked on Frax. "In his company, the woods might let us within, but it could still send its creatures against us. By freely shedding first blood, he ritually offers himself as security for our safe passage."

Kaphri's chest tightened with dread, but she could not tear her eyes away as the commander shifted the weapon into his left hand while holding his right poised at shoulder height before him. Slowly he raised the knife and drew the blade across his palm so that his blood ran in a thin trickle to drip onto the forest floor. Velacy hissed in displeasure beside her. She glanced over at him, following his gaze to where the Frax's blood pooled brightly on the leaves of the forest floor. A dark mist began to rise from it, coiling and spiraling like some living thing. It snaked up through the air along the path of the falling blood until it enwreathed his hand. Swirling and growing denser, a small cloud of dark smoke clung hungrily to his flesh. Then it evaporated into nothingness. Frax closed his hand and turned back to face them, expressionless. "By offering my blood to the Grimmen, I've identified my lineage and declared that we do not seek to challenge the woods. The Grimmen accepts that and will allow us to enter." Velacy's uneasy curse went ignored as he continued. "It does not mean we're completely safe. This remains guardedly hostile territory. It will wait and watch. We must not do anything to make it question our intentions." He shot a glance at Kaphri.

She met his look without reaction, but a flicker of unhappiness ran through her. After the incident in the tower, did he think he had reason to doubt her? He did not need to concern himself with her; she was back in control of her thoughts and emotions again.

The Geffitz commander's eyes moved on to the others as he continued. "Despite the Wyxa's intentions, they were ironically generous with supplies, but we'll still have to ration carefully for the time we're in the woods. Meanwhile, don't eat any fruit or plants from this place. I've heard tales that the wood can turn them poison between the vine and your mouth if it chooses, and I don't think any of us wants to test that. Also, there'll be no hunting. It's no secret that the Grimmenwood thrives on blood: if we come as hunters, we make ourselves part of that game. We can't risk it mistaking a food kill for a challenge or an assault.

"Water is the lifeblood of Kep and sacred to all her children; even the Grimmen will not tamper with that. It should be plentiful and safe to drink. But, as with many other places, we should be wary of what may dwell in any pool.

"We'll be able to move fairly fast once we pick up a trail, but we still have a long distance to travel. We'll walk in pairs. I'll take point with Seuliac to my left. Uri, you're the next closest in Cadarnian blood: you bring up the rear with Velacy on your right. The Priestess will be in the middle. We'll watch in teams for now: Velacy and me, Uri and Seuliac. Velacy and I will take first duty. Everyone stays close—and, most importantly, be sure you know where the Priestess is at all times. Nobody assumes that she's with someone else." He glanced at Kaphri again. "*I'm sorry, but what little privacy you've had is a thing of the past. If we lose you, we lose the battle.*"

"So what do we do now, start walking and wait for something to attack us?"

The corners of Frax's mouth lifted in hard humor, making Kaphri think Velacy's question was probably a closer summation of their situation than the heir suspected. "There's a clearing a league north of here. We can pick up an eastward trail from there."

"You expect to find a trail after twenty-odd years?" Velacy gave him a dubious look. "We've been shut out of the south for a long time, Kitahn."

"It will be there. Cadarn did not make the trails that run throughout the Grimmenwood, Velacy. We only use them."

"Only a trail? Not a road?" Seuliac's question was faintly mocking, but Kaphri could read the sharp interest in his eyes.

All trace of humor disappeared from Frax. "The war roads are no myth, Seuliac. The Grimmen allowed Cadarn to make them ages ago. But, by their very nature, the Ways of Blood are broad and exposed to the sky, rendering them useless in light of our pursuit. And they lead to... other places."

Kaphri caught the image of broad, white-paved roadways cutting through the forest. The thought of vast armies of Cadarnian warriors moving over them to do battle caused her to shiver despite the sun on her back. She did not have to be a military strategist to understand the advantages a clear, protected way through the Grimmenwood would give Cadarn against any other army forced to move around the wood's immense boundary. And "other places," as Frax so delicately put it, would mean toward the strongholds of the enemies of Cadarn.

"Not so eager to find the Holy Land as you were to find the rest of us, were you?"

Frax made a broad, sweeping gesture that took in the forest in front of them. "Why, Warlord, this is Holy Land right before us."

Seuliac's eyes narrowed. "A warrior's shrine?" he asked warily.

"A killer's shrine," Frax corrected him.

The white-locked warrior raised an eyebrow in an elegant gesture of mocking surprise. "Do I detect a note of bitterness in those words—from the Commander of the Edge of Cadarn?

For a moment, tense silence hung over them as they waited for Frax's reply.

When he finally spoke, it was as if he chose his words very carefully."How many of your people have been lost, Seuliac? How many of mine? How many more will die before we are through with this? If we're successful, our people will return home—but they will be greatly diminished. There is much healing that needs to be done."

Seuliac stiffened, his chin lifted, his expression wary. "Are Kitahn's forces so severely diminished?" he asked, his eyes sharp as he watched his counterpart.

"You know better. They are no less than Rhynog."

The words had a surprising effect on the warlord. He abruptly relaxed with a sigh. "It's true; there will be enough to do just keeping common folk from killing each other over the setting of a fence stone. Dull work for a warrior." A shadow seemed to pass over his features, and Kaphri was surprised by how weary he suddenly looked. "It has changed, hasn't it?"

In the next moment, however, he squared his shoulders and, with a flick of his raven and white locks, transformed once again into the cold, cynical warrior. "Then we may be going to the last real battle we'll see for a long time, Cadarn. We'll have to make it a good one."

A grim smile twisted Frax's lips. "And high time to begin it, too."

Seuliac nodded agreement, and without further comment, Frax turned, gesturing for them to follow him.

A nerve-shattering shriek ripped the air above them.

Uri thrust Kaphri behind him while Seuliac and Velacy dropped low, bows strung and ready. A heavy thrashing in the branches overhead rained leaves down on them.

There was another piercing scream, and something took wing above them, flying off toward the caer. Kaphri twisted to see it, but Frax caught her by the upper arm and dragged her deeper under the trees beside him. For a long, frozen moment, no one moved.

The cry came again, faint with distance.

"Kep!"

She was not sure who muttered the word. Uri and Velacy nervously scanned the branches overhead as they lowered their weapons. Seuliac remained immobile, watching the sky toward the caer. He came out of his stance with exaggerated slowness, muscles rigid as he lowered his bow to his side. He threw his head back and drew a deep breath. The knots of muscle in his shoulders flowed away to rippling flesh as he eased the air from his lungs.

"A cursed pyanth!" He spat the words. His eyes smoldered with unreleased tension and fury as he turned back to glare at Frax.

"No." Frax shook his head. "That's one foulness that was never brought here."

"Maybe so, but you have them now."

"The spawn of Omurda," Uri murmured. Kaphri caught an image of a large, black bird with an evil-looking hooked beak and terrible claws. "The dark power under the Maugrock is extending its reach."

Was this pyanth-thing acting as a lookout for that darkness?

Kaphri watched Frax frown.

"All the more reason to push ahead swiftly," he said. "Let's move out before something else comes to check out the disturbance."

Wrapped in their individual misgivings, they followed him into the shadows of the Grimmenwood.

WHEN, AFTER THE FIRST few heartbeats, horrible, monstrous things did not fall upon her to rend her limb from limb, Kaphri allowed herself to breathe again. But she still could not allow herself to relax as she followed Frax and Seuliac.

At the edge of the woods, dense patches of plants, their round, drooping leaves centered on single stems that made them look like so many small, massed green mounds, covered the forest floor. She moved through them cautiously, fearful of what might lurk beneath the canopies of their shin-high caps. Meanwhile, the warriors plowed through without a downward glance.

The trees were not as tall as she had imagined when she gazed at them from the tower watch, but their branches grew well above the ground so that the way was clear and unhampered. The filtered sunlight gave them a clear view of their surroundings, and the morning air was surprisingly cool and pleasant—not tainted and foul as she had expected. It was the same as any other woods she had passed through, except for one thing: no bird sang, and no small animal stirred the greenery or rustled on the ground.

The crunch of dried leaves beneath their boots sounded unnaturally loud in her ears. It brought back a memory of the woods above the barrier, and she shivered.

"*This place doesn't seem different from any other woods I've seen,*" Velacy observed tightly after a moment, "*except for this cursed silence.*"

"*Yes. I've never heard tale of the Grimmenwood being silent,*" Uri agreed. His footsteps slowed. "*Frax?*"

The Geffitz leader had already stopped, his eyes searching the treetops above them. He shook his head and looked around at Kaphri. "Priestess?" He spoke aloud.

At first, she was confused, but then she realized what he meant: he wanted her to scan the area around them mentally. Acutely aware of the watcher's presence, she had refrained from curiosity about what did or did not move in this place.

When she sent him a mental sensation of reluctance, he continued to regard her with flat expectation.

Plainly, he did not intend to accept a refusal.

Time drew out as her reluctance warred with his pressing demand until she finally acquiesced. Wiping moist palms on the white cloth of her breeches under the tabard and shivering inwardly, she reached out.

Resentful of his demand as she felt, she was still able to contain her surprise and confused relief at what she discovered. *"There are living creatures all about us."*

"This is a forest. What kind of observation is that?"

She pointedly ignored Velacy's acidic comment, looking again to Frax. His expression remained unchanged as he continued to regard her.

He wanted more? Surely he didn't want her to speak any further about what she'd found. It would reveal to the others how she could do more than merely touch minds. That she could also actively invade their thoughts. He must realize that.

But again, her sense of reluctance met unmoved expectation.

Cold fear closed about her heart. Why was Frax showing this sudden change in attitude, especially in front of the others? Was he angry with her for the weakness she'd displayed in the tower room? Did he blame her for their situation? For Tobin's anger? Tobin's loss?

No. None of those things. A Geffitz warrior would not lay blame in that way.

Then why?

Nothing but cold, rigid expectation answered her mental touch.

Very well, then. She would give him exactly what he asked, and he could cope with the results.

Confusion and resentment rising inside her, she reached into the tiny minds in the trees around them. "*They are not frightened. As we approach, their minds slow and blur as if they fall asleep. The ones at the edge of the forest where we entered are beginning to stir again, almost as if awakening. They do not seem concerned about it. When they wake they go on with their animal thoughts.*" For the first time, she realized the forest wasn't entirely silent: the sounds were simply so faint with distance as to be missed.

"*You can't know anything like that. Animals don't send!*" Velacy protested hotly.

"They don't have to send," Seuliac said. His gray eyes were bright as he studied her. "*She can get into their minds.*"

Uri gave Frax a quick, penetrating glance, but since he didn't react with surprise, Kaphri suspected the commander had already made him aware of her skill. Velacy, on the other hand, appeared shocked. His gaze flicked to his fellow Aedec.

Seuliac's eyes remained steadfastly locked on her. "*You can do that with us, too, can't you?*" He put the question out for all of them to hear.

Control. Despite her thundering heart, her mask of inexpression gave away nothing as she stared back at the warlord. Control! Oh, Hredroth! Why was Frax doing this? He just stood there, watching and listening without any reaction. She reached out mentally, seeking something—anything—to guide her in how to respond.

A further jolt of shock ran through her. The Kitahni Commander was shielded against her!

"*Answer me, girl!*"

She twitched as if the warlord had stung her flesh with a lash. Anger welled inside her. "Yes," she spoke aloud in their language, her voice taking on an evenness she did not feel as her eyes swept over them all. "*Yes, I can. Anytime, anywhere. Even through shields.*" She took a deep breath and added. "*And you would never, ever know it.*" Let Frax cope with their reactions to that statement for a while.

Velacy's expression of revile as he took several steps backward did not bother her. It was hardly a change in his response toward her. But the expression in Seuliac's eyes made her feel like she should seek some shelter.

"*That is not a concern, Warlord. She won't use it on us.*" Frax gave her a hard glare as he rejoined the exchange.

She drew no comfort from his presence now. His action of shielding against her had been a clear message.

Seuliac gave a short, humorless laugh. "*Nonetheless, Kitahn, it is interesting. It could be of use.*"

The Commander shrugged. "*Yes. But it's served its usefulness for now. We have our answer. Let's move on.*"

Kaphri was seized with a feeling of cold isolation as the others fell in around her with thoughtful silence. It was as if she had violated some sense of trust between the warriors and her.

Seuliac glanced back at her once, his gaze cold and calculating, and Kaphri's sense of resentful confusion heightened. Something about being the object of the warlord's interest stirred a reaction in her that nearly equaled her uneasiness of the watcher. She could not bring herself to meet his eyes.

Instead, she turned her attention to Frax. "*What purpose does this silence serve?*" she demanded irritably.

It was not the question she really wanted to ask.

He shook his head without looking back at her. "I don't know." He spoke aloud. "But it will certainly make it harder for anything to stalk us, won't it?"

No one responded.

Chapter 60
Frax and Kaphri Talk

Frax Kitahn had no way of knowing what to expect when he stepped into the shadows of the Grimmenwood. Shock? Recognition? A cold sweep of evaluation?

Childhood tales filled with fear and probably inflated for terrorizing effect ran through his head. They, coupled with the numbing effects of the Cyrwin song he still suffered, made him move inside a nightmare of potential disaster.

The fact he experienced nothing when he stepped inside its dark border left him as disconcerted as an all-out attack would have. It felt the same as any other forest on this world.

That was a dangerous, deadly deception. The shadowy guardian that jealously encircled Caer Cadarn with dark and deadly arms was not going to release its charge today. The Grimmen knew a son of Kitahn stood at its edge. It knew he was freely in the company of an enemy it had worked to protect Cadarn against since the establishment of its guardianship.

The Grimmen was not pleased.

Frax never doubted that sometime in the past, one of his forefathers had made some sort of pact with the force, demon or whatever dwelled inside the wood, though what form the binding had taken, he was unable to say. The Lords of Cadarn then—as today—were willing to do anything they deemed necessary to secure the power and strength of their line. It was Caer Cadarn, and nothing came before it. But, despite any ancient pact, blood did not guarantee his safety here. There were the occasional stories of how the Grimmen had acted with cold capriciousness against someone of the blood. Strange, unexplained hunting accidents scattered Kitahni history. As Uri told Kaphri, the woods made its demands upon the family—more than even the Caspanis, close allies as they were, were aware. Soft-spoken curses often followed expressions of fierce, defiant pride the alliance historically stirred in the Kitahns. But to give voice to any doubt outside the family would have been an unforgivable betrayal. And among family, only a look, a sound, or a single word was tolerated.

Forced beyond the wood's shadows at the tender age of six, Frax had never sensed the power of its presence. Others with more experience had been content to let the place fade in their memories, finding more pleasant things of which to lament the loss. So the Grimmenwood had never been more than a shadowy, mysterious thing to him.

Until today.

Now, suddenly, the Grimmenwood stood before him in magnificent, dark reality, waiting to discover what a son of Kitahn, in the company of Aedecs, wanted of it.

He had no idea if the ritual he performed would work. Uri might guess his trepidation, suspecting no situation like this had ever risen in Kitahni history, but the Aedecs and the girl must not know. He had recalled a snatch of an ancient story while desperately seeking a way to secure safe passage for his dangerously mixed company. An ancestor once offered her blood in an attempt to appease the Grimmen for some offense given. Legend said the act served its purpose and the offender hunted the woods for many years afterward.

But as he moved the blade across his palm and his blood flowed, he knew the wood was accepting his request with conditions. As the dark wreath of smoke curled up around his hand, a frosty cold sank into the flesh around the wound, numbing the nerves with its chill. It simmered through his blood to his heart, then flashed out to every part of his body. Before he could flinch, it vanished and the dark smoke around his palm dissolved away, taking all traces of blood, leaving the hand unblemished, the cut healed. The Grimmen recognized him, the healing said. It weighed the sincerity of his intentions and found them acceptable. It would allow him to bring these enemies within its sanctum, but there would be a price. A high, bitter price.

He accepted without hesitation.

In that instant, Frax learned something of the Grimmen's nature. The force had gambled on a level of loyalty he could not give, and it would never forgive his choice. Too late, he remembered his warning to Kaphri: he had bargained with an Eldren, and it did not think the same way as he did. Its rules were different. Now he would have to stay on constant alert to circumvent any treachery the woods might attempt.

Frustration ran through him, genuine, true frustration, with its source inside him—he made sure of that before he gave in to a brief moment of self-indulgence. How was he supposed to know the right choices to bring this thing to a successful conclusion? To him, they were all in the wrong place and moving in the wrong direction. Taking her to the Ly Kai city would not remove the barrier. That didn't change what he had to do: he could only move forward the way he'd done since the first, fateful moment Tobin detected that little flit of movement back in the dimness of Omurda. Trusting his instincts, trying to anticipate the infinite possibilities. Trying to deal with each twist of manipulation as it came. Frax broke off from the line of thought before...

Too late.

A pang of bitter resentment ran through him.

Tobin was gone, taken by the Grimmenwood.

How many good sons of Kitahn had its demon-creatures claimed away in one manner or another? Kep forbid his brother should become another of their number! He bargained with the Grimmen for the rest of this group, but for Tobin, he could only wait.

Like so many others of the blood had waited down through time.

The Cyrwin song rang in the back of his mind as he struggled to keep his thoughts focused on the task before him. It was bad enough the call still affected him, fuzzing his mind so that everything around him appeared slightly remote, but its cursed effects still coursed hotly in his blood, too.

Once inflamed, he was finding his passions difficult to extinguish. Just the memory of Kaphri and him in the tower room sent a tingle of heat through him. Allowing just a brushing thought of that sweet mouth, the gentle touch of those lips—what it might have led to—sent the blood roaring in his brain.

How long would the cursed animal reaction persist? He struck it aside in disgust, understanding now what the Cyrwins had done to him.

Lewd, salacious beasts! Had they enjoyed seducing a son of Cadarn to an enemy? He'd heard enough stories about the demon-horses and their lusty mental touch that mortification stung him now in retrospect. Any son of Kitahn knew the Cyrwins used their telepathic ability to stimulate the erogenous centers in the brains of other creatures. And that they had none of the moral restraint to stop them using it. The Cyrwins knew exactly what they did, and they had used it on him.

They had complicated everything! He and the girl had begun to share an easy companionship in the swamp. They'd been able to talk and discover truths beyond anger and bitterness, so he did not think of her so much an enemy as an individual with shared enemies and goals. Even during those early hours in Cadarn, she had been nothing more than a fellow warrior.

But now! Now he couldn't look at her without lust firing in his veins.

Damn the Cyrwins! Now, more than ever, he needed to work with her. He needed information about what she sensed from this place. He needed to discuss her encounter with the treacherous Wyxa, what they might have revealed to her about the Winisp's cursed prophecy, and their prospective roles. But right now, the thought of speaking with her brought an uncomfortable flush to his skin that made him clench his teeth.

He fully understood Kaphri's frustration with the depth of manipulation around them. He felt it too. Acutely. Pointless to fume over. For the sake of his world, he must endure it.

He wasn't helpless against it, either. There were things he could do, something he'd already set in motion, something he had serious doubts about.

What he was about to do would take him out of direct influence over the priestess just when he needed it most, forcing him to become a bystander. Unfortunately, their safe passage through the wood demanded his entire focus. She required much, much more attention to prepare her for what lay ahead. The battle that would come down to Klandar Bayne's simple reasoning: that either she could or she could not. He must expose her to as much warrior training, mentally and physically, as possible.

He'd chosen a drastic action. Uri would object strongly for more than one good reason. Frax squelched a sudden burn of jealousy at the thought of the other's easy relationship with the girl. Regardless of how any of them might react, he knew it was the right thing to do. He'd paid a high price to gain them access to the Grimmenwood—one none of the others could imagine. It was time for someone else to step up and bear some of the burden, too.

We do what we must do: he allowed himself one quick image of Kaphri's face, the weary resignation in her sending as she'd expressed her understanding of the task before them. Somehow, it seemed appropriate. Then he set about with cold, ruthless precision, isolating his personal feelings to his deepest depths, preparing for the things to come.

We do what we must do.

SHE WAS HURT, AND SHE was angry. Try as she might, no amount of self-admonition or reminders of the lessons in control impressed upon her so rigorously in Kryie Karth, helped. If she had not feared the woods so much, she would have screamed aloud to release some of the tension coiled inside her.

For the last several hours, Kaphri had managed to keep everything locked away. That, at least, was something she had mastered very well from her earlier years. Now, however, as the quiet of the woods slipped past in an endless vista of trees, everything was catching up with her, ruthlessly forcing itself to the forefront of her mind. Between the Wyxa and what they would have done, Gemma, the crystal, the illusions of attack she'd experienced, the dead in Cadarn, the Cyrwins and Tobin's abduction, the presence in the woods, Frax exposing her mind-invading ability to the others. His kisses...

No. Not the kisses! They were something strange and unexpected but good. Something she would not allow to mix with the rest of the things distressing her. Besides, they would add too much into her already churning emotions. They must stay separate and locked away.

But the rest! Her thoughts spun with misery. Of all the things in her head, the worst was the memory of how the fear had driven her to say such cowardly things in the tower. It didn't matter if Frax said the Ankar Mekt had been working on her; she'd said them. The Wyxa had gotten to her so easily, and she hadn't recognized it. What must Frax think of her, cowering and threatening to run like that? How could he ever trust her again?

But she'd been so afraid!

Helpless anger twisted in her gut. Why? Why this tangled mass of manipulation that was being woven around them?

Beneath the stinging pain and humiliation of the Wyxan attack, another fear was beginning to claw at her. Would the Grimmen work against her too? Would it attack when she least expected it? The sense of the watcher, coupled with the illusion of the attack on their arrival, made her wonder if it was trying to warn her away. When she searched her senses, however, she found only uneasiness and caution. The watcher remained out there, a heavy presence in its silent observation, but if it wanted her driven away, why did it allow Frax to lead her deeper into its realm...

Kaphri's heart gave a sudden, painful jerk. The commander was slowing his pace to drop into step beside her. Treacherous heart! It pounded so hard she feared it would leap from her chest.

What did he want? What should she say? What could she say? Her face colored as she found the ground before her very interesting.

Her resentment over his earlier treatment, exposing her ability to invade the minds of the others, followed quickly on the tail of a secret rush of breathless sensation. She gave herself a stinging mental lash of reproach. Did he want to exhibit her skills before Seuliac again, as if she were some trained animal?

Perhaps she was reacting unreasonably. She didn't care. He had betrayed her. She wanted him to go away and leave her alone, but she knew he would not.

"*Priestess, we need to talk.*" He sent tightly, for her mind only. "*Is the presence you sensed in the tower still with us, or did it disappear with the pyanth at the edge of the wood?*"

His question surprised her. "*Surely you feel it?*" The presence in the wood was nearly overpowering.

He shook his head, missing or choosing to ignore the sharp tone of her reply. "*It may be something of Cadarn, Priestess, but it does not choose to reveal itself to me.*"

"*Or perhaps it cannot mask itself from me.*" Or perhaps it did not choose to: the realization sent a chill through her.

His eyes narrowed. "*Perhaps.*"

Regardless, the sense of being under constant observation wore on her mind and numbed her alertness. "*All I know is I've felt it since the moment we arrived, but I only became aware of it in the tower room. I can tell you it knows we are here, it knows I am aware of it, and it watches. Constantly. And, no, it is not a pyanth,*" she added as she sensed the beginnings of another question. Did he doubt her ability?

"I must ask you again: do you sense any evil in it?"

"No. But it is very similar to the Wyxa."

They walked, the pause between them growing more strained.

"The Wyxan," Frax began again. *"The one called Klandar Bayne. He spoke with you at some point during our capture?"* His sending was stiff now, awkward.

"Yes."

"What did he say?"

The wariness in his question surprised her. She looked over at him. He met her gaze flatly, without expression, which sent another wave of frustrated resentment running through her. What did he think Klandar Bayne told her? "*That I cannot completely sever myself from my people, no matter how I feel about them. That this world went through a terrible crisis in the distant past. That I must take charge of my own life. Then—just as I managed to take a step forward by re-securing the crystal—something snatched my progress away by whisking us here.*"

"*Nothing more?*"

"*Nothing more!*" What was he looking for? "*Let's see, Lord Geffitz. They took my whole being apart in the thing they called Ankar Mekt, invading every piece of me. They held me as a solitary prisoner for days. They read my mind at every opportunity, suppressed my emotions and reactions at every turn. They planned to suspend my life indefinitely and take away everything I'm familiar with. So, no, nothing more.*"

She watched a telltale muscle in his jaw tighten. He was not satisfied with her response. She wondered again what he was searching for. What question did he really want to ask?

Not so long ago, the thought ran through her mind, he would not have hesitated in this way.

The cool remoteness of the whole exchange struck her, sending a shot of apprehension through her. Why had he forced her to reveal a mindskill that he had so adamantly warned her not to use? What changed between them?

"*In the guard tower—*" he began.

The guard tower! Oh, Hredroth! Was that it? The things she said in the tower? Quick humiliation burned in her. How could she ever explain the horrible fear that crept over her in the tower while they talked? How could she make him understand? Saying the Wyxa caused it would be placing the blame for her weakness on someone else.

Bitter frustration with her failure ran through her. "*I reacted with unreasonable fear,*" she interrupted. "*It was a display of weakness we cannot afford. I'm sorry. It won't happen again.*"

HER APOLOGY CAUGHT Frax off guard. He'd expected the topic of her upset in the tower to be much more difficult to broach. She seemed almost relieved to discuss it.

She was watching him closely, with a posture that almost bordered on a challenge. Kep! For someone who reflected no emotions outwardly, her reactions were suddenly all over the scale.

He nodded slowly, trying to ease any thoughts she might have that he was attempting to reproach her. This was so damned awkward and difficult. But, now she had opened the subject, her choice of words caught his attention. "*Reacted? To what? It was the Wyxa, wasn't it?*"

"*I failed to recognize their attack.*" How could she help anyone if she didn't recognize when she was under attack? How could they depend on her to help save their people? She looked away with a shielded sense of misery. She'd been so afraid! What had he said once? Heroes and stuff of legends?

All she wanted was to be away from all of this. There must be someplace where she could take refuge against the outside manipulation of everyone and everything.

"*Don't be too harsh on yourself. What you said back in the Palenquemas—how outside forces were manipulating us. You were right. And it seems more keep adding all the time.*"

The image of the great stone beasts that guarded the gates of Caer Cadarn loomed before her. The screaming, the slashing hooves, the illusion of attack... She should tell him. "*The Cyrwins—*"

"*I know you felt the effects of their song. They can mesmerize and paralyze. And they have other skills. Abilities...to do things to people...to affect how they feel. It's a useful weapon in battle because it can make an enemy run in mindless fear... I think they used it on Tobin to incite his rage.*"

There was something in his expression—something more than he was saying. Her heart began to thunder again, what she intended to say before he cut her off forgotten. "*They used it on you, too.*"

He looked at her, his eyes cold. "*Yes.*"

"*You did not feel fear.*"

"*I felt...something different.*"

"*I see.*" The secret joy in her earlier thoughts withered to dust. "*Something besides fear.*"

"*Yes. But that's not important.*" He shifted the subject. "*I need to talk to you about other things.*"

HER FACE WENT PALE. So pale that, for a moment, Frax feared she might faint. He resisted the urge to reach out and touch her, forcing hard non-reaction instead.

"*Oh, Hredroth!*"

Did she whisper the words? Send them? Perhaps he only imagined the exclamation. But he sensed she understood what he was trying to avoid saying.

"*Priestess, what happened in the tower... I must apologize. What I did...was a mistake.*" He studied her, searching for some hint of reaction in her dark eyes, in her expression, bracing for anything.

She gave away nothing.

What did he want from her? Kep! He cursed himself in frustration. "*Priestess...*"

"*It's all right.*" She came back to life with a shrug. "*I know the strength of what I felt.*" Her sending tapered off into a mental whisper. "*It made me say and do things I did not want to do, too...*"

He hadn't said— "*Priestess...*" He lifted a hand. Dropped it again, knowing he couldn't trust his reactions if he touched her while the Cyrwin song rang in the back of his head.

It doesn't matter! It doesn't matter what you—or she—or any of us—wants! Just accept the situation and move on, his brain shouted.

"*The Wyxan influence is gone now and I am in control.*" She looked at him, her sending firm. "*I still feel fear, but I won't embarrass myself again. I'm sure it's the same with you.*"

"*Yes,*" he agreed while savagely cursing himself for mishandling the whole situation. It had gone wrong, and he couldn't just leave it alone: he was getting ready to add another complication.

She was staring into the woods. "*You should know the geas is still with me. It has a heightened sense of urgency, but as long as we move eastward, it doesn't pain me. I believe it does have origins on the plateau, but I don't know anything else.*"

"*What do you expect to find there?*"

"*I try not to think about it.*"

He had suspected as much. "*If you don't believe you're walking toward an enemy, then what? Will it help you, or is it trying to snare you for some purpose you cannot yet imagine? What can you do to protect yourself against the possibilities? You have to consider those things. A warrior must always be prepared.*"

She looked at him. "*What is this leading up to?*"

He braced for the resistance. "*Instruction in the art of battle.*"

"*No!*"

"*Yes.*" He came back firmly. "*You can't imagine for a moment you're prepared for what's to come. There'll be no argument . Your training begins at our noon rest today. I've put Seuliac in charge of instructing you.*"

"*Seuliac!*"

The strength of her dismay and disbelief caught him by surprise. A flame of unreasonable jealousy blazed up inside him. Kep! Was she so attached to his cousin?

"*Uri does not have the time!*" he snapped.

For the briefest moment, she stared at him, then turned her head away, the color in her cheeks darkening.

Was that a display of emotion? For the hundredth time in an hour, he bitterly cursed the Eldren, Wyxa and Grimmen alike, for the awkwardness their actions had inserted between him and her.

"*Families fervently petition the Warlord of Rhynog to instruct their sons in the arts of war. He accepts few, and then only at the direct behest of the Lord of Rhynog. His students do return alive from battle. He's a master in the art of war, better than anyone in Cadarn.*" She must understand the impact of what he was trying to do here. They could hold no illusions about her chances of triumph at her current skill level. Araxis was ruthless and experienced far beyond her measure, even without a physical form. Their only hope of success in defeating him would be to raise her level of tactical and fighting skills.

"*But—* "

"*But what?*"

SHE LOOKED AWAY, SHOCKED and bitter. But what? He had kissed her? He could not hand her off to his enemy like this? He could do anything he damned well pleased, and her protests meant nothing. He had made her situation abundantly clear long ago. "*Nothing.*"

"*No, I thought not. Your lessons begin without delay. Be prepared. He's my enemy, Priestess, but he is skilled. Listen to him and learn. For the sake of our world.*"

She continued to stare at the trees as if he were no longer there, until he stalked back to his position beside the warlord. Inside, however, she felt as if she might shatter with a single word. She breathed shallowly, focusing hard. Trying to reason.

Fighting to keep her thoughts above the pain.

A mistake. He said the kiss was a mistake. Oh, Hredroth! How could she be so stupid? How could she have allowed herself to think... To draw some tiny secret pleasure in a thing he considered a mistake?

But he held her so tightly—

Oh, Hredroth! She didn't want to feel this pain!

Tears blurred her eyes. She blinked them away, not daring to brush at them for fear Uri, behind her, would see the action and guess at her upset. She couldn't face his gentle concern right now. Hredroth, why couldn't Frax be the one who cared what she thought and felt? Tears flooded her eyes again, and she drew a deep breath through her mouth, exhaling slowly and silently as she tried to force calm. Change focus, she told herself. Change your thoughts. Move on to the rest of the discussion.

Seuliac? Uri? The pain twisting inside her chest made thinking difficult. She concentrated, drawing on her resentment instead.

What did she care of Geffitz families?

Frax was right, of course: she had learned a great deal from these warriors, but there was still much more she needed to know. She had no idea what the geas was drawing her to, and Araxis would come eventually. She needed their help to prepare for the challenge. But,Seuliac?

She had just thought perhaps the Kitahni commander might... In the Palenquemas, they were... Tears flooded her eyes, and she chastised herself for being a fool. What had she been thinking? Of course, the thought of instructing her himself had never occurred to Frax. Why should it? In the Palenquemas, it had been just the two of them. A contact forced by Wyxan interference. Now there were others to see to her. The Kitahni commander only needed to give an order and Uri would carry it out.

Or Seuliac.

Was that why he had pushed her to reveal some of her mind skills when they first entered the Grimmenwood? To give the warlord a preview of what she could do?

Memory of the cool interest Seuliac displayed stung her now and sent another surge of resentment running through her. Her sense of betrayal and humiliation deepened. Why would Frax do such a thing? He claimed Seuliac was an enemy of Cadarn. How could he coldly hand her over to his enemy like this?

Why shouldn't he? The bitter thought crept into her mind. After all, he thought of her merely as a means to an end. Seuliac was fighting for the same end.

Maybe the Wyxa were right. Maybe Frax was only willing to work alongside her to achieve his desired end. He could stand before his Goddess and all the other creatures of his world and deny it, but he didn't see her as anything more than a tool for restoring his world. A thing to use. To work and improve; to be taken care of, certainly—as a weapon, but nothing more. What did the Geffitzi call it? Warrior right? He claimed her by warrior right, as a spoil of war. His possession to use as he saw fit.

Suddenly, desperately, she wanted Gemma. It had been so long since she had experienced the serpent's comforting presence. Always before, the little dragon had been there to share her thoughts, her pain. Now she was gone.

Overwhelming despair washed over Kaphri. Had she seen Gemma right before she moved them out of the Palenquemas, or was it a trick of her imagination like the warriors claimed? Did Gemma have a hand in guiding them here, or had she used and abandoned her, too?

No. She refused to believe that. What did the commander call Gemma? A Guardian? Well, Frax might question Gemma's motives, but the little dragon had been with Kaphri because she chose to be there. She listened because she chose to listen. Gemma, at least, saw her as another living being. She would not willingly abandon her without reason. Something had happened to Gemma at the edge of the Palenquemas.

Realization shook her to the quick: Gemma had been missing for fourteen days. Fourteen days! Why did it take her this long to realize...?

As she thought back, the peculiarity of her companion's disappearance struck her. From the point at the edge of the Palenquemas where they fell into the grasp of the Wyxa, concern for Gemma's whereabouts had barely existed in her mind. Did the Wyxa do something to block her memory of Gemma? If so, why?

No matter! She remembered now. She would find her.

Her instincts flared warning as an urge to seek out for Gemma rushed through her. She must not reach out with her mind here! This was unfriendly territory, and she did not want to stir the Grimmen's interest any more than the current level.

Not even to search for Gemma.

Not so long ago, she had believed she couldn't survive one day without her small companion. Today she had no choice.

Kaphri realized she was clutching the crystal that hung from the chain around her neck, trying to draw some comfort from her contact with it. A sense of betrayal ripped through her and she released it to fall back to the red fabric covering her breasts.

Whatever the crystal might be, it was not a substitute for Gemma.

But what had become of her small companion? If the Wyxa had done something to Gemma...

Her fierce thought was wasted anger.

Besides, if what Frax told her in the swamp was true, Gemma was also one of the Eldren Races.

Now that she had the opportunity to think about it, the Wyxa had been remarkably incurious about the little dragon, acting as if they did not recognize what Gemma was when Kaphri asked them about her. It was as if they were unaware of Gemma's role in any of this.

Until last night on the Moonplain—

Someone was pressing insistently at her mindshields. Frax.

Hadn't he already said enough? She hid behind a carefully calculated coldness before she opened her mind to him again. "*What?*"

"*What are you sensing?*"

She sent out a quick, light questing. "*The watcher is out there, as always. Otherwise, nothing. Why?*"

"*Because we're approaching a place of ancient power. I wondered if you sensed it.*"

A place of power of this wood? Her heart gave a thump. "*What sort of power?*" After everything else that had happened this day, she did not want to touch anything else from this place unexpectedly.

She realized the appearance of the forest was changing. The trees were taller and further apart, with few branches between the ground and their spring-leafed canopies. The dappled light was bright, and a lush carpet of long, pale, thin-bladed grass covered the ground. Clumps of dense fern hugged the bases of some of the trees or grew in lush drifts. The appearance was almost garden-like in its order.

Instead of answering her question, Frax came to a stop. He motioned for the others to draw up beside him.

"*We are approaching the Ilex, the meadow from which the east-west trail begins,*" he told them. "*It's a sacred place of the Grimmenwood, and we must exercise the caution and respect due a holy place.*"

"*Why can't we just go around it?*" Velacy asked.

"Because, for me to come so close and not pay my respects to the forces dwelling here might be taken as an insult by the Grimmen, something we can ill afford."

"Then what?" Seuliac looked about curiously.

"The trail we seek begins at the eastern end of the meadow. If everything goes well, we should be able to relax our vigilance a bit once we get there. We never made this common knowledge, but the Grimmenwood has always respected the trails and certain clearings as neutral ground for us."

"So, why are you so free with the information now?" challenged Velacy. *"Do you think your secret will remain here, hidden with our bones?"*

Frax smiled without amusement. *"When this is done, Velacy, you have my blessing to share the knowledge where you will. Just remember, the problem for anyone other than a Kitahn will always remain staying alive to get to the trails first: they neither begin nor end at the wood's edge. Like Kitahn, you must have the Grimmen's approval to get to them."*

He continued quickly before the younger warrior interrupted again. *"We should be able to follow a trail to the escarpment above the Silverline in five days. We can reassess our situation there. Meanwhile, the Ilex is not one of the safe havens I mentioned. We'll skirt the edge of the clearing down to the trail. Only to the area. Don't put a foot on the trail until I return. With Uri in your company, you should be safe from attack for the short time this will take."*

Kaphri nodded silent understanding along with Uri and Seuliac. Velacy merely glared.

Satisfied, Frax led them on.

The thought of a holy place dedicated to the presence of this wood did not fire Kaphri's enthusiasm. Her mood lightened, however, when she saw a sunlit meadow ahead through the trees. She could almost feel the heat of the sun on her skin.

With each step, the air around her seemed to grow warmer. And warmer.

In fact, the air was growing downright stuffy.

She put a hand to her throat, and her steps slowed as she tried to draw a deeper breath. In front of her, she saw Seuliac move his head from side to side as if he, too, were feeling some discomfort. He lifted his right hand to his brow and took several quick, shallow breaths. Beside him, Frax appeared oblivious to the temperature rise as he continued walking.

Two steps later, Kaphri was gasping for breath. As she faltered to a stop, she heard a startled exclamation behind her.

Uri called out, his voice strident with concern. "Frax, I think we have a problem...!"

Several steps ahead of the rest of them, Frax looked back. Kaphri saw the questioning expression on his face turn to startled disbelief as she crumpled to her knees.

Ahead of her, Seuliac slowly collapsed, too.

"What's happening, Frax?" Through the distant roar in her ears, Uri's question bordered on panic.

Fighting for air that refused to come, Kaphri toppled into the grass.

"I don't know!" Frax was suddenly kneeling beside her, his hands rough as he pulled her up to a sitting position to help her get more air. His fingers fumbled with the clothing at her neck to no avail. It wasn't her clothing that kept the air from coming; it was the Grimmenwood.

"*Kep, breathe, Priestess!*" Frax gave her a light shake, his sending bordering on desperation in her fading mind.

"They can't breathe, dammit, Frax. It's the Woods. It's killing them!"

From the corner of her darkening vision, she saw Uri, his expression helpless as he bent over Velacy. The Aedec warrior was on the ground, his body arched with the effort to breathe, his booted feet tearing at the grassy surface.

"No!" Frax's angry exclamation was a distant sound as her mind closed in on darkness.

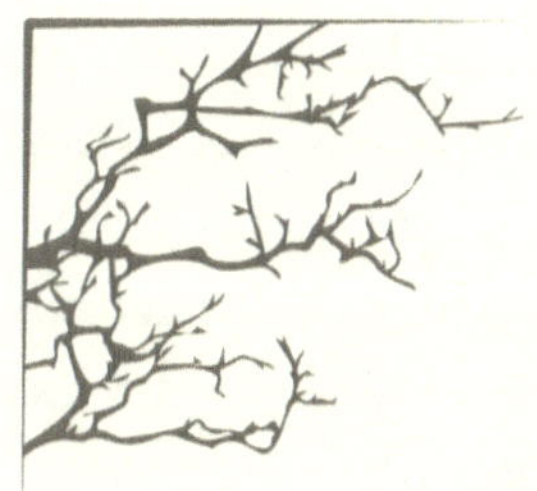

Chapter 61
First Blood

The girl sagged lifelessly.

The wood was taking them all. But why? If the Grimmen doubted their intentions, why didn't it act at the edge of the forest before they entered instead of waiting until they were in so deep? Now there was no retreat...

Which was exactly what the Grimmen intended. It wanted something more, and Frax had to figure out what it was. Fast. Or Kaphri, Seuliac, and Velacy would die.

His mind churned in wild turmoil. Had he missed something in his offering? It wasn't as if there were written instructions for him to work from. No situation like this had ever arisen in the history of the caer that he was aware of. Kep! Yes, he had brought the enemies of Cadarn into this place, but they were necessary in the battle to protect this world. What did he have to do to stop the Grimmen from killing them?

There was only one thing the Grimmen seemed to place value in.

"Blood, Uri! Like I did earlier, give their blood to the wood. Maybe it wants them identified before letting them access the trail's sanctuary."

"Identified?" Uri managed to look even more stunned. "They're not Cadarnian. For them, that would be—"

"Do it! Otherwise, they're dead."

The Geffitz commander did not wait to see if Uri followed his instructions. He seized Kaphri's slim left wrist and rolled it upward. Her veins showed darkly against the bluish pallor of her cream skin.

"Another battle scar, little one," he whispered as he pulled his knife and ran the blade across her flesh. Blood welled in its wake, warm against his fingers as it flowed out to drip on the ground.

Seconds dragged by while Frax waited for a response.

He heard a rattling gasp behind him, and Velacy began to cough. Glancing back, he saw Uri hover over the younger warrior long enough to assure he was out of danger, then move over to the warlord's side to repeat the act of bloodletting.

Still, there was no response from the girl.

"*Priestess? Kaphri*!" His mental prod met only emptiness.

The cold control that had held him in check since he'd seen her collapse began to slip. He pulled her higher, drawing her against him, so her head lolled heavily on his chest, and turned her wrist down to let her blood fall directly on the forest floor, into the bright little pool accumulating there.

One drop. Two. So agonizingly slow. She was dying in his arms.

The cough penetrated his thoughts again. He looked over to see Velacy, flat on his back, bring a knee up and push over on his side. The younger warrior began to vomit. At the same moment, Uri expelled a heavy sigh of relief as Seuliac made a choking sound.

The big Geffitz's eyes met Frax's. "They won't thank you for this," Caspani said. "It waited until we were too far in to do anything else. Damn this woods, Frax, and damn Cadarn!"

Frax glanced away angrily, not caring if the Aedecs questioned the cost of saving their lives when they discovered it. At least the Grimmen allowed them the option. They were recovering while Kaphri still lay limp and unbreathing. The Grimmen was killing her!

Why?

A horrible thought struck him. Did it think he wanted this?

All the anger, frustration, and resentment that had built inside him... Kep! What had he been thinking over these last hours? Of course he resented the prophecy of the Winisp that Klandar Bayne had revealed to him. Of course he felt frustrated with the sensations he was experiencing at the whim of the Cyrwins. He was angry at being manipulated on a grand scale! But most of all, he was furious with himself because he feared, deep inside, that the thoughts the Cyrwins stirred in him were not the results of their finagling but his own, deep-seated desires.

She was the enemy, for Kep's sake!

He froze. What was he thinking? Was she really the enemy? Had he brought her here as a prisoner, forcing her to his will—or had she come willingly as a partner?

She couldn't be both. The Grimmen would not allow it.

The sole mission of the lurking presence the Priestess felt was the protection of Cadarn. It had invaded his mind in the tower, responding to the Wyxan threat, and he never questioned that purpose. Why should he expect it to do less inside its domain? The thing in his head was simply reading his thoughts, perceiving the threat, and acting.

Small wonder his ancestors had earned a reputation for convoluted, twisted dealings. They played the same game daily, defensively, against their greatest ally and protector, the Grimmenwood. How had he been so careless? And, the more vital question, how could he stop it? How could he undo the damage he'd done?

Giving the Grimmen what it demanded, access by blood, wasn't saving the Priestess. The wood had misread his unguarded, confused thoughts and was acting in what it must regard as his, and its, best interests. Killing her was the solution to his resentful anger. He had to correct the error.

He was willing to do anything—believe anything—think anything—to stop this. But what did the Grimmen want? His blood? A show of binding with her?

Releasing her, he snatched his knife and cut his wrist deep. As the blood swelled, he picked up her wrist again, turning them both down to let the crimson flow into the pool already coloring the grass.

The puddle grew larger, but the girl lay lifeless.

No! Horror boiled up from the very bottom of his being. They had come so far. Fought through so much. Now the Grimmen was destroying the only hope they had because he was a fool in his emotional, unguarded thoughts.

He threw back his head and howled, his rage and frustration echoing across the woods.

The silence that followed was heavier than anything they had walked through in the past several hours, as if the whole wood had stopped to listen. On his knees in the grass, oblivious to Uri's stunned stare, Frax lowered his head and gathered the limp body to him, blood smearing them both in long scarlet slashes. The sense of defeat that rose to engulf him was the most terrible, harsh thing he had ever experienced.

For what seemed an eternity, the silence reigned, petulant and thoughtful, blocking out the sounds of the recovering Aedecs. Then there was a soft intake of breath near his ear. A shudder ran through the body he held pressed against him.

The sound of Seuliac's coughing was like a physical blow, Velacy's weak stream of hoarse curses like a rough edge drawn across his flesh. He didn't care. With a silent shout of triumph, he loosened his grip and lowered her gently to the grass, positioning her head to help her breathe clearly. He watched, willing her recovery as she drew deepening, hungry breaths. Then, as her color began to return, she gave a terrible shudder that racked her whole body and began to cough. Each pain-wracked sound was a shot of pure triumph to him.

As her strength slowly returned, Frax helped her sit up. When he took his hands away, she sagged like a child's broken toy but remained upright. A moment more, and she moved, turning her wrist to see what he knew must be a source of stinging pain. She stared dully at the slash.

"*It's just a surface cut,*" he told her hastily. "*It'll heal quickly.*"

Nothing came from her mind as she continued to stare at the congealing crimson.

Frax got to his feet, eyes sweeping the rest of the group. Velacy was on his knees now; head bowed forward as he breathed. Seuliac was sprawled in the grass, his arms rigidly propping him up from behind. He pulled in deep, controlled breaths, his head thrown back, face skyward, and eyes closed. Uri stood by, watching them with a troubled expression.

"*It tried to kill us, Cadarn. Why?*" The warlord's sending burned with anger.

Frax avoided Uri's eyes. "*If the Grimmen intended to kill you, Warlord, you wouldn't be asking that question now.*" The situation would be easier for him if they let the matter end right there, but hiding the truth would only invite future disaster. Uri was right; they would not thank him for what he had ordered done. The alternative had been to let them die.

Unpleasant as what he had to tell them was, there was no benefit in delaying it. "*No,*" he continued. "*The wood wanted something from you.*"

"Wanted?" Seuliac's head snapped forward, his gaze fastening on him. "What are you saying, Kitahn?"

Even though Kaphri had not moved, Frax knew Uri was sending the exchange to her. "Because of what I ordered done to save your lives, the Grimmen holds a certain power over you now, sealed by the bond of your blood. You owe it for your life."

"Owe it for my life? It tried to take my life!" Velacy exclaimed hoarsely.

"The only thing the Grimmen recognizes is that your blood was offered as the price for your life."

"That's a fine piece of duplicity, Kitahn!" Seuliac growled in low, tight anger. "What will we owe the next time this thing decides it wants something from us?"

"You better pray to Kep that doesn't happen." Uri's soft interjection drew their attention. Hearing the rest from Uri would soften the blow, and Frax was grateful for his help. "It would not do to shed your blood in this wood again."

"Meaning what?" Velacy glared.

"The Grimmenwood demanded blood to identify you. Now it can track you anywhere within its depths. If you shed blood again, its power will build and it will be able to send its creatures out to attack or assassinate you in other parts of the land."

"What!"

Uri shrugged. "Early Lords of Cadarn were accused of drugging their guests and stealing samples of their blood while they slept, and of stealing the blood of injured foes on the battlefield. They stored the samples underground in cold caverns in case they needed to use them later to give the Grimmen's creatures targeting information."

"This is a betrayal, Kitahn," Velacy snarled.

Seuliac looked quietly unhappy. "I've heard the story. You have quite a clever collaboration with this wood of yours, Kitahn. One I would not have chosen to participate in."

"I didn't ask you to come into the wood, and I gave you no guarantees." The Kitahni commander told him coldly. "I only had done what would save your lives." Frax didn't add that he'd forgotten the part about his family's blood-stealing history until Uri brought it up. His ancestors had done so many treacherous, nasty things it was hard to keep up with them all.

He relented slightly. "Uri's right, though. Don't shed blood in this place again if you can avoid it. Doing so would deepen the tie." Frax looked over at Uri.

"It's said that blood given to the Grimmen once is obliged; twice, tied; thrice, applied," Caspani explained.

"What's that supposed to mean?"

"Shed blood a third time, and it will establish a mental bond with you. The Grimmen will invade your thoughts. Within its realm, it might even control you."

"I find myself beginning to admire your scheming ancestors." The warlord's voice cracked and he coughed.

"Rhynog has its share of treachery and scurrilous methods," Frax replied.

Seuliac's attention shifted to the girl. Kaphri had not moved during their exchange. "She doesn't appear to have been treated as much of an ally."

She was listening to every word despite her listless appearance. Frax wished there was some way he could comfort her, to let her know he recognized how difficult this experience must be for her, but he dared not. He had to remain firm and remote. There could be no confusion about their relationship again.

He shrugged. "The woods will recognize her now."

She raised her eyes and turned her head to look at him. He waited, nerves strung to snapping, for what she would say.

Before she could respond, however, Velacy filled the void. "You knew this would happen, didn't you? We're lucky we're not all dead!"

She closed in on herself again, whatever she was on the verge of saying lost.

Damn Velacy's timing! Frax turned his frustration on the Aedec heir. "Then you can revel in your luck while you walk. Now the wood has accepted your presence, let's move down to the trail."

As the Aedec warriors climbed to their feet, he turned back to Kaphri. Before he could extend a hand to help her up, she moved a half-turn away from him, out of his reach.

He understood, but his action was not wholly altruistic: he still had the safety of the whole group to tend to. "*The presence. Do you sense any change?*"

When she looked at him, her expression was calm, her sending without emotion, but he did not have to guess at the anger and resentment seething inside her. "*Don't ask that of me now. Not after what just happened.*"

Her fear and mistrust of the woods had deepened. So had his. "*I have to know, Priestess.*"

She closed her eyes, her body rigid as she braced herself for the encounter, then she looked at him again. "*It's the same. It watches. Nothing more.*"

All too aware of the coldness in her sending, Frax nodded. "*Very well. That's all.*"

"*Frax.*" Uri was suddenly beside him, his mental touch urgent.

The commander delayed responding, watching as the girl moved away, noting the move took her closer to the Aedecs and away from Uri and himself. He turned to his cousin.

"*All trace of the Aedecs' blood disappeared, but hers...*" The other Geffitz moved a boot toe, subtly drawing his attention to the crushed grass at their feet.

A knot of cold twisted Frax's gut when he saw the blackened char where her blood had fallen. The Grimmen had taken the blood of Cadarn's age-old enemies but destroyed hers. Why? The muscles at the corners of his mouth tightened. "*She is not of this world, Uri.*"

"*True.*" The other warrior was not so easily satisfied. *"But I watched. Your blood's in that mix, too. What happened here, Frax? The Grimmen accepted your pledge of blood for our safety. Why did it attack the others?*"

He suspected the answer. He had requested an immense breach of the rules to bring the Aedecs into the woods—a request that carried a very high cost. The Grimmen thought he would fold on discovering it. He hadn't. So, the Grimmen had decided it wanted more. It wanted an unbreakable binding over Cadarn's age-old enemies, regardless of oaths or agreed-upon prices. So it had waited until they could not turn back, then struck, leaving them no choice but to submit to its additional demand.

He could not fault the Grimmen for the move. It was serving its role as protector of Cadarn.

But the problem with the girl's blood... "*It's a warning, Uri. The Grimmen has tied my fate with hers.*"

"*What the hell does that mean?*"

"*It will kill me if it thinks I'm failing its agenda.*"

Uri swore. "*Then it will kill the rest of us. Kep, Frax, have we done the right thing, putting ourselves into the hands of this thing?*"

"*The geas that grips her would not allow anything else. At least we know the Evil One cannot follow us in here.*"

"*The geas. Have either of you gotten any hint of what its plan is?*"

"*No, but I suspect it has something to do with the Ly Kai city. She agrees that Araxis may have located it on the plateau overlooking Pterfellen.*"

"*So we have a destination, but still no motive. What if it only wants to shove her back through to her Homeworld, Frax? What about the barrier?*"

"*That is secondary.*"

"*Not to us!*"

"*For now, Uri, it must be.*"

"*There's more going on here than you're saying.*" Uri met his gaze levelly.

"*Let's hope the Grimmen doesn't feel compelled to attack again, Uri. I don't know if I can find anything else to appease it.*" He knew the response did not satisfy his cousin, but he had nothing more to give him.

Uri stiffened. "*Listen!*"

From the sunlight beyond the trees came the raucous sound of two birds quarreling as they fluttered in the grass. Nearer, a small, colorful bird took wing, chirping merrily while several more added their twitters to the mix.

"*Well.*" Relieved by the sudden diversion, Frax glanced around. "*Whatever happened here, we passed some test.*"

"*What comes next?*"

Frax looked at the sunlit meadow. After all this, he dared not appear remiss or disrespectful to the force that ruled this place. "*Take them over to the beginning of the trail, Uri, and guard them.*" The Grimmen had not attacked Uri, signaling that, at least for the moment, he was acceptable. "*I still have unfinished business here. Then we go east and hope for the best.*"

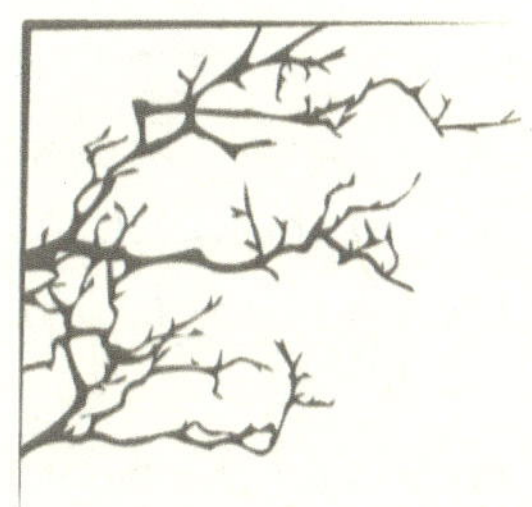

Chapter 62
First Noon

Seuliac Aedec did not hate Frax Kitahn with any violence of emotion. The Commander of the Edge was merely a Kitahn and, as an enemy, dispassionately to be destroyed if he threatened the security or interests of Rhynog. He did not harbor any resentment toward Frax for forcibly securing his oath of cooperation after they fell through the barrier. Given the same situation, it would have been that, or death, with him, as well. Enemies though they were, they were much the same, and Seuliac, as a soldier, abhorred the waste of a good fighting man at any time.

Especially the waste of himself, he thought with a flash of wry amusement.

And Especially now. He had sworn he would seek vengeance at the end of this. Cadarn must never be allowed to think it could conscript a warrior of Rhynog without paying a deadly penalty. Kitahn would pay, but he must delay any action for now. No major upset for him: the business of the holds could wait for a later, more convenient time.

In counterbalance to that delay, he found himself faced with the most exquisite, unexpected situation.

Who would have anticipated it? When Hraben Aedec stepped outside the authority of the Two Circles and allowed him to make his own investigation into the rumors of renewed activity at the Maugrock, Seuliac had already suspected something was seriously amiss. The Holderlord of Rhynog had scoffed mightily at the idea of any threat, declaring it a devious attempt by the Illians to manipulate the Geffitzi clans into assisting them in a petty local squabble. Seuliac could not afford the luxury of that easy dismissal, however. As Warlord of Rhynog, he bore responsibility for the hold's protection, even in the face of derision from its lord.

He never expected, in carrying out his duty, to find the key to a strange and provocative power placed within his grasp, knowingly and willingly, by a highborn of Cadarn!

Hours before, on the road along the base of the caer, Frax Kitahn had stunned him by saying he was turning the girl over to him for tutelage in tactics and defense. From the first day fate had thrown them together, Kitahn had gone out of his way to deny him contact with the girl.

The abrupt switch in strategy, declaring that Seuliac was the best, most logical choice to train her, while he must turn his focus elsewhere, nearly dumbfounded the warlord. But a master strategist's cool calculation swiftly took over. He must have this!

But not too easily. It must be on his terms.

He let his first reaction to the idea be outright refusal. Only pressure exerted by Lord Hraben ever compelled him to tutor a private student—and Kitahn rated nowhere near the status of the Holderlord of Rhynog. Necessary that point be stricken home clearly. However, Seuliac burned with the fire of intrigue during his rejection. To accept the responsibility, he demanded complete control over her lessons.

To his surprise and growing perplexity, Kitahn agreed.

Working with her, having an opportunity to mold the outcome of this venture, was better than observing from the sideline, waiting for some bad result. Still, he didn't completely trust Kitahn. There had to be a self-serving motive behind the action. That was how things worked.

But the nasty incident at the edge of the Ilex changed his perspective, highlighting Frax's argument in blazing clarity: Kitahn needed to focus every bit of his energy on getting them through this cursed place!

It would be his first opportunity for direct contact with the small but deceptively dangerous creature who walked with them. He foresaw all sorts of problems, but the possibilities were mind-boggling.

Why would Kitahn agree—even force—this task on him? Surely he was aware Seuliac would take advantage of every opportunity to subvert the girl to Rhynog's interests.

He would never have allowed the situation if their roles were reversed.

Then again, he reminded himself, Kitahn knew more about the waif-like creature who had appeared, up until the dawn of this very day, to be helpless. The Commander of the Edge had spent days alone in the swamp with her. Perhaps he had taken the opportunity to poison her mind against Rhynog.

Was the Commander of the Edge that confident in his success? Under Seuliac's skilled hand, such confidence might prove misguided.

Common sense argued against Kitahn devoting his time in the swamp to poisoning the girl against Rhynog, however. From the commander's condition upon arrival in the Wyxan cell, basic survival had been their sole priority.

Apparently, the things Kitahn told them at their first encounter were true: there was a resurgence of ancient power occurring—enough to even draw the attention of the Wyxa. If it was also true that the future of their world rested in this one small female, he wanted to know if there was any hope. How intelligent was she? Could she handle herself? He must not underestimate her, and trust was not an option. Many questions needed answers, and he intended to test her to the fullest. If Kitahn wanted her tutored, it would be in his way, by his measure.

Now to discover something about what Kitahn said the Guardian claimed was the 'only hope of the Geffitzi Clans'.

He turned to Kaphri.

She sat on the ground close to Uri and Velacy, fiddling with the last crumbs of the midday meal and displaying no interest in his activities. As he finished inspecting the path for irregularities that might cause treacherous footing and turned his attention to her, however, she looked up.

He jerked his head, indicating she should join him.

She ignored Velacy and Uri's startled, inquisitive expressions as she stood, but shot a resentful glance toward Kitahn. Sitting off to one side, the commander seemed lost in thought and oblivious to them all.

Although her face betrayed no emotion, the warlord read stiff defiance in her bearing as she walked over to position herself before him.

Intriguing. That inscrutability might help her survive life in Rhynog. If she survived him first.

Without any mental comment to guide her, he stretched forth his hand. Kitahn had spoken with her about this. Would she realize he wanted to examine the blade she carried beneath the red tabard?

Kaphri looked at him warily, then slowly pulled her knife and laid the leather pommel in his hand.

So, she was focused on the task at hand. He did not react, although he was mildly pleased. Instead, he held the blade between his fingers, testing the balance. It was an excellent weapon. It was one of Frax's and he had expected no less.

With a quick movement, he flipped it end for end, catching the tip lightly with his fingertips then rolling it through a series of quick maneuvers that put the pommel back in his grasp. The girl's eyes widened slightly as she watched the display, and he realized her people did not use such weapons to any degree.

But then, he reminded himself grimly, her people didn't have to.

His flicker of amusement at her reaction hardened. He caught the knife, shoved it into his belt and held out his right hand again, his attention locked on her.

She looked up questioningly to meet his hard gaze.

The darkness of her eyes sent an unexpected pang of pleasure running through him. His first impression of her on the hillside below the black tower—of a thin, ragged and dirty urchin—had stayed with him despite her recent transformation at the hands of the swampdwellers. He had never taken the time to look at her—never had the opportunity really, with the others hovering so closely around her.

So, she might be considered rather pleasant to look upon if he overlooked her strange red crop of wild hair. That would make incorporating her into the power structure of Rhynog sometime in the future a much easier task. Right now, however, that wasn't the issue. He brushed the thought aside as he stared down at her, refusing to let her break eye contact now that he had established it.

The issue right now was whether she could save their world. He continued to hold out his hand, waiting.

After a brief hesitation, she raised her right hand and put it in his.

Seuliac seized it with a quick movement, causing her to flinch. She wanted to pull away from his grip, he felt the tension in her muscles, but he would not allow it, any more than he would allow her to break his gaze.

A FLICKER OF PANIC ran through Kaphri.

Of the five warriors, this white-locked one frightened her the most. He was so cold, so remote. Yet he observed everything, and he always seemed to be thinking. She also knew he would not have agreed to this training without having some purpose of his own in mind.

As she placed her hand palm-up in his, she had the sudden sensation that she might be a small animal staring up into the eyes of a plains cat.

She escaped the plains cat, she reminded herself. She was not some simple quarry for this Geffitz warlord.

Let us see what you will do, Lord Geffitz, she thought as she forced her hand to relax in his grip.

HE SAW GATHERING CONFIDENCE chase the uneasiness from her eyes and it stirred a deepening interest in him. Perhaps there might be something here to work with after all.

Confident beginners, however, were the slowest to learn. First, he must crush that out of her.

Although his grip on her hand had loosened with her lessened resistance, his eyes bored into hers with cold intensity. He allowed a slight tightening of an eyelid. Her hand jerked to pull away, but not before his fingers closed tightly about hers again.

"Good," he said. He dropped his eyes to her hand, examining it thoroughly as he had done the blade, turning it, running his fingers over the flesh. It was a good, strong hand, small and well shaped, but used to work. No court lady's life, this little one.

"What is your name, girl?"

"Kaphri."

He had spoken aloud. Now he dropped into mindspeech. "*Is that what he will call you?*" He felt her confusion. She was thinking he meant Kitahn and Caspani, totally ignoring the reason she stood before him. He looked up, locking eyes with her again. "*The Evil One. When you finally face him.*"

She drew a shallow, quick breath, her cheeks pinking. "*I don't know.*"

Such a simple question and her self-assurance shattered. His reaction bordered somewhere between disgust and irritation. Still, it was no more, or less, than he should expect from her at this stage. Now to get rid of the rest of her hollow boldness and defiance, so he could begin his work.

"*Any time you face a challenger you must remember one thing above all else: always watch the eyes. The eyes are the secret, girl.*" He ran his thumb along the base of her fingers at her palm, feeling the calluses there. "*The eyes always prelude the action.*" He had purposely positioned her with her back toward the others. He wanted no interference. No distractions. His thumb slid lower, caressing the mound at the base of her thumb. It was a sensual action calculated to distract. "*Always watch the eyes.*"

The girl tensed, blinking. He smiled mockingly at the unguarded reaction. So this little one had some fire in her veins. Did Kitahn know that? She hadn't, judging from her reaction.

"*You must concentrate.*" He continued to let his thumb make the gentle cycle, knowing now that the sensual stimulation it caused would confuse and make her uncomfortable. "*Let nothing distract you.*"

KAPHRI EXPECTED HIS hands to be as cold as his gaze, but they were warm, his fingers firm and light. They traced over her skin, stirring startlingly pleasant sensations inside her. She had to fight to maintain eye contact, to keep from looking down at her hand, knowing, unspoken, that the action was forbidden. Did he know the confusing sensations he was causing—?

Anger and defiance shot through her. Let nothing distract her? Of course, he knew the reaction his hands were stirring in her! What game was the Aedec warlord trying to play here?

"*No game!*" It was as if he read her thoughts. The thumb pressed into the soft flesh of her hand, tearing a gasp of pain from her. "*The eyes. Watch them! Let nothing distract you.*"

Kaphri forced her eyes back up, locking with his gaze.

"*There will be pain again, unless you react swiftly enough to prevent it. Just a twitch of reaction in your hand will be all that's required of you for now. But a false start,*" the thumb pressed cruelly once more before she could react, causing her to gasp again, "*Will be equally unacceptable. Do you understand?*"

She nodded, her eyes not leaving his now.

It began again, the fingers lightly exploring her hand. Abruptly she realized that he used both hands now. The thumb found its pressure point again and anger curled in her. What kind of cruel lesson was this? And why did Frax Kitahn sit by, watching this abuse?

The pain came again, bringing tears to her eyes, but the grip on her hand did not release. She blinked them away. Seuliac's gaze did not waiver.

"*Kitahn will not help you, girl. He requested this. If he makes such a request of me he knows he must abide by my methods.*"

This time she saw it—some slight change in the depths of his eyes. She jerked, hard, but his fingers caught hers firmly. He did not hurt her.

"*Good. You are not a child, girl. Your lessons must be quick and hard if you are to survive what will come.*" Again she reacted, and he nodded, satisfied.

A false start in the silence that followed brought pain once again. They had not moved one step from the spot on which they had begun, but a fine sweat covered her body as she locked eyes with him once more. Her insides quivered with the effort, but she would not allow it to pass on to her hand. She was successful once again, then failed. Anger at the pain drove her concentration. The next time her hand was gone before his fingers closed.

"*You're not reading my mind, are you?*" He said it in jest, but he was curious. She flinched again and saw a gleam of amusement. His fingers changed their touch, becoming a caress once again.

"*Yes. Your master will be proud,*" he murmured.

Her whole body tensed. "*My master?*" It was the first time she had entered the exchange. His fingers caught at hers, then continued their seductive work.

"*Kitahn. He is your lover, is he not?*"

The question stunned her. She expected him to accuse her of acting for Araxis or Bithzielp. Any number of terrible things. But not of coupling with the Kitahni commander! At that instant, his thumb drove the pain home with more intensity than before, bringing a cry to her lips. Something snapped inside her, unleashing her fury. Instinctively she brought her knee up for his groin, but he anticipated the move. His left hand dropped, dragging her captured hand down as he countered her knee, throwing her off balance. His right hand came around in a broad-handed slap, and she tumbled to the ground as he released her.

The blow was a sharp crack, more sound than pain; Seuliac could have broken her neck if he chose to, and they both knew it. But it startled the others.

Uri leaped on him with a roar of fury. The white-locked warlord made no attempt to resist as his arms were pinned behind his back by the infuriated warrior.

Velacy had sprung to his feet, but he hung back, his expression uneasy as he glanced over at Frax, sitting off to the side, still seemingly lost in his thoughts. For a moment, the air about them seemed frozen.

The Kitahni commander finally looked at them with irritated impatience. His gaze flicked between Seuliac and Kaphri, searching their faces several times before he made a slight motion to Uri. "*Let him go.*"

"*What!*"

"*Let him go. He has agreed to give her some basic instruction—*"

"*No!*"

"*—in strategy and warfare. Let him go.*"

Angrily, the big Geffitz released the warlord.

Seuliac shrugged away elegantly and smoothed his clothing with several flicks of exaggerated exactness. During the whole incident, he had managed to keep his eyes locked with Kaphri's.

"*Never react in mindless anger,*" he told her calmly. "*Ever. No matter what is said or done to you.*"

Kaphri's eyes narrowed, but she remained silent as she continued to glare up at him.

"*Your lesson is ended.*" He reached down and grasped her arm.

Uri moved to seize him again but a warning look from Frax stopped him.

AS KAPHRI TUMBLED TO the ground, she felt a shocking sense of triumph. How dare the warlord strike her! Now Frax Kitahn would see the mistake he'd made in giving her over to this cruel, vicious barbarian. Now he would lash out in outrage at his enemy.

He would regret his decision and things would return to the way they had been.

During the whole incident, Seuliac held her eyes with a silent mental command that would not allow her to break away. Crouched on the ground, hand to a stinging cheek, she waited for the explosion to come.

Frax's calm order for Uri to release the warlord left her stunned.

How could it be that only Uri's disbelief and outrage matched her own? How could Frax accept this behavior toward her? How could he allow such brutality? Uri was properly outraged. Why not Frax? Why was he turning a shoulder on this misuse?

On her.

As he repeated his order to release the warlord, cold reality penetrated her disbelief: Frax did not intend to challenge Seuliac over his actions.

She nodded numbly when Seuliac took her to task over her anger, her mind shifting from a sense of betrayal to a chilled realization: Frax really was giving her over—abandoning her completely—to Seuliac Aedec.

When the warlord's hand clamped on her arm, the truth of her situation snapped into place around her: either she accepted it and got to her feet with his assistance, or rejected it and faced the further humiliation of an awkward stumble when he pulled her up. And that was only the first sure thing her rejection would bring down upon her.

Anger, the anger Seuliac had just warned her against, took flame inside her.

Very well. If this was the way Frax Kitahn wanted it, then this was the way it would be. She would rather have gotten to her feet on her own, but the final step in this drama had to play out, and she was not about to suffer another indignity at Seuliac Aedec's hands by falling on her face.

Once she gained her feet, however, she jerked free of his grasp.

But not quickly enough.

"Your Kitahni blade, milady." His fingers caught her wrist, turning her hand upward. He pressed the knife haft into her palm, the blade pointed outward toward his belly.

She closed her fingers about the grip, the stinging humiliation and rejection of the whole incident welling in her. He was boldly taunting her. Daring her. He knew that, despite his warning, she still wanted to react, wanted to lash out in some way. And knowing that, he diabolically pushed her to it, mocking her as he held her gaze.

Fury flashed in her mind. Damn these Geffitzi. Did he really think she was that stupid? That vain and untried? Did he think her so incapable of learning? He knew nothing of her. Nothing of her previous training, of her endless lessons in...control...

The word struck her almost like a blow.

What in the name of Hredroth was she doing? She knew better than this. The Ly Kai had etched the lessons of self-control upon her very soul in Kryie Karth. Yet, here she stood, wanting to lash out, wanting to brawl like a common creature of this world. Like a...a...Geffitz.

A mental switch snapped closed inside her. The angry rigidity of her muscles flowed away. If the warlord thought he could taunt her into another stupid reaction...

Seuliac watched her for a moment longer, then nodded, as if to himself. When he released her hand, she quietly slipped the blade back under her tabard.

"*My first lesson is ended*," she corrected him flatly. Before she could hesitate she plunged on, "*I obviously have much to learn*."

Seuliac's mouth twitched at the corners as he nodded again. "*Much.*"

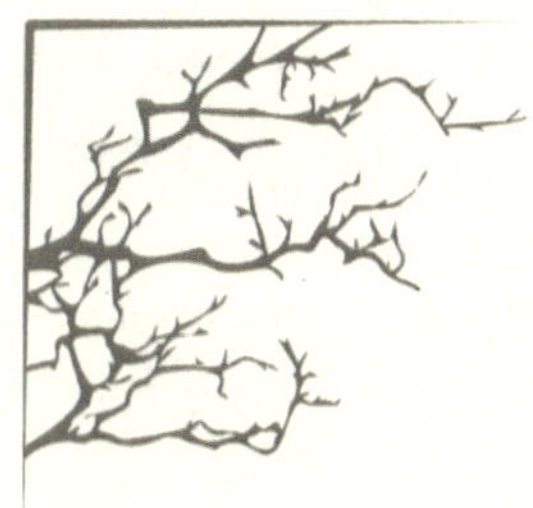

Chapter 63
Abandoned

So, the warlord had challenged her and she'd taken him up on it. Well finessed, Seuliac Aedec.

But was he as clever as he thought? She knew he'd manipulated her. The mark on her cheek was darkening, and there was a glimmer in her eyes when she looked at him. Hearing her declare the lessons would continue, Frax wondered if she would keep her reaction in check if the warlord dared to touch her again. Seuliac Aedec was playing a dangerous game.

The cold, bloody bastard!

Frax was not surprised when Kaphri's eyes raked him with the same resentment when she turned to walk away.

Did she think he would interfere? Defend her? To her, it must look as if he had abandoned her, giving her over to his enemy like that.

She could have no idea.

He disapproved of the warlord's methods, but he had separated himself from that part of their situation. She must learn to fight, and Seuliac Aedec was the most skilled at teaching the art.

"All right," he climbed to his feet. "Let's move out."

"CASPANI," SEULIAC DID not look at Uri, standing beside him, as Frax and Kaphri stalked off in different directions. "If you ever place a hand on me again, I will kill you."

Uri turned to scowl at him. "You know, Seuliac, I could tell you the same thing if you ever lay a hand on her again, but I don't need to. She can take care of herself."

"Then what's your concern? You must realize the situation was under control."

"Honestly, I don't care if she burns a hole through you, Seuliac." Uri paused for a moment to watch Kaphri gather up her pack. "But Tobin puked for a quarter of an hour, and it took him two days to fully recover from a mental shot she leveled at an attacking ahmdulak we encountered in Omurda. All because he failed to shield. And Frax and I got singed, even with shields. I didn't like the feel of it then. I don't want to experience it again."

Seuliac finally looked over to meet Uri's glare. His perfect white teeth glinted in a humorless smile. "Really?" His tone made it clear he was dismissing the implicit threat in the Caspani Geffitz's words, but that what Uri said intrigued him. "Such power?"

Uri shook his head in disgust and walked away.

Behind him, Seuliac laughed to himself. A second priority had just risen to the top of his agenda. The first had always been to survive this ordeal unscathed; the second just became a mission to subvert the girl to Rhynog. Provided, he gave a mental sneer, she proved worthy.

Cavalier as he had treated Caspani's warning, he was no fool. He might need to reconsider parts of his strategy with the girl. Perhaps this might even become...interesting.

"An intriguing creature and a most opportune development for Rhynog."

The comment pulled him out of his thoughts. He looked over to find Velacy beside him. The younger Aedec studied him for a moment before he continued. "She must be secured for Rhynog, of course."

"Of course," Seuliac agreed stiffly. He wished the other would move on. Velacy was an Aedec and blood, and against Cadarn, they would always present a united front. But Seuliac would have never selected his company by choice.

Velacy, however, did not seem inclined to go. He searched Seuliac's face with sharp, calculating eyes. "I can see no need for Cadarn beyond that point." When Seuliac did not respond, he pressed further. "You do not foresee a problem with that, do you?"

Seuliac gave an irritated sigh. "I see a great many problems, Velacy, not the least of which is just staying alive to get to that point."

"I remind you of the oath you made when you bound us to these misbred dogs, Warlord," Velacy snapped. "You will fulfill it, or I'll see you stand before the Lord of Rhynog on a charge of treason."

Treason! The audacity of this young pup, even daring to suggest...! Seuliac bit back the flash of fury that ran through him. Arguing with Velacy Aedec was beneath both his rank and his dignity. He couldn't let the remark go unanswered, however. There were always the little intricacies one must be mindful of in every situation. One learned swiftly in the caer if one intended to survive, much less to wield power successfully. He smiled thinly at the other as if dealing with a child too young to understand the reasoning of an adult.

"And I remind you, Velacy, it's pointless to discuss some things before their time. First, you must survive this."

"Are you threatening me?"

The fool! Seuliac gave a short, harsh laugh. "Look around you, Lordling. I wouldn't wager one copper for our lives right now. Not just Rhynog, but any of us. And I won't plot vengeance against a warrior who stands at my side in battle. It weakens us. That's something for another time and place. If we survive."

"Surely you don't believe what Caspani said earlier about the woods being able to control us?" Velacy looked incredulous.

"All I know is, I couldn't breathe and it wasn't because of anything I'd done."

"Kitahn could have arranged it! Some trickery—"

"I don't shed blood lightly, Velacy. It generally involves injury to my person. There are other, more subtle ways of doing things, ways that don't include open confrontation or obvious conspiracy.

"You're not exactly renowned for your plotting skills at this point, anyway." Seuliac gave the other Geffitz a direct, meaningful look before he turned away.

"Wait!" Velacy's hand shot out to catch his arm, stopping him mid-step. "What's that supposed to mean?"

"Unhand me, Velacy."

The coldness of the command caused the younger Geffitz to pull his hand away before he could stop himself. He bristled in anger and embarrassment at his reaction. "Don't forget who you're addressing, Warlord! There will come a time when you'll answer to me as Holderlord of Rhynog ..." his words tapered off under the warlord's impassive gray stare. He floundered for a moment.

"Lord Hraben..." He faltered again under the warlord's continued steady regard, then he paled. "No!" he breathed in a rush of air. He looked as if the warlord had struck him in the stomach. He made an attempt to regain his shattered composure, but words still seemed to elude him.

Finally, he gritted his teeth, an ugly scowl passing over his features. "I'm not supposed to return from this little excursion, am I? He sent me out so you could kill me."

Seuliac's features twitched in elegant distaste. "Kill is such an ugly word, don't you think? 'Execute' sounds much more civilized. And, yes, we do execute traitors."

Velacy opened his mouth to protest; thought the better of it. He smiled grimly. "So, why haven't you carried out your orders?"

"My orders—"

"To take me out and discreetly kill me, Warlord. Don't mince words with me."

Seuliac shrugged. "My orders, Velacy, were to ensure you did not survive our excursion into Omurda."

"If Lord Hraben gave orders for my elimination, why didn't you let the Balandra take me at the Maugrock when they were chasing us down? That would have tied everything up nicely without you getting your hands dirty—not that that would ever bother you. Your reputation for loyalty to your warriors is renowned. No one would question if I were lost under such circumstances. But you lost four of your best men, instead."

"Do you think I need a lesson in strategic thinking, Velacy?" Seuliac's smile flashed ice. He had lost four men: four well-respected warriors and comrades, but that was between him and Kitahn—who had stirred up the Balandra while helping the girl escape the Maugrock—for a future reckoning. He did not intend to discuss the subject with this young pup. "If you must know, I was forced to delay my orders in case a different situation arose where sacrificing you would serve to better advantage. The Balandra would not have stopped pursuing me if you had fallen to them. Consider it your good luck we ran into Kitahn. You might even say he saved your life." The warlord savored the other's reaction to the mockingly ironic remark as Velacy's face went white in a mixture of outrage and disbelief.

"I've always known you were ruthless and calculating, Seuliac. I just never guessed the depths of it."

"What do you want, Velacy? I serve Rhynog and her Holderlord." He made another move to walk away.

The younger warrior, careful not to touch him, quickly stepped around to block his path. "So I am not to die yet—for the sake of Rhynog? How kind of you, Warlord. Why?"

"I just told you—"

"Why was the order given?" The younger man's voice rose slightly.

Seuliac frowned. He was enjoying the other's discomfiture, but the timing was terrible. "Velacy, this is not the—"

"What? The time? It is as good as any, for all I see. It's only my life, Warlord, and you, the executioner. Why did Hraben order my execution?"

Seuliac glanced toward their companions. Kitahn and Caspani, locked in what appeared to be a rather intense conversation of their own, had not reacted to Velacy's raised voice, and the girl stood at a distance from them all, lost in thoughts of her own. He leaned close, his face nearly pressed against the younger warrior's, and said harshly, "Compose yourself. You are in the presence of our enemies. And don't do me the discourtesy of playing innocent. You plot and scheme like a pegin farmer, Lordling, with clumsy, bungling incompetence. You live in the most treacherous, powerful hold of all the clans, in one of the bloodiest families, yet, you have learned nothing. The next time you plot to assassinate the designated heir so you can move up into his place, choose better and fewer conspirators. Macre' spilled his guts—literally and figuratively—before he died. Believe me, I was there, and he left nothing out."

Velacy's face went stiff with horror. "I—Kep! Hraben didn't have to—"

"What? React so strongly? Yes, he could've ignored your involvement in the incident: you're his grandson and an Aedec. He didn't choose to. You not only attempted to assassinate the heir-designate; you went against the will of the Lord of Rhynog. The penalty for that is death. It's what any traitor to our clan deserves.

Unfortunately, I'm forced to consider myorders temporarily suspended because Rhynog has a greater need here and now, and you are an Aedec. You will live up to the name and serve her. I expect your full cooperation and loyalty. Consider it a favor when I tell you that if we are successful and survive this, I will not stop you from walking away. Go far to the north. Find a way to live there. Don't show yourself anywhere near Rhynog, or I promise, I will execute you.

"And, by the way, you'll have to find some new friends. All your co-conspirators are dead. They were dispatched an hour before we left the hold, and they thanked me for the mercy."

Velacy flinched at the warlord's matter-of-fact statement. "Gods! You killed Tapeen?" He paled. "You gave the order to execute your sister!"

Seuliac's expression hardened. "Foster sister," he corrected. "She plotted with you against the heir-designate to the Holdership of Rhynog. She knew the penalty."

"What a marvelous, cold piece of work you are, Seuliac." Velacy smiled, but his eyes glimmered with fury. "When this is all done, yes, I can run. It wouldn't be difficult for you, under new orders from Hraben, to come after me, would it?"

Seuliac shrugged. "If we live, I will speak to him on your behalf for your role in this. But, ultimately, I serve the Holderlord of Rhynog."

"And right now, you take orders from a Kitahn, our enemy," Velacy lashed bitterly.

"I cooperate because it's necessary. I will not have Rhynog left out of this."

"Rhynog! It's always Rhynog with you. You live it, breathe it, eat it—"

"And desire to control Rhynog was enough to make you conspire against her Lordship, Velacy, so don't get self-righteous with me. I don't owe you any explanations. I warn you this: what we speak of right now is the business of our clan, and I won't have Rhynog seen to be in a power struggle, especially in front of Cadarn. You will see this task through to the end. Then, if you live through it, Velacy, I won't stop you from walking away."

Velacy glared at him, seething. "I will live to give you orders one day, Warlord."

"Maybe," Seuliac shrugged. "But not here, and not now. Until that day, you're obliged to take orders from me. This conversation is at an end. If you value what's left of your life, don't bring it up again. And stay away from the girl. One ill-timed word from you could destroy anything I achieve."

He started to walk away, then paused to look back at Velacy. "Don't lust for power too much, Velacy. It might not be all that you imagine."

The younger Geffitz glared after him in impotent rage.

"I never thought Cadarn would surrender such a valuable resource to Rhynog without a fight. Look at them. They're over there with their heads together, plotting something for the first opportunity they get. What are you thinking, Frax?"

He probably should have discussed his decision with Uri beforehand, but his cousin would have presented compelling arguments against his actions. Arguments that might have swayed his decision. Arguments that could get them killed if he tried to divide his attention over too many things.

With the woods playing at the edges of his senses again, stirring a raw sensation of unfocused anger that set his teeth on edge, he didn't want to discuss it now, either. But Uri would not let him walk away without an answer.

He kept his eyes locked on the woods. "*She's not a resource, Uri. She's a weapon. Not yet, but she must become one. There's no better person to teach her.*"

"*What? I suppose beating her will improve her mettle, like a fine weapon on the forge?*"

Frax swung about, the fury in his eyes causing Uri to take a step backward. "*No one,*" Frax's sending was low and tight, "*is more conscious of this giving over to Rhynog than me. But this is not about Rhynog and Cadarn. It's about our whole world. And nothing else—nothing!—can enter into this. He can work with her with an impartiality that you cannot.*"

Before Uri could respond, Frax looked around at the others. "We've wasted enough time here." He spoke aloud so they all would hear. Turning, he started down the trail without waiting for the rest of them.

"Me?" Uri stared after him in perplexed surprise.

TORN BETWEEN ANGER and confusion,Kaphri stared into the forest, ignoring Frax's order for as long as she dared. When she finally turned to follow, the warlord was standing behind her.

"*I thought you were aware of things around you at all times,*" he remarked dryly.

"*Not always.*" She managed a light shrug despite her suddenly pounding heart. She had no desire to discuss what had preoccupied her with this Geffitz.

Seuliac continued to study her. She suspected he might be testing her again to see if he could make her exhibit some uneasiness. She returned his gaze levelly, refusing to be intimidated.

"*You're sure you want to give yourself over to my instruction?*"

"*Do I have a choice?*"

The Geffitz warlord's eyes narrowed. "*An unwilling student will not learn. Of course, it must be your choice.*"

She kept her thoughts carefully neutral as she looked at him. Why was he offering her this second chance to change her mind, away from the others? Was it to reassure himself, and her, that this was what she actually wanted? Or was it a way of tightening the binding of her commitment?

One thing she felt sure of; he was not acting out of any gracious concern for her."*And if I say no?*"

"*It's your choice. But it is a decision which should be made with careful thought—not in the heat of anger.*"

No, this was not concern. It was a subtle challenge. The drawing of a line in the dirt between them. He would not allow her to retreat if she dared step over. The sudden flash of insight surprised her. How did she know that? Then again, why shouldn't she? She'd spent enough time with these warriors to know a bit of their personalities and what moved them. And she had lived in Kryie Karth, surrounded by the Ly Kai men, each with his own cynical motives and hostility. Even at her most innocent she had recognized that an ulterior motive moved Rath. Maybe not which one, but still, she had known.

So, what motivated Seuliac Aedec?

"*Know thy enemy, Warlord?*" She sent the question before she could stop herself.

Seuliac shrugged. "*I won't lie to you: you intrigue me. If you can get us through this, if you actually have the power that Kitahn believes you do, you would be a worthy asset to any hold.*"

A 'worthy asset to any hold.' Was he recruiting her for a time after this was over? Of all the cold, calculating... Kaphri almost laughed aloud. Rath had been relentless in his intentions, but he had never been so obvious.

Still, he was talking about her life after this was over, something none of the first three warriors had done beyond asserting 'warrior claim' over her. Why shouldn't she consider the future beyond the next few steps on this forest path? Having a safe place to live was why she fled Kryie Karth with Gemma in the first place. With Gemma... the thought caused her throat to tighten.

She could brush off his offer. She could say 'I told you I agreed' and walk away, staying at her present level of commitment, remote and untouched. Or she could take up the challenge he was laying before her, the challenge that lit his eyes with a strange, intense fire as he watched her and waited for her reply.

Two different levels of commitment to choose from.

Watch the eyes, he said. She was already finding the lesson useful.

What more did he have to offer? There was only one way to find out. "*I want you to teach me.*"

"*What did Kitahn tell you about me?*"

"*You are renowned for getting results.*"

"*Do you think that includes babysitting a silly girl-child who indulges in temper tantrums?*"

She felt her cheeks pink. "*No.*"

"*It will not happen again.*"

"*No.*"

"*I train Geffitzi warriors. I will not be easy on you.*"

"*He says you are the best. Teach me. I want to survive this. I want to live.*"

HER SENDING WAS FIRM. Sure.

Seuliac allowed himself a moment of fascination. He had not missed the slight coloring of her face. Without any hint of expression, he found it impossible to be surewhether it was it caused by anger or humiliation. Despite what he might have taught her today, whatever went on inside her brain did not betray her through her eyes.

She was not socially sophisticated, however. Her physical movements and gestures spoke volumes. She was afraid, confused, and defensive.

She was also very angry with Kitahn.

He was satisfied. Whatever those unreadable thoughts in her head, she had committed to him at a basic level without the anger and melodrama that overshadowed the earlier incident. That was what he was looking—hoping—for. Only one thing cast a shadow over it. 'He says you are the best.' He. Kitahn. Still the influence. For now.

He would rid her of that soon enough.

This was going to be a difficult mental task, demanding a lot of telepathic contact. The sooner begun, the sooner mastered. "*There are conditions. First, you will not walk away from me again until you are given leave.*"

"*I—*" She thought better of her protest.

"*Second, it will be my way in all things. You'll do whatever I tell you to do, the moment I tell you, without question. Third, I want you to focus exclusively on the task at hand. Put anything else out of your mind. Fourth, you will be at my side when we are not on the trail. Learning is a constant thing: you will devote every available moment to it. Fifth, you'll answer any question I ask fully and truthfully, no matter how personal or painful. You'll withhold nothing from me. Sixth, you'll be mentally accessible at all times. Beyond that, I will advise you of new requirements as they arise.*

"*These conditions are not negotiable. I will accept nothing less.*" He regarded her closely, waiting for a reaction.

THE WARLORD'S REQUIREMENTS were no surprise: being open to him at all times was nothing more than Frax demanded. Uneasy as Seuliac made her feel, she did not fear committing to it with him. When he spoke aloud, it was with a mental backup, so there would be no mistakes in interpretation, and there was a slight mental pressure of warning preceding his sending, unlike Frax's abrupt mental intrusions that dropped into her mind unannounced. His manner might even encourage her to relax a bit around him. If she thought she could trust him, which she didn't. No doubt he was every bit as dangerous as the Kitahni commander, perhaps even more so, but he was much less formidable with his telepathic skills. She did not fear getting caught up in mind games with him.

Most importantly, this situation took her out of Frax's realm of control. A tiny bead of rebellious anger—and satisfaction—burned hot inside her at the thought. If the Kitahni commander wanted to put her within the sphere of his enemy's influence, fine. She would embrace it wholeheartedly. Whatever made him happy.

Had the warlord told Frax he planned to take complete control over her? She suspected he had not. Frax hadn't relinquished anything in his conversation with her, and he wouldn't. She didn't need him to tell her that. Still, he was the one who had given her over to Seuliac, and he couldn't have it both ways.

Would it anger him to see her so occupied with the warlord? Would he regret what he'd done? She hoped so. Perhaps it would stir some of the same cursed feelings in him that had begun to constantly grip her. Would he think of the time they had shared in the

Palenquemas? A wretched time, to be sure, but, somehow, pleasant in her memory—when he saw her sitting beside Seuliac, devoting all her attention to the warlord instead? A tiny blaze of spite tingled through her. The Geffitz commander was going to wake up to find she was beyond his reach.

She brought her attention back to the Geffitz standing before her. "*I understand, milord.*"

"*You will address me as sir. For me, that means teacher.*" His mouth quirked. "*You may as well get used to the word; it's in your future in one form or another.*"

He was referring to Frax's warrior claim on her. It made her resentment burn even hotter.

Those gray eyes were watching her, trying to read her reactions. Why? To discover some weakness he could use against her? So he could try to manipulate her? That would not happen.

She forced calm over her rampant thoughts.

Although her face did not convey her emotions, the slight flush of her skin was beyond her control. She only hoped the light in the forest masked it from him. "*Yes. Sir.*"

"*Lastly, be sure you understand what I say,*" he continued. "*I don't expect to have any conversation with you twice.*"

"*I understand, sir.*"

"*Very well. You have nothing to do for the rest of the afternoon but walk; I want you to think about our two peoples, how they are similar and how they differ, so we can discuss it tonight. It is your only focus. Now, I see our Kitahni friend has already started down this cursed trail without us. Go.*"

FRAX HAD THE WATCH, so Seuliac was able to focus on the things that had just taken place as he fell into step beside him.

He'd been unsure of this little one, not knowing anything of her culture or people. But, despite the bold defiance he'd observed in her encounters with the Kitahni commander, the girl had taken everything he put to her with an amazing lack of resistance.

She was an innocent. He'd recognized it within seconds of laying hands on her earlier. No one had ever attempted to take that from her, though she seemed to sense there was something between a male and female and it made her uneasy. And, as he suspected from the beginning, she felt a strong attachment to the Kitahni commander, although she did not seem to realize it. All she knew was an inexperienced ineptness of emotion that only served to heighten her frustration and resentment toward Frax because of what must seem to her, his hard rejection. That sense of rejection had been her primary motivation for agreeing to his stipulations just now.

Ah, the treacherous female mind. He was no novice to those intricate workings. A favored son of a great hold, he had enjoyed all the advantages and education to which his name and position claimed entitlement, including the companionship of court ladies and courtesans. He had always savored the unpredictable fire that burned in the feminine mind. It was so different. So intriguing and dangerous.

But, there was a time and place for everything, and the close companionship of the fairer sex had never been a priority for him.

Still, a woman scorned... She was furious with Kitahn; he must realize that. The commander's exploits with the fairer sex were a common source of gossip even around Rhynog's campfires, and Seuliac felt sure he would have recognized her developing feelings. Perhaps the handoff was part of an attempt to cool that interest by putting some distance between them.

Emotions were always such nasty, tricky things, particularly in the young and inexperienced.

A sudden thought struck him. What if it was not only the young and inexperienced involved here? What if Kitahn was trying to distance himself from his feelings, too? Now, that offered some interesting possibilities. He had seen no indication, but, of course, the commander would do his utmost to hide it.

Unspoken fact: they both wanted her exclusive alliance to their holds when this was over. How much more rewarding would it be if he could take something more personal away from this son of Cadarn?

Kitahn had presented him the opportunity: the girl was in his hands by Frax's request. It would certainly do no harm to probe for a sensitive spot or two in Kitahn's armor while he was about it.

The warlord gave a short, soft laugh. If his suspicions were correct, this could play so deliciously.

Oh, yes, the next several days were going to be very interesting.

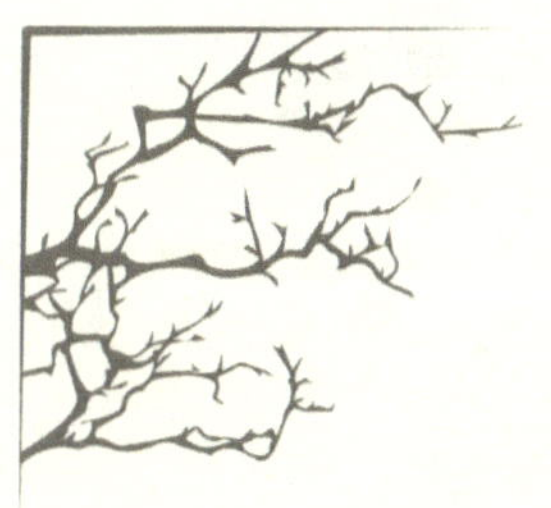

Chapter 64
First Camp

The Grimmenwood grew steadily darker and denser, the presence of its creatures noisy but more scattered and distant.

As Frax assured them, even in Cadarn's absence something kept the trail open. Although the warriors walked two abreast, the way was wide enough to easily accommodate four, and clear of debris or encroaching undergrowth. Despite the width of the path, the trees closed tightly over their heads, creating a tunnel of protection from prying eyes that might fly above the wood. There were still complications. The thin light made it difficult to see any distance around them, and scattered dense patches of undergrowth sometimes grew up to the path's edge. The branches never intruded onto the trail, but they blocked the view of the woods beyond them, sometimes for several lengths before they gave way to the open forest again.

They made ideal places for an ambush, thought Kaphri. And that was a strange observation, indeed, for someone who had once wandered about for weeks in an oblivious haze. She smiled secretly at the irony. Gemma would appreciate it.

The thought of her lost companion sobered her to their situation. This Grimmenwood was a dangerous, treacherous place. It made her wonder which of the two forces she should fear the most: the one pursuing them or the one that held them within its green grasp. She glanced down at her left wrist, suddenly aware of a stinging sensation from the cut the Geffitz commander had made at the clearing.

Which force, indeed?

As they approached another clump of heavy side-growth, Frax looked back at her. She responded automatically, her resentment toward him eclipsed by her uneasiness with their surroundings. Mentally reaching into the brush and the woods beyond, she searched carefully. Finding nothing, she shook her head.

Just as they began to pass the bush, however, a blood-curdling scream tore the air above them. Branches overhead jerked and swayed, leaves and twigs showering down, then once again, the sound of heavy wings thrashed the treetops.

Arrows bristled around her as Geffitzi twisted about, their eyes sweeping the forest canopy. There was no movement in the dimness now.

"Damn! Damn, damn!" Velacy exploded when Frax made a motion for them to lower their weapons. A sharp glare silenced him, though they all would have admitted that a little of their own tension had vented in his release.

Guilt flashed in Kaphri. Caught up in the threat of the woods around them, she had not thought to scan the branches overhead. One or more of them could be dead at this moment if it had been something other than a pyanth in the canopy.

"Is this to be a war of nerves?" Even Seuliac's calm demeanor appeared shaken.

"If it is, it promises to be effective," Frax said. "But we are bound by oath not to spill blood here. Don't raise your weapons again."

"You can't be serious!" Velacy stared at him with a stunned expression. "What're we supposed to do, stand weaponless while this cursed place attacks us?"

"We weren't attacked, Velacy," Uri pointed out. "But," he looked at Frax, "if the pyanths weren't brought to the Grimmenwood by the

Lords of Cadarn, we should suspect they're acting as advance spies for the Evil One."

"All the more reason to kill them!" Velacy exclaimed.

"Agreed. But you can't kill what's already flown beyond your reach," Uri said.

"There will be no killing," Frax repeated. A few more starts of the caliber they'd just experienced, and the morale of this group could suffer severe damage. "We must be better prepared. An occasional scan of the canopy seems to be in order." He looked at Kaphri. "See to it, Priestess."

He must know she had thought of that. Besides, she was not accountable to him now. She glanced at Seuliac.

FRAX DID NOT HAVE TO sense the brush of mental activity or observe the slight nod from the warlord to recognize what transpired in front of him.

Seuliac had already inserted his authority between him and the Priestess.

He turned his attention back to the trail without reaction when she sent him a stiff sense of affirmation.

The pyanths struck twice more before the end of the day. Kaphri successfully gave them a warning before the creatures took a screaming flight each time. It made it easier on their nerves, but Frax could see the constant state of watchfulness taking a toll on her.

They needed rest, but they couldn't randomly set up a camp in this place. The Grimmenwood had rules—rules only a fool would break. He had no choice but to press them on in the gathering darkness until he found what he sought.

Finally, as he began to feel serious concern, a small clearing opened alongside the trail. The trees grew tall around its edges, bending their tops inward to thickly weave them in a dome-like cover. At the center of the space stood a squat, ancient tree, the grass beneath it cluttered with fallen branches.

Frax dropped his pack and turned toward the others. "We'll spend the night here."

"Is it safe?" Velacy looked about uneasily.

"As long as we stay within the cleared area and keep a fire burning, yes."

"How do you know?" The younger Aedec was not convinced.

"Because the clearing is an extension of the trail." Frax gestured. "See how the whole length of it opens directly off the path. It's one of the safe places I spoke of earlier."

"What about that tree at the center?"

"It's for our convenience."

"Firewood?" Seuliac's eyes gleamed with mocking humor. "Oh, you are too pampered by this demon wood of yours, Kitahn."

Frax shrugged. "Nonetheless, it's here for our use. Uri, there should be a fire pit. If not, we can dig one. The heavy growth overhead will obscure most of the light from the blaze. Velacy, you're with me. Priestess, you—"

"Will work with me," Seuliac inserted smoothly.

Frax nodded. However, he would not let the warlord have the last word on the matter. "You take the right side of the clearing; we'll take the left. Stay well away from the edge of the woods. Gather all the firewood you can: we want to avoid moving around after dark."

Kaphri dropped her pack and flexed weary shoulders during their exchange. Power struggles, even over her, were, at the moment, of little interest. The late spring air was growing cool, and the thought of resting beside a blazing fire sounded appealing, regardless of whether it meant she must submit to a mental grilling by the warlord later.

Relief ran through her when Frax moved off to the western side of the tree without sparing a glance in her direction. Bitterness, resentment, and regret had warred inside her all afternoon, pulling her one way and then another until she was emotionally exhausted.

He had given her over to his enemy. She had no choice but to make her alliance there. Seuliac was her mentor now, and she answered only to him.

Her heart twisted as she moved to follow the warlord.

A stab of pain lanced through her. During the day, while she'd walked eastward, the geas had lurked at the edge of her consciousness, pressing her forward, but she had been able to contain it. Now that she had stopped moving, it was trying to re-assert dominance by filling her with a painful sense of urgency. She fought back, closing her eyes as she drew the burning, frantic urge deeper inside her. When she had gathered it all up, she shoved it into a place at the back of her mind and closed it firmly away. She would never control the geas completely. But for now, she could force it down to a tolerable level so that, if she were not alone with her thoughts, she could focus beyond its gnawing need.

She wasn't sure how much longer she could contain it in that manner, though.

Perhaps the rising pain was a good thing, she thought as she bent to gather up rotting bits of wood strewn about the grass: it would keep her mind off Frax.

They worked silently and efficiently, the warriors breaking the heavier branches into usable lengths and the pile of firewood growing. After contributing several armloads of wood, Kaphri surrendered to the weariness of the day and collapsed into the thick grass among the twisted roots of the ancient tree in the center of the clearing.

A shadowy form paused nearby. It was Seuliac.

"*I agree,*" he sent softly. "*This is enough for one day. Come, Caspani has built an excellent fire.*"

She moved to push herself to her feet, then froze. "*Warlord!*"

"*I see it.*" Two quick steps brought him over to where she crouched.

He slipped a foot between her and the tree, leaning his shoulder against the trunk so that she found herself huddled between his knees. Any other time she would have been uncomfortably conscious of his action, but right now, it was an added security against the fear that slithered along her spine.

They stared at the light that had appeared in the distance. It moved about jerkily, flickering as if a torch was moving between the trees.

Uri came over to join them. She twisted to look up at him, missing the sidelong glare he shot the warlord in the gloom.

"*What is it, Uri?*" she asked. "*Could it be other Geffitzi? Cyrwins?*" The image of the rearing, serpent-skinned creatures guarding Cadarn's gates made her heart race.

"*No.*" Uri shook his head. "*Those are what we call ghost-lights, Willow. If you tried to approach them, they'd only move further away, luring you deeper into the woods until you became hopelessly lost.*"

Seuliac snorted. "*Oh, come on, Caspani, you're the renowned storyteller. You can do better than that. Our warriors say they're demons with tiny bits of coals from the fires of hell to light their lanterns. They wander the forest searching for lost souls to carry back to their dark domain.*"

"*You're just a real bright spot, aren't you, Seuliac?*" Uri snapped irritably.

Seuliac straightened away from the tree. "*Whatever they are, Caspani, I have no desire to see what walks in the darkness of this place.*"

"*Don't want to know or don't care?*"

"*Don't know. Don't care. Some things are best left alone. You should learn that.*" Carefully extricating himself from his position above Kaphri, the warlord withdrew to the fire.

Uri heaved a long, hard sigh.

Kaphri twisted to look up at the big Geffitz again. She knew he was scowling as he stared over his shoulder at the warlord's retreating back. "*Are you sure, Uri?*"

He pulled his attention back to her. "*Whatever it is, Willow,*" he told her gently, "*Seuliac is right about one thing. You don't want to know. This is the Grimmenwood.*" He let his fingers brush the top of her hair affectionately. "*Come back to the fire.*"

"*I'm right behind you, Uri.*" Kaphri shot him a quick sense of reassurance, but she stayed nestled in the roots, staring at the flickering lights that moved in the darkness.

Sometimes there would only be one glow, then, suddenly, as many as four. They carried an almost hypnotic quality as they wove about, sometimes joining together, sometimes moving apart in opposite directions. Sometimes they would move away, growing faint with distance, but they always came back, as if they were performing just for her. They danced their silent dance, beckoning her to come and join them.

Drawing at her.

She gasped, and jerked out of her half-trance as fear shot down her spine.

"*What the...?*"Frax's glare was furious in the firelight as he looked for her. *"Priestess! Get over here."*

She got to her feet, sulkiness making her movements slow and calculated as she went over to where she had dropped her pack in the grass. Behind her, she heard Frax furiously take Seuliac and Uri to task for allowing her to remain behind them at the tree. Cheeks burning with humiliation, she picked up the bag and made her way around the now-blazing fire to plop beside the warlord. Seuliac ignored her, but Frax gave her a mental rake before turning his wrath back on the two warriors again. She didn't dare look across the flames at him: her new position put those strange, dancing lights at his back, and she feared they might lure her attention again.

Her defiance evaporated with a shiver. The distant glimmers of light had held her so transfixed that she'd failed to notice how the chill settling over the wood had deepened. She edged closer to the flames and nibbled at one of the Wyxan-supplied, mildly flavored wafers.

The food inevitably brought her thoughts to the swampdwellers. She reluctantly focused on Klandar Bayne, trying to force the dancing lights from her mind.

What would the moon find when it rose over the mists in the Palenquemas this night? Was Klandar Bayne dead? Was that why the Ankar Mekt had tried to ensnare her with fear in the guard tower? It was hard to comprehend that less than one full day had passed since they had found themselves on the Wyxan Moonplain. So much had happened since then. They had escaped from the Palenquemas to Cadarn and beyond, to this strange place; they had lost Tobin. And Frax had given her over to his enemy with no apparent reason or explanation.

And Gemma... Her hand stole to the crystal beneath the red and green tabard.

She could not probe that. Not yet.

So many forces pulled at her. So much emotion. Surely, she would go insane.

That was self-pity, and self-pity was an indulgence she could not afford. She moved away from that stream of thought, forcing her attention to the conversation going on around her.

"I never really appreciated the wonder of walking into the hold kitchens at any hour and getting decent food until the last few weeks," Velacy growled. "I can tell you; I will never take it for granted again."

"This isn't so bad," Uri turned over the wafer in his hand with a thoughtful expression. "I've eaten much worse."

"The Hrsst serve dead rats to their unwilling guests," Frax said.

"Well, I've served myself a few insects out on the Writhing Steppes and was damn glad to have them." Uri grimaced at the recall. He and Frax laughed.

"And what is the worst thing our little companion has had to eat?" Seuliac's attention locked on her. "Was it something that she found while wandering the Palenquemas?"

Frax's humor disappeared in a thoughtful frown. *"Yes,"* he said after a pause. *"Priestess, it's a good time for us to hear what passed with you in the Palenquemas after the Wyxa—"*

"From the time of our separation at its edge, if you please." Seuliac's white teeth flashed a disarming smile at Frax. *"I've heard the account of an experienced Geffitz warrior. Now I wish to hear her observations—to compare how well she performed, of course."*

She tensed, waiting for Frax's angry response to the veiled insinuation that he might have been less than open in his accounting of events.

The commander merely smiled. *"Of course. From the time of our first separation, at the edge of the Palenquemas, then, Priestess."*

All attention shifted back to her.

Well, she thought, only her foolish emotions could be called into question in the swamp, and they were no one's concern but her own.

Re-wrapping her food, she laid it aside and commenced her account in the flat, emotionless narrative the warriors used when they made a report.

If any of the things she said surprised Frax, he did not reveal it as he settled back comfortably across the fire. And if failure to draw a challenge or refusal disappointed Seuliac, he did not show it.

She faltered when she came to the Kitahni commander's disappearance after the sigalithe' attack, fearing she might let slip too much of her distress at the fear of his death. She explained the hesitation away as the memory of feeling so helpless and moved on.

But the next part, her first encounter with the Wyxa, was even more difficult to relay. She knew experiencing the Ankar Mekt had put terror of the swampdwellers into the heart of more than one bold Geffitz warrior. She was grateful for a gentle mental brush of support and reassurance from Uri as she broke off her narrative to regain her composure.

"*Go on.*" She'd barely collected herself before Frax's prod dropped into her mind.

A flicker of anger ran through her. She had to do this, but he didn't have to be so cold about it. She was not one of his warriors!

No—she knew what his response would be—she wasn't one of his warriors: she had to be more than that.

The anger flowed to resignation. Fortifying herself, she continued her story in the flat, precise tone.

Frax sat up sharply when she described her initial encounter with the Wyxa. "*Wait. You actually used the crystal against the Ankar Mekt*?" He gave a sharp, harsh laugh when she nodded. "*I knew it! The Swampfather lied to me. They didn't fully assimilate you! You and the crystal stopped them cold. No wonder they wanted to put you away. You must have scared them out of their minds.*"

He immediately withdrew into his thoughts, leaving Uri to explain what he meant.

As she came to the end of her story, Kaphri allowed herself the briefest sense of relief at having gotten through that part of the ordeal. Now would come the probing questions, the putting together of pieces.

"*You had every intention of letting the Wyxa put you away, didn't you*?" Seuliac asked.

"I knew they did not plan to free me. I thought it was more important for you to return to the north, especially after they told me your people were under attack. I didn't know where they planned to send you until last night on the Moonplain. Then I was horrified."

Seuliac eyed her thoughtfully for a moment. "*Such selflessness. I've never met a martyr before, but I'm told they have powerful motivation for their self-sacrifice...*"

THREE PAIRS OF EYES locked on him.

Uri, Kitahn and the girl. Velacy, of course, was frowning in confusion. But the other three... Seuliac leaned forward, his eyes riveted on her. "*What?*"

The girl twitched as if he'd stung her. Her eyes flicked to Kitahn for guidance in her reply, and Seuliac cursed. Throughout the afternoon, she'd begun to defer to him, but the commander's hold on her remained strong in spite of the resentment she harbored toward him. It was going to require more work to break it.

This was not the time to drive the wedge deeper, however. There was something hidden here: something critical.

He looked across the fire at Frax. "*You owe us the truth.*"

Frax, obviously, did not disagree. "*Tell him, Priestess. From the very beginning. Why you fled the northern tower.*"

A rush of triumph ran through Seuliac. At last, the truth was coming out!

Over the next hour, the warlord's sense of triumph stiffened to dismay, then to disbelief.

Frax watched warily as the girl came to the end of her narrative. Seuliac knew the commander had a hand on his knife, ready to use it at the slightest hostile reaction. It did not diminish his outrage.

"You knew what she was—how she fit into all of this—and you kept it from us. You bound us to an oath without telling us the full truth of it!"

"You weren't ready to hear the truth," Frax answered. "You would've had one solution."

Kill her. Even now, at first glance, it seemed the most reasonable thing to do. Yet, his gut instinct told him Kitahn was right. Even if he chose to ignore the words of the Guardian—and he couldn't do that any more than the Kitahni Geffitz had—it was clear they had no other option if they wanted to reclaim the south.

For the first time since their encounter at the barrier, Seuliac felt the full weight of the forces behind their situation. He stared into the fire, frowning.

"This has all been a bundle of lies and deceit, right from the start," Velacy said.

"Be silent," Seuliac growled at him. He looked back at Kaphri. "He can do that—take your form away from you? Your mind? Everything?"

"He's done it with other Ly Kai."

"Has he tried it with you?"

"He was forced to act before he was prepared. I escaped."

He looked at Frax. "She's like the Evil One."

"In a manner of speaking, yes; she is exactly like him."

"But not as experienced or as ruthless." Seuliac looked at her and shook his head. "We are going up against the Evil One. And the swampdwellers think we must also add Bithzielp into the mix! These are two forces that nearly destroyed us separately, Kitahn. Now there is reason to think they have combined their effort. There are only five of us. I begin to think we are too bold."

"You doubt our ability to succeed?"

"We must succeed. No. I think we need to have a better plan than our enemies."

"We don't know what their plan is," Velacy protested.

"Their plan is to restore the Evil One to power through her, open the gate beneath the Black Tower to Bithzielp, then reduce this world to hell as revenge for the past," Frax said. "Even if we destroyed her, they can do that last part—he already has a Ly Kai form and power, even if it is weaker. She, on the other hand, is a change in our situation. Something we haven't had on our side before. A possible equal to him. It would be a senseless waste to destroy her."

"I want to talk with her,"Seuliac told Frax

If the warlord harmed her now, he was a bigger fool than Frax believed him to be. "She's out of the watch cycle from now on. Just remember, we're up and moving before first. That will seem very early after the luxury of lying in a Wyxan cell." With that, he turned his attention away.

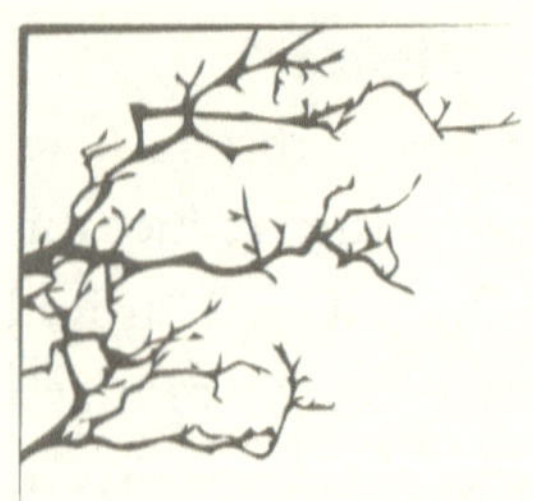

Chapter 65
First Talk

Seuliac stared into the fire, his mind racing, while Frax and Velacy settled to rest, and Uri took up first watch. The warlord had requested third watch, knowing he would never be able to sleep after he talked to the girl.

Kep. What task had he taken on? The girl was equal to the being who had decimated his world. Yet she claimed she didn't know how to use that power to defend herself, much less the rest of them. Had he picked up the tail of a waking tarmeuth? Or a dead one?

"*Do you regret your agreement to teach me?*"

His skin prickled. Caught up so intently in his thoughts, he almost forgot she sat beside him. He looked at her squarely, wondering what was behind her question. Kep! This creature was a potential Evil One! How did one react to power on that scale? Did he actually want to awaken it?

To return his people to their lands? Yes. But, such power! Should he change his usual approach to warrior training?

No. She was the same as any other youngling who ever stood before him: capable but ignorant of her potential. Potential waiting for him to mold and influence. No one was better suited for the task than he.

Time to address his biggest concern first. "*You can't read my mind?Or do you desire clarification on some point?*"

The girl stiffened. "*I do not intrude into the minds of others.*"

A sensitive subject for her. Good. Principles gave him a targets to work on. "*Why not?*"

"*Violating others' minds is wrong.*"

"*Really?*" The hair on the nape of his neck stiffened with wariness. She hadn't bothered to deny she could read his mind. What circumstances might push her to think she was justified in doing it?

"*Are you saying you never...?*"

"*No.*" She answered before he finished his question.

That was the type of thing he was searching for. She'd done something with her power that she thought was wrong. He had to begin his work somewhere, and putting her at a disadvantage was an easy way to dig in fast. He pressed forward, taking advantage of her agitation. "*Then you have invaded other minds?*"

She had the grace to feel remorse; he picked that up from her mind, although she did not reply.

"*Why'd you do it?*"

"*I have only used it on the animals of this world!I have never gone deeper than surface thoughts on the Ly Kai.* "

"*Why did you do it?" he repeated. "Was your life in danger?*"

She looked away, her mental shields suddenly up.

His anger, the anger of one accustomed to ultimate control, flared. "*How dare you shield in the presence of a superior!*"

She flinched, and the shields disappeared.

"*Never do that again! I asked you, was your life in danger? Was a world at stake?*"

She stared down at her hands, clasped in front of her. *"No."*

He leaned forward, putting his face close to hers, and spoke aloud. "Tell me why." His breath brushed her cheek with each sharp, clipped word. The action was calculated to intimidate and to emphasize their respective positions. He was teacher; she was student. He could make demands of her most intimate thoughts and expect a complete and honest response.

"I only looked at their memories," came the mental stammer.

"Their memories'?"

"I peeked inside their private thoughts. The things they remembered about the Homeworld were so different from life in Kryie Karth!"

She had her eyes closed. He watched as, unable to shield, she tightened physically against him.

"*Ah, yes.*" His mind flashed back to her story, when she first, supposedly, discovered betrayal and lies around her in the tower they called Kryie Karth. The area was a barren circle in a near-desert, mountainous region. It had surprised him to learn any of the invaders survived in the place. "*Did it help you in any way?*"

She opened her eyes. *"Yes. The images showed me something I will never see. They helped me understand the men's loss."* It was a mental whisper.

"So. Advantageous. Why not read my mind?"

"*I—Because it is wrong to violate others so.*" Again, the same protest.

He leaned back to regard her with an overtly bored expression, but beneath his calm exterior, his whole attention was riveted on her. Such an advantage, to be able to access the thoughts of one's enemies! Yet, she bound herself with rules against its use. Rules someone thought had a sound basis. Rules he was sure her people put into effect to protect their society from chaos.

This was not their society. This was one individual with a monstrous and unique ability. And this was war.

And it was not the answer he wanted from her. "*Who told you it was wrong?*"

"*I just know...* "

"*But you did it anyway.*"

"*Yes.*"

"*Then why not now?*"

"*No!*" Her outburst was nearly a mental blow. "*This is not the same! I only asked you a question.*"

Behind the protest lurked a deep sense of misery.

The Kitahni commander had not exaggerated on the road at the base of Caer Cadarn when he said she had power and refused to use it. Grudgingly, he conceded a sliver of respect for Frax's decision: no one was better at shaping a warrior than he, and she definitely needed shaping.

At last, the warlord allowed the curiosity, kept under control since their first encounter at the edge of Omurda, to flare. What was she capable of doing? What were the limits of her abilities? His imagination and ambition ran rampant with the possibilities. Did Kitahn realize what he'd done in giving her over to him for tutoring?

Her dark eyes searched his face for a clue to what he was thinking, a clue she could easily steal from his mind. A clue he was actually encouraging her to steal. He shielded swiftly in reaction, then experienced a sinking sensation of realization. If he pressed her to use her powers to probe minds, he would never be sure she would not invade his thoughts if she felt the need.

The obvious conclusion to their discussion so far: he was not currently a significant enough threat to require her to use those skills.

And that was how she must continue to think of him.

Perhaps this was going to be more difficult than he anticipated. Well enough. He always sought out the challenge. He dropped his shields with a twist of amused realization. Oh, yes. Kitahn was very aware of what he had given over to him.

He had brought her face to face with her current, helpless ineffectiveness. Now to discover possible things they might build on. "*To answer your question: I do not regret my decision. We have no time for that. Our focus is on preparing you to face what you meet.*" Defining "face" as destroy. "*You claim you forfeited your power. Why?*"

"*Because power draws power.*" She seemed relieved he hadn't outright rejected her. "*He seeks me constantly... sir,*" she stumbled awkwardly on the word. He nodded, and she continued. "*... sensing out over great distances for some trace of my presence. The crystal blocks his seeking, but its ability is limited. If I draw starpower, he will know. He will find me.* "

Again, the insanity at this task flashed in his mind. Wouldn't it be wiser to destroy her and eliminate a significant portion of the threat?

They would still be in the same situation they were now, with nothing resolved. Araxis had succeeded in pushing their world to the edge of disaster already. Losing her might set his plans back but would not stop him or the dark force behind him. Meanwhile, she was their best hope of defeating him.

"*When you were at Geron Maed, the place you call Kryie Karth,*" he chose his words carefully to avoid stirring a strong emotional reaction in her, "*before this present situation came about, how did you use this power?*"

Just when he thought he would have to demand a response, a tickle of sad amusement touched him. "*Do you know,*" she sent in a rueful tone, "*it was so natural, so much a part of me, that I have to think hard to remember what I gave up? One of my tasks was to supply the kitchen with water.*" She paused again thoughtfully.

Supplying the kitchen with water was a task any Geffitz child with a bucket could do. He bit back the sarcastic observation as she continued.

"*Durim's power was not strong enough to fill the large stone vats on the fourth level of the tower, so each day I would pull enough water from the lake for his needs and drop it in.*"

"*Drop it in? You carried it?*" This time he made no effort to disguise his impatience.

"*No.*" Kaphri looked at him.Her sending was perplexed, as if physically carrying so much water was a horrific thought. "*I reached out with my mind, determined how much I wanted to take, and moved it inside, dropping the water into the vats for him. Sometimes I would even heat it. Other times,*" she blushed, "*I would purposely splash some on the floor, mostly when he acted very demanding. That might sound childish, but making a mess was the only way to strike back at him.*"

She moved volumes of water with her mind. Hiding his stunned reaction behind a mask of inexpression, he nodded. "*Go on.*"

"*I can project a strong illusion as part of my telepathy. After—during—my struggle with Rath, I learned I could also project a volume of energy. It's how—*" she drew a deep breath. "*I killed him.*"

"*That's part of your telepathy?*"

"*No, otherwise, I'm sure you would have discovered it, too. This energy comes from somewhere else inside me...*" she floundered for a moment. *"Maybe it has the same source as my starfire."* She had never considered where the light she projected came from, either. *"Some things I'm telling you seem rather small, but you must remember they are a child's tasks. As I said, the mindblocks put in place during my infancy to protect people around me have not been removed.*" Her sending carried sadness. "*There may never be anyone to guide me along the Paths of Power to take those blocks away now the Twenty-five are all dead. I did find my way through a few of them by myself in the tower. But only tiny ones. If I could free myself of them...*" she looked at Seuliac, and the light in her faded. "*Well, then I might even open doorways between worlds.*" It was the barest whisper.

Open doorways between worlds. She had, indeed, stirred feelings in him, but they were not the feelings of scorn and impatience she suspected. They were ones of shock and fear. The things she said she could do... Things she so innocently described... They were the small things! A child's tasks! What she might accomplish without the restrictions her people had placed on her was beyond imagination!

"*What are these 'Paths of Power'?*"

"*A coming-of-age ritual performed to remove the mindblocks. I fled Kryie Karth before I underwent the ceremony. I had no choice; if I hadn't left, he would have bound me so I could never have escaped him.*" She shrugged. "*It doesn't matter. No one would have performed the ritual, anyway.*"

"*Why not?*"

"*Because they knew. They knew Arylla was my Birthstar, and they lied to me! They hated and feared me for what I am—for what they believed I would become.*"

There was resentment in her sending. Very good. He could work with that. But not yet. "*You said you heated water. How?*"

"*I channeled power into it.*"

"*So, in theory, you could burn something by doing that?*"

"*When I was young, I set twigs afire on the lake shore. Freya is powerful enough to allow that.*"

"*Nothing larger? No living thing?*"

"*No!*" Her sending was horrified.

"*Don't be too quick to discard an idea, girl,*" Seuliac reprimanded. "*This is war. You must consider all the options open to you.*"

"*That is not how the Ly Kai use power!*"

"*Don't tell me how the Ly Kai use power,*" he snapped. "*I've seen it first hand, which is more than you can say, and it wasn't the benign thing you insist it is.*" He sensed her shock and forced himself to tone down his anger. "*You've been misled. Protected. Which is why you're under my tutelage—to learn how to use your power. You must prepare to do whatever is necessary.*"

Whatever is necessary. "*But...*" She shuddered.

"*What? Does the thought of using such force offend your sensibilities?*" Seuliac allowed his outrage to seep through. "*What about the people of this world? I suppose it's acceptable for them to die horribly, as long as you don't violate your delicate sense of morality."*

"Do not try to make me feel guilt, Warlord. There is nothing you can say I have not already thought about. It eats at me every day." The response was the snarl of a cornered animal defending itself.

So, she could respond in anger in the place of whispered protests. *"I don't want your guilt. I want your anger. Your outrage! I want you to sink into the pain of this world and feel justified to use whatever you have, in whatever way is necessary, to end this violation!"*

THERE IT WAS AGAIN: the ever-echoing Geffitzi refrain. Whatever is necessary.

We do what we must do.

She had fled out into this world seeking a safe place where she and Gemma could live free of the starvation and hostility that surrounded them in Kryie Karth. Instead, she'd fallen captive to these Geffitz warriors, Gemma was gone, and her evil uncle, Araxis, had gathered an army to capture her.If he succeeded, he would destroy her mind and steal her physical form, restoring his access to Arylla's power.

He had brought her to this world. Killed her parents. Sentenced her to a life of misery. Now he wanted to steal everything she was and use it to finish decimating this world.

The warlord had every right to demand her anger and outrage.

"Earlier today, I told you to think about how our two peoples differed. What did you find?"

During the day, between her scans of the leaf canopy above the trail, she had considered, compared, and re-thought old situations and things she'd experienced in her interactions with the Ly Kai and the Geffitzi. It had been a revealing exercise.

"*I think,*" she replied at last, "*The biggest difference I found is the Ly Kai have a need for order that overshadows everything else. Geffitzi, on the other hand, thrive on change. Some of it has not been good for you,*" she hastened to add, thinking of Araxis, "*But, unlike the Ly Kai, you do not fear the new and unexpected.*"

"*Did you think about why this difference exists?*"

"*Perhaps because the Ly Kai do not need to adjust to the differences of other beings.*"

UNEASINESS STIRRED in Seuliac . "*Why do you think that? How did the Ly Kai defend their lands and people?*"

"*Defend?*"

His lips tightened with impatience at her confusion. Given their experiences over the past several weeks, that concept could not be unknown to her. "*Protect themselves.*"

"*Oh! They had no need. There is nothing on the Homeworld to threaten them, and, although I'm sure they occasionally disagree among themselves, they are forbidden to raise a hand in violence against one another.*"

"*What about the other beings on their world?*" In his observations, the world did not long tolerate the placid and unchanging. Someone or something was always ready and willing to shake things up.

She looked at him. "*There are no other beings.*"

It had also been his experience that the world did not tolerate singularity in its creatures. Not naturally, at least. "*What happened to them?*"

"*There are no others. It has always been the Ly Kai.*"

"I seriously doubt that."

It was Kaphri's turn to mentally frown. *"No. They... The history of the Homeworld is ancient. I studied it daily. There are no other people."*

Seuliac smiled without humor now. *"I'm sure there weren't. History and genocide don't compliment each other."*

Catching the implication of his comment, Kaphri shot him a sense of doubt. *"The Ly Kai would never do such a thing."*

"Really? Where did your Araxis get the ideas for what he did to my world? The Evil One did not suddenly spring from a saint. A banthu will always be a banthu, and a field lily will be a field lily, no matter where you place them. I haven't seen anything to make me think the Ly Kai are different from any other people. Your short history on our world certainly doesn't support it."

"Perhaps not," she conceded doubtfully. *"But if they fought this thing you call a war, it must have occurred long ago. Araxis and Alexar were the first to be born to Arylla in two thousand years, but Ly Kai history is much older."*

"If they were the first born in two thousand years, how did they learn to use their power? Who taught Araxis the things he needed to open the gate?"

"I heard some of the men argue once. They said when Araxis and Alexar were young, they were so precocious the priests indulged them terribly. As they grew older, they boldly invaded the inner sanctums of temples, searching for information on Arylla. They uncovered forbidden knowledge before the priests became aware of their activity. The Council was supposedly furious with them, but Araxis was so charming and persuasive that he took control of the situation. He extolled the wonders of the things they'd found. He persuaded them to have an open meeting of the Ly Kai people. Of course, he stirred their imaginations with his stories and overrode the Council's will."

Forbidden knowledge. *"Forbidden by whom and why? Hasn't that ever made you wonder a little bit?"*

SINCE HE MENTIONED it, yes.

Seuliac continued. "*This Homeworld must be excruciatingly boring with such a lack of variety and challenge. I can see how he stirred their imagination and support. What kind of things did they do there, anyway?*"

Even as a child, she had sensed the Homeworld had not been a challenging place. There had been breathtaking art, music, and beauty, but little else. After encountering these warriors, she could hardly imagine how the Ly Kai ever endured it. Of course, on those days when she was cold and hungry and dirty, such a world seemed appealing, but deep down, she didn't think she would want to live in such a place. It seemed small wonder the Ly Kai were so rigid in their ways.

For the first time, her resentment toward the survivors of her uncle's betrayal softened. Their shock at becoming trapped on this world must have been horrific. No wonder they cringed and fled for refuge. Considering their history, it was surprising they had been able to mount any united resistance against Araxis.

Seuliac was studying her. "*Your thoughts,*" he demanded.

"*I don't know what to believe or how to feel.*" A wave of confusion and frustration threatened to overwhelm her. "*Based on what I've learned, the Ly Kai may have done some questionable things, but I still find it hard to believe the men I knew acted to steal this world. They acted wrongly in many things: sometimes through innocence, sometimes not. But I felt their pain and their sense of betrayal,*" she flushed at the admission, "*in their unguarded moments, and they were victims, too.*"

"*Do you feel sympathy for them?*"

The coldness behind the question threatened harsh judgment.

"*Would that help them, or me?*" Her response was a little too heated. She hastened to soften it. "*No. I'm trying to understand what's happening to me. I've learned many things from the Ly Kai, the Wyxa, the Geffitzi, and Gemma. I've seen through the eyes and minds of others. I even have the geas working to influence me. How am I supposed to know what to do? How do I choose the right thing to do?*"

"*By using what's in here,*" Seuliac touched his forehead with a finger. "*Listen, observe; think. Be aware of what is happening now. Just remember one thing: you can think about it, turn it inside out, weigh it, agonize over it. Weep. None of that matters. You can't change what has happened. You can only affect what will come. Prepare for that. It's why I'm here: to teach you to use the remarkable skills you have.*"

She stared at him. "*You think invading another's mind is a marvelous ability you wish you had.*"

"*I can see its advantages.*"

"*You realize if anyone knows what you can do, all trust is lost, even from your family. People hate and fear you for it.*" Back in Omurda, when Frax had discovered how she'd escaped the Lake God he'd been shocked and furious at what she could do. He had warned her never to use mind invasion on a Geffitz on pain of death. Then, today he had exposed her ability to them all.

Seuliac shrugged. "*People will always find a reason to fear and hate.*"

"*Do not desire this thing, Warlord.*" Panic fluttered inside her. "*Do not desire it or any other power! It is most urgent you all listen to me! Craving power is how he gets into you. He feeds the need and seeps in to fill you up until everything that is you is gone. I know; it has happened twice.*"

Seuliac studied her. "*You're afraid of it. You have this power, and you don't want it. Well, things don't work that way. How long do you think you can run before you are forced to take up the hand fate has dealt you?*"

"*Afraid of my power? No. I was once, when I believed what the Ly Kai had taught me all my life. That Arylla was a source of evil. But not now. Not since I finally experienced it firsthand. Arylla is not evil. Power is simply a tool to use. I did not let it go lightly, Warlord. I let it go because I was afraid of Araxis. I'm still afraid of Araxis. Deathly afraid. I know what he can do. I will not willingly draw his attention down on me.*"

"*There's a small animal in the northern steppes called a niejo. It's a tasty, meaty little creature predators favor as food. When it's hunted, it hides in a dark place, with its head turned away from the attack. It thinks because it cannot see the hunter, the hunter cannot see it. The niejo is also a very prolific breeder, which is good; otherwise, it would have disappeared long ago. Do you think the Evil One will stop looking for you because you do not draw his attention? There are pyanths in this wood, girl. Kitahn says his family did not bring them, yet they are here, and they're agents of evil if ever a creature was. Think about that. How much longer can you turn your back?*

He cut off her protest with an abrupt gesture. "*No more discussion. Rest well tonight. You'll need it. Tomorrow we begin this task in earnest.*"

Chapter 66
Frax and Seuliac Talk

"The boy's a wilding!"

"Let him be. He'll find his way; it just won't be the same as the others."

No.

"He has a gift—"

"Animals. He must learn more than just the care of animals."

No!

"Why? He's Kitahn."

"Precisely because he's Kitahn! He's the heir next behind Riftkin. He must learn what that means."

No, not that. Tobin opened his eyes with a jerk.

Nausea assailed him. He tried to roll over to his side but the pain of the movement sent him rigid. He dropped onto his back, the nausea evaporating in the struggle to breathe.

Kep! What the hell had happened to him? Something had knocked him about. He closed his eyes, forcing slow, shallow breaths. Anything deeper locked his muscles, making him gasp in agony and pitching him into a vicious cycle almost beyond tolerance. Kep! He'd been in fights before, but even the ones he'd lost never left him feeling like this. It hurt to move.

If he could lay immobile...

But he couldn't. Gut instinct, memory that wouldn't come, told him he was still in serious danger.

What the hell was going on?

He opened his eyes again, this time only a slit. Light stung and caused him to tear, but he managed not to tense his muscles a second time. Tensing caused agonizing pain. Just lying still and using his senses was better.

There were sounds of the forest around him. Birds sang, and he heard a skittering sound, followed by a warm brush of air and the scent of dust: the wind, blowing a loose leaf. And a sense of heat on his skin: that would be the sun. It felt good over the background ache that gripped his whole body. Maybe he could just lay here. Rest. Fall back into oblivion...

Kep, he hurt. What had happened to him? This was worse than a day in the stable, breaking horses.

Horses.

Cyrwin.

He groaned. Cyrwin? Not possible. He opened his eyes again, ignoring the painful glare of sunlight. Blue sky above. Now, if he could only master the pain enough to sit up...

That would take a bit of effort. First, he should find what hurt him the least to move.

A leg. Push the pain down. Push it away. Focus on the movement. He drew his left leg up, pausing between gasps of pain until he had his foot flat, and then shoved himself on his right side.

Ah! That hurt! It hurt a lot! Every muscle in his body screamed protest. But he was on his side.

Now, to push himself up.

Slowly, slowly. Move the arm and place the hand. He paused, his body quivering under a fine film of cold sweat. Push.

Very slowly he levered up off the grass. That took a little more time to master the pain in order to focus on anything outside of his body. Meanwhile, he stared at the area around his hand. Grass. Grass and dirt, churned up as if a stampede had passed over it.

Very slowly, careful not to move his head, he let his gaze rove.

More churned turf. Hardly worth the effort.

The soft sound of a footfall behind him sent him rigid, threatening to throw his whole body into a spasm. He clenched his teeth to keep from crying out. "*Frax?*" He sent a sharp inquiry. There was no response.

Kep! He couldn't turn around and look at what was behind him. Pain locked him in place. His imagination ran rampant. His heart felt as if it would leap from his chest as he strained to hear.

Bird calls. The whisper of the breeze. Sweat, half born of pain, half of nerves, now beaded his flesh. Pain warred with fear of the unknown at his back.

"*What do you want?*" he sent in his best effort at calm. "*Who are you and what do you want?*"

Behind him, a dried twig snapped. He flinched, throwing his muscles into another spasm.

The arm that propped him up rebelled under the strain of his awkward position. The agony of falling onto his back was lost in the overall seizure as pain exploded in his brain, sending his mind into whiteout.

A long, narrow muzzle nudged Tobin's limp shoulder. "*They are so fragile. I always forget that on the first encounter. We played with him too hard.*"

"*Is he dead?*" The question was deep, musical.

"*I should hope not!*" The irritation turned to indifference. "*But, if he is, then we made the wrong choice.*"

A small golden form climbed up to perch on the unconscious Geffitz's shoulder and glared at the speakers beyond the warrior."*You have your way of doing things. I have not disputed that, though I think it extreme. But, I remind you, you acknowledged he passed your trial. There is no need to test him further.*"

"*You do not frighten me, sister.*" The whispery voice took on a petulant, querulous air.

"I am sure I do not. But you will respect your own affirmation."

"*This is my domain.*" A glow flared to stain everything in the area with a bitter green light.

"A lovely place. It hangs by a thread, like the rest of the world. We have no time for your cruel, ungracious games. He withstood your twisted tests. Do not subject him to further abuse."

"*Abuse?*" The whisper rose in outrage. Checked itself: went petulant. "*Oh, very well, I suppose you will insist on having your way.*"

"PROGRESS?" ACTIVITY between the warlord and the priestess during noon rest of the second day certainly looked a disaster. If the subject hadn't been so deadly serious, Frax would have taken a moment to savor Seuliac's frustration.

"Depends. If you mean discovering the possibilities, yes. If you mean getting her to consider them, no. As you warned, she's afraid to use what she has." Seuliac shook his head.

"Aggression is not natural to her. I would bet it was bred out of her people ages ago."

"Obviously not bred far enough, or we wouldn't be in this situation right now. They're still capable of inflicting great harm."

"Yes. But in a different way. I don't think you'll be able to teach her our methods."

"Perhaps you should be doing this, then."

"If you can't..."

"Don't try that on me, Kitahn. The transparency insults us both. I need more time to do this."

Years wouldn't be enough time to accomplish what they needed to do.

"We don't have time," Frax said. "We reach the escarpment in four days."

"We should have begun this weeks ago," Seuliac complained.

"Yes, we should have. Would you have agreed to arm an enemy in such a manner four weeks ago?"

"No."

"Neither did I." It had been a rough night for Frax. Strange dreams of walking a gray, misty plain, and his mistrust of the woods had made his sleep a broken stream of fitful starts. That he recognized the scope of the task Seuliac had undertaken did not help, either, sleeping or waking. "Kep! Anything you teach her is an improvement, Warlord. The girl was a sheep when we took her. She ran from the north tower, she ran from the Black Tower. She ran during that attack at the edge of the Palenquemas. She even ran two nights ago, during the attack on the Wyxa. He'll expect that. If she picks up a stick and hits him over the head, it will be a marked improvement. Stabbing him would be better."

Frax could almost see Seuliac's mind working. Kep protect the Priestess: there was no knowing how the warlord would twist her if he could find a way to affect her thinking. If she was successful and made it out the other side... He caught the thought and changed it. If she was successful. She did not have to make it out the other side. Their road was already paved with the dead. Another casualty wouldn't matter if their efforts were a success.

"She has free time while we walk."

"She has to keep watch for those damned pyanths. Otherwise, they'll exhaust us with frayed nerves. As of now, you're both out of the night watch rotation. That will free up some time in the evening, but that's the best I can do. You do what you can, as you can, but we keep moving. The spacing of the safe havens controls us. If one comes up early, you can take advantage of the extra time." It was a near-impossible situation and they both knew it.

Seuliac nodded. "All right. And by the way, stabbing him would not be better. If it wasn't instantly fatal, he could escape the body. Hitting him would be best, if she hit him hard enough. If she knocked him out we could finish him."

Frax gave a short laugh. "If she would. But," he sobered, "she wouldn't. She needs a jolt of hard reality to make her see that she has no choice."

And what was hard reality? Seuliac gave him an intense look. "Clarify what you mean. Where are you drawing the line on what I can do?"

No lines. No limits. They were past that. "We need results, Warlord."

Seuliac's mouth twitched. "A warning, Kitahn: you won't like what I have to do. Your precious little piece of 'warrior right' might get broken."

Frax ignored the taunt. "We both know what you have to do, Warlord. I understand that you need to isolate her from the rest of us to do it. But, I also know that if you push her too far in one direction without giving her a way to bend, she really could break. She trusts Uri. Let him offer her some balance."

"Doing what, wiping her nose? No. I won't have him undermine what I do."

"We need her intact, Warlord. We can't have her freezing up or losing control at the wrong time, or worse, turning against us because she can't reconcile what she's doing with something she learned earlier in her life." That was an intimidating thought! "She hasn't got the cursed dragon to fall back on anymore. Let Uri keep her centered."

The warlord looked annoyed but didn't argue. He shifted tactics. "Have you re-considered simply killing her? She would let us, you know. She really would."

The idea sickened Frax. Not Seuliac's suggestion, but the truth of his words: that she would stand there and let them take her life. But to just lay down one's life as a solution to a problem—and an inadequate solution at that... Frax's mind recoiled at the thought. He would give his life for Cadarn. He was willing to do it right now if it achieved something. But, giving up instead of trying? No. "That's a half measure," he snapped.

"True." Seuliac shrugged. "But it might be the best way to handle this."

Best? Safest, maybe, if you were satisfied with frustrating your enemy's plans with no countermeasure on your part to regain the things you had lost. "Not an option, Seuliac."

"I didn't think it was. Still, she may offer it again."

"An empty, useless gesture. Emphasize that. We don't need or want it. Let her pay for her people's mistakes. The cost to her is negligible beside what has been done to this world."

"Kitahn, you surprise me. You're quite adamant on the issue."

An uneasy chill ran over Frax at the comment. Did he sound defensive? He met Seuliac's narrow-eyed, calculating gaze. Don't read too much into it, he told himself. "See it gets done, Seuliac."

"Oh, absolutely." A cold smile lifted the corners of the warlord's mouth and a chill settled into Frax's gut. "Tell Caspani he will be needed."

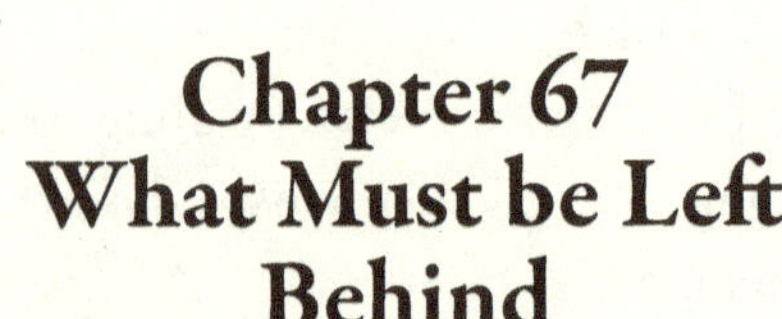

Chapter 67
What Must be Left Behind

Seuliac had not spoken or sent to Kaphri all afternoon. He was thinking, and that scared her. Two days had taught her that when he and Frax had talked on the trail, their discussions did not bode well for her.

The warlord was irritated. Their efforts during noon break had been a disaster. It was not that she feared the knife she carried; she had been the weapon's target more times than she cared to count. And she had used it in the Palenquemas to rescue Frax. But she could not take the weapon coldly in hand for the sole purpose of killing.

She understood the situation: their time was growing shorter with every step they took, and she had to learn to defend herself. The Geffitz warlord had to produce results. She accepted that. She wanted to respond appropriately. But not with the knife.

She shivered in the growing darkness, drawing his attention. Torn out of his thoughts, Seuliac glanced at her. "*What happened to the damned lizard of yours?*"

"*Gemma?*"

Seuliac gave her a withering look. "*Was there more than one?*"

"*She disappeared at the edge of the Palenquemas the night the Wyxa attacked us.*" There was no point in bringing up the flicker of gold she'd seen before their jump to Caer Cadarn. The warriors would not listen.

Her hand stole to the crystal. She had decided to wear it outside of the red tabard since she found her hand searching for it more frequently as she walked. The cool surface of the little bead against her fingers made her heart ache.

The whole day she had clutched it close while she tried to make contact with what was locked inside. Gemma had escaped its binding once. Kaphri had to find a way to help her do it again.

"*I wonder what the sneaky little creature is up to.*"

Frax had said something similar in the swamp. It seemed her missing companion drew as much distrust and dislike as she did. "*She has not abandoned me.*"

Sitting across from him, Kaphri was struck by his similarity to some of the Ly Kai men. The Warlord's features were sharper and more refined than the rest of the warriors'. There was also an air of fastidiousness about him. Not that the others were slovenly; Seuliac just seemed more precise in things, from his clothing to his food, to tasks he performed during camp. He also spoke differently: his pattern was terse and direct when he spoke at all. Did that come from his being older? Uri had told her the difference in age between the warlord and Frax or Uri could not be more than ten years, approximately the same difference between her and Frax.

Making Seuliac twice her age. The realization surprised her. The other warriors had been children when Araxis struck, but Seuliac must have been a young warrior. Had he been involved in the Geffitzi attacks on the Ly Kai as they fled northward?

"*She is not your focus. Pay attention,*" he said. "*We have work to do.*"

His tone reminded her of another time and place, where people spoke aloud when they addressed her. That had been by her choice. "*You don't trust mindspeech, do you?*"

It was a trivial, personal question. An attempt on her part to alleviate some of her tension. It was not the sort of thing to ask this Geffitz.

It was too late to remedy the error and unthinkable to back away.

Seuliac studied her in silence for so long that she began to think, with some relief, that he would not reply.

"*I don't need someone else in my head,*" he finally sent.

She should let the conversation end there, but something perverse would not allow it. "*Do you have a lifemate?*" Hredroth! What was she thinking?

The Warlord lifted his head to stare down at her through narrowed eyes. It was a calculated, intimidating movement, but Kaphri read a flicker of defensive surprise in it. Even the cool smile that twisted the fine lips conveyed wariness. "*My lady's kiss is cold; her arms are hard as stone. My passion would dash itself against her unyielding strength.*"

"*Rhynog is a harsh mistress,*" she observed stiffly, unsure how to react to such an uncharacteristic, poetic outflow of words from the warrior beside her.

She realized he was silently laughing.

The humor vanished as he leaned forward. "*That's what you expected to hear, wasn't it?*"

"*I wanted to hear the truth,*" she replied tightly.

"*It is the truth. I'm the Warlord of Rhynog, sworn to protect her. It's what I've chosen. There's no room for anything else in my life. You must do the same.*" They were back around to her again. "*Your only focus is the task at hand. There's no room for anything else in your life. You are alone. Accept it. Anything you might care about is leverage to be used against you. It makes you vulnerable.*" Did she see a flicker of emotion behind those gray eyes, or was she projecting the pain his words caused back onto him? "*You should consider yourself lucky: you have nothing to weigh you down, nothing to bind you to this world.*"

Nothing to weigh her down. What was that supposed to mean? That she had no one to care about? What about these warriors? Her throat tightened. No matter her status with them, she actually did like them. She cared about what happened to them. And what about Gemma? Did people who cared for someone shrug them off so easily in their absence? Frax said Gemma... No. Never mind what the commander said. Guardian or not, Gemma was her friend first and foremost. She could not forget her.

Seuliac's hand closed around her upper arm. "*Stop indulging in self-pity and listen to me.*" He shook her lightly for emphasis. "*This is not your world. You don't belong here. You and your kind have invaded and destroyed. Now you must make amends for that. Anything which distracts you from your purpose could inflict more damage on us.*"

True. But his words were like blows striking her heart.

"*I understand you, Warlord,*" she gritted back at him. "*You're saying this should be simple for me. I have nothing to turn my back on.*"

He had stopped shaking her, but his grip still hurt. "*What? Do you mean unlike me?*"

"*You were born into family and position...*"

His quick flash of scorn surprised her. "*Like Kitahn and Caspani? No.*" He looked away, staring out into the woods for a heartbeat before returning attention to her, his eyes hard. "*I wasn't born to caer-luxury. I'll tell you something few people know, even inside Rhynog, because it's a perfect example of what I'm telling you that you must do. This is no one else's concern, and I forbid you to speak of it. Ever. I was taken in a harvest of candidates when I was very young.*"

"*Harvest?*" Her sending was the barest whisper. His whole demeanor had changed so abruptly that she felt a sudden dread of his revelation. This was something too personal for comfort. "*I—*"

"*Silence. Listen! It was during the fading years of an age-old practice in Rhynog. Every eight years, a select group of the best warriors of our clan would go out, forming liaisons—consensual or not—and impregnating select women of the clan holdings.*" He shrugged. "*During that time, they also harvested the talent and potential—the fruit—of the previous excursion. They found me, without a father, in a small village in the Eryni Mountains. Something about me caught their attention. Was I a result of their seeding? Possibly. My mother never spoke of my father, but I was only six years old, while the others were seven.*

"*It took four men to wrestle and tie me so they could take me away.*" She felt the anger in his sending. "*I escaped Rhynog three times—found three ways out of her no one else had ever found before. Each time they dragged me back, their impatience growing.*" His eyes were distant as he stroked his left forearm absently with his thumb. "*Each time, the punishment was worse until the day they brought the matter before Lord Hraben. The captains of the harvest candidates wanted to know if they should execute me or send me back to my village.*" He smiled tightly at the recall. "*Lord Hraben was outraged to think they were so shortsighted, to consider such actions with a child who had escaped Rhynog three times. He asked me what drove me to act so, and I told him I worried for my mother. He told the captain in charge to "see to it." Bound and set upon a horse, I was taken back to the village, where they drug my mother out into the street and cut her down right before my eyes. Then they unbound me and gave me a choice: I could return with them, or I could stay. I knew if I stayed, I could swiftly elude them: they would never catch me again in my home territory. But, I also knew if I chose to stay, they would slaughter everyone else in my village before they left. I rode back to Rhynog. I loved my mother, but because I put my love for her before my destiny, she died.*"

Kaphri was aghast. "*You feel an obligation to this man, Lord Hraben?*"

"*He did what was best for Rhynog. I was something special. My talents could work to protect her. It doesn't matter what I feel about his action. Sometimes there are things higher and more important than one person, and the individual gets lost in the process. That's fate. You can't fight it. A cruel lesson, but you learn to deal with it if you want those around you to survive. If you want to survive. It's time you learned that."*

"I don't want to be that person!"

"I just told you; fate doesn't care what you want. The irony is that those you sacrifice the most for don't know and don't care. It's simply your destiny."

Seuliac pulled her to her feet. "*Come with me.*"

"*What's that about?*" Uri watched the warlord walk the priestess a short distance back down the trail away from them.

"*Time, Uri. We don't have enough of it.*"

"*And you trust him with her?*"

"*No. He's an Aedec. Not to mention he's an expert at working people's minds. But, he can get what we need out of her.*"

"*Get what we need,*" Uri's expression was cautiously neutral as he broke a wafer. Velacy was sitting nearby, so their sendings were narrowly directed. If the younger Aedec wanted to eavesdrop, his only recourse would be to read their expressions and guess their cause. "*She's been learning and developing all along. Wouldn't it be better if she cultivated her own skills?*"

"*Do you want to rely on that strategy at a critical moment?*" Uri glanced down with a sigh as Frax continued. "*We have to know there's something there, Uri, a solid base to give her an option other than running to act on.*"

"Weagree on that, Frax. But, Kep, Seuliac Aedec?"

"I can't do it, Uri. Gray dreams plague my sleep, and the Grimmen constantly tries to intrude into my thoughts. Who was I going to pick to teach her? You?"

Uri laid the wafer aside and looked at him. *"That's the second time you've said that to me. Are you trying to accuse me of something?"*

Frax closed his eyes wearily. "*No.It's just me, Uri. Never mind.*"

"*No. Something's bothering you. We've been friends since we were born. I deserve an answer.*"

"*I don't want to talk about it.*"

"*Well, I do! If you suspect me of something, then say it!*"

"*I don't suspect you of anything, Uri. Kep! I just don't... I just don't understand how you can be so easy with her, and I can't.*" There, it was out. He scowled.

"*Easy?*" Uri blinked, confused.

"*Comfortable.*" Frax corrected. "*With you two, it's all smiles and conversation. With me, it's instant, cold hostility. No matter what I say or do, we end up at odds.*"

Uri stared at him for a moment. Then he grinned. "*Kep, Frax, you're jealous!*"

A flicker of annoyance touched Frax's expression. "*No. I'm frustrated because I can't work with her better. Right now, when everything is so critical, she and I are like two banthues meeting on a trail.*"

"*You don't think I...?*"

"*I don't think anything of you, Uri. I told you, it's me.*"

Acutely aware that Velacy was watching the silent exchange, he guided the conversation onto a different topic—the one he really wanted to discuss. "*Besides, the fact she likes you works for us. Especially now. Things are going to get tough.*" His irritation changed to earnest concern. "*Seuliac has to shake her up. I don't like it. You won't like it. But it's necessary. She's going to need help putting things back into perspective when he's done. You've kept her calm and centered from the very beginning. We need that relationship intact. I want you to keep it going with her. She—we—have to rely on your support more than ever.*

I'm asking you to be there for her. Keep her together—without getting too involved."

"*Without... If you mean don't react to what Seuliac does, don't ask me, Frax. I can't do that.*"

Frax put his face in his hands, his fingers digging into his hair, his eyes closed. Uri was too damned close. He had no perspective.

Ha! What? Like he did? "*Uri.*" Looking up, he tried again. "*I have to have your help on this. Help her, but don't interfere.*"

"*Is that an order, Commander?*" The sending was flat.

Kep, Uri! Frax nodded. "*If that's how you must take it, yes, it's an order.*"

Uri was a warrior: he nodded in acknowledgment.

His cousin was not quite ready to end the conversation, however. He tilted his head, eyes narrowing, and Frax felt a tingle of panic. Had something in his words revealed too much of his own conflicted thoughts? He did not want to be the target of that shrewd Caspani brain as it broke down words and observations to deftly reassembled them in his very skilled way, based on knowledge gleaned from those years of friendship.

If Uri formed any conclusions, he did not reveal them. "*I'll be there for her, Frax. But if Seuliac makes a problem of it—*"

Was it possible for Uri to have a bigger problem with the Aedecs than he did? A ridiculous wash of relief ran through Frax. "*Don't take him on, Uri. Come to me. Please.*"

Uri scowled, but he didn't comment further.

THE SAFE HAVEN THEY found for the night allowed them space for sleeping, but nothing in the form of privacy. Seuliac decided to dare the so-called sanctuary of the trail as he pulled the girl twenty paces away from where the others sat.

"Sit." He gestured to the hard-packed surface, positioning her, once again, with her back toward the others. He settled cross-legged before her, their knees almost touching, his expression grim.

"*The time is coming when you will have to act. What are you going to do?*"

She knew the answer he wanted to hear: she just wasn't sure she could say it, much less do it. "*I must defeat him.*" She cringed inwardly, knowing that was not the right choice.

"*Defeat. That's what you think you must do?*"

She avoided his eyes. "*No. It's just hard for me to think about t-taking the life of anything.*" Not the knife issue again, please.

"*And what about all the lives he's taken? Is any Geffitzi child worth less than he?*"

She had braced, expecting an explosion of fury from him. The flat, emotionless question cut much deeper. She stared into smoldering gray eyes. "*No.*"

"*What are you prepared to do about it?*"

"*I must end the threat.*"

"*You must kill him,*" he corrected.

She swallowed hard, uncomfortable with the bluntness of his statement. He knew what she was thinking. It was humiliating that she would seem weak to him.

"*Nothing else will do. Can you do it?*"

"*Yes.*"

"*Say it.*"

"*I can do it.*"

"*No. Say it!*"

"*I can—I can kill him.*"

"*Why am I wasting my time with this?*" He looked away in disgust. "*You don't have what this takes!*"

"*I must kill him.*" She relented angrily.

He did not appear convinced.

Hredroth! What did he want from her? She was sitting here, declaring she would take the life of another being! It should be enough she said it. Did he want her to be happy about it, too?

No. He just wanted it done.

She drew a deep breath. "*I must kill Araxis.*"

"*Do you even know what you're saying? Do you know why you're saying it?*"

"*It is either him or me. I want to live, so it must be him.*" She could see he was still not satisfied with her response.

"*You have to believe it in your heart. You have to walk with thoughts of death.*"

Did that mean she should grow callous to the thought of death? "*I am not like you, sir,*" she sent bitterly.

"*No.*" He gave a sudden harsh laugh. "*You are definitely not like me. But you must learn to be.*" His tone became brusque. "*Death comes to us all, girl. It may seem ridiculous that I find it necessary to point out such an obvious fact to you, but I've seen warriors who glamorized the ideal of battle and did not realize the simple truth until it was too late: beyond all the bravado and boasting, people die in battle. Any of us here could fall. Are you prepared for that?*"

"*I could die.*" She had always known that. "*I have accepted it, Warlord.*"

"*No. If you go into battle prepared to die, you are already defeated. We'd be better off killing you now and reducing our risks of your failure. We don't need a martyr. We need someone who can end this threat to our world. We need someone willing to strike the necessary blow. Can you do that? Are you prepared to do that?*"

We do what we must do. The Geffitzi refrain. "*I am prepared to do whatever I have to do to defeat Araxis.*" There. She'd said it.

He abruptly shifted topics. "*I indulged your curiosity earlier; now indulge mine. Is it true your mind-imaging is as clear as Tobin Kitahn's?*"

Comparing her mental skills to the young Cadarnian warrior's had never occurred to her. How he utilized his mental abilities had been startlingly new and fascinating to her, but—yes. Now she thought about it, Tobin's maps had also been an amazingly clear and detailed form of mindsharing, but her long years with the Ly Kai in the northern tower had taught her another, much more complex form of the same type of imaging. One that twisted reality.

She felt a sudden stir of uneasiness. Did Seuliac want her to do some type of mindshare? Her only mental communication with him had been scattered contacts over the last day and a half. Only Frax had ever...

She shoved the thought away and met his piercing gray stare. "*Better,*" she answered.

His eyes gleamed with speculation. "*We'll see. Face me and focus on what I tell you. Do exactly as I say. Understand me, girl: this is no game.*"

Fearing a replay of what had happened yesterday, Kaphri felt cold nausea seize her.

Seuliac was already speaking in a low, intense tone and sending, too, so she would understand clearly. "Listen to me carefully, girl. You are arrogant at times, defiant, even. That is a desirable trait in a warrior—we must know we are the best. But you must leave all that behind when you enter battle. In battle, arrogance is blindness to truth; defiance is foolhardiness." He leaned forward slightly. "In battle, emotion can be death."

It was a well-calculated movement. Kaphri sat, mesmerized, watching the even white teeth cut through the last part of his statement as if the warlord had bitten into a juicy, ripe fruit and was savoring its flavor.

Seuliac's lips curved upward, enhancing the effect with the wolfishness of his smile. *"No anger. No hatred. No attachments of any kind. In battle, you have only two purposes: to conquer your foe and to survive. You must focus single-mindedly on those things. There is no Rhynog or Cadarn in the equation. See everything only in relation to your purpose. Will it aid you? Does it hold you back; does it stand in your way? Must it be sacrificed for the greater purpose?*

"But," he leaned back, causing her to blink as he shifted the focus of their discussion again, *"that is for later. Right now, I want you to do something else. Close your eyes and clear your thoughts. Listen to what I say and place an image in your mind, subject to my direction."*

He waited for her to follow his instructions. *"Now, I want you to go back to three nights ago in the swamp, on the Moonplain. Do you see it? The moon is so bright, almost like day. The fog gathering there glows with the cold light of Kep's Daughter. The grass is wet; your feet are chilled from it. Your breath steams. The shadows of Wyxa move in the fog wall surrounding you. One of them, inside the circle with you, looms close, but it does not touch you. Do you see it?"*

"Yes"

"Now you see the rest of us. We stand as we did that night, across an open space. Metal glints in the moonlight. We are clad for battle, our weapons drawn as we face you. There is a breathless silence over everything. We are waiting. We are watching you for a signal. I am watching you for the signal..."

The chilled damp of fog slid over her skin, and dread tightened in her chest. The Wyxan standing beside her shifted at the edge of her vision. Across the way, the Geffitzi warriors were watching her, ready, waiting.

"Share your image with me."

Obediently she reached, found his mind, and sent the image.

"What the hell?" Among the knot of warriors across the moonlit space, she saw Seuliac look about in disbelief. *"What sorcery is this?"*

His reaction of suspicion startled and disappointed her. "*This is what you requested.*"

"*No, You treacherous little— You've moved us back in time!*"

His anger confused her. "*Shielding will sever the mindlink, Warlord. You will find you are still sitting on the trail in the Grimmenwood.*"

His image went still and lifeless.

In a heartbeat, she felt the warning pressure of mental contact, and his form came back to life with a laugh of pure exultation.

"*Oh, Kep! This is amazing!*" Seuliac raised the knife she had remembered into his hand, brushing his fingers over the fog-dew settling on the blade. "*Absolutely amazing. Are you doing all this?*"

She realized he had expected, in the manner of Tobin's imaging, to be an observer in her mind. He had never expected to become an actual participant.

Too late, she realized she had given away too much of her ability to him.

She looked around. It was a shocking scenario, with, of all things, a Geffitz sharing it. Still, it was only a variation on what she had participated in daily in the stone dining hall of Kryie Karth.

"As a stronger telepath, I support the framework," she answered his question, *"but we share the structure. You control some of your external sensations with your expectations."*

"*Yes.*" The knife's metal gleamed in the moonlight as he consciously dismissed the moisture from the blade. For someone relatively weak in telepathic skills compared to the Kitahni warriors and her, he seemed to adapt and master the situation remarkably well. He lowered the blade and glanced about. "*Do you see what I see?*"

"*I do. A mental link makes this sharing possible. Either of us can change the things around us as long as the other does not resist.*"

"*If I thought I died here, would I die in the real world, too?*"

A typical Geffitzi question and one she disliked intensely. "*I think if you believe you die, your mind might accept it and shut down your body. I would not test it.*"

"*No,*" he smiled humorlessly. "*I don't think I will.*" Separating from the knot of frozen warriors, he strode across to her.

She flinched when he caught up her left wrist in his hand. He flexed her arm experimentally. "*Warm,*" he observed. "*And with substance.*"

"*It is what you expect to feel.*"

He released her arm to pinch his flesh, then nodded. "*Yes. Very convincing. Does Kitahn know you can do this?*"

"*No.*" She controlled the flicker of hostility his question ignited in her. Why should he care what Frax knew about her skills?

He nodded, satisfied. "*No need to discuss it, then. Can you take us back to the moment just before the Balandra attack?*"

She drew a deep breath. "*I do not want to.*"

"*I know.*"

It was pointless to argue. She drew on her memory. The green glow of the Ankar Mekt flooded the circle, and Klandar Bayne materialized close by. The light dimmed as the Balandra swarmed over the moon. She left them hanging, motionless, and wondered if there had been so many of them or if her fear magnified their numbers.

Seuliac considered the results and nodded. "*Very impressive.*"

He gave the weapon in his hand several experimental swipes as he mentally made adjustments to its weight and balance. "*Ah! Better. Now, listen to me. We are going to change things a bit. The Wyxan chieftain still has that crystal you value so highly, but before negotiating for its return, we have discovered we are coming under attack—just like then. We are all still in the open.*" He gestured to the area behind her. "*Your task is simple. Help the Swampfather get to a place of safety. You were a prisoner, the same as us; you must have built some image in your mind of where we were. What the place must have looked like. Take him to safety. We'll cover your retreat."*

She stared at the wall of fog surrounding them. A place of safety? She had no idea how to begin the task. Did the Wyxan stronghold exist on this plain? Before she could protest, however, a form began to take shape, bulkingout of how, during her confinement, she had speculated the place might look, rising above the fog until she stared at a huge plant-like structure. Even as she observed, parts of it moved and adjusted to a believable reality.

"Good enough." Seuliac walked over to rejoin the other warriors who were still eerily frozen at the distant edge of the fog circle. He motioned to the space between them. "*The chieftain should be there, midway between us.*"

There was a disorienting sensation in her head and the form of Klandar Bayne faded from one place to re-appear where the warlord gestured. Kaphri's uneasiness heightened sharply: Seuliac had just manipulated a part of the image that was much more complicated than a simple detail.

Perhaps this whole thing was not a good idea.

He gave a smile of satisfaction and nodded. "*Good. We, and his people, will fend off the attackers while you take him—and your crystal—to safety. It's your only purpose. Remember that and let this unfold as it will.*"

"*But how can I maintain the illusion if—*"

Seuliac gestured impatiently. "*You can do this. It should be just like placing the grass in this illusion; you know what color grass is without having to give each blade individual attention. Give everything the freedom to move the way you know it should.*"

*"Yes."*Saying 'I will try' would not be an acceptable answer.

"*One question: will the illusion fail if I am not in your line of sight?*"

"*Not as long as you participate in the mental link with me.*"

"Where is your weapon? You should have automatically armed yourself."

She found Frax's knife in her hand, an automatic response to the warlord's angry observation. She flicked her wrist, feeling the awkwardness of the weight against the muscles of her arm. This was not the right thing for her to have here.

"I do not need this type of weapon." She shoved the blade into her belt.

His irritation flashed, then he shrugged. *"Very well. On my command. The Balandran horde is approaching. I'm sure you realize these are the creatures who butchered the last of your people at the barrier."* He glanced upward. *"Don't let that affect your thinking, though."*

She should have prepared for the attack. Instead, she found herself staring at the warlord in sudden anger.

The bastard! He had baited her, and she had fallen for it so easily. She tore her gaze away from him and cleared her mind.

"Let them come." Seuliac's command dropped into her head.

The screech of the Balandra tore at her ears as the winged darkness flowed across the face of the moon and began its descent toward them.

"The battle begins!" With a crash of sudden noise, everything around them burst into action.

Kaphri did not see the Wyxa move to fight; she only knew they did. She had thought they might fly in short bursts—their winged bodies had indicated that might be possible—and so they did. Forms swooped and surged in a battle she created.

It was a battle she quickly realized was running without her complete control. She knew what should happen, but how it should unfold, the details, were too myriad and overwhelming for her to manipulate. Once set in progress, it played out with a life of its own, like a dark nightmare.

The Balandra were upon them, their sharp, jagged spears slicing the air. Their long, clawed fingers tearing and slashing. The Wyxan who stood beside her earlier was still there. It lashed out with a stick-like weapon she hadn't even been aware it carried, stunning the winged attacker descending on her. The Balandran fell at her feet in a crumpled heap, mangled by the force of the blow.

She stared, shocked at the horrific sight. The thing was obviously dead, but how could that be? This was beyond her imagining—

Seuliac! She spun about in outraged protest.

He met her eyes as he thrust his blade into a thrashing figure on the ground in front of him. "*Oh, you are so good!*" There was a bright, hard sense of exhilaration from him as he twisted the blade.

"*This is not mine, Seuliac!*"

"*Of course not. You've never been in battle. You can't know...*" he paused and her stomach lurched as everything around them came to a stop, waiting for them to resolve the issue between them. "*This is your image. You created it. But you don't have experience in battle. Besides, you can't control such a monstrous thing. It must unfold around you. Things simply happen because you know they must. Unlock your consciousness and let it run. Resume your task.*"

What he said made sense. A sudden shot of fear ran through her. This was a battle. Creatures would die because that happened in combat. It was not real, she told herself frantically. This was not real! Things would die here, but this was not real.

Sound was a thunderclap in her ears.

"*Resume your task*!"

Klandar Bayne! She found him in the glare of the moonlight. He was out in the open, exposed to the Balandran attack and looking about as if he were unsure what to do. He clutched his hands close to his breast as if he held something of tremendous importance.

The crystal. She must not let the enemy have it. "*Swampfather.*" She started toward him, stepping over the twisted and mangled body that had appalled her moments before. The Wyxan focused his huge eyes on her. "*Come. We must get you away from this.*"

A shout caught her attention. She spun about, the knife instinctively in her hand. A sensation of the blade meeting flesh and bone nearly tore the weapon away, but she succeeded in holding on, letting the momentum carry her body with it. Hot liquid gushed on her skin, and a scream rent the air. The blade pulled downward with the weight of the collapsing Balandran. The creature thrashed and hissed in rage on the ground before her, its hands fumbling to pull the knife from its belly. Kaphri felt the sting of its clawed toes rip her leg. The impact of its other foot striking her shin almost swept her off her feet.

The pain was real. The noise was real. Cold steam billowed from her mouth as she jerked her weapon free of the thrashing creature. It nearly blinded her as she spun around, meeting another Balandran plunging toward her. She stepped sideways, away from the ugly, tubular spearhead thrusting for her. The point rammed past, into the dirt, throwing the second Balandran forward. Kaphri heard the sickening crack of bones as the creature tumbled out of control. She felt the tug on her breeches leg again as the first one continued to kick at her. She reached, grasped the shaft of the deflected spear, jerked it out of the earth, and turned, thrusting blindly downward at where the thing writhed in the grass. There was a horrible sensation of the weapon sliding through resisting flesh and bone. Hot blood spewed onto her shins as the gray man screamed. Its limbs gave a spasm then it went limp.

Fighting the urge to vomit, she spun to find the Swampfather still standing helplessly in the center of the melee. Her focus locked back onto her task. "*Come on! You must get to safety!*" She grasped his elbow and began to pull him. "*You must move!*"

"*My people—*"

"*Are fighting to save you. You must move!*"

The creature started forward, slowly at first, then his pace quickened. Running beside him, Kaphri twisted around to check for pursuit.

A Balandran was hobbling after them, its pained, limping gait deceptive as it closed the gap between them.

"*Keep going,*" Kaphri turned to intercept the dark form. As the Wyxan continued forward, Kaphri planted her feet firmly in the grass and watched the wicked spearhead swing up toward her.

The scene behind her attacker snared her attention. The Geffitzi warriors were fighting back-to-back. A ring of fallen bodies circled them, building steadily, but the sheer number of their attackers was overwhelming them. The gray men swarmed, thrusting and picking with their spears. She saw a blade catch Tobin in the upper arm, viciously slicing his flesh. The young warrior's teeth flashed in a snarl of pain and outrage as he brought his blade around to knock the offending weapon away, but he could not follow through to slay his attacker. Kaphri saw him sag; his arm injured beyond use. Several more Balandra moved up, closing on the weakened warrior.

Over the bobbing heads, Frax turned, his features twisting in fury as he lunged to Tobin's defense. Dark forms wove between her and the warriors, breaking the commander's movements into slow frames. There was a glint of light near his chest. The silver starburst? Kaphri knew in an instant it was something far more deadly. He came to an abrupt stop, his rage going to shock and then relaxing into blankness.

A dark stain spread over the front of his tabard. She did not see the Balandran attacker, but she saw the dull, stained spearhead protrude through Frax's chest.

"No!" she screamed.

"WHAT THE HELL—!" URI twisted around.

Down the trail, Seuliac suddenly grasped the girl by her shoulders; his head bent forward so their foreheads almost touched. He was talking rapidly and quietly. The girl was shaking her head.

"Leave them alone, Uri." Frax's soft warning cut across his mind in a narrow sending. Uri spun back to focus his outrage on the commander, but Frax was watching the other two, his expression hard. *"I just told you, he's working with her."*

"Working—! I've never heard anyone scream like that!"

"It's necessary."

"Necessary." Recalling that Velacy still sat nearby, Uri tempered his expression of outrage. *"She is not a weapon to be honed and hammered."*

"I told you yesterday; she must become a weapon, Uri. She's the only one we have. You've known that since we captured her in Omurda. The Guardian told us as much. And yes, she must be honed and hammered. Even the Wyxa said if she can't help herself, she can't help us.

"It's necessary," Frax repeated. He looked over at Uri, catching and holding his eyes. *"Either she can do it or she can't. And, if he judges she can't, he's to execute her on the spot."*

Uri appeared stunned. *"That's ridiculous! You can't let Seuliac Aedec—"*

"Judge her fitness? I can't think of anyone better qualified. He has the experience. And he'll be ruthlessly objective in his judgment."

"Meaning he's the only one fit to make the decision?" A flush of anger rose in Uri's face.

"Yes. We're warriors, Uri. The best our holds have. But we're too close to this, you and I." Frax's anger softened. *"We may not be able to make the right call here. Look at us right now. We're fretting over the fate of a dangerous enemy."*

"I don't see you doing much fretting, Frax. You've just handed her off to Rhynog and turned your back on the whole thing."

What could he say? You're wrong? It eats away at me with every breath I take?

"Just do what I ask, Uri," he said. *"Please. For all our sakes."*

SHE WAS BACK IN THE Grimmenwood. Seuliac was leaning close, his hands gripping her shoulders. He was furious, speaking aloud, his tone low and tight with anger, but she couldn't hear him. She wanted to turn, to reassure herself everything was all right. That Frax... But she couldn't. Seuliac's hands wouldn't let her. Tears spilled down her cheeks.

"Get control of yourself, right now." The warlord had reached the end of his patience.

Control. Control was the magic word. With control, there was no emotion. It was a refuge from this horrible, unexpected pain. Wiping at the tears and sucking in gulps of air, she fought to compose herself.

"What the hell just happened?"

The question shattered her thinly limned, barely gained composure. *"I—he—killed."* Words failed her.

She had regained control of her emotions, but somehow, the tears would not stop. With shaking fingers, she wiped at new ones.

"So? Didn't you hear what I said to you earlier? Listen to me! People die in battle. It happens. You can't stop what you're doing! If you do, a lot more people could die. Do you want that?"

"No." Hredroth, the thought came to her dully; she had failed abysmally.

"The only thing you can carry into battle is the purpose that brought you and the will to see it through to the end. You can't worry about anything else. If you do, it will kill you and the ones you try to protect.

You have to keep going, no matter what. We've all prepared for that fact. You must, too."

Coldness sank into her flesh as the meaning of his words penetrated. Now she understood: it didn't matter if she accepted her own death; she had to accept that some of the others might not survive. She drew a deep, sobbing breath.

"Precisely." Seuliac released her. *"You'd better ask yourself some questions and be honest with your answers, girl. Why'd you take on this struggle? How do you want this to end? How high a price are you willing to pay? You'd better find the right answers quickly. If you can't handle it—"* he shrugged.

If she couldn't handle it, they would be better off killing her now. She felt herself sinking under the implications of his words. What was too high a price? The death of Frax? Of any of these other warriors? It might horrify her, but Araxis would see to it they all paid the price if he survived.

She could not allow that. *"I understand."*

"Then get over it so we can continue. I told you, there is no place for emotion in this. Why cry over a Kitahn, anyway?"

The question stunned her. *"I would feel pain over the loss of any of you,"* she snapped as she wiped the last of her tears.

Seuliac hissed in disgust. *"Oh? Would you now?"*

"Yes!" Defensive outrage boiled up in her. *"Any of you."* seeing his cold expression, sudden suspicion lanced through her. *"Is that why you did it, Warlord? To see how I would react to—to..."* He wanted to see how she would react to the loss of Frax Kitahn? He wanted to play with her emotions?

"And how did you react? Do you really want to discuss it?"

She stared, shocked speechless as much by her reaction as his deviousness. He was right: her responses had betrayed her.

"I warned you, girl. You are the enemy here. Kitahn does not forget, and neither should you. Get rid of any attachments, real or imagined.

They weaken you. Focus on what you need to do. That's your only purpose." He gave her a cold, mocking smile that made her want to tear at his face. *"Do you think your tears could help anyone in this world?"*

Fury was the only defense she could find against his decimating words. *"Am I dismissed?"*

"For now. But this matter is not ended."

No, indeed it was not.

URI AND FRAX HASTILY moved apart as Kaphri stormed back up the trail, her whole body radiating fury. She swept between them without a word or glance. Seuliac followed behind at a leisurely pace.

"What the hell was that about?" Uri demanded as the warlord paused beside them.

"A large jolt of harsh reality," Seuliac's self-satisfied smile sent a chill through the other two warriors.

Frax turned to watch Kaphri spread her blanket on the ground. Her eyes flicked up as if conscious of his attention. The glare she shot him was one of pure hatred. He heard Seuliac chuckle softly beside him, and his stomach tightened.

What had the Aedec warrior done?

Chapter 68
My Enemy's Enemy

Hredroth! How could she be so stupid? Stupid, stupid! Kaphri fought the urge to pull the blanket over her head and hide her humiliation from the world. How could she let Seuliac manipulate her so—into betraying...?

Betraying what? Something even she did not know?

Well, she knew now! And Seuliac did, too.

A terrible chill settled in around her heart. How could she let herself develop feelings for such an insensitive, manipulating, ruthless, heartless, bloody... A tear trickled down the side of her face. She made no effort to wipe it away; fearing the warriors—fearing Seuliac—might see her movement and know.

She never suspected in all the emotions, anger, irritation, and frustration, to find she cared so much for Frax Kitahn. Of course, her heart had raced more than once in the Palenquemas when she looked at him, saw the small gestures, and heard the things he said. But he had no choice in those interactions with her; he had to keep her stress down to prevent the Wyxa locating them. Besides, the rare kindnesses did not counterbalance the times he had torn her world apart with his words. And that secret sense of breathless joy in her, once the shock of his kisses wore off, had been a waste. It was all a mistake. He already told her that.

There would always be the indifference, the ruthless control he would exercise over her. The cold naming of her as a spoil of war made her status in this Geffitzi world clear. Yet, even knowing that had not meant anything to her.

Until the warlord viciously ripped away the veil of self-deception and exposed the truth.

Hredroth. She wanted Gemma so badly! Where was her small companion of so many years when she needed her most? Where was the only creature on this world she could talk to, who could offer her some clear perspective on this stupid, emotional mess she suddenly found herself immersed in? Gemma would make her concise, gentle observations. Gemma would offer her some little handhold of reason she could use to pull herself above this terrible emotional fray.

Another tear trickled, the salt in its wake burning her cheek. Oh, how she missed Gemma. This stupid, unexpected sense of affection—it was only affection, after all—had only developed to fill the gap left by Gemma's absence. The Geffitz commander had been there in the swamp, a surrogate for her only friend and ally.

Besides the constant gnaw of the geas, now her heart hurt. Her mind ached. She couldn't think, and her stomach felt as if she might be ill.

Kaphri fought the sickness down, refusing to give in to it. If she got up or moved in any way, Seuliac would know he had scored cruelly. She would not give him the satisfaction.

But Frax did not know what she felt: the thought shot through her like an arrow of clarity. He did not know about this "affection" she had developed for him. And he must never know. None of the others must know. Her heart raced, her thoughts grasping for a solution.

In spite of what Seuliac had done, she knew he would not tell. His whole purpose had been to expose her weakness to her, to make her see what she could not see: what might distract her and cause her to fail. Exposing her 'attachment' would run counter to what he sought to achieve.

The warlord said there was no room for anything else in her life. He'd shown her what a distraction could do. This terrible misery told her he was right. So, if she eliminated her feelings and treated Frax as she would have treated one of the Twenty-six, she would be fine.

She could do that. She could do better than that. Hredroth knew she had reason enough: the Geffitz commander had betrayed her and given her over to his worst enemy. Her resentment took fire. This stupid emotional attachment ended now! She would be resolved and steadfast in her decision. She would overcome an embarrassing affection that threatened the security of a whole world.

It did not make her feel any better. As she lay in the darkness, staring at the canopy of the Grimmenwood above her, images ran through her mind. A quiet smile, a flash of sudden wariness in gray eyes. She replaced each one with a familiar sense of fury, pushing the warmer feelings away. And failed miserably, reminded with each attempt that she only felt her particular temper for one being—the one she sought to forget.

Her blanket did not offer much warmth against the cold night air. She tried to use that, focusing on her physical discomfort, but her mind drifted to other times of misery, other cold nights and the warmth of another body in the darkness, the scent of a warrior's flesh...

Hredroth! What was she doing? She had never, ever, thought such thoughts before. Why now? Ignored in her misery, the tears trickled in a steady stream, dropping onto the blanket.

Dropping onto the leaves on the floor of the Grimmenwood.

THE PRIESTESS WAS IN deep despair. He hated the knowing, but he couldn't block it. Somehow, her misery and loneliness edged their way along his mind and seeped inside. It was nothing clear, just a general sensation of unhappiness, but it made it hard for him to focus during his watch. Frax rubbed his temples and cursed in silentfrustration.

He wanted to put his hands around the warlord's neck and throttle him for causing the upheaval in the Priestess, even though he was the one who suggested it.

When questioned, the warlord had only sent an irritating sense of intrigued amazement and given an enigmatic smile. He had unearthed something unexpected in the incident, and he wouldn't reveal it to the rest of them.

Clearly, she had experienced something equally unexpected. Whatever Seuliac had done, it had driven her into a sense of isolation she did not seem inclined to break. She had stormed up the path past them, radiating fury, and retreated to her blanket, where she instantly dropped into dark mental despair.

Damn them all! Frax forced his thoughts back toward cold rationality. He couldn't have the Grimmen misinterpreting his emotions and taking another disastrous action for what it might conclude was his benefit.

He must trust that Seuliac knew what he was doing, beyond any vendetta he might personally harbor toward the Cadarn clan. The warlord would put the safety of their world first.

He also must trust Uri to keep Seuliac's actions from driving her over the edge.

It was a delicate and disgusting game of intrigue and balance worthy of the finest ancient Caers.

There was no other way forward.

"*Willow?*" From his place on watch, Uri studied the dark form balled up in the blanket a few feet away. It was late; she should be asleep, but he knew she wasn't.

There was an open, blank response.

"*Willow, are you alright?*"

Still no response.

"*You are not alone, Willow.*"

"*Yes, Uri, I am alone.*"

"*We are here with you.*"

"*I do not belong here, Uri.*"

So cold and distant! What had Seuliac done?

"*No. We all know that, Willow.*" Carefully. No matter what he thought, he mustn't undo whatever the warlord had impressed upon her. Though he detested Seuliac, the man was a highly skilled commander of men, genuinely deserving of respect. "*But you are here, and so are we. And we're here with you by choice. Otherwise, we would be back at the barrier, beating our heads against solid air, trying to find a way through. But we're not. We haven't given up. We're that stubborn, you know.*"

He caught a quick sense of choked, bitter amusement as she relented a tiny bit. "*I'm sorry you're here, Uri. Do you hate me for it?*"

"*Hate you? Why would you think that?*"

"*My people caused this: the barrier, all this death, your separation from Ladrienca. My existence puts your whole world in danger.*"

Ah! "*Yes. That's undeniable. But, I don't hate you.*"

"*But I am your enemy!*"

"*If you insist. But we Geffitzi also have a saying: the enemy of my enemy is my friend.*"

She lay very still, obviously turning his words over in her mind. "*Araxis is your enemy as well as mine. And I am trying to act against him.*" There was the tiniest sense of rising hope. "*Do you really believe that saying?*"

"Believe it, yes. And live it every day, just as Frax, Seuliac, and Velacy do."

He felt her emotions lurch with a shift in perspective. "*Rhynog and Cadarn are enemies.*"

"Deadly enemies. Have been for a thousand years. Yet they've found a way to form an alliance in this situation."

"An alliance? Do I have an alliance with you?"

"Willow, we have had an alliance since the day Frax declared our intent to protect you while you followed the geas."

The sense of relief that ran through her sending was nearly overwhelming. "*My enemy's enemy is my friend.*"

"Uh-huh."

"Uri, can you really accept me under those terms?"

"I can live with it if you can."

The rush of pure gratitude made Uri grit his teeth and curse Seuliac Aedec to hell. He didn't care if the warlord was managing the task to the best of his ability.

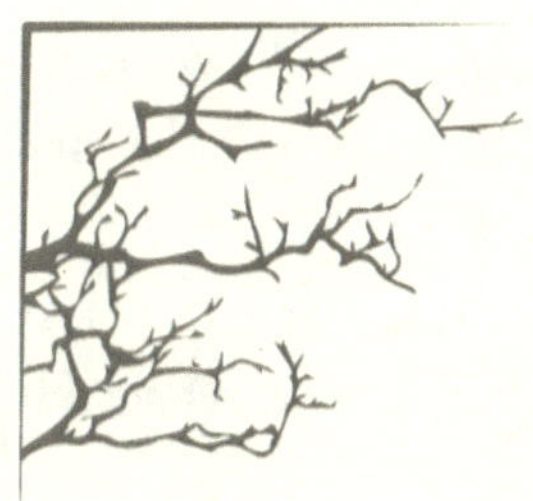

Chapter 69
Ambush

"Ow!" Pieces of dirt and leaves crumbled under Kaphri's fingers when she brushed her left shoulder. She looked around to check whether any of the warriors breaking camp had seen or felt anything. Frax, Uri, and Velacy still went about their business, but Seuliac stood, watching her fixedly.

He threw another clump of debris at her, striking her hard on her thigh.

"*That hurts!*" Was this some type of retaliation for her behavior last night?

"*Don't whine. You have the skills. Make it stop.*"

She stared at him in disbelief. Nothing she'd done last night would make him think something like that. Another clod stung her wrist. "*Stop!*"

"*It's a problem. Find the solution. But,*" his eyes carried a dangerous glint of warning, "*don't think of doing anything stupid.*"

Stupid. Like attacking the source? She rubbed her wrist.

The other warriors had paused, watching with curiosity as Seuliac picked up another clump and lobbed it at her. Seeing it coming, she easily sidestepped the chunk this time. Uri gave the warlord a look of disgust and turned away. Velacy looked perplexed, but Frax watched with interest as Kaphri shot the warlord a sense of triumph.

"*Not even close to the correct solution. Use your brain.*" Two more clods of debris followed in quick succession. She dodged the first one, but the second struck her hard on the shoulder.

"*Hredroth!*" she swore while fighting to contain her confusion. What was this new torment? How did he expect her to react? He was throwing dirt at her, for Hredroth's sake!

Frax shrugged and resumed tightening his pack.

Her reaction to Seuliac's antics was irritation, but outrage boiled up inside her at the commander's response. What did these creatures want from her?

Seuliac came up beside her. With meticulous, exaggerated care, he flicked some debris off her shoulder. "*This is very simple. You have a problem: you must find an equitable solution.*"

"*How do you know there is a solution*?" she snapped.

"*I'm sure. Find it. Until you do, the lesson is in effect at all times.*" He took her upper arm and drew her out onto the trail. "*And if you take too long, I'll recruit help.*"

Her eyes widened. "*The others would never—!*"

"*Chuck a piece of dirt at you? Of course they would! Probably harder than I'm throwing. You're lucky they haven't done much worse to you. I told you: you're the enemy. We don't forget; neither should you. Now, concentrate on solving your problem.*"

FRAX AND SEULIAC WERE less inclined to conversation this day. Kaphri eyed the warriors darkly as she stalked along behind them. Last night, Uri's words helped settle her mind, but Seuliac's behavior this morning, coupled with his ploy of the previous evening, left her agitated and with a heightened sense of anger. She doubted Frax had a hand in the warlord's little tricks. It didn't matter: he was the source of her humiliation and, therefore, the direct object of her hostility. And he had turned his back on her again today while Seuliac pelted her with dirt. He didn't care what happened to her, no matter how ridiculous; why should she care what happened to him? How many times had she asked herself that question last night? The warlord was right: she had exhibited a dangerous weakness. There was no room for attachments of any kind here. They diverted her attention from her task. They made her unhappy. She was better off alone.

If Gemma were here, she wouldn't be alone. A wash of angry sorrow ran through her. Gemma was gone, right when she needed her the most.Meanwhile, as long as the two Geffitzi warriors in front of her walked in mental silence, she did not need to wonder what torments they were plotting for her next.

She paused, eyes snapping to the heavily-leafed branches over the trail ahead of Frax and Seuliac. There was something there. A strange sensation...

Another pyanth preparing to take screeching flight? The creatures had struck twice this morning, erupting in a cacophony of shrieks that set the group's collective nerves on edge despite her quick alerts. The last few hours, however, had been uneventful.

Cursed harbingers of evil, she thought wearily, using the warlord's description. Each time she twitched to their cries now, she twitched to thoughts of Araxis.

She searched the leaves. Nothing. Yet she was sure she had felt it—a sharp sense of surprise, like a silent exclamation abruptly snuffed out.

Perhaps it was nothing, but she should warn Frax.

The thought sent another twist of resentment through her.

Control, she thought firmly. She had spent a miserable night thinking it through. Seuliac Aedec wanted her to break all ties. She knew how to cope with that. Remote aloofness, respond when appropriate, do not touch, keep her purpose foremost in her mind: those things had worked for her before. They would work again. She and the warriors had an alliance against a common enemy, but personal feelings would not be an issue.

"*I—*" she cut her sending to the commander short as Seuliac batted the air above his head with a sense of irritation. Something warm and wet struck her cheek.

"*What the hell...?*" The warlord stopped in the center of the trail and stared at two crimson streaks on the back of his hand.

She put her hand to her face. It came away with a similar smudge.

Blood!

The warlord took a quick sidestep toward Frax as several black feathers floated down from above. Then something larger tumbled from the branches to land in the dust where he had stood.

They stared in stunned silence at the severed wing.

Seuliac made a snarling sound and ran his hand across the top of his head, picking up more blood from his hair. He swore vehemently.

"Looks like a pyanth wing," Uri observed. "Wonder what happened to the rest of the damned thing."

It had fallen from the very place above the trail...

"*I felt it,*" Kaphri murmured, half to herself. She stared down at the tattered remnant. Araxis' harbinger of evil. And something had killed it. She shivered.

Uri glanced over at her. "*You all right, Willow?*"

"*Yes.*"

"Well, if that's a pyanth, it's certainly flown its last spy mission," Velacy said nastily. Uri gave a soft snort of uneasy amusement as the younger Geffitz edged forward to nudge the feathers with the toe of his boot.

"It can't have happened that long ago, with the blood still fresh like that." Frax gestured at the gleaming red dots speckled about the dirt.

Leaning down to snatch up a handful of dirt, Seuliac gave him a half-accusatory glare. He rubbed his hands vigorously to remove the drying blood. Frax shrugged and looked up, studying the dense foliage from which the wing had dropped.

"*I felt it,*" Kaphri repeated, louder.

They all turned to stare at her.

"*There was a sensation. It felt startled, like something came upon it suddenly. Then,*" she made a vague gesture with her hand. "*It was...*"

"Dead," Velacy finished for her with a tone of satisfaction. He met Frax's eyes defiantly. "One problem solved."

Frax nodded. "For once, I agree with you, Velacy." He focused back on Kaphri. *"Could you tell anything about what was happening when you felt it?"*

"*Nothing. Only surprise.*"

"*The watcher?*"

Oh, yes, always the watcher. Perhaps if she were some monster of the Grimmenwood she might stir his interest, too. She choked off another surge of hostility, realizing it might draw Uri's curiosity. She did not want to search her soul in response to the big Geffitz's kindhearted, intensely probing questions.

"*Unchanged.*" It was still there, doing what it always did: observing.

"*I don't want to take anything for granted, but there's nothing we can do except feel grateful the damned thing's gone. Maybe it'll be enough to warn whatever's behind their presence.*" Frax unceremoniously kicked the wing to the edge of the trail.

"*Whatever attacked it is still around,*" Kaphri protested as the warriors moved to resume their trek.

"*Can you locate it?*" Frax glanced at her.

"*No...*" Animosity swirled back in like a veil between the two of them.

"*Well, then,*" he shrugged and started walking.

Uri reached out to touch her shoulder gently. "*Are you sure you're all right?*"

"*Yes,*" she answered stiffly. He cocked his head, studying her, his expression troubled. She was acutely aware of Seuliac watching their exchange and was glad he did not have the skill to send the disapproval she read in his face. Uri pointedly ignored him, but her situation did not allow her that luxury. "*It was a strange sensation. There was life, and then it was gone...*"

"*It's not healthy to be too curious in here. Let's keep going.*" Frax snapped back at them.

The pace he set was brisker now. They barely settled into it when he held up his hand for them to stop again.

"Now what in the hell is that?" Seuliac asked softly. Both the lead Geffitzi were staring directly ahead. Kaphri edged forward to peer between them. In the gloom of heavy shadows, she saw a dark mound blocking the center of the trail.

"*Priestess?*"

She had already sought out. "*Nothing.*" That did not mean it wasn't alive, only that it had no mental presence. Memory of the creature lying in wait along the narrow path in the mountains of Omurda flashed in her memory.

"*Easy,*" a caution flicked in her head. Somehow, Frax had picked up the tingle of panic in her thoughts.

He was shrugging out of his pack. "*Guess we'd better find out what we're dealing with,*" he sent to the warriors around her.

"*It could be whatever killed the pyanth,*" Uri suggested uneasily.

Frax walked forward cautiously. He stopped with the mound a few steps beyond him and studied it. Kaphri could see it was large, nearly to the Commander's mid-thigh, and she had no idea how far down the trail it extended. After a moment, he lifted a hand to motion them forward. "*This isn't pretty,*" he warned.

As she drew closer, Kaphri gasped. A large pile of bones with gray, withered flesh clinging to them, blocked their way. Bits of leather armor and rags were mixed in with black bows that were snapped like green twigs and pieces of black-shafted arrows that were tipped with familiar, wicked barbs.

"Oh, Hredroth." Her eyes traveled over the jagged edges of the weapons with a rising mixture of awe and horror. *"Balandra!"*

"How long, would you say?" Seuliac glanced over at Frax.

"It looks like years, but I can't believe that."

"It's not," Uri broke in from behind them. "It's been minutes." He was standing at the edge of the trail, staring at the trunk of the closest tree. A dark, wet rivulet ran down the side, glinting in the furrows of the bark. Uri touched it with his fingertip and held it up, so they could all see. It was bright crimson. "Still slightly warm."

Frax's eyes flicked between the pile of remains and the wet bark. He nodded. "Impossible as that seems, I think you're right."

"Stripped to the bone," Velacy breathed. He retreated a few steps back up the trail. "What could do a thing like that?"

The commander shrugged. "There are things here that even my family has never seen."

"Or didn't live to tell about," Seuliac added.

"Whatever. It appears as if something spared us from a lethal attack."

Frax, Uri, and Seuliac moved forward to stare at the jumble of bones. Kaphri remained at a more cautious distance, closer to Velacy.

"It would make it easier to count if there were heads," Seuliac observed after a short silence. "And where are the wings?"

Kaphri's gaze went to the branches overhead. The thought of dead Balandra parts dropping on her made her queasy. The warriors continued to study the bones.

"Maybe they aren't Balandra."

"Look at those barbs. We saw that on the shaft we pulled from your shoulder."

"Does the Grimmen take trophies? Maybe it trophied the wings and heads."

She listened as the conversation continued between the three in cold, removed speculation, as if they were staring at a pile of brush blocking the trail.

"I'd say at least a dozen Balandra," Frax finally declared.

The other two nodded.

"And not a sound, even though we were only footsteps away," Uri said. "They must have been perched up there, ready to rain destruction down on us. Now they're just one neat, ugly pile."

Twelve Balandra dead without a sound. A shudder ran over Kaphri. What was this Grimmenwood?

"This was a large force." Seuliac nudged the vicious barb of a broken arrow with his boot. "Considering what this place is, this seems a desperate measure on their part."

Frax grunted agreement.

"Why attack us now?"

"The pressure to act before she got somewhere?"

"Possibly. Kep! That might've been our bones lying here."

Kaphri wrapped her arms around her body to hide a shiver. Araxis was not searching; he knew where they were.

"Are we to take this as a sign from your Grimmen that our passage is to remain unthreatened?" Kaphri jerked back to the present when Velacy spoke up behind her.

"I wouldn't take this as a sign of anything except the Balandra are here." Frax frowned as he glanced around. "Much earlier than we calculated. We have to leave the trail."

"What?" Velacy stared at him in shock.

Uri and Seuliac managed to contain most of their dismay.

"Is that wise, Kitahn?" Seuliac spoke up quietly. "I don't want to spill more of my blood ten steps off this trail."

"Wise? I don't know. But I don't know if we can trust the woods to defend us if we stay on the trail after it's given us such an obvious warning, either. Or if it could contain a larger strike. All the Balandra need to do is grab the girl, and everything is over."

"You said we would be safe on this trail." Velacy sounded accusatory. "Why leave it?"

"We have no choice, Velacy." Uri was grim. "They know exactly where we are today and where we'll be tomorrow. We can't take the risk."

"We'll leave the path here." Frax nodded at the pile of dried remains, "That will give them second thoughts about following us into the woods, so they'll have a harder time picking up our trail again. We'll go sharply southeast, away from the path." His attention turned to Kaphri. "*Can you manage that for a while*?"

The geas would fight the change in direction. "*I'll manage,*" she sent shortly. She would manage it or die trying.

Dread made her heart beat like thunder in her ears. The warlord was right; they could have died here. Three days out of the Palenquemas, Araxis' forces had already found them.

"*We'll adjust back true east as soon as we can. We must move as far and as fast as possible. We'll take a break at dark, then move out again.*" He ignored the moans of dismay. "*This is a vast place: the further and faster we go, the more territory they'll have to search.*" Frax bent to pick up his pack.

"Wait! Southeast?" Velacy radiated sudden suspicion and anger. "Azay Rhiad lies southeast of here, doesn't it?"

Kitahn paused, half-slid into his pack, and gave the Aedec heir a flat, cold stare.

Seuliac actually laughed. "Kep, Velacy! We have a whole mountain range between Azay Rhiad and us. You know that." He gave Frax an exaggerated, apologetic smile. "He excelled in diplomacy, not geography."

"Indeed," Frax murmured dryly. He finished shouldering his pack.

Velacy flushed with rage. "Damn you, Seuliac! I—"

"Should be silent," the warlord inserted deftly. He reached out and caught at the other Aedec's shoulder in a friendly manner. Velacy tried to hide a wince as fingers exerted painful pressure. "Don't make this political, Velacy."

There was a sense of furious, private mental exchanges, but Seuliac's uncharacteristically pleasant expression never faltered. The younger Geffitz's color darkened further. He gave a snort of anger as he twisted out from under the other's grip.

Uri was watching the exchange with a mild interest she knew was deceptive. "*What is Azay Rhiad?*" she shot at him narrowly.

"*Nothing that affects the here and now,*" he responded. "*Get back into place, Willow. Our way just became a lot more difficult.*" He put out a hand to guide her off the trail.

"*Is Azay Rhiad important?*" A silly question, with the tension seething around her.

"*To some of us, yes. It's too detailed and politically sensitive to talk about right now. Ask me when we break for the day.*"

"*I will,*" she promised.

SEULIAC HAD COMMENTED more than once over the past three days about how ridiculously easy their passage along the trail was. That ended within ten steps off the path. The trees were not a problem: the massive trunks were frequently spaced more than five path widths apart. But the ground hidden beneath the thick carpet of leaves was damp, steeply gullied, and rutted with roots, making their footing treacherous and slippery. Obstacles blocking their way quickly became another issue. They had to fight through or go around clumps of fern tall enough to qualify as small copses of trees, while broken branches and the occasional massive fallen tree made for time-consuming detours.

Frax took the first severe fall while climbing down into a dry stream bed. Cursing furiously, he picked himself up. No one laughed: they all had to get down the same bank behind him.

The stream bed, however, proved a fortunate encounter. They followed its winding, stony course roughly southward for almost an hour before Frax thought to check Kaphri.

He stopped in his tracks. "*Priestess, are you all right?*"

Teeth clenched against the geas, she nodded. She didn't trust to send lest the pain filter through, and she was determined that would not happen. It had started the moment she stepped off the trail. Every step became a gradual, growing agony, the ache in her body and mind slowly ramping to constant, consuming pain. Only the rare turn eastward had allowed her short periods of respite.

The stream bed was currently running at an almost true north-south course, and she was struggling so hard for every step that she had fallen back to a place almost between Velacy and Uri.

"*You should have told me you were having a problem.*"

Not likely, she thought. She said she would manage, and she would.

There was no debate, however: they had to change direction. They could see her shoulders twisting eastward while she stood in place.

Climbing out of the rocky stream bed proved more difficult than climbing in. The banks were higher now, the walls soft and crumbling from recent spring rains. The effort developed into a three-person task involving a rope; a Geffitz pulling from the top of the bank and a third pushing up from the bottom, with Uri and Frax pulling Seuliac out last. They were all muddy, sweating, and irritable when they collapsed on the ground.

"Kep, I want a bath," Seuliac growled. His usually immaculate hair was stringy and tangled. He brushed back the damp strands with his hand, leaving a smudge of dirt on his forehead.

Hardly looking better,Uri chuckled. "Ah, for a plunge into one of the seven crystal lakes surrounding Pen Gerrig."

"The ocean," Velacy corrected. "The waves strong enough to slap your thighs and make you fight for balance, and the spray hitting you full in the face, making you gasp with its chill."

"The waterfalls at Ameth Thiem. Standing on the rocks under the tallest fall, the icy water pounding you as if it would peel the flesh from your bones," Frax said.

"Or a dive off the red stone cliffs of the steppe country, plunging deep into one of the secluded blue-green pools, the water temperature perfect for a long, leisurely swim," Seuliac finished.

Moving eastward up the bank had eased the persistence of the geas enough so that Kaphri was able to unshield. Her heart squeezed at the beautiful, vivid images and the accompanying sensations that came from each of the warriors in turn.

"*What are they?*" she asked, her resolution to remain distant forgotten in the face of curiosity.

"*Memories, Willow. Some of our most pleasant, in this case.*" Uri gave a short laugh. "*It's a friendly form of competition, sort of like seeing who tells the best story.*"

"*Competition?*" She looked around at the others. "*Who won?*"

Seuliac shrugged. "*We don't actually choose. We just experience and consider. Warriors are sometimes judged by their peers on the experiences they relay.*" So, the Aedecs could use certain modes of telepathy quite efficiently when it suited them. "*What's your best memory of a swim?*"

Recalling her decision to remain aloof, she shook her head. Uri caught at her mind before she could shield. "*No, you're part of this group. You have to share.*"

Memory of the Lake God flashed in her mind. "*I have only bad memories.*"

"*Can't be true. Share,*" he persisted. "*Something simple will be fine.*" Four pairs of gray eyes rested on her expectantly.

"*A swim?*"

"*A pleasant one.*"

She swallowed hard and focused, recalling warm summer evenings, the pebbly shore beneath her bare feet, the sky above rose and amethyst long after the sun disappeared over the mountain wall. "*A swim in the lake surrounding the tower after a hard day in the field. Washing away the dirt and sweat in the cold water.*"

A chorus of groans and laughter interrupted her.

"*Stop, stop. You started out well, but you ruined it.*" Uri laughed. "*You're supposed to divert our attention away from our current plight and make us forget about the dirt and sweat, not remind us!*" Laughter rippled around again.

"*You didn't say that!*"

"*Well, now you know.*" Frax gave her a short nod as he got to his feet. "*Next time, we'll expect better.*"

The groans around her as the others struggled up went unheard. Next time. Warmth spread over her. The next time they expected her to participate without hesitation—as part of the group. She sat for a moment longer, secretly savoring that little scrap of camaraderie.

"*Don't get too comfortable, girl.*" Seuliac shot her a sidelong look as he twitched his muddy clothing back into place with expert precision. "*Something will change, even if it's only the weather.*"

Seuliac was right: he or Frax would take the tiny secret pleasure from her at their next encounter.

When she bent to pick up her pack a clod of dirt struck her square in the back.

DODGING THROWN OBJECTS became a tedious struggle. She learned to expand her mental sensing to the area around her to get better at discovering objects coming toward her, but it was still hard to move out of the way fast enough. Uri watched, frowning, but he neither protested nor participated. Frax either ignored or observed in weary silence, too preoccupied with the Grimmenwood and their safety to comment.

She flinched at every sound. Twisted to avoid an insect that buzzed too close to her head. Staying alert was wearing her down, making her reactions slower. Things she might have dodged were making contact again until she was so frustrated and angry she thought she might scream. She began to fear her own reactions. Seuliac was pushing hard, forcing her into a corner. What if he pushed her too far? What if she struck out in retaliation?

She had agreed to this torment, affirmed she wanted him to teach her. Now she feared her response.

Finally, after a series of successful evasions, she gave him a defiant glare.

He nodded grimly. "*So, we move to the next stage.*"

And that was...?

She found out when a lump of hard dirt struck her behind her right ear, almost knocking her to her knees. She spun about to meet the eyes of a smirking Velacy and a stunned-faced Uri.

"*You!*"

"*Leave him be!*" Seuliac snapped.

Instantly her rage shifted. "*You bastard—*"

"*You bastard, sir,*" he corrected. "*Do you think you'll always know where an attack is coming from?*"

"*How can I watch for things randomly flung at me?*"

"*The same way you sense the presence of other things around you. Broaden your awareness.*"

"*I should not have to watch my back all the time!*"

"*Why not? Is there some rule that exempts you from attack? You have abilities; use them.*"

She blinked back tears. The place where the clod had struck burned painfully. It was not fair, making her watch her back constantly.

She knew better than to protest further. "*Hredroth reject your return!*" she snapped at him. It was something she had heard once during a strong disagreement between the Ly Kai men. She knew it was a serious curse for the Ly Kai from the reaction it had stirred among them.

Here it meant nothing.

As she got better at moving out of the way again, the objects came harder, faster, and from more unexpected directions. During one break, Seuliac swept a stick out as she walked past, catching her in the back of the knees and bringing her to the ground.

She huddled there, her mind caught between outrage and pain. "*You hit me?*" Her sending was a whisper of disbelief.

"*You should have sensed the pending strike,*" he returned unsympathetically. "*Kep! What does it take to make you react?*" He got up and stormed away.

FRAX OBSERVED HER STRUGGLE. All the warriors around her had schooled under a weapons master, a skilled hold officer charged with their training. They'd all endured the repeated bruises and humiliation necessary to reach the point where they learned to react instinctively in the right ways. Everyone mastered the harsh lessons in their own way, in their own time.

He held his tongue, feeling the warlord's frustration as the day dragged on without any indication that she had moved toward the reaction he sought.

She was slow, too slow in picking up the lesson. If she didn't catch on soon...

SEULIAC'S PROJECT WAS not her most pressing problem, however.

As they progressed deeper into the untracked woods, the geas was intensifying its hold on her again. At the slightest turning away from the east, it sought to overwhelm her thoughts to the exclusion of anything else. She tried everything, from dwelling on her feelings of loss for Gemma to reciting from the laws of the Ly Kai. Always, the geas insinuated its need back into dominance and stole her focus.

Sometimes, when they were moving eastward, she gave in, blanked her mind, and let it flow through her.

"*Willow, this way.*" Uri's hands gripped her shoulders and turned her in the direction Frax and Seuliac had taken, down a slope between the enormous trees. Without realizing it, she had fallen back from her usual position until she was walking between Uri and Velacy.

This was how many times now?

"*I'm sorry.*" She tried to look up at Uri, but she found it too difficult to turn her head.

"This is insane!" Velacy fumed, his clod-throwing forgotten for the day. "What are we supposed to do with her when we stop?"

Uri tightened his grip and she realized she was trying to push through Velacy because he would not step out of her way.

During their next break, Seuliac tried to work with her, but her attention kept drifting until, scowling in frustrated fury, he finally gave up.They walked in tense silence into the evening, Uri and Velacy guiding her while Frax and Seuliac focused on lookout duty.

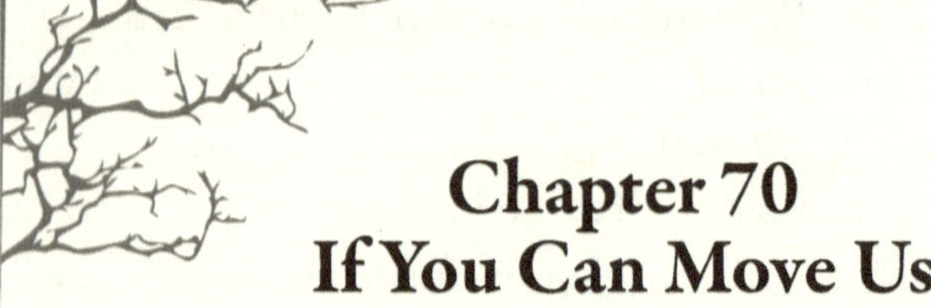

Chapter 70
If You Can Move Us

"I*'ll take the firswatch.*" As the others dropped to the ground in relief, Frax climbed the bare roots of an immense tree and wearily settled his back against the trunk.He couldn't sleep, so he may as well save duplication of someone else's effort.

Stepping into the woods the second time had been a vastly different experience than back at the edge of the field in Cadarn. The effects of the Cyrwin song had never left him, but this! This felt like he had pushed through an insulating membrane into roaring flames. The low, nagging sense of urgency that had plagued him since first entering the Grimmenwood had ramped into hot, raw emotion. The Grimmen wanted... the Grimmen wanted... wanted... wanted... Angry, red, blazing need—that was the closest description he could find for it—hammered inside his head. The Grimmen never clarified what it wanted and it never let up. It just sent an endless, relentless blast of emotion, like a jealous, angry lover screaming into his face, trying to insert its presence between him and anything else that might occupy his mind. If not for the presence of the others, it would have driven him to move without stopping, to find some way to appease it. They acted as a brake against it. They needed to rest. They forced him to think and to speak. At least for now, their needs pushed through the raw sendings and gave him a focal point outside his head. Tomorrow, who knew? If the need ramped any stronger, he didn't know if anything could hold him back.

That was self-defeating, he thought wearily. How did it benefit their situation if he became physically unable to continue because of exhaustion, or if the others fell behind because they couldn't keep up with him?

"*Back off a bit!*" he snarled in the direction he imagined the Grimmen. "*Let me be for a while!*"

That might have been enough to bring him some relief if Seuliac had not chosen that moment to walk over to the Priestess. The Grimmen responded with another twist of urgency that set his teeth on edge.

KAPHRI SAT FACING EAST to ease the gnawing sensation of the geas.

The ghost lights floated in the distance. The flares were a familiar sight now, appearing as soon as darkness settled over the woods to dance their slow, alluring dance far into the night. What would they do tonight, she wondered, when, very shortly, she and the others picked up their packs and moved on? Walking at night would be a new and daring thing. Would the ghost lights follow? Dance ahead? Disappear in a fit of pique?

Silly to put a personality to such things, she chided herself, but this place did have its own presence. The watcher's attention never left them. Day or night, any time she dared reach out, it was there, hovering at the edge of her mind. Earlier, Frax had expressed concern with its reaction to their leaving the trail, but she could not detect a change. It just... watched.

If only the same were true for the geas.

Her head hurt, she was dirty, itchy, sore, and so tired she could hardly move. She didn't want to think about Frax, the watcher, or

Seuliac, with his sudden, outrageous habit of throwing things at her, but the irritation they stirred in her kept her mind off the grinding need that plagued her now that they had left the trail.

And a chief source of her irritation was approaching. She suppressed her dismay as the warlord dropped to the damp, mossy ground beside her.

"*What are you doing?*" Scruffy as any of them, he still seemed remarkably unaffected by physical discomfort.

Despite the geas and the added challenge of dodging flying objects, he really expected her to focus her thoughts on the next encounter at all times. "*I'm wondering what the demon lights and the watcher will do when we start moving again after dark.*"

"*Does it advance your skills in any way?*"

"*We have placed ourselves within their domain.*"

"A legitimate observation. But that's Kitahn's problem." He laid an arm on a bent knee and relaxed forward, giving her the look of undisguised curiosity she had learned to associate with pending trouble. "*So, you can include me in a mental image as real as life and move us around at will. You can invade the depths of someone's mind undetected, and you can project a mental image and physical sensation. What else can you do?*"

Certainly, not stop a clod of dirt from bruising her arm! Oh, Hredroth, what did he want from her? She didn't want to go deeper into another problem of his making. "*The crystal helped move us, and the rest is a part of my telepathic abilities. I cannot do anything with starpower. Araxis would sense immediately if I did—*"

"*Relax. I'm just asking.*"

She dropped her shoulders and turned her head away.

"Don't be testy."

She looked back at him. "*I want to sleep.*"

"*We'll stop again in a few hours. You can sleep then. Meanwhile, we have things to discuss.*"

"*Discuss? Like what? Sir.*"

"*Like last night.*" His smile would have been quite dazzling if she didn't know its nasty implications. She was sure many Geffitzi would judge the warlord's fine-boned features very pleasing, sans smudged dirt and sweat, but she had been subjected to the mind behind the face. "*I know you thought about what happened. Did you find ways you might prevent what you saw? Did you play out any scenarios in your mind where you were the great hero?*"

He thought she should dwell on saving an image of Frax from a death blow he machinated? Other than dwelling on an intense desire to make the warlord suffer for humiliating her with his underhanded trick, no, she had not. She fled the incident, too distressed to consider anything outside her upset. Now, belatedly, she realized the wave of emotion she had ridden might have carried her to solutions not normally part of her mindset. Instead, all afternoon, when she could draw a focus, she had desperately searched for something to fix her mind on while wallowing in anger and self-pity.

She had wasted a valuable portion of his lesson.

"*No.*" Again, she bit back the urge to add she'd been too busy dodging thrown objects.

His sending carried a sense of impatience. "*That particular ability offers you a perfect opportunity to learn from your mistakes without injuring anyone. You must explore every possible option for honing your skills.*"

What had he come up with now? Not another mindlink with him! She snatched at her only defense. "*I don't know if experimenting with power in mind-conjured scenarios is safe. I told you: power attracts power. We are born to the same star. He might find me if I use it.*" She wondered if she feared detection by Araxis or the next situation Seuliac might place her in more.

"Well," Seuliac leaned in to murmur conspiratorially in her ear, "in case you haven't noticed, this place is crawling with Balandra. I think the secret is out."

It did not matter how well she kept the anger and resentment out of her mind; he knew he'd upset her. He didn't care. His mindset was unrelenting. "*So, what else can you do with this power of yours?*"

"*I cannot think of anything else I can do.*"

"*You lack imagination.*" Irritation flickered over the fine features.

He thought he knew as much about her power as she did. She was born to it, and he was a Geffitz. A Geffitz not even comfortable with mindspeak. Their first real encounter, three days ago, still burned fresh in her mind. She held her emotions in check, but she could not ignore his challenge. "*And you can do better*?"

"*Oh, yes.*" This time he smiled the lean smile of a hunter sighting in on its prey, and she realized she should not have asked the question. "*I could do so much better. I want you to listen. Keep your mind open to the possibilities. Don't rule anything out.*"

This was a bad idea. This Geffitz was an expert at dealing in death. But Seuliac had already begun. "*Think about this: if you can move us, why not move your enemy? If you can project pain or illusion into a mind, why not paralysis? How far can you send: if you can invade unseen from nearby, why not from afar? If you project energy, can you withdraw energy? How strong a blast can you manage? How wide a sweep? Can you control more than one thing, cast illusion on more than one mind, strike out at more than one target? Can you cross over open spaces, such as water, forests, or valleys if you can see a destination on the other side? Can you steal a destination from the mind of someone else? If you can manipulate illusion, can you give someone exact instructions, as if they were there, or a false image to trick them? Can you concentrate your power into a weapon to burn or slice? Can you use mental projection as a shield; can you form an unbreakable field around you?*"

She listened with mounting horror. So many things, so many ideas, and all of them so aggressive and dangerous. It sickened her to think power might be used in such horrific ways, yet, she wondered: could she do them?

Her thoughts had never moved in this vein before. Absently she wrapped her arms around her body to fight off a deepening chill while her mind raced. And why had her thoughts never inclined in the same sinister directions as the warlord's? He didn't possess power, yet he came up with all these ideas. She had power, and nothing of the sort had ever occurred to her. Was it because he was crueler, more savage, or less compassionate than she was? No. She knew now the Ly Kai and the Geffitzi were not so different in how they acted. The Twenty-six had proven that. Araxis had proven that.

Was it because of her association with Gemma? After her conversation with Frax in the Palenquemas, she knew Gemma had wielded a great deal of influence on her life. But this was something different. She shivered again, the cold sinking deeper. Why did the ideas he presented horrify her to her core?

The memory of Hyfas, his sendings hostile and cold, flashed in her mind. Hredroth! Every day, reciting, over and over again laws strictly stipulating how power should be used. Laws telling her and everyone else in their society how to behave; what to do; what to say.

They told her what to do, but they never listed the forbidden, the things she should not do. Ly Kai law steered completely away from the remotest thought of such things.

There were things she had done: eavesdropping on other minds, negative thoughts, mischief. But doing anything major outside acceptable behavior had never crossed her mind. Until she tried to flee Kryie Karth...

Hredroth! The headache ramped with a vengeance. She massaged her temples while she struggled with the thoughts warring inside her head.

What had gone wrong with her? Why had she reacted and killed Rath? Was she defective in some way? How was she able to accept these volatile, violent warriors without feeling complete appall? Was there something that made her a renegade or flawed?

A shaft of terrible cold sank into her. Of course, she could do the things Seuliac suggested. She had already taken a few paltry actions with the plains cat and the ahmdulak, responding instinctively to a threat that confronted her. What could she do if she applied trained calculation to those actions?

She recalled the fury she'd faced on her first encounter with Frax, Tobin, and Uri. How they accused the Ly Kai of murder, and how Seuliac, on the night they spoke for the first time, told her with intense bitterness that he knew what the Ly Kai could do.

Seuliac was older than Frax and Uri, at least in his late teen years when the Ly Kai had fled to the north, invading the warriors' land a second time. How much of what he'd just listed had he witnessed firsthand in Geffitzi encounters with the fleeing Ly Kai?

Her skin was suddenly clammy, her heart fluttering. "*You saw those things. They did them.*" Her sending was a mental whisper.

"*Your people are not innocent, girl. Far from it!*"

"*The Ly Kai are not a violent people. They have no weapons—*"

"*They don't need physical weapons! They have something far more effective. You tell me how the Geffitzi could fight against what the Evil One did, sending a plague on us.*"

"*I can't do the things you suggest. They would be wrong.*"

"*You'll be guilty of a greater wrong if you don't learn how to do them. Saying you're sorry doesn't help us. Lying down to die for us doesn't fix the greater wrong. You have to do something to fix this.*"

"*If it means using the power of Arylla, I can't.*" She wanted to help them. Gemma said she might be their only hope. But the thought of facing Araxis and failing terrified her. "*That would be surrendering to him.*"

"Then why are we wasting time with you? Either you can do something to make this right, or you're useless."

She was not useless, and she did not need the warlord sitting here, reinforcing her deepest doubts! Her anger flashed. At the same moment, her head gave an agonizing throb that blanked her thoughts and darkened her vision.

"Priestess?" Seuliac's sending was calm. Forced calm.

Another stab of pain drove deeper into her head, striking the cold, black place at the center of her brain that had lain quiet for weeks. It was followed by nine more, all driving straight and deep. Her body jerked with every stab as they drove straight and true. The blackness swelled, shredding and tearing its bounds until it burst free, sending a wave of terrible, ebon cold surging outward. She drew a ragged, gasping breath, arched her back in agony, then twisted, throwing herself sideways as everything in her belly came up.

"Kitahn. Caspani. Both of you come here. Now."

"Shit!" she heard Uri exclaim. There was a wild scurry of movement, but she was blind, her brain seized by the pain, her body wracked with violent heaves.

"What happened?" Frax's voice was close.

Blackness rolled through her head. Another wave of violent nausea followed it.

"Uri—!"

"I don't know! Wait a moment; maybe it will pass."

There was nothing left in her stomach to purge, yet her body kept trying to empty it. She spat to keep from swallowing and having that come back up again in violent rejection. Another wave of pain rolled through her brain, pushing away organized thought. Her body began to tremble uncontrollably.

"Kep! Someone get a blanket. Velacy. Quick!"

In the middle of another wave of dry heaves, something dropped across her shoulders. It did not warm her. *"Priestess."* Firm hands tugged the blanket, pulling it tight about her shoulders, then easing her back on the forest floor. She shuddered. Her stomach twisted and she cried out.

Hredroth! What was happening to her? Something was tearing her brain apart...

A silent explosion inside her head blanked all conscious thought.

When she regained awareness, one of the warriors was talking to her. She couldn't understand what he said. She blinked, trying to focus, trying to see, but her vision was blurred. She tried to speak, but she was unable to form a thought. All her senses were caught in a jumble of confusing input.

Another silent explosion ripped deep inside her head.

She might have screamed. She didn't know. But when she finally regained some small fraction of organized thought, she was no better than before. What was happening to her? Hredroth, she was helpless, so helpless! If something attacked right now... Panic surged inside her.

No! Reason fought back. Whatever was happening, panic would make it worse. She was among allies. She could trust these warriors. They would protect her.

Something seized her brain and stretched it. The cold darkness pulsed and tried to expand. The pulling sensation broke with a snap, and she screamed and writhed in agony.

"Get her arms! Get them secured under the blanket. Stop her thrashing before she hurts herself! Seuliac, find something to put between her teeth."

Hands forced her jaws open; shoved something into her mouth. She bit down. Tasted leather. Animal skin—oh, Hredroth!

The darkness pulsed again, sending out a wave of cold. So cold! She gave a silent mental scream and went rigid.

"AH! HOLY KEP!" FRAX swore as a brush of strange blackness moved across the outer edges of his mind.

"Frax!" Uri broke in, ignoring his exclamation. "Is this the woods again?"

Frax stared down at the small body trussed up in the blanket.

She had gone quiet, so mentally quiet. "No." This was nothing of the Grimmenwood. He looked at Seuliac, on his knees beside the girl. "Food?"

"She ate and drank with us, the same as always. You saw."

Uri rounded on him. "What did you do to her?"

"Be careful, Windmer," Seuliac warned. "I did nothing to harm her."

"What were you doing?" Frax asked.

"I made some suggestions on how she could better use her abilities to help us."

"Such as?" After conversations over the past few days, he could well imagine what mind-twisting suggestions the warlord might have put forth.

"Such as transporting the enemy over a ravine and loosening her hold on them, or concentrating that force of hers into a weapon."

Hardly suggestions to become upset over. "Nothing more?"

Seuliac shook his head.

"It didn't need to be anything else!" Uri exploded. "Don't you people see? She's never contemplated using what she can do for harm."

"Doesn't really amount to much unless you can use it," Velacy observed acidly from behind them.

"She doesn't think like that. How many times do I have to tell you?"

"Well, it's time for her to start thinking like that," Seuliac shot back.

"It could be done more subtly, Warlord."

Seuliac rocked back on his heels to glare at Uri. "We don't have time for subtle, Windmer. Like it or not, she's got one purpose. One! And it's to get rid of that—that thing—out there. If she dies in the process of learning how to do it, well then, she wouldn't have succeeded anyway, would she?"

"Damn you!" Uri's face darkened in rage. His muscles bunched for attack.

"Stop it, both of you!" Much as he would like to see the big Geffitz successfully take on the warlord, they could not afford an injury to either one. "Arguing isn't helping her. Uri, what diagnosis?"

"I don't know," Uri snapped. "It looks similar to battle shock, which is strange. She could die," he shot another glare a Seuliac, "or she could pull out of it. We can't move her, and we need to keep her warm. Seuliac, gather up all our blankets. Velacy, make yourself useful! Put her feet up in your lap. Keep them warm and elevated. Do it." Ignoring the young warrior's scowl, he put a hand to her neck. Her pulse was rapid and weak. He did not have to touch her mind to know her breath was barely enough to sustain her body. "Frax! You've done this before. Get inside her head. Talk to her. Don't let her fade. And be careful what you say, for Kep's sake. Don't do anything to drive her deeper into retreat."

Considering the level of hostility she exhibited toward him lately, Frax thought Uri probably should rethink his choice. But what Caspani said was true: he had saved men from dying of shock during battle. And Uri knew he'd taken some pleasure in mentally tormenting her early in their encounters.

That did not promise to make the task easier—or safer. "*Priestess.*" She was open. That was good. He moved quickly, slipping into her mind as he had done so many times before, but never for so dire a reason.

"*Priestess?*" He moved cautiously, carefully. Searching. Searching. He found no sense of physical pain, so whatever had happened had not affected her body. He should have felt relief, but he didn't: the touch inside her head was so cold and dark—nothing like the warm vibrancy he equated with past mental contact. Her presence was gone, retreated beyond the wall she used as a refuge. He could not go there. Even when he taunted and threatened her in Omurda, he'd known he could not intrude upon that place unless she allowed it. He didn't dare invade there now, even to save her life. It wasn't self-preservation that held him back: it was fear of what she might do if she mistook his act for aggression. He had the grace to feel a fleeting sense of remorse for his past bad behavior.

She might hear him if he could draw her attention. He just needed to be quick enough to evade any bolts of mental fury, if that was the response he happened to draw.

"*Priestess,*" he mentally called again.

Nothing. No glimmer of response, no sense of presence.

Damn Seuliac! What had he done? If the Priestess died, the warlord would not be long for this world.

That line of thought was a path to failure. He had to find a way...

Gentle was not working here, regardless of what Uri advised.

Frax shifted tactics, releasing some of his frustrated anger into his thoughts. "*Found a way to run away and leave us again, Priestess?*" he taunted while desperately searching for a flicker of response. "*You said you wouldn't run. You said you wouldn't do it again. Was it a lie? Was it a delay until you found another excuse?*"

No response.

He pushed harder, drawing on his memory of their conversation in the woods before the incident at the Ilex. "*I believed you when you told me you wouldn't do this again. I believed you!*"

Still nothing.

Kep! What was he supposed to do here? What was going on with her? If they could have talked over the last few days, if the situation had allowed, he might have some idea. But he didn't.

He let his frustration and anger trickle out, replaced by sadness. "*Perhaps you consider surrender better than the risk of defeat. It's not. It's worse. It's the coward's way out.*"

A flicker of emotion. The merest brush, but still a response. He could sense her behind it, but nothing of what she thought. He hovered, afraid to say more for fear of creating another rift between them, for fear of extinguishing the tiny spark.

There was no time. She had to come out.

"*I thought—I hoped—better of you.*" Kep! The flame was dimming! "*Damn it, Kaphri! You said you wouldn't run again!*" The fierce blast of accusation and frustration was out before he could stop himself.

A spark! A spark of anger flared. He held his breath, waiting while a millennium seemed to crawl by. The spark burned, sometimes flickering to briefly stronger light. It was only a spark, but it did not extinguish. "*The lies...*" the sending was weak, sorrowful. "*I am back to the beginning.*"

"*What lies?*" His heart thumped painfully. "*What beginning?*"

"*The laws... I am back to the beginning, to the savagery before the laws.*" The light steadied but remained pale with sorrow.

"*What are you talking about?*"

"*The violence. What they could do... It's why they wrote the laws—to raise the Ly Kai above the violence. But if I live by those laws, you will all suffer...*"

"*Suffer what? At the hands of one of your people?*" Sudden anger made him sharp. "*What do you want to hear, Kaphri? The truth? Your laws don't work. If they did, we wouldn't be here in this situation. I understand you might need to reconcile some things, but you damn well won't do it by hiding. We have a whole lot of dead Ly Kai, a whole lot more dead Geffitzi, and you and Araxis. We have to do what we can, or a whole lot more innocent people will die. Damn it! Lapsing into a mental state is a coward's way out, and you can't have that. I told you in Omurda: I won't let you off so easily.*

"*Look at you! You have a piece of dead animal skin stuck between your teeth to prevent you from biting your tongue off—and you'd better do something before they start brewing a healing broth for you out of one of those little fuzzy creatures you're so fond of listening to. Stop whining and make the best of it, Kaphri.*" Kep, Uri would never approve of this method. "*You owe us.*"

He felt a wash of shock, then rising resentment. It flared, sending out a blast of anger. "*You made your point, Geffitz. Now, get out of my head!*" She severed the link between them like the slice of a knife.

Frax jerked back, cursing. The others looked at him, startled, but Kaphri drew a long, deep breath and they refocused their attention on her. She spat out the leather knife sheath Seuliac had jammed between her teeth.

Behind them, Frax got to his feet and returned to the perch he'd chosen for his watch. Under cover of the darkness, he pressed his palms to his temples, seeking relief from the pressure. That blast of emotion had been stronger than anything he'd thought she could produce. It hurt.

It also set him to thinking. What were they trying to do? She said her people put things in place to keep her power in check. They were trying to tear those checks away without any of the precautions the Ly Kai would take. Were they unleashing something they would later regret?

Cold feet, Kitahn, he asked himself, or uneasiness at finding something so powerful not as much under your control as you would like?

Even worse, his family's worst enemy held as much influence over that power as he did.

The Grimmen snatched up the ends of every strand of stress inside his body and gave them a twisting jerk so hard he thought he would cry out. Jealous bitch, the Grimmen; it allowed him no other focus for long. Clenching his teeth, he directed his mind back to the watch.

Thank the Goddess he had the others to rely on for things that needed doing...

Chapter 71
Putting the Pieces Back Together

"*You should stay under the blankets.*" The Caspani Geffitz was a dark silhouette at the base of a nearby tree, where he sat guard.

Someone had tucked them too tightly. She struggled out and sat up, the night air cool and heavy on her skin.

"*Uri?*"

"*You're obviously feeling better.*"

"*My head aches,*" she fretted.

"*I'm not surprised. You gave us quite a scare.*"

She got up, stepping cautiously over a sleeping warrior to join him on the mossy hump of ancient tree root. She hesitated at the last moment, "*Is this all right?*"

"*To join me? If you're strong enough. Everything's quiet.*"

She sat down carefully so as not to jar her head. Though the wood was still dark, the ghost lights were gone. "*How long—?*"

"*It's getting close to sunrise. What happened to you last night?*"

Just the memory made her head hurt worse. "*I'm not sure. The dark coldness is back, stronger than before. My head hurts, but it feels different somehow.*" She searched inside herself. "*Like something is missing, but I can't say what.*" Too bad it wasn't the pain. "*I'll tell you when I figure it out.*"

"*I know.*" He meant his mental pat as a gesture of comfort, but it made her wince. The warrior did not appear to notice.

She looked around slowly, careful not to set off more pain. "*We're in the same place?*"

"*It didn't seem a good idea to move you.*"

Frax would not be happy with her causing this delay. *"Do you have anything for the ache in my head?*" Best to prepare for a long day.

"There are a few doxentler leaves left." He dug some from a pouch and handed them to her.

An image flashed in her mind, of Gemma dropping wilted leaves into her palm at the edge of another forest the day after they had fallen through the barrier. Her heart twisted with sadness.

She chewed the leaves thoroughly before spitting them out. "Ugh!" Doxentler leaves became bitter with age, and these were weeks old, brittle, and crumbling.

The warrior laughed softly. "*They may taste awful, but it's not as bad as not having them when you need them.*"

"We should search for fresh ones." They had not dared invade the Grimmenwood from the trail to replenish their stock. Now that they were walking in the heart of the woods, they'd seen little beyond moss, fern, and fungus growing in the shadows of the trees.

"*Oh?*" He shifted to look down at her. "*You expect to have the pain awhile?*"

"*It's similar to what I experienced before Windmer.*" She felt a pang of guilt about having evaded his questions back then. "*If it is the same, it may linger.*"

"*You haven't taken the chain off?*"

"*No.*" The crystal was a link to Gemma. She would not relinquish it again.

"*Do you think the pain is related to Araxis?*"They had learned those headaches were caused by Araxis searching for her, and that the crystal worked to block his search. When she took the chain off he almost captured her.

"I think it is related to my starpower." She hesitated. Telling Uri about the situation was better than answering the commander's questions directly. Frax disdained her enough already. *"Please don't misunderstand this, Uri. I don't want to sound weak. But, last night, the things the warlord suggested—they were terrible, violent ideas on how to use my power. For me—not for you!"* That didn't sound right, either, but Uri would understand. *"They shook me. Not because of what they were, but because I became aware I could do those things. That the Ly Kai had done those things. That Seuliac actually witnessed them. I realized,"* her throat tightened, *"the Ly Kai were not the innocent victims I always believed. That was when the pain hit me, as if something was ripping my brain out of my head. I hurt so much, and I was so afraid..."*

"Well, clever and conniving as he is, I really don't think Seuliac Aedec can do anything to affect your power."

"No," she agreed. But Seuliac had forced her to touch on something that did.

"Do you know why it happened?"

"I know when it happened. It happened when I realized if I did the things he suggested, I would be acting outside Ly Kai law. I realized the laws the others had ground into me so ruthlessly were written to prevent those kinds of things from happening. It was a harsh revelation. But it was worse to realize the Ly Kai might have had good reason to subject me to such arduous studies. That I could do..." She gave a mental shudder at the recall. *"That they... Then the cold seized me. Maybe after the laws are forced into our heads every day for so long, we cannot accept the thought of violence."*

Maybe, but she doubted that was all of it, and so did Uri. She had acted with a degree of violence in her own paltry way when the situation called for it, and nothing had happened to her in retaliation those times.

It had never stopped Araxis...

Resentment toward the Geffitz commander and her own self-doubt swirled inside her. "*I know Frax thinks I'm weak and incapable of acting.*" The thought slipped out before she could stop it.

Uri's expression was solemn in the growing light. "*What do you think? That's what's important.*"

"*I think he is wrong.*"

"*Ha! Wouldn't be the first time he was wrong. We won't tell him, though. Are you sure you're all right?*" She nodded. "*You will tell me if anything changes or begins to worsen, right?*"

"*I promise. The doxentler is beginning to work.*" She could finally move her head without stirring a jarring pain.

"*You should rest some more.*"

"*I will be fine.*" She wanted to ask him something. "*Uri, when we left the trail, you said you would tell me about this Azay Rhiad Velacy was talking about.*"

"*It's a long story, Willow.*"

"*It will take my attention off the headache. I can help you keep watch.*"

"*All right,*" he acquiesced. "*But if you begin to feel ill again, you must tell me.*"

"*I will.*"

"*You understand the title of Holderlord is generally inherited by the oldest child of the blood family; in more recent history, also subject to approval by the Two Circles.*" She sent an affirmation. "*Well, the Circles reserve the power to keep one clan from gaining too much influence. It's a recent development, precipitated by certain Cadarnian activities.*" Of course, it would be Cadarn. "*Frax's mother, Kesshri Glastig, is the direct heir to a hold south of the mountains called Azay Rhiad, or Mist Home.*" She caught an image of a stone structure with delicate towers sitting high on a cliff above a sheer drop. To its right, a massive waterfall tumbled off the mountain heights and fell past the hold into a wall of mists. The place was a stunningly beautiful image. "*It's the southern-most Geffitzi hold. So far south, in fact, few of its people got out during the plague. The heir-designate, Kesshri, escaped because she was in Windmer at the time, visiting her sister, Adiel, my uncle's wife, with her two young sons. Those sons, my cousins Frax and Tobin, are the progeny of her marriage to the Holderlord of Cadarn. Several holds, including Rhynog, opposed Kesshri's marriage to Frax's father, claiming it gave Cadarn influence over two holds. They were not out of line: if she names her firstborn, Frax, as heir designate, which is her absolute right by all Geffitzi law, she will place a Kitahn in holdership of Azay Rhiad. With the death of so many of her hold's bloodline, objections have become more strident. When you open the barrier, people will move onto those empty lands, and they will likely be citizens of Cadarn. Many people already fear Caer Cadarn will eventually swallow Azay Rhiad."*

"Frax is the heir? But I thought he was bound to Cadarn. Isn't his brother, Riftkin, Holderlord?"

"Yes. But Riftkin is his half-brother, and because Frax is the firstborn to the heir of Azay Rhiad, Tobin follows Riftkin in the lineage for Cadarn, and Azay Rhiad claims Frax."

"What would happen to him if he doesn't inherit?"

"He would retain some position in Cadarn's military, I'm sure."

"Frax wants this hold?"

"It doesn't matter what he wants, Willow. You know how that works. It's the business of power. The Inner Circle will make a decision and the rest of us will go along." Uri sighed. *"I'm also an heir designate since my uncle's son and my father are gone."*

"Frax told me. He said you hoped to become a scholar and historian, but now you cannot."

"Well, yes, I still can. I'll just have less time to devote to it. Meanwhile, I have time right now."

"You can hardly be a scholar in this place."

"Ah, but I am, Willow. Don't you see?" Uri's sending was earnest. *"Who could better tell this story? I'm living it firsthand. I'll know the truth because I'm here inside it."*

Kaphri laughed. "*Then you can be a great hero!*"

"*Yes, and you shall be a great lady.*"

"*A great lady,*" she gave another laugh, this one sad. "*I don't think anyone would believe that. I fear I already own the name 'that sorcerer filth.' Will you at least correct them that it should be "sorceress," Uri?*"

Uri picked up her hand and placed a light kiss on the back. "*I will tell them you were sweet and gentle, that you struggled beside us as an equal to any warrior, and that you knew great pain.*"

Pain. She pulled her hand from his, putting it in her lap and covering it with the other. "*Why do you do that?*"

"*Do what?*"

"*Talk and make plans about after?*"

"*It reminds us of why we're doing all this.*" Uri's smile faded as he looked at her. He knew there was nothing for her on this world. "*What about you? Have you thought about what you will do when this is over?*"

Frax had asked her the same question once, back in the swamp, beside a stream. Despite the heat, dirt, and insects, that was a good day in her memory. She had told him she wanted to be left alone. Now, being alone did not seem so appealing. It sounded lonely. If she stayed on this world, it was exactly what she would be: lonely. The others would go rushing off to their people, helping to organize a return to their lives before Araxis. She had nothing like that. There was no 'before Araxis' for her.

"*Willow.*" Fingers brushed her arm. She looked up, her tears blurring the Geffitz's image. "*Don't think sad thoughts.*" She couldn't see his expression, but his sending was gentle.

"*I have nowhere to go, Uri. I have nothing.*"

"Hey.You can't think that way. You must believe something will work out. That there will be a place for you."

"Where?" She couldn't stop the bitterness from creeping into her sending. *"I understand what 'warrior right' means, Uri. It has been made very clear to me. I'm a spoil of war. A claimed object! Will I be hidden away in the stone cellars beneath Cadarn, brought out as a weapon when tempers flare? Or will it be Rhynog? Seuliac wants me there, you know. I could be the jewel of their weaponry."* She gave a short, angry laugh and raised a shaky hand to brush away an escaping tear.

Uri was still, his mind carefully neutral. *"Did he say that?"*

"He doesn't have to say it." She met his eyes. *"But it's all right, Uri, really. I'm not going to Rhynog or Cadarn. I don't want to go to Windmer, either. You have Ladrienca and so much more ahead of you. I just want to know there is a place for me too. Where I am wanted. Where there will be someone glad when I'm there and who will miss me when I'm not."* She had hoped that would be Gemma.

"There will be, Willow. Believe that."

She gave a short, broken laugh. *"We are wasting our time even talking about this—"*

"I don't think so. You've come this far; you can't give up hope now."

She was silent.

"Willow, it's all right to be afraid of the future."

"Uri, how can a Geffitz warrior know how I feel? You stare death in the eye without flinching."

He snorted derisively. *"You know better."*

Kaphri sighed. *"Yes, I do."*

"It's all right." Uri put an arm around her shoulders and gave her a light squeeze. *"We all have doubts. It would be stupid to expect you not to experience them too. But don't let them overwhelm you."*

There was a groan and the sound of movement to their right. The rest of their companions were beginning to stir.

She wiped at her eyes. "*I'll be all right, Uri.*"

"*Come to me if you have a problem. I don't care what it is. You hear me?*"

"*I will, I promise.*" She patted a hard-muscled arm as she got to her feet.

"*Headache?*" She could feel his concern as she moved off to fold the blankets.

"*It has eased.*" Her brain still felt tender to head movement, but it was better.

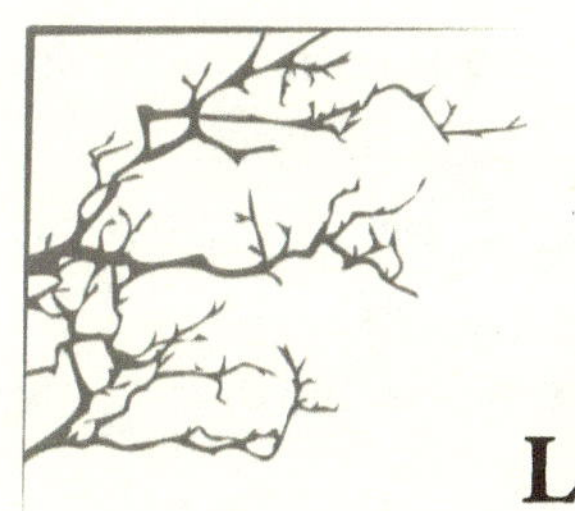

Chapter 72
Life and Death

"*Priestess.*"

Now what?

The warriors had had their heads together, quietly debating something for the last several minutes. They were in disagreement. Again. Although she sensed varying degrees of excitement and caution in them, their discussion did not pertain to her, so she had chosen to ignore them.

Frax shook his head resignedly as the others moved off into the woods in a scattered, disorganized pattern.

Seuliac paused long enough to glare back at her. "*Come!*"

"*Why?*" She picked up her pack, wincing as a wave of pain rolled inside her head.

"*Velacy and Caspani have found something of interest. It promises a break in our endless feast of brittle-paste.*" The warriors had given the dry breadstuff the Wyxa had loaded into their packs a name that described it succinctly. Something offering a bit of variety might not be a bad thing.

She followed the others through the forest to the edge of a shallow, misty meadow. A dense, low-growing plant, its leaves heavy with dew, covered the entire surface of the place. The sun would not touch the area, sheltered between low, tree-lined ridges, for hours yet.

The others stopped at the border of the trees, their packs dropped and forgotten, while Frax, scowling, walked out among the plants and stooped to brush some of the leaves aside with his hand. He pulled at something, stood up, and walked back to them.

"Now, which of you will dare to try them?" He thrust out his hand. "I certainly wouldn't, and they are safest for me."

Kaphri leaned forward with the others to stare at the plump, red berries he held.

Seuliac drew a breath beside her. "I hear your warning, Kitahn," he said. "But I don't think this wood of yours let us come this far just to end us with a mundane bit of fruit. Where is the pleasure in such a kill? It lacks finesse."

A hint of amusement briefly lifted Frax's expression. "Perhaps the Grimmen appreciates the irony. At your risk, Seuliac. I will not recommend this."

Recalling Frax's warning on how some Geffitzi claimed the wood could turn food or water to poison between the source and the mouth, Kaphri stared at the bright red fruit. Then the tangy scent assailed her nose. Hredroth! It smelled so tempting that she salivated. But... Frax had warned them, and they had enough experience to back his warning: this wood was not a gentle, benevolent entity.

The warlord lifted one of the berries from Frax's palm and studied it critically.

Seuliac had better sense than to trust this place, she thought. He would not gamble his life so recklessly.

"Nothing attempted, nothing accomplished." Seuliac popped the fruit into his mouth and began to chew.

They all stared at him in reluctant, horrified fascination.

He chewed slowly and deliberately, then swallowed while they all held their breath.

He smiled. "My compliments to the gardener."

Now the rest of them must consider their risk and whether they were bold enough to try their fate with the Grimmen. After a pause,

Uri shrugged, walked out among the plants, picked a berry, and cautiously nibbled. He looked over at Frax. "He's right; they're as good as any I've ever tasted, maybe better."

Velacy hung back a bit longer, looking torn, but hunger finally won out. He waded into the patch beside Uri, reached down in the leaves, and snatched the bright fruit. Kaphri took a quick step after him, sliding past Frax before he could restrain her, knowing the thought of her putting herself at risk would be more than he could tolerate. She felt the surge of his displeasure in her mind and moved to shield against him. As the warlord observed: where was the pleasure of destroying them in this lonely, isolated place?

Morning dew ran in rivulets off her hands as she picked a cluster of the berries. She popped one into her mouth with hard determination. The fruit broke in a burst of tangy sweetness, and she closed her eyes, the ache in her head forgotten in a moment of bliss. Hredroth! Such a pleasure!

After another long, furious moment, Frax gave in and followed them.

"*What are these things?*" Kaphri appreciated the advantage of being able to send when her mouth was too full to speak.

"*Spring runnerberries.*" Uri brushed aside the dense growth and pulled two more fruits off their stems to pop into his mouth. "*Treat the plants gently so they will return next year.*"

Not that she would be here next year: gloom tried to descend upon her thoughts. She pushed it away and bit into another fruit. Whatever their situation, now or a year from now, nothing was going to rob her of this simple pleasure.

The warriors obviously agreed as they moved through the low-growing plants, picking and eating with gusto. At least one of them, however, was always standing upright, checking their surroundings.

The runnerberry patch was large and everyone had ample opportunity to eat their fill before Frax raised an arm to shield his eyes. With a troubled expression, he stared westward at the low ridge beyond the meadow. A thin, widespread line of trees edged the crest, with little undergrowth, so the morning sky showed through with an uncharacteristic clarity. After so many days of sheltering beneath the dense canopy of the Grimmenwood, the brightening light was startling.

"*What?*" Uri sent.

"*The thin area. Is there a cliff over there?*"

"*We didn't check.*"

"*There should be more trees, not sky. Something's not right.*" He started up the far slope.

Uri and Velacy moved quickly to follow, but Seuliac hung back to wait for Kaphri. "*Stop dawdling,*" he snapped peevishly. "*You are not last. You are never last.*"

Why? So he could throw something at her? Now that their focus had returned to the woods, the ache in her head had reasserted itself. As she hurried to catch up with the others, Uri gave her a light mental brush, questioning her physical state again. She sent back a quick sense of reassurance, despite d failing to tell him the effects of the doxentler had already worn off.

She would readily admit the dull ache put her out of sorts, but the warriors seemed edgier than usual this morning, too. Frax had been pushing them hard, trying to maintain their progress over the rough terrain. Plus, they were bone-weary, filthy, and their nerves felt stretched to the limit from a constant state of alertness, which had probably contributed to their rebellious invasion of the berry patch.

The risk of eating the berries hadn't lessened the sense of threat. But, now their bellies were full, shouldn't their spirits have lifted a bit?

Ahead of them, the Kitahni commander dropped to the ground and slithered the last short distance to the top of the ridge.

"*What the hell?*"

Even she recognized that hurrying toward what might be trouble wasn't the smartest move they could make, but his mental gasp brought them swiftly up beside him.

The small, shallow valley cupped between the steep green hills of the Grimmenwood was a scene of devastation. The few trees that remained upright were stripped of bark far up their trunks. Most were shattered stumps, splintered, with deep scores in their sides. There was no grass, only dust, dirt, and rocks. A rank, acrid smell hung in the air.

Kaphri had to look around at the heavy growth of the Grimmenwood behind them to reassure herself she was still in the middle of the forest.

There was a sudden stir on her right.

"*Kep!*" Velacy exclaimed, horrified. "*We have to get away from here!*"

"*Wait.*" Kaphri thought the youth would have actually gotten up and bolted back down the slope if Uri hadn't caught his arm and held him pinned to the ground.

White-faced, the young warrior tried to wrest free. "*We have to get out of here! Now!*"

"*Why? What is this?*" Frax demanded. They all knew this place wasn't right, but something about it struck terror in Velacy.

"*Tarmeuth, damn it! It's probably too late already.*"

THE LORDS OF CADARN had played with the balance of wildlife in the Grimmenwood for centuries. But, a tarmeuth? Of all the cursed things they could have brought into the place, that would be the most deadly.

If it was a tarmeuth.

"*It's here,*" Velacy hissed, reading his doubt. "*The proof is down there below us. I'll never forget that smell. You've led us into the heart of its lair, Kitahn, damn you!*"

Frax stared down into the small valley. The place was a wasteland of shattered, dead trees and stinking, bare earth. What kind of creature would have such little regard for its own environment?

Meanwhile, Velacy was on the verge of panic. He pulled against Uri's grip on his forearm. They all knew the young Aedec would sooner swagger with false bravado than react with reasonable caution any day.

"*What is this tarmeuth?*" Kaphri asked.

"*A dangerous hunter,*" Frax answered. "*Withdraw. Carefully.*" He motioned for them to return to their previous night's camp.

"*They're killers.*" Velacy snapped at her as Uri finally released his arm. "*It will make short work of us!*"

IF IT WAS A TARMEUTH, they had already put themselves in mortal danger by entering its territory. But who knew when, in the last few days, they crossed that line? The big cats claimed huge areas for their hunting ground. Stumbling right to the edge of its lair only shortened its hunt. It would follow their scent and slaughter every one of them unless they could kill it first.

Uri looked at Velacy. "*You speak as if you have firsthand experience with the creatures.*"

"*I was assigned to a patrol exploring the Wastes in the north. We stumbled across a pair. We ran for days. They stalked us day and night, killing horses, killing men. The cries—*" a haunted expression passed over the young warrior's face. "*There were eighteen of us. I'm the only one who made it back alive.*"

"*There's no record of such an encounter.*" Uri's sending was puzzled.

"*Well, consider this your record. I was there!*"

They had returned to the small meadow. The others stopped, all eyes riveted on the young warrior, the runnerberries at their feet forgotten. He glared back fiercely.

Uri could see the younger warrior wavered on the edge of some difficult decision. Velacy's reticence intrigued him. If the Aedec heir spoke the truth—and he sensed Velacy did—what would hold back the normally boastful youth?

"*And...*" Uri prompted.

Velacy shot Seuliac a look of defiance, as if he expected the warlord might make an effort to stop his reply. The warlord regarded him back calmly.

Velacy drew a deep, distressed breath. "*Three of us made it to the Tazzia River only steps ahead of them. The damned things followed us into the water. A swift current caught us, pulling us away, but the cats still took the other two survivors before we hit a broad section of deep water. That was the only thing that saved me.*" He swept them all with an angry gaze. "*I ran. We all ran. Eighteen of us. We kept moving and moving. We tried to rest the first night, but they took two of us. So we got up and we just kept going after that. No sleep, except in the saddle, until the horses died from exhaustion or fell prey. Nothing we did stopped them. We tried laying traps, but they were on us before we could complete them. They just kept coming. And killing.*"

"*Kep! How is it no one's heard of this? Seventeen warriors. They deserve some accounting,*" Uri said softly.

The young Aedec stared at the ground. "*It's not important.*"

"*Not im...!*" Uri twisted to glare at Seuliac. "*You knew about this?*"

Seuliac lifted an eyebrow coldly. "*No. However, if Lord Hraben decided the matter would not be reported, I will respect his wishes.*"

"*That's garbage!*" Uri snarled. "*We have an obligation to share information on such events. It's warrior code.*"

"*Apparently,*" Seuliac returned icily, "*Lord Hraben did not consider it necessary.*"

"*That's—*" Uri stopped, too angry to go on.

"*It's not important now,*" Frax cut in. "*With any luck, the creature is hunting in a different area of its territory. We must get out of here before we draw its attention, or everything else becomes a dead issue, along with us.*"

Seuliac shrugged indifferently, while Velacy scowled with impatience.

"*The lair appears abandoned,*" Uri observed.

"*Let's pray to Kep it is.*"

"*So, what do we do?*" Uri cut Frax a sidelong look as they began walking eastward again.

"*We can't run, screaming with fear through the woods. We go on, try to cross some running water—for what that might be worth.*" There were no rivers east of them until they reached the escarpment and, with the geas binding the Priestess so tightly, their range of movement was extremely restricted. "*All we can do is move fast and hope it's on the other side of its territory.*"

"*Does the Grimmenwood extend its protection over us to include tarmeuths?*"

"*Judging from that valley, it doesn't look like the Grimmenwood can protect itself against tarmeuths.*"

"*Is this Grimmen manipulation?*"

"*Using the runnerberries to lure us and put us on the edge of danger? No. I can't believe that's the Grimmen's intention after what it's done so far.*"

"*You can't believe we can just walk away from a tarmeuth, Kitahn,*" Velacy looked back at them, his eyes haunted. "*You'll see it at the edge of your vision, slinking in shadows, just out of weapon range. Once you see it, it will always be there, waiting for a chance to run in. Waiting for darkness.*"

"*What would you suggest?*" Frax asked quietly. He could sympathize with the warrior, placed in another such nightmare situation, if his story were true. But sympathy would not help them survive.

The younger Aedec only shook his head.

"*We could separate. Some of us might make it,*" the warlord suggested.

"*We'll stay together,*" Frax said. "*Maybe our numbers and scent will discourage it long enough for us to make the escarpment.*" Kep, seventeen dead Rhynogian warriors! It would be a mistake to think they were anything but Rhynog's best if they had an Aedec heir with them. "*You all know the threat. Keep your weapons ready. Under the circumstances, I don't think the Grimmen will fault us a defense. Priestess.*" He indicated with a jerk of his head that he wanted her to wait for him. "*You feel well today?*"

"*A slight headache.Other than that, I am fine.*"

So she seemed. He had watched her all morning. She was testy and a little slow to respond, which could be attributed to the headache. Still, something didn't seem right. He just couldn't pin it down.

"*This creature we stumbled on, it's similar to your plains cat, only much larger. And it has hunting habits even worse than the kitsk. As Velacy says, once it scents us, it will not be content until it slaughters us all.*" In this wood, it could stalk them for hours—might already be stalking them—without them being aware of it. "*I need you to watch. To sense for it.*"

"*Does it have a mental presence?*"

"*I suspect if you touch it you will know.*" No comfort in that observation.

"*Is there any hope of evading it?*"

"*There is always a chance, Priestess. It could be on the farthest side of its territory, away from us. It might not know we passed this way for many days.*"

"*But you do not think so.*"

She knew the kitsk. She must know how serious this threat was. "*Do an occasional sweep, Priestess. Keep alert. If something happens, grab whoever you can and get out of here.*" They would have to take a risk that the Ankar Mekt would not snatch her away.

"*You...*"

You what? You should tell the warlord what you want and let him relay it? He had set things up that way, after all.

She had the grace to cut short the thought, unformed. "*Yes, sir.*" She shifted restlessly. "*Is that all?*"

Was that all? It was a huge problem! A tribute to their control that they weren't all running mindlessly right now. Added to the problems they already had. Added to the problem of her. And Seuliac. And the Grimmenwood. And the rest of this mess he had muddled them into. Insolent little—! "*Yes, that's all. You let me know if you sense something. Me, Priestess. Not Seuliac. This is no game!*"

Her dark eyes flew to his face. They were wide. Unreadable. But a frosty sensation tingled deep inside his brain. She thought him the game player, and his words made her furious. Kep, she was shielded, but he could almost hear her thoughts! It shook and outraged him even more.

"*As you say, Lord Geffitz.*" She gave a slight bow, a minute, stiff forward movement of the upper half of her body.

So like a hold-bred Geffitz. Kep, where the hell did she pick that move up? Was the warlord already coaching her...? He broke off the thought, staring after her and cursing his lapse in control as she walked after the others. Why in Kep's name had he let his temper flair? He had driven another wedge into things. Was it jealousy? Frustration? Pressure? And why the hell should he know what she was thinking? Kep! What was happening to him?

Damn the Wyxa. Damn their predictions! Damn their interference! Damn the day Tobin caught that little flicker of movement in Omurda!

Whatever was going on, one thing he knew for sure: none of it would matter one tiny grain if a tarmeuth found their trail. He had to focus on the task—tasks—at hand. With the new threat of the tarmeuth, they must move faster. And the straighter their path eastward, despite the terrain, the faster they could cross the natural barrier of the Ysgubar River and move beyond the animal's territory.

He saw Uri hand the Priestess some doxentler and frowned. "*Priestess, come here.*"

Radiating impatience, she turned around and started back toward him.

He stared. Holy Kep!

"SO, OUR LITTLE PRIESTESS has managed to slip the geas that's crippled her for months."

"It seems that the headache diverted her attention away from the change. She didn't even realize it until you noticed."

"What a convenient development."

"You don't believe it?" Uri frowned.

"I find it troubling. Something that held her ruthlessly in its influence is abruptly gone. Why? Did it lose interest? Did it find it was unable to maintain a hold on her for some reason? Or, is this another tidy bit of manipulation disguised as a convenient twist of fate?" Twists of fate were not generally as opportune as they appeared on the surface. In fact, Frax thought cynically, they usually had an unforeseen price that came at you from a direction you did not expect. "When did it happen?"

"She was in its grip when we stopped last night."

"What does she think happened?"

"She says she doesn't know. But she went through a really bad experience last night, Frax."

"Perhaps, but something that exerted a strong control over her is gone, and we don't know who or what was behind it."

"She will not falter in her purpose, Frax."

"As we get nearer the city and the reality of this task takes on its true dimensions, she'll rethink her situation. All of us will. The thing that bothers me, Uri, is the source of the geas might realize that, too. If whatever happened last night forced it to release her, it might send something else to regain control."

Uri looked dismayed. "What can we do?"

"Warn her. I'll talk to Seuliac. We need to talk about any changes immediately, Uri," he added. "I want to be wrong, but none of us know what happens next."

Uri sighed heavily. "She doesn't deserve more difficulty."

"We didn't deserve to walk into a tarmeuth's lair, but we did. It's just the way things are."

His cousin gave him a sudden, penetrating look. "What is the Grimmen doing to you, Frax? Don't deny it: it's twisting you all up."

"It's not anything I can't handle, Uri. Just keep an eye on her."

Because he couldn't do it.

Chapter 73
On Time and Power

Her release from the geas allowed them to move faster, but their passage remained difficult. They reached a series of ridges that ran eastward, but they couldn't stay on them long for fear of the sharp eyes of Balandra flying above them. They had to plunge into the valleys and cross rougher but more protected terrain for a while before climbing out again. The good thing was the water in those hollows—cold streams for filling water bags and quick bathing. But the warriors said none of them would stop a tracking tarmeuth. Safety would only come at the base of the escarpment when they crossed the Ysgubar River.

Kaphri was on constant alert, sensing for any mental activity around them that seemed out of place. So far, the big cat had not shown. Perhaps the animal was leagues away, and they'd had a mere brush with disaster.

Or, perhaps the Grimmenwood was not yet ready to cast them into the cat's jaws.

In the interest of their own preservation, Seuliac and Velacy stopped chucking dirt at her.

They had an hour of daylight left when Frax called a short break. The constant fear and pressure of watching for the tarmeuth had strained them to exhaustion.

Kaphri wanted to snatch a bit of sleep. Seuliac had different ideas.

"*Sleep when you are dead,*" he growled as he settled to the ground beside her. The maxim had been bantered between the weary warriors since they left the trail. Uri said it was a common retort of Geffitzi commanders, meant to rally hard-pushed, complaining warriors.

This was Seuliac's first real opportunity to talk with her since her collapse the previous night, and he wasn't going away. Resignedly, she turned away to hide her shaking hands while she picked out two brittle doxentler leaves. She kept her movements slow so as not to appear too eager as she put them in her mouth.

The warlord had seen Uri give them to her earlier. "*Ah, Windmer. You like him, don't you?*" Picking up a stick, the warlord casually broke it into two pieces and held them up side by side. "*Don't be fooled by that gentle demeanor. He would cut your throat in a heartbeat.*"

"*No quicker than you or any of the others.*" Hoping the earlier leaves had simply been too old to be effective, she swallowed the bitter juice,

"*True.*" Seuliac smiled enigmatically as he continued to examine the sticks. He pressed his thumb along their length to test their rigidity. "*Why do you need the doxentler? I thought you would be running through the wood after getting rid of that geas.*"

"*A headache.*" The prickly residue of the leaves burned her mouth; she twisted aside to spit out the debris.

"*Caused by your little fit last night?*" He finally looked at her, examining her with the same critical expression he'd used on the sticks in his hand.

A little fit caused by him and his mind games. Irritability seethed below a pain-thinned surface. "*You could say that.*"

"*What precipitated it?*"

"*What?*" Hredroth, the doxentler juice had not yet taken effect. She didn't want to talk right now.

"*What precipitated the fit?*"

She checked her hostility. Hating him. Wondering why she had agreed to endure this and knowing she had to answer. "*The things you said...*" she tapered off, wishing she could change the subject but knowing he would persist. "*They made me think. I realized the Ly Kai laws had been made to prevent people from doing the things you were suggesting.*" She met his grey eyes squarely. "*But they didn't stop them, did they? You saw the Ly Kai do those things.*"

He did not answer. "*So, the Ly Kai have many laws?*"

"*Many.*" For nearly everything they did.

"*A people who need many laws must have many reasons to make them. You studied them?*"

"*Every day, for many years. Apparently, they wanted to impress them strongly upon me.*" She instantly regretted the statement. She did not want him to explore anything to do with her right now. She made an effort to shift the topic. "*How many laws do your people have?*"

"*Enough to keep order. And, yes,*" he added with a wry grimace, "*there are some who devote a lifetime to the study and application of what we have, too. But, enough of that. What happened to the geas?*"

"*I don't know. It was gone when I awoke. My head hurt, so I didn't realize until Frax called my attention to it.*"

"*Hard to imagine something like that just disappearing.*"

Indeed it was. While it was an immense relief not to have insane need battering her with every step she took, its mysterious disappearance terrified her.

"*I think we'll try something different today. You teach me something for a change.*"

Tension ramped higher inside her. Now what tactic?

He smiled as if guessing her thoughts. Obviously, it pleased him that she had learned a wary fear of him. "*Tell me how your people determine this thing of stars and power.*"

Her people. The words struck a hard chord inside her. She had never claimed the Ly Kai as her people. She had gone out of her way to put distance between them. This time she bit back her instinctive objection. She could deny it all she liked, but, in the end, she was Ly Kai. Not proud to acknowledge, because of what they had done, but finally able to accept it. Being Ly Kai was not the be-all or end-all of her existence: it took more than that to define her.

"*I've told you all I—*"

Seuliac cut off her protest with a wave of his hand. "*Teach me.*" He smiled disarmingly.

A chill ran down her spine. The warlord at his charming best did have a certain deceptive appeal, and she didn't like the sudden sensation of heat on the surface of her skin or the slight catch in her throat. Those were reactions she felt in Frax's proximity. Frax made her angry. He was dangerous, and he made her life difficult with the things he said and did. He hurt her, and she hated him. But Frax also made her feel safe. Frax... She caught herself. This was not Frax. This was the warlord. He was dangerous, too, in his own way. He did not make her feel safe. "*Teach you what?*"

"*Something about the Ly Kai. Teach me about their culture.*"

"*I don't know anything about their culture. I've been in this world all my life.*"

"*Of course you do. Show me their calendar. They had one, didn't they? Explain how it worked.*" He proffered one of the sticks he held.

"*Calendar?*"

"*How they record the passage of time as their world moves around their sun. They have a revolving pattern to mark important, repeating events, right?*"

"Yes."

"*Tell me about your birthdate. How that fits in their calendar.*"

"*Oh,*" comprehension dawned, "*The Hierarch.*" Getting to her feet, she took the stick and drew a line in the mossy dirt in front of the Warlord. She drew another, shorter one above it, then another, ten more times. Each line was shorter than the one before until the last tiny, almost imperceptible dot at the peak.

She squatted at the top of the triangle. "*This,*" she said, pointing to the dot with the stick, "*is Arylla. Everything below, in descending order, represents the rest of the Hierarch. It's the Star Ascension: the order in which the Stars of the Homeworld ascend the sky and the length of their influence. Weakest is lowest and has the most days and the most births.*"

"*And you were born in the little time allotted Arylla's influence at the top.*" Seuliac stared at the shape for a long time, frowning, and then shrugged. "*I can't work with that form. Lay it out on a straight line.*"

Kaphri hesitated, confused.

"*Draw a straight line, and mark off the sections as if you have unfolded the thing. Each section will be shorter than the last, right? Until you get to the little bit that is your Star, at the end of the line.*"

"*Oh.*" It was a very different way of looking at the Ly Kai calendar. She drew the line and marked the Birthstars off, beginning with a tiny dot for Arylla, extending the line several times as she miscalculated and ran out of space. When she finished, she studied her work. It was not like anything she had ever considered before, but the warlord appeared more comfortable with it.

Seuliac mulled it over in silence for a while. "*How many days from the beginning to the end?*"

"*Five hundred and forty-three.*"

"*Longer than ours.*" He continued to study the line until she began to drift into sleep. He nudged her. "*The Ly Kai have days of celebration?*"

"*Yes.*"

"*Any here?*" He pointed to a section half the length of the line from Arylla.

She did a quick mental calculation in her head. "*Yes.*" How had he known that? "*That is the High Sabat when Regis reaches the height of its pass across the sky.*"

Seuliac smiled grimly. "*How do they celebrate?*"

Kaphri hesitated. "*The people journey to the temple complexes to renew their bond with their Birthstar.*"

"*Renew their bond. What does that mean?*"

"*It involves a complicated ceremony that begins within the home. Then everyone must go to their Birth Temple. There are roads the women must take to theirs and roads exclusively for the men, to theirs.*"

"*The men and women are completely separated?*" He gave her an intense look. "*Does everyone participate?*"

"*Yes. Everyone.*" His reaction stirred uneasiness in her. "*Mixed company is forbidden during that time. If that law is broken, the woman must go through a ritual purification and remain at the temple for many days afterward, doing penance.*"

"*Ha! And the ritual? Do you know what it is?*"

"*No.*" She replied, perplexed.

"*I'll bet I can guess.*" He returned to studying the line. "*I'm also willing to bet the timing of your birth was no accident of nature, although someone may have committed a high crime against your people.*"

Kaphri felt the color drain from her face. "*What are you saying?*"

"*Look here.*" Seuliac gestured as he slid forward to squat in the dirt. "*Unless I'm way off, this,*" he broke his stick and stretched his arm to jab the shorter piece into the dirt, marking the tiny space she had made for Arylla, "*doesn't mean much to your Hierarch. It's a birthdate, nothing more.*" He waved his hand dismissively when she started to protest and turned his attention to the mark he'd made on the line in front of them. "*This is what's important.*" He took the remainder of his stick and circled the holiday emphatically.

"*But I was born—*"

"*Doesn't matter. It's not when you were born. It's when you were conceived.*" He looked at her. "*You know what that is, right?*"

"*Yes.*"

"*How long do your women carry their unborn?*"

"*I—I 'm not sure,*" she gave a mental stammer.

"*Your women do carry their unborn inside their body?*"

She gave a weak affirmation.

"*Well, physically, you don't seem much different than a Geffitz female. I'll bet the gestation time is approximately the same. On your calendar, from here,*" he jabbed the circled holiday again, "*to there, is how many days?*" He gestured at the stick marking Arylla's time reign.

"*Two hundred and seventy-five.*"

"*And the big holiday lasts?*"

"*Ten days.*"

Seuliac stared at the line. "*Unbelievable,*" he said slowly. "*This is just too obvious.*"

"*What?*" Kaphri's heart raced with dread. What did the warlord see in that line in the dirt?

"*Your people are segregated during this period to prevent any possibility of pregnancy,*" he mused. "*Someone knew how to bring about a birth from Arylla and scrambled everything up to hide it. Then they put safeguards into your religion to prevent accidents. The priests know it, though—or at least the highest echelons do. They would have to. They would use their stories and temple rituals to deceive the populace. Kep! This is all religious hoodoo to prevent births from Arylla.*" He rocked back on his heels, studying the line in troubled silence.

Kaphri's mind was trying to grasp what he said. Pregnancy? Conception? Days? What was he talking about? Her eyes ran up and down the line in the dirt, from the rough circle to the bit of stick at the end. She knew a little of how a child came into existence. But she had nothing to compare it to, nothing about which she had ever needed to think. What was the significance of the gap between the two spaces? What did it span...?

Her back stiffened. "Oh," she breathed.

Seuliac glanced at her. "*Precisely. Someone figured it out and set this all in place.*"

"*But that's impossible. Our birthdate determines our Birthstar.*" She stared at the line, looking from one stick to the other. He couldn't be right, could he? She looked at Seuliac in appall. "*What you are saying would mean my parents broke the laws of Hredroth!*"

He cocked an eyebrow, coolly amused. "*And the parents of the Evil One, before that.*"

"*No.*" She shook her head firmly. "*No one would do that. It's forbidden.*"

He snorted in disdain. "*As if that ever mattered to a bunch of power-hungry priests. They probably engineered it, at least the second time. Which was why there was no penalty,*" he added thoughtfully. He considered the circle on the timeline. "*I wonder how long that holiday's been in place.*"

"*Thousands of years.*"

"*Always the same days?*"

"*Yes.*"

"*What happens on those days? Not on the Ly Kai world.*" He made a dismissive gesture. "*What happens in the heavens? Anything special about the stars? Their positions, maybe?*"

"*High Sabat begins five days before Regis, the Ninth Star in the Hierarch, reaches the apex of its pass. On that day, the apex, Arylla is also at its farthest point, on the far side of our world. The High Sabat ends five days after Regis begins to fall toward the horizon again. The stars increase their influence as they rise to their zenith in the sky and lose influence in decline. The stars decline for half a year and rise for half a year.*"

"*So, at that time, Arylla is just beginning to re-assert influence?*"

"*It is at its furthest point of influence,*" she repeated, puzzled at where his thoughts might be leading.

"*It is also beginning to re-assert power, Priestess. Think about that. You said the Hierarch declines for half a year and rises for half a year. At what point do you think Arylla begins its rise to greatest influence?*"

She hesitated, confused.

"*Here. Look at this.*" Seuliac drew a circle on the ground, then intersected it vertically with a line. "*This is the Ly Kai world. Anything on the left half of the line is rising in influence, and anything on the right is declining.*" He punched the line above the circle. "*This is the point of greatest influence—the apex of its path.*"

"*Yes.*"

"*Then where is its weakest point?*"

That would be... She slowly reached forward to put her finger on the line below the circle.

"*Also, the point where Arylla begins to wax influential again.*"

She stared at the impression, trying to grasp the meaning.

"*How does the rise and fall of your stars affect their power?*"

"*The change as they drop below the horizon is perceptible, but not extreme.*"

"*Why doesn't Arylla hold more influence?*"

"*Because there are only hours during which Arylla dominates the sky. Freya follows close behind and takes zenith immediately after Arylla. Even so close, the difference is very distinct. Only those born to Arylla can use its power. It would burn away a lesser starborn.*"

"*But you can use any of the lesser stars?*"

"*Anyone can use the ones below their own, but not the ones above.*"

"*Tell me about the births to Arylla.*"

"*I know once there were many, and they stopped after the Reclamation.*"

"*The Reclamation. That sounds ominous. What is that?*"

"The establishment of the High Sabat: the holiday we're talking about. I don't know the story behind it, but I sometimes caught mental whispers from the men. Bits of ancient history, when they thought our people were greater. But they always acted uneasy with their thoughts, as if they were indulging in something improper. I know there was a time of terrible turmoil and conflict, and it ended with the Reclamation."

"I'll bet there was turmoil and conflict! People like the Evil One, in number, vying for power: I'll bet it was a bloodbath. The weaker ones must have been slaves or died en masse as casualties of power wars. Until someone stepped up and put an end to it."

"Hredroth."

"What?"

"Hredroth. He is the only other Ly Kai born to Arylla, other than Araxis, Alexar, and myself, that I ever heard mentioned by name. He was born a long time ago. And he did something huge related to the Reclamation. Saying his name is like calling on a great power for aid."

"What became of him?"

"He died ages ago. He was a leader of the High Council, the High One. He was also a historian."

"Of your current recorded history, no doubt," Seuliac observed wryly. He gave a short laugh. *"Amazing, but not surprising. Tell me about this Reclamation."*

She shook her head. *"It was not part of my studies."*

"You'd think they would talk about an event which immortalized a person in your culture. Was there a celebration when you were born?"

His question caught her by surprise. *"I don't know."*

He clicked his tongue reproachfully. *"Think, girl. The potential for all the power you're supposed to have, wrapped up in one little girl. Someone had big plans for you. Two thousand years, then, suddenly, three of you. What were your people thinking, I wonder. What were your priests plotting? What happened two thousand years ago during your Reclamation?*" He stared down at the line moodily. "*You said Hredroth was a High One. Wasn't that what you were to become?*"

Kaphri felt the color in her face heighten.

"*What?*"

"*It is hardly appropriate to compare us. He reigned over an entire world...*" She had no regrets about missing the opportunity to claim the title. How paltry her prospects had been compared to the history of the title!

"*You had twenty-five miserable old men to cope with. What did they expect from you?*"

"*I would have conducted certain ceremonies, made decisions, arbitrated in disagreements. Very little, actually, as the men already performed the tasks I might have delegated. All I could have done was bid them continue their work. As the strongest, I might lend power to their efforts when—if—they asked. A real High One would do much more.*"

"*Two thousand years, denied their greatest power,*" Seuliac marveled. "*One wonders how they could resist for that long. Don't you find it strange your people hid your Birthstar from you instead of encouraging you to fulfill your potential?*"

"*The Ly Kai of this world hated and rejected me.*"

"*The Ly Kai 'on' this world,*" he corrected sharply. "*They were never 'of' this world.*" She flinched at his rebuke. "*Why did they treat you differently?*"

"*They thought I might become evil like Araxis. They hated and feared Arylla.*"

Seuliac looked dubious. "*Why would they think that? Were they afraid of Arylla all along? No. They didn't begin by expecting Araxis to behave badly, did they? What happened to the brother?*"

"*Alexar? None of the Ly Kai of—on—this world seemed to know. I was curious enough to explore the question.*" A flicker of guilt ran through her at the memory. "*Many of the Ly Kai resented him because he opposed some of Araxis' activities. They thought he was dull and uninteresting, while Araxis stirred their imagination and sense of adventure. When they found themselves trapped here, they began to say Arylla was evil and Alexar was part of the betrayal. That he and Araxis planned it all. From what I gathered, they didn't believe anyone attempted to rescue them."*

"Perhaps the ones left on the Homeworld didn't think they were worth rescuing."

"Or they couldn't find where they went."

"Would this other one set himself up as leader back on your Homeworld?" Seuliac frowned.

"They suspected that."

"What do you think?"

"I don't know enough about the betrayal to form an opinion. The memories and thoughts I stole from the others sometimes conflicted between the survivors. But I learned Arylla is not evil. Araxis used its power for his own purposes, but it is only power, to be used as the wielder would use it."

"The others must have realized that."

"All I know is that from my earliest memories, they hated, feared, and resented me. It's not something a child can mistake." Not a child with the ability to read other peoples' minds.

"*Who were the Ly Kai who came to this world? What positions did they hold on your Homeworld?"*

That was something she had never thought about before. It took some rummaging through old memories to find anything. She started with the most painful one first. *"My parents held high rank in one of the governing houses. But my mother died here when Araxis made the fatal strike to save his essence. My father..."* she could not finish that thought.

"The others?"

"There were healers, educators, many of high position. They anticipated celebrating a new age for the Ly Kai when they came here. One filled with adventure and new experiences." She did not see the flash of pained expression her words caused him as she struggled to remember something she had never considered important before.

"Any priests?"

"None that I'm aware. So many people died when they rejected him—all the women and children..."

"I still don't understand. They had you from infancy, and they wasted you. Why try to deny you when you could be so valuable to them?"

"I told you, they feared Araxis. They even refused to look in the southerly direction for fear they would draw his attention. They lived in terror of his retribution after they rejected and attacked him. They just wanted to hide."

"For good reason. But with the right education, they might have used you against him."

"They believed the power of Arylla was evil."

"They didn't believe that when they followed the Evil One to our world. Maybe they were afraid they would lose control of you, the same as happened with Araxis."

That was a sobering thought. *"I don't know."*

"I guess we won't ever know what was in their minds. Not unless we can ask that last one. And he's not capable of answering, is he?"

"No." Ving might still be a mental presence in his own body, but he was not in control of it, or, likely, his sanity, by now.

"And this one you killed—Rath. How was he taken over?"

"Through a desire for power. And Ving, too. That's how he invades the mind. None of us must desire power of any type. To do so will leave us open to him. " In her need to make him understand, she reached out and gripped his arm. *"Please, Warlord, none of us must desire any*

form of power in any way!" Realizing what she had done, she quickly released his arm.

Seuliac smiled. *"I'll see Velacy is warned."*

"YOU DIDN'T EAT." Uri was no nursemaid, but common sense told any Geffitz warrior that he should keep a close eye on the people around him, especially those he might depend on the most.

"I'm not hungry." The sending was short.

Frax continued to stare into the woods, but Uri knew he wasn't seeing the forest. He could almost feel the internal battle raging in the other warrior. *"I'm afraid there's no substitute for food and water."*

"We must move faster, Uri."

"Are the Balandra still following us?"

"Not directly."

"What does the Grimmen want?" Uri was aware the wood was working on his cousin from the moment they arrived at Caer Cadarn, but Frax was even more tense and distracted since leaving the trail.

"It wants her off this world, Uri," Frax spoke aloud, refusing telepathy and any peripheral information that might reveal.

"Dammit, Frax! Don't shut—"

The other Geffitz looked at him, eyes cold. "Nothing else matters."

Uri stared at him.

For a fleeting moment, Frax's rigidity softened. "You can't help me on this, Uri. Really. You can't. This is my problem. Just keep the others away from the edge of disaster. That's what you can do." He turned away again, shutting him out.

Uri walked away, leaving his cousin in Kep-knew-what kind of hell. 'Edge of disaster,' he thought in frustration. What was that supposed to mean? With the Grimmenwood surrounding them, every one of them had their own personal potential to turn this thing into a disaster... He abruptly stopped and glanced around.

Seuliac and the Priestess were engrossed in conversation while they marked busily on the ground with a stick. Velacy, however...

Velacy sat to one side, alone, sullenly watching them.

A sudden chill ran down Uri's spine. How often did they ignore the heir of Rhynog? How frequently did they leave him alone to mull his resentful, hostile thoughts? While they were wrapped up in their concerns, most of which seemed to revolve around the Ly Kai Priestess, Velacy had the least involvement of any of them. How close to anything like an edge, as Frax might define it, was the Rhynogian heir?

"Velacy! I was wondering..." Uri walked over to him.

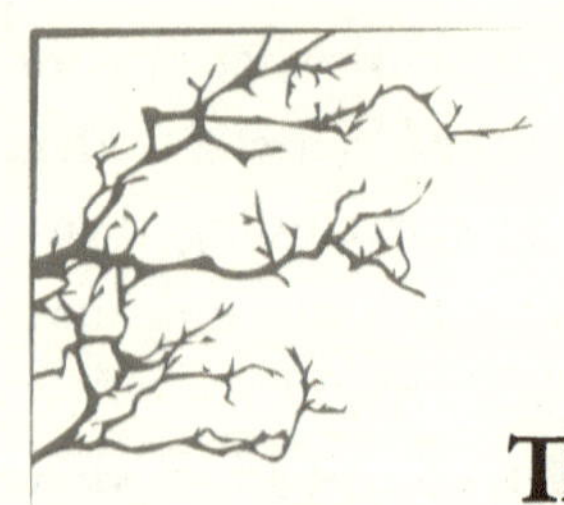

Chapter 74
The Escarpment

"It's beautiful!" Kaphri whispered.

A silvery strip, glinting in the sun, wound sinuously through a lush valley of forests and meadows to meet foothills, then mountains, to the east. As the silver curved westward to run parallel to their perch on the cliff top, Kaphri saw it was a broad band of trees that edged a river. Their leaves caught intermittent beams of sunlight breaking through the clouds scudding above and glinted in a dazzling display as the wind rustled through them.

Her hand stole to the symbol on her left breast. "Oh," she gasped with a sudden flash of insight.

"Very good." Frax had come up to stand beside her.

She had avoided contact with him over the last four days, secretly trembling in fear over what he might pick up from her thoughts in an unwary moment. She should continue to ignore him, but her curiosity about his comment would not let it go. She looked over at him. *"What?"*

"You've made the real connection between the symbol and Cadarn. It's not sunlight glinting on a weapon, as most people think, though that does sound good and reasonable, knowing Cadarn. It's really the sun sparkling on the leaves of the Silverline. Of course, since this is hidden deep in the Grimmenwood, very few people have the opportunity to put that together." He drew a deep breath, his eyes traveling over the vista before them. *"This valley is named Pterfellen, and that's the Silverline that divides it from the Grimmenwood."*

Pterfellen: the sacred land of the Geffitzi goddess, Kep. Tension tightened inside Kaphri, and the magic of the view dimmed.

"This is the only place the trees grow, and only on the Grimmenwood bank." His arm swept out, his hand tracing the winding strip of silver through the forest below. *"They mark the path of the Ysgubar River, down from the mountains in the east. The plateau we seek is over there."* He gestured toward the north, out across the land he named Pterfellen.

"See the massive gray cliffs over to the left?" He directed her attention to a sheer wall of towering stone that edged the northwest side of the valley. *"A cold, deep lake lies along their base. Stories say the heart of one of Kep's lost daughters, Twyfel, fell there. The place is surrounded by an overgrown bog, rendering it nearly inaccessible. See that dark slash?"* Frax pointed farther left, toward a darkening in the gray wall that was almost blocked from their view by the trees atop the escarpment. Even from this vast distance, Kaphri could feel the cold threat of the gash in the walls. *"That is the Gwmladd, a sheer-walled gorge and the second most dangerous place on this world. The Uchaf River hurls through that crack and eventually tumbles down the hundred-foot drop of Tiannon Falls to the High Lech, then runs to the sea."*

"Geffitzi do not live here?"

"A small religious center with a few priests once existed somewhere close to the lake. Otherwise, no. It's sacred land. And, beautiful as it appears from up here, most of it's a miserable, treacherous place. The whole area around the lake is marsh, and there are creatures that dwell there..." Frax's sending tapered off, leaving her to draw from her imagination. *"We're going north and east, across Pterfellen to the mountains. The bad thing is, we lose the protection of the Grimmenwood as soon as we cross the Ysgubar."* She could see the darkness of the currently cloud-shadowed foothills in the east and the darker jag of the mountain chain behind them.

"We still have all that to cross?" Velacy asked glumly as he, Uri, and Seuliac joined them. *"How long is this going to take?"*

"You have something better to do?"

Velacy shot Uri a scowl.

"The tarmeuth remains a threat," Seuliac reminded them. *"What's the plan?"*

"Get down the escarpment and across the river. We'll lose the protection of the Grimmenwood, but the Ysgubar is the only substantial water barrier against the tarmeuth we'll encounter until we reach the foothills."

Seuliac heaved a sigh. *"I never thought I'd view leaving the Grimmenwood with uneasiness."*

"There'll be forest for cover; it just won't be active cover." Frax shifted his attention to the drop before them. *"We need to move fast here. The climb is tricky, but once we're out on the cliff face, we're vulnerable to attack, and we might be visible for miles."*

"Can we climb down after dark?" Seuliac asked.

"Too treacherous without moonlight, and there won't be any tonight. But we can't move in daylight, either. We'll take shelter and wait until sunset."

"The question is: will the weather hold?" Uri glanced at the sky. It raced with puffy clouds that were condensing into a solid, darkening mass behind them. A distant rumble of thunder carried on the wind.

"Be still!" Seuliac went rigid with a sudden hiss of warning.

"What?"

"There." The warlord gave a slight mental gesture, directing their attention to the west, out into the open air of the valley. In the distance, barely visible, black dots were circling against the gray sky.

"Balandra," Frax said. *"Watching the area where we would have exited the woods if we'd stayed on the trail. Fall back to the tree line."*

They retreated across the bare rock that topped the escarpment into the bordering trees, where there was a swift sorting out in the deeper shadows. Frax and Velacy moved off to the north, toward trees offering a better view of the winged fliers, while Uri disappeared to the south, following the opposite line of the cliff, leaving Kaphri and Seuliac.

She looked around to find herself alone.

Was this a form of reproof, to remind her that if she had stayed closer to the warlord instead of engaging in conversation with Frax, she wouldn't need to search for him now? He would not go far, but he wasn't making an effort to draw her attention, either. Cursing herself for an idiot, she sent out a narrow seeking.

A slight sensation of response flickered a few steps off to her left, and she ducked in that direction. Seuliac might not be as greatly skilled in telepathy as the Kitahns, but he still managed to imbue his acknowledgment with a scathing sense of impatience.

She expected some cutting remark when she settled into the leaves beneath the bushes where he'd taken shelter. Instead, he said, *"your watch,"* and fell asleep.

How she envied his ability to push everything aside so completely. If she slept, she could avoid her dread of the pending climb down the cliff face and everything else beyond that. The earlier beauty of their surroundings had dimmed with the Balandra sighting and the significance of their presence. She rested her chin on her hands and watched the dust on the stone shelf in front of them swirl in tiny whirlwinds while she monitored the woods around them.

The sky grew steadily darker as the afternoon passed.

She fell asleep just as quickly as the warlord had when Uri returned and offered to take over the watch.

The sound of the rising wind woke her.

"A bad storm is blowing in." As if to confirm Uri's sending, a gust picked up dust from the stone surface and peppered them with grit in spite of their leafy cover. Thunder rumbled in the distance.

"*Excellent.*" Seuliac's eyes were open now in dark slits.

Kaphri brushed the dust from her cheeks. *"Why?"*

"The winged devils will be reluctant to fly in lightning and high wind, especially around this rift, with the dangerous updrafts. That'll give us a chance to move more freely."

"Something is moving at the edge of the woods north of us." Panic edged Velacy's sending. His position put him furthermost down the tree line to the northwest.

The three of them froze, listening to the exchange between Frax and Velacy.

"Air or ground?"

"Ground. It was tan. I saw a flicker of movement along the cliff top west of us."

A cold chill ran down Kaphri's spine. Was it tarmeuth or some other creature of the woods?

This was not the time to wait and find out. *"Pull in, Velacy,"* Frax ordered. *"Uri, the descent you favor, is it far?"*

"Just beyond that boulder." The blonde warrior sent an image of a big rock thrusting up from the cliff's edge about a hundred paces to the south of them. *"There are some rough spots, but we can handle it."*

"If we are caught out on skree in a deluge, it could be a disaster," Seuliac warned.

"It'll be a worse disaster if we sit here talking," Velacy responded sharply. *"We need to cross the river. Fast!"*

A nudge in Kaphri's back sent a flash of panic lancing through her before she realized Seuliac was on his feet. Leaves rustled and shadows loomed as the warriors converged around her.

Frax nodded. *"Uri, can you give us an image of the way?"*

"I'm not Tobin, Frax. I don't possess the gift for carrying maps in my head."

Of course. According to the Geffitzi warriors, Tobin's skill in projecting maps and terrain was a rare gift—and a very useful one the commander must wish he had at his disposal right now.

"Then each of us must project an image of our path to the one behind him as we go. Uri, you lead, then Velacy, the Priestess, and Seuliac. I'll bring up the rear."

Another blast of dust-laden wind struck them, this time more heavily, and a large splat of rain hit the surface of the cliff. Kaphri looked up at the sky. In the time they talked, it had darkened considerably, giving the light a dusk-like quality, even though it was only late afternoon.

Clinging to the cover of the woods, they made their way to a spot parallel to the boulder where they would make their descent. The rock was taller than a Geffitz and several spans wider, offering some shelter from the prying eyes to their west. The stone of the escarpment was peppered now with dark, wet splotches, but the rain had stopped.

"Try not to string out too far apart," Uri warned. *"Take it slow and don't forget to send an image of your path to the person behind you, especially if it looks rough."*

Velacy would be sending to her, and she to Seuliac. Kaphri acknowledged tersely.

Uri darted across the short span of bare rock to the boulder and disappeared downward. Velacy followed. An image of a steep, narrow game trail flitted through her mind as she ran for the boulder, Seuliac close on her heels. Sheer, open space loomed before her, and she stopped, grasping for the rough surface of the rock.

"You're not afraid of heights, are you?" Seuliac asked sharply.

"No." The huge openings in the walls of Kryie Karth had never bothered her, but she couldn't shake the sense of uneasiness that gripped her. She briefly considered telling him, then dismissed it. They were all uneasy. Why should her jitters be any more significant than theirs? She started forward again.

"Take no chances. If you need help, I'm right behind you."

She sent back a quick sensation of acknowledgment and gratitude.

Concentrating on the descent pushed her uneasiness to the back of her mind. The path Uri had chosen was nothing more than a shallow rut that twisted down between brush and boulders. The first ten feet descended the slope steeply, but the boulder also extended along their left, offering support. Kaphri clung close to it and moved after Velacy's disappearing form. Small clods of dirt and rocks rolling past her feet told her when Seuliac started down behind her.

The supporting wall of stone came to an end, leaving her in the open. The wind buffeted her hard as she inched down the rock-strewn decline and around a shelf of broken stone to find a treacherous-looking mix of small rock shards and dirt. Gouges and clumps showed where Uri and Velacy's boots had slipped during their passage. Alarmed, she flashed the image back to Seuliac.

"Skree," he sent back. *"Move slowly and carefully. The surface can break and slide beneath your feet."*

The trail led to the left. She inched her way across, ignoring scratches from the prickly brush she clung to for support. Seuliac was just appearing behind her when she caught a flash of an image from Velacy: the skree sloped down to a tree jutting out from the cliff face. From there, she would have to climb down a ravine.

She sent an uneasy question to the younger Aedec warrior: was the break composed of the same loose stone as the slope? The rock beneath her feet, easily chipped and broken, looked almost rotten.

His reply was reassuring. The ravine resembled the solid stone surfaces they were used to seeing in the hollows, with water-worn pocks and layers to offer hand and footholds. She should have little trouble moving down the narrow crevasse if she were careful.

Hardening her determination, she passed the message to Seuliac and moved on.

It was growing darker. The thunder had become a near constant, distant rumble, and occasional flashes of lightning sent cracks of noise bouncing off the surfaces around them. Though the rain held off with surprising restraint, the wind gusts unnerved Kaphri. More than once, she was forced to crouch and turn her face away from flying dirt and debris. The thought of getting caught out in the open by a strong blast, with nothing to cling to, made her speed up her steps. By the time she reached the bottom of the next section and found herself on a narrow rock ledge, her muscles were trembling from exertion.

She snatched a moment of rest while she sent the warlord an image of the place. The ledge across the face of the cliff was ample, though not excessively wide, the surface smooth and hard like the crevasse she had descended. He took it with silent, firm efficiency. She was becoming accustomed to the sense of that in him; nothing was wasted.

A light drizzle began as she moved forward again. Within seconds, the stone around her beaded with wetness. She paused uncertainly. With the film of dust that coated everything, the rock would be slippery and treacherous. Should she continue or stay where she was?

A rattle of loose stones warned her that Seuliac was coming down on her, which meant move or cause a dangerous delay. Resolutely she inched on, her back pressed against the cliff face. She had made it nearly half the way across, about three double-arm-lengths, when she came upon a small, twisted stub of a bush sticking out of the cliff. For the Geffitzi warriors, its placement would not have mattered; they would brush past, protected by their clothing. But on Kaphri, it projected out at the bare, unprotected area at the back of her head. It forced her to lean forward, removing her back from the wall. She had just begun to maneuver around it when Seuliac came out of the ravine. She glanced back nervously.

"Take your time," he sent.

"It's just so nar—" A loose pebble rolled under her boot. She lifted her foot, throwing all her weight back onto the other foot. The action left her body thrust forward, leaning out over the edge. She stared downward. Caught an impression of tree branches in a flicker of lightning.

"Kep, girl, be—"

Her boot slipped on the wet surface, and she pitched forward off the ledge without a sound.

She did not have time to cry out before she felt the jab of branches as she crashed through them. They slowed her fall, rebounding under her weight and thrusting her sideways so that she twisted toward the rock face of the cliff. That threw her over on thinner limbs, which gave way, and she plummeted downward again. This time her instincts took over, causing her to grasp out. Her fingers found a limb, gripped, and held.

"Oh, Kep!" Seuliac's sending was tight with concern. *"Are you all right?"*

Lightning flickered, but all she saw was the cliff a few inches from her face. *"I caught a branch. But I can't hold on for long."*

"Yes, you can," he snapped. *"There's a bit of ledge below this one. I'm coming down to pull you up."*

Please hurry. She kept the plea to herself.

After what seemed a lifetime, she heard a stir of movement above her; then, she felt Seuliac's mental presence again. She risked tilting her head back to look up. He was peering down in the dimming light. He thrust her an arm, but too much space gaped between them.

"Put your feet on the rock in front of you for leverage, push upward and give me your left hand."

Terror at the thought of letting go held her muscles frozen. *"I can't."* Her fingers felt melded to the branch.

Anger shot through Seuliac's sending. *"You have no choice, girl! Do what I say! When I tell you to, I want you to give me your hand."* He leaned out another fraction, straining toward her.

She was not conducting herself in the manner of a warrior—disgust at her display of weakness seared her to the quick. But to let go...! She closed her eyes and drew deep breaths to compose her mind. Her brain screamed protest at what the warlord wanted her to do. The wood under her fingers was all that kept her from plummeting to the rocks far below. The ridges and cracks in the surface of the bark burned beneath her flesh. Still, she knew she could not hang there indefinitely. The way the warlord was straining forward put him in jeopardy, too.

Very slowly, she brought her legs up to touch the rock with her feet. She scrabbled, seeking frantically for projections or pits. Her toes caught on a narrow outthrust, and she pushed down, trying to lift her body upward on the bobbing limb.

Her boot sole slid off the smooth surface, and she lost her breath in a sharp exhalation of terror. The branch rocked under her weight, and for a breathless moment, she hung helplessly, afraid that her swiftly numbing arms would betray her.

"Find a better foothold." The warlord's order cut across her mind.

"I'm trying!" Furious, she raked out with her feet again. This time her right foot found a narrow slot in the face of the stone. Cautiously putting her weight on it, she brought her left foot up and groped about, fighting rising panic until the left toe found anchorage. *"I have it."* She was surprised at how getting contact with a firm surface, even vertically, calmed her.

"On my word I want you to put your weight on your feet and push up while you lift your left hand to me..."

"Will this work?"

"It will. Now!"

Snatching a quick breath, she thrust hard against the cliff, forced herself to release her left hand, and reached up for him. For a breathless moment, their fingers brushed, then Seuliac surged forward to cover the last bit of space. His hand wrapped around her wrist.

Kaphri cried out in terror as her feet slipped off the rock, throwing all her weight on her extended arm. Stones showered down on her from the cliff edge above.

Seuliac snarled a curse, but his grip remained firm.

She held her breath, afraid to move.

"I have you. Release the branch so I can pull you up."

"But I might pull you over!"

"No, you can't. I've lashed myself to something to keep that from happening. Now, do as I say."

Heart pounding, she slowly let her fingers slip from the bark.

She swung free, her weight running through her arm and shoulder, her toes curling desperately for niches in the cliff face. More dirt and gravel showered down on and past her. She cried out, afraid for a moment that she was dragging the warlord over the edge, before pain forced her to realize she was not falling. Her one arm in the warlord's tight grip felt as if it were separating from her shoulder.

As she fought for calm, she heard the sharp clack of a stone striking the rocks below. She looked up, squinting against falling dirt, at Seuliac. He was all that stood between her and death.

Her eyes must have revealed her thoughts. In the flickering light, Seuliac smiled coldly. *"It's really too late to come to that realization now, don't you think?"*

Her heart turned to ice.

The mocking smile turned hard. His sending came to her flat and firm. "*Quickly now. You're going to have to walk up the cliff. I want you to get solid footing and push upward when I tell you to, so I can begin to pull you up. But whatever happens—if you slip or miss—don't panic. I have you."*

Kaphri closed her eyes and fought to calm her pounding heart. Bastard Geffitzi. Always the mind games.

Still, he hadn't dropped her.

"Alright. I think I am ready."

"You think...?"

"I'm ready," she snapped savagely.

"Good. Catch the stone with your feet and walk yourself up."

She caught the surface with the fingers of her free hand and her toes and inched her way upward. She thought her arm would pull from the socket as she used the warlord's grip to lever along, but after a few precarious moments, his other hand fumbled across hers and wrapped around her free wrist.

"Don't fail me," he gritted. *"I'm going to lift you up until your arms are on the edge, then I'll grab your clothes and boost you the rest of the way. Don't panic when I let go of your arm. I'll warn you first."*

Kaphri's feet scrabbled wildly for purchase on the cliff face, finally finding an outcrop that allowed her to push upward again. There were a few more breathless seconds as a toehold crumbled under her weight, then she was dragged up to cling against the ledge with her arms, and Seuliac was reaching to grab the cloth of her breeches. He hauled her unceremoniously up on the shelf and collapsed beside her.

For a time they lay panting and silent, then Seuliac pushed to a sitting position and loosened a rope from between his waist and the scrubby tree to which he had anchored it.

"Well, I passed up the perfect opportunity if I was ever going to see you dead as the solution to all this." He sighed and shook his head as if he wondered at his sanity. *"We have to move before the rain catches us and this all becomes a wasted effort."*

Carefully, painfully, they got to their feet.

"It's a short climb back up," Seuliac sent her a vague image of a series of broken stones, like a natural stair, along the rock face. *"Let's go."*

It was almost dark. Kaphri squinted, trying to see through the flickering light, but the wind picked up loose dirt from the stone beside her and sent a spray blasting into her face. Gasping in pain, she twisted to put the wind at her back and brushed at her eyes.

"Turn around and start climbing," Seuliac hissed in her head.

"I'm trying!" As she lowered her hand, the lightning flickered around them again.

She froze.

"Warlord," Kaphri tried not to breathe. *"There is an animal on the ledge behind you."*

She sent him the image of what she had seen, and he snarled a curse. *"Tarmeuth."* She had feared as much. *"How far?"*

"Several lengths past where you pulled me up. Do you think it has seen us?"

"It doesn't track by sight, Priestess. It tracks by scent."

"What do we do?"

"You get up on the trail. Find the others. I'll draw it away."

"Draw it away? No! Seuliac, it will kill you!"

"Just do it." Lifting her bodily, he all but thrust her up the stone face. *"Move!"*

"No!" Kaphri twisted in his hands, refusing to grasp the surface. *"I will not run away and leave you to die. There is another way. Put me down and give me your hand."*

"There's no time."

"There is! Do it!"

It was either give in to her demand or fall from the ledge in the ensuing struggle. Seuliac dropped her back down beside him.

She snatched his hand in her small grasp. *"The boulder on the cliff top where we came down,"* she hissed in his head. *"Picture it!"*

"Do it now, Priestess!"

Kaphri looked to where she had seen the tarmeuth. Lightning cast a glow into a pair of animal eyes and illuminated teeth as long as her fingers. The tarmeuth, bunching its muscles to spring, was exposed like some terrible image from a nightmare, then it was gone, plunged into blackness again. A massive clap of thunder split the air.

"Oh, Hredroth!" She drew on the crystal.

At the last second, she remembered the others.

"Frax!" She sent out a mental cry. *"A tarmeuth! We..."* The power of the crystal jerked them away.

SHE STUMBLED AND FELL to her knees. Trees loomed in the darkness, and wet leaves oozed beneath her boots. Thunder rumbled.

She looked around. Where was...? Where was...? What? She couldn't remember!

The escarpment! Yes. Her fingers still felt the wet stone. She—and Seuliac! She had used the crystal to move them back to the top of the escarpment.

This was not the top of the cliff. This was the Grimmenwood, and she was gasping for breath and fighting terror of a different kind. A terrible sense of loss gripped her heart.

Disorientation must be a side effect of using the crystal for a jump, she thought fleetingly. She sucked air and fought to bring order back into her thoughts.

Thunder rang in her ears, and Seuliac was suddenly beside her, his hand still grasping hers. The boulder where they had begun their descent down the escarpment stood solidly on their right.

What had just happened?

The warlord jerked her to her feet and put an arm across her, pinning her to the rock as he peered around its edge toward the north. "*Damn it! Priestess, are you all right? Can you run?*"

"*Yes.*" Why? What was wrong here?

"*When I give you the word, run for the trees. Keep low. Get inside and keep running.*"

Her heart leaped into her throat. "*Another tarmeuth?*" She could not move them along again. She had no clear images of any places up here.

"*Balandra. At least five, a short distance up the escarpment lip. If we're quick and luck keeps the lightning away, we can reach the wood. They won't even know we're here unless they pick up our scent. But we have to move fast. The tarmeuth may come up the cliff behind us.*"

Lightning illuminated the area in a series of slow flashes. Thunder rumbled and rain fell in icy drops. Kaphri shivered in fear and confusion.

Seuliac glanced back at her. "*The storm will muddle our scent.*" He drew the long knife at his belt. "*I want you to stay on this side of me, out of their sight. If anything happens, you keep running. I don't think they'll follow us into the wood. Ready?*"

The brush that edged the forest was less than ten steps away. In another flash of light, Kaphri's eyes found the gap they had moved through earlier in the day. She nodded, forgetting the warlord wouldn't see her as the blaze died to darkness.

Seuliac took another look around the rock then his hand was on her arm, pulling her forward. "*Now! Go!*"

The lightning caught them four paces from the boulder, blazing out in a long flash that illuminated everything around them as clearly as daylight. She heard Seuliac swear before the clap of thunder deafened her.

She did not have time to send the mental question as a sixth Balandran, undetected on the opposite side of the boulder, billowed startled wings to take flight.

She knew it screamed even though the wind tore away the cry. Knew its companions were warned. Seuliac shoved her toward the tree line while he slowed and turned to confront the creature.

The storm chose just that moment to change to a torrential downpour.

She wanted to stop. She wanted to fight. Her hand was fumbling with the blade at her waist when Frax's words came to her: 'swear to me that no matter what happens to the rest of us, you will continue with your task.' With a sob of terror and frustration, she kept running.

She slipped in the wet leaves and fell hard on her left hip when she ducked under the cover of the bushes. Ignoring the pain, she twisted to stare back at the scene on the cliff top.

Through the gray curtain of the downpour, the other Balandra stumbled and scrambled along the rock, their movements made awkward by the wind and pounding rain as they came toward her. But the sixth Balandran, the one from the other side of the boulder, had managed to take to the air and was grappling with the warlord. Seuliac had it by one wing, pulling it downward, but it was making use of the fact that it towered above the Geffitz with both its hands free. Kaphri watched in frozen horror as its twisted blade rose into the air, then flashed down.

"No!" The horrified protest boiled up inside her. Before she could think, she lashed out, sending a lance of power at the creature.

Blue-white fire exploded from the Balandran, causing it to jerk backward, its wings giving a mighty flap that ripped it out of the warlord's grasp. A scream of agony tore at her ears. Seuliac threw up his hands to shield his eyes from the light as the creature slammed into the boulder, then crumpled to the stone surface of the cliff top. A drift of white smoke rose eerily from it despite the driving rain.

Seuliac stumbled backward a step and Kaphri realized with horror that she had stunned him with her attack. Meanwhile, the remaining Balandra were closing on him. She saw the nearest one spring forward, snatching at his hair as it leaped upward, its wings billowing. Two others were trying to work their way around behind him, their weapons raised for a strike.

Not all the Balandra were focused on the warlord, however. Two had spun about and were looking for the source of her attack. With a motion to the one behind it, the nearest of the creatures started toward her hiding place.

Kaphri froze, torn by terror and indecision. She wanted to help the warlord, but she was helpless. The blast of power she had thrown had been an uncontrolled, gut reaction to a threat. She couldn't recreate it. She simply didn't know how to do it. And any new defense she might come up with would require more time and thought than she had left to her.

And Seuliac had ordered her to run...

The choice was abruptly taken from her as a dark, lithe form came bounding up over the cliff's edge. She watched in helpless horror as the tarmeuth plunged into the battling group on the escarpment, its raking claws catching the Balandran that held Seuliac, dragging it down to crash into the warlord. The three fell in a tangled heap of limbs while the other Balandra made a sudden, wild attempt to escape.

With a sob of helpless terror, she fled into the black depths of the Grimmenwood.

Chapter 75
Danger On All Fronts

Frax could curse Seuliac Aedec's poor telepathic abilities, but he should have anticipated the warlord's sendings would weaken dramatically once he moved out of the line of sight. He'd received an occasional flash of a fuzzy image during their descent. Now that had disappeared too.

He was searching intently, trying to detect any scrap of mental presence, when Kaphri's shout of warning, that a tarmeuth was stalking the ledge, hit him. He froze, stunned to discover that, somehow, he'd passed the other two on the trail without realizing it.

His first instinct was to turn and charge back up the cliff to help them. He swiftly rejected that as only adding to a developing disaster. If Kaphri had carried the two of them out of danger, as her sending indicated, he would be running back into the jaws of a very angry tarmeuth. If she had not reacted quickly enough... But, no, he would already know that. She was with the warlord. Together they could handle it.

He caught another flash of an image. This one drove a chill of panic through him. They had made it back to the top. But what he thought she saw in that flash—

He waited for something more.

Nothing.

Kaphri had called out a warning. Had the others heard it and started back up the rocks via some other route to aid her? That might compound the disaster!

Whatever was happening above, he couldn't stay where he was. An angry, frustrated animal stalked the cliff behind him, and it might be turning, picking up the scent of his passage and following the rest of them down.

The rain broke into a hard torrent, turning the air into an impenetrable soup as he hit the last bit of gravel slope and almost collided with Uri.

The other warrior stood in the darkness, staring up at the cliff heights.

"*You heard?*" The noise of the storm forced Frax to send to the other warrior.

"Yes. What the—?"

"We've got trouble, Uri."

"*The tarmeuth...?*"

"She jumped them back to the top. But there are Balandra up there."

"How do you know that?"

"*Sometimes I catch a quick flash of what she sees or feels.*"

"*By the Goddess, Frax!*" Uri's sending was a mix of horror and appall.

He probably should have told his cousin that earlier. "*Berate me later, Uri. Right now, we have to do something—*"

An earsplitting crack of thunder rent the air. "*What? What can we do?*"

Frax raised a hand to shield his eyes against the rain as he stared upward. "*We—Oh, Kep!You're exposed! Get out of there, Priestess! Don't—*" A sudden blaze of light, white and unmistakably different from lightning, flared on the cliff above them.

His expression was bleak when he looked at Uri. "*The tarmeuth followed them back to the top.*"

"*Then we go back up! Velacy...!*"

Velacy! He had forgotten about the other warrior in the disaster unfolding above them. Frax looked around, reaching out mentally.

He touched on the young Aedec warrior standing a few paces away, cloaked in heavy shadows.

"*Let's go!*"

"*I can't,*" Velacy said sullenly.

"*Why?*"

"*They won't let me.*"

The younger Aedec took a stumbling step forward as if something had shoved him from behind. The thick shadows around him began to move and expand, taking on the outlines of four large creatures.

Cyrwins! Frax found it suddenly hard to breathe as he watched the animals fan out to form a loose, half-circle around the three of them.

"*Frax?*" Uri's sending was tentative beside him.

The commander stared at the huge, dark forms, unsure how to respond to the expanding catastrophe. Were the Cywrins hostile or was this an offer of assistance? These creatures were servants to the Grimmen, but the Grimmen responded to Cadarn. Of the four, which should he address as the leader? Choosing the wrong one would lose him credibility with them, something he could not afford.

A tingle of instinctive warning shot through him: something stood at his back! Tarmeuth? The question flashed in his mind. He fought panic. Any loss of control would mark him as weak. Besides, he reasoned in another flash, these Cyrwins would never stand still for the immediate threat of a tarmeuth. He turned to face the fifth Cyrwin, behind him.

It blocked his way back up the escarpment.

"*You stand between us and our companions in distress,*" he said.

"*The way back is forbidden.*" The sending fell into his mind, flat and truculent as if he were dealing with a surly child. The Cyrwin remained firmly fixed between them and their path back up.

"*As a trueblood of Cadarn, I order you to let us pass.*" Frax moved to step around the animal.

He felt a sizzle of warning in his mind. The Cyrwin jerked its head up, towering high above him.

"*Frax! Wait!*" He felt a pull on the strap of his quiver as Uri tried to stop him.

Too late. The animal dropped its head in a broad sweeping motion, striking him hard across the chest and flinging him backward. He collided with Uri, and they both went down into the mud in a tangle of limbs.

"*The Grimmen forbids it.*"

"*Son of a—*" Frax shouldered Uri's weight aside and tried to pick himself up. He froze with a gasp.

"*Frax? Are you all right?*" Uri rolled to his feet in a half-crouch and was staring at him.

"*Gods, Uri.*" Shocked pain filled Frax's sending. "*I think the bastard broke my ribs.*"

"*The Grimmen forbids it.*" The creature shook its bony head and repeated the warning as it glared at them.

Uri straightened. "What the hell's wrong with you?" His angry shout was audible above the noise of the storm.

"*Uri...*" They didn't need two people with broken ribs.

"*No!*" the other warrior snapped. He turned his attention back to the Cyrwin. "What the hell is wrong with you? He's Cadarn! You're supposed to be on his side!"

"*It's all right, Uri.*" Frax caught his arm, using him for support as he climbed to his feet. "*Stay calm,*" he pressed into his cousin's mind as he straightened to face the Cyrwin blocking their way. "*Our companions on the cliff are in danger. We have to help them. Perhaps the Grimmen could...*"

He and Uri stumbled back a hasty step as the animal swept its head down again in warning. "*You will wait here. The Grimmen has ordered it.*"

"*Frax, what's going on?*" Uri shot an aside to him. "*We can't—*"

"*Sit!*" The creature tossed its head again.

Uri retreated another step, but Frax held his position. "*No.*" These creatures specialized in killing Cadarn's dismounted enemies on the battlefield. It went against every instinct in him to put his companions down on the ground. "*We'll stand.*"

"*Can we at least find some shelter?*" Velacy asked from behind.

"*Sit!*"

Frax continued to glare at the Cyrwin blocking his path.

"*Sit!*" The other four Cyrwins moved in around them, tightening the circle.

"*Frax, it's pointless to argue and risk further injury.*" Uri pressed his shoulder.

His cousin was right. That didn't make it easier to accept. He made a downward motion and the three of them squatted where they were, into a steadily deepening pool of water and mud.

"*I thought these demons were your allies, Kitahn,*" Velacy muttered.

"*What's happening up above? Can you tell?*" Uri broke in tersely.

"*I don't know. She's with Seuliac. It could be worse.*"

"*You can't see...?*"

"*It only hits me every once in a while. I have no control over it.*"

There was a long moment of silence.

"*Has the Grimmen changed alliances?*" Uri sent.

"*Changed to Araxis? No.*" Frax was sure of that. "*But we've never claimed to understand what motivates the Grimmen.*" He glowered at the animals, making no effort to mask his frustration. "*Do you have others on the escarpment? Are they helping our people?*"

The Cyrwins ignored him.

Kep! At least one of them had to get back up the cliff to help their companions. The only way to achieve that was by creating a big distraction.

He didn't know if the Cyrwins could pick up sendings not specifically directed at them, but he had his suspicions. Nothing that invaded other minds as cavalierly as these creatures did would have qualms against eavesdropping. He would need to rely on the others' quick wits and experience. Uri would protest if he realized what he planned. The possibility of cracked ribs did not make him the best candidate for action, but he was the one the Cyrwins were least likely to kill if they reacted badly.

Abruptly he leaned forward with a loud groan, as if seized with sudden pain. At the same moment, he sent to the other two. It was a warrior signal, a sensation rather than a complex thought, and, hopefully, something the Cyrwins would not notice. Generally, commanders used it to draw the attention of warriors scattered in the field when their concentration might be otherwise occupied. It demanded a focus on the matter at hand.

"Kep!" Velacy sprang forward instantly, reaching out to check the pulse in Frax's neck. The younger warrior looked up. "He's hurt. Bad."

Uri surged to his feet. "We can't just sit here! He needs our help!" He began to shrug out of his pack. The Cyrwins shifted their attention uneasily between his quick, exaggerated movements, Velacy, and the moaning Kitahni warrior. "Don't just stand there. Help us!"

Frax gave another tortured cry and curled his body. What appeared to be a reaction to intense pain, however, was really a shift to put him in a better position to get his feet under him.

The Cyrwins, curiosity mixed with concern, shifted their attention to the agonized warrior. Meanwhile, Uri managed to place his body between Frax and the creatures by bending to open his pack—a risky move depending on how they reacted to what was about to happen.

Frax launched into action, throwing himself forward. The pain in his ribs grabbed at him and darkness played at the edge of his consciousness as he rolled between the legs of the Cyrwin blocking the path back up the cliff. At the same moment, Uri gave a cry, and Velacy began to shout at the creatures.

It was a perfectly timed distraction.

Frax had barely taken two running steps when something whistled through the air behind him. A flick of slicing pain struck the back of his upper left arm.

Two more steps and he crumpled to the ground, unconscious.

"Oh, shi—" From a view beneath one of the Cyrwin's bellies, Velacy saw the Kitahni warrior fall. He settled back into the mud with a solid thump while Uri erupted in a mental wave of frustration and fury.

"*Damn you! What have you done to him?*"

"*He lives.*" The animals moved unhurriedly, widening their circle to include Frax's sprawled form. "*Attend to him now. Water could invade his nostrils.*"

The two warriors got to their feet and edged forward, careful not to incite another attack. Uri dropped to his knees, lifted Frax's head onto his thigh, and rolled his body half over to inspect the Cyrwin sting. In the darkness, he had to examine the wound by touch. "*You fools!*" he said bitterly as his fingers probed the swelling puncture. "*We have companions in deadly danger. You should let us go back up the cliff.*"

"*The Grimmen honored the petition of Frax Kitahn but do not push the situation. There is nothing that requires we spare you pain or discomfort.*"

Uri made one last attempt. "*If you'd just listen—*"

The barb of a Cyrwin tail flicked within a fraction of his face. "*It would be better if you remain silent. We will be here a while longer.*"

He settled into the water and mud, his anger a bitter taste in his mouth.

"*What the hell's going on, Caspani?*" Velacy sent tensely. "*Shouldn't they be on our side?*"

"*I don't know, Velacy. Just be quiet.*"

"*Have they turned against Cadarn?*"

Velacy would persist despite everything. "*I don't know.*"

"*Be silent!*" The Cyrwin's order ended further conversation.

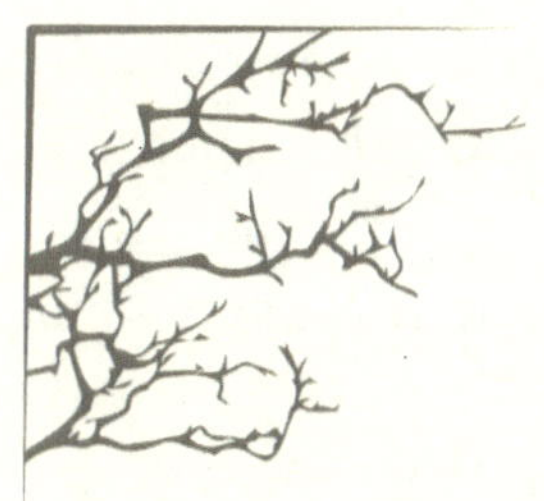

Chapter 76
Seuliac

The tarmeuth cleared the cliff's edge and leaped for the first creature in sight. It caught the Balandran with its claws and sent it crashing into Seuliac, bearing them both to the ground. A snap of jaws crushed the Balandran's throat.

Seuliac held himself breathlessly frozen, the weight of the cat and the hapless Balandran pinning him. Smoke from the charred body of the other Balandran, lying against the boulder, drifted slowly before his eyes, and he wondered if it would be the last thing he ever saw. The tarmeuth, however, gave a passing sniff at his pack, found nothing of immediate interest, and charged after the two Balandra now trying to flee into the woods. It bore down on them swiftly, bringing them to ground with a slash of disabling claws, then spun back toward the boulder and the two creatures who were already airborne. It easily snagged the first one out of the air with a ruthless snap of jaws and flung it aside. The second gained height faster, its black wings pumping desperately.

Rainwater sprayed off the surface of the escarpment as the tarmeuth slid to a halt. Its eyes locked on its target and massive muscles bunched. Seuliac watched it leap, shooting straight into the air, rising to almost twice the height of a Geffitz warrior. The cat reached, claws extended like hooks, snagged the Balandran out of the air, and carried it down. Seuliac heard a brief keen of terror before a horrible crunch of bones silenced it.

The whole attack took place in less than sixty racing heartbeats.

It was time for him to move before he became the next casualty. Seuliac flexed the muscles down his body, testing for damage he might have sustained when the cat knocked him down. Sections—his ribs, belly, and left thigh—protested, but nothing screamed the sharp pain of a broken bone.

Kep, he hurt! The blast the girl had leveled at the winged warrior had been like fire dancing on his nerves—and he only caught an edge of it. He was grateful he wasn't the poor bastard over by the rock she'd left a smoking cinder. Now he fully understood Uri Caspani's warning of days ago.

Too bad he might not ever acknowledge it to the other warrior.

The Balandran that had saved him from the tarmeuth's crushing jaws lay sprawled over him. The body and the smoke from the burning flesh had masked his scent, saving him from the giant cat's attention so far, but if he stayed where he was, that would not last. The tarmeuth would sate its initial hunger on its last kill and begin to browse among the other carcasses.

The flexed wing of the Balandran warrior blocked his view to the north. Cautiously he levered himself up to peer over it. The tarmeuth had its back to him, its tail flicking rhythmically as it fed on the downed body of the last Balandran. As long as the tail continued to flick he was safe.

A blaze of lightning showed his long knife, knocked from his hand when he'd fallen, lying a short distance to his left. Easing sideways, he strained against the weight of the body on top of him to reach the weapon. His fingers closed about the pommel, and he drew it back to him.

The thin, leathery wing still blocked his view of the tarmeuth when his head was down, but he could hear the snap of bones above the noise of the storm. The edge of the woods was only a few lengths away. If he could make a quick dash in darkness... Steeling his resolve, he pushed over to hands and knees in a single, smooth movement, his muscles bunching for flight.

Thunk!

He caught movement from the corner of his eye as something flashed through the air to connect solidly with the carcass he had just shrugged off. Just as quickly, the thing was gone.

He froze, his chest suddenly so tight he could only draw air in quick, shallow gasps. Ripples of cold horror rolled down his spine.

The sound of the feeding cat stopped, and a low growl came to his ears.

There was a whiz of something passing through the air again and another solid sound of connection. This time he saw the snaky movement, the spearhead point that struck the dark flesh of a lifeless arm right in front of him, sinking in. With horrified fascination, he watched body fluids seep from the puncture and wash away in the pounding rain. Another flick and the shape was gone again. The corpse barely twitched with the movement.

He could feel the tarmeuth's attention now, riveted on the spot where he lay. Its growl sounded like a roar in his ears.

"*A challenge to its kill.*" The voice was a deep, husky contralto whisper in his head. "*Perhaps we should withdraw and leave it to reclaim its feast.*"

And bring death down upon him. Now that the tarmeuth's attention was drawn to where he lay, he had no hope of escaping those deadly jaws.

Dire as the thought was, he had other problems.

Something brushed his jaw. Slid lightly forward along the bone. He held rigidly still as the barb of boney flesh came to hover before his eyes.

"*But it has also been so very long since we have tasted this meat....*"

Seuliac became aware of the splashing sounds of several creatures moving through the rain. The tarmeuth gave a scream of enraged challenge, snarled, and then there was silence. He knew without seeing that the big cat had skulked off, driven from its feed.

Only one creature would have that effect on a ruthless killer like a tarmeuth: an even more ruthless killer.

He watched the barb that still hovered before his eyes with horrified fascination. How many warriors of Rhynog had fallen by that weapon over the centuries? Every Geffitz warrior knew how deadly the horny tip of a Cyrwin's tail was.

"*Just a tender caress and I could make you so ill.... Or I could make you die.*" The sending had a rich, seductive sound that made Seuliac want to wretch.

The barb dropped slightly, a feather touch against his right cheek.

"Enough games. If you're going to kill me, do it and be done," he gritted between clenched teeth.

"*Oh, it will not be that simple.*" The thing disappeared from his sight.

Horrified, he felt the hard edge at his throat. The Cyrwin's tail coiled, wrapping around his neck and gliding so the tip came back up to poise before his eyes. It tightened with an ominous squeeze.

"*While you are on your belly, slide your blade into your belt, behind your back, out of reach. Then slowly get to your feet. You will keep your hands below your waist, crossed in front of you. If you lift them, you'll die.*"

Slipping the knife into his belt, Seuliac stood. He refused to display a reaction as he turned to look into the red, snake-slit eyes of the Cyrwin that held him captive.

They stared at each other for a moment, cold gray meeting mad crimson, then the creature shifted its attention back to the activity around them.

Four other Cyrwins were moving about in the rain, thrusting their tails deep into the bodies scattered about the cliff top. He flinched as one of the winged warriors near the edge of the woods gave a sudden scream of pain and thrashed about spasmodically, pinioned on a barb, before growing still.

Likely, it harbored the same scheme for escape as he had.

He continued to watch, hiding his reaction when the animals began to trample the bodies beneath their sharp hooves. They were ruthlessly thorough in their destruction, crushing flesh and grinding bones under their heavy weight until nothing was left but a large, shapeless mass oozing dark stains into the rainwater. It was a harsh, explicit warning to any other invaders who might find their way into this place.

He realized all their attention had shifted to him.

What came next? A long, slow death? Writhing agony as poison coursed through his veins? Five pairs of red eyes burned into him, the malevolent hatred radiating from his captors nearly tangible.

He lifted his chin, his mouth tightening in defiance, rain sheeting down on him.

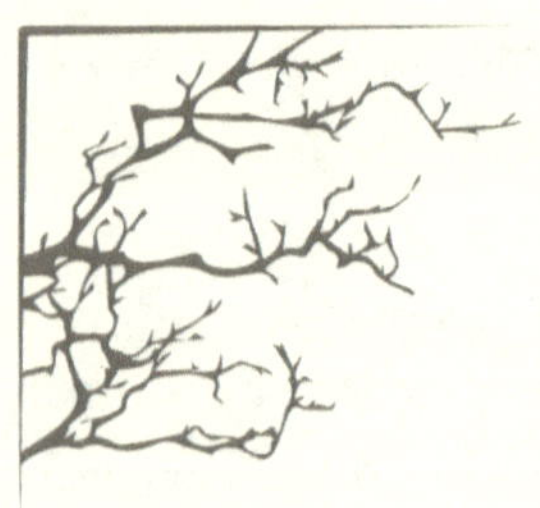

Chapter 77
Kaphri Runs

As the tarmeuth charged over the rim of the escarpment and snagged the attacking Balandran in its claws, Kaphri ran, her mind churning with horror and bitter despair. She left the warlord of Rhynog behind, fighting to buy her the time she needed to escape. Her task, the promise she had made to Frax, must be to get as far away from the danger as she could, as fast as possible.

So she ran as swiftly and as far into the wood as her body would allow.

She finally collapsed against a tree, fighting to ease the agony in her side. Her breath came in great, burning tears and her eyes searched the dark for a stealthy movement, for a lift of a wing, while she fought to slow her pounding heart.

Had the Balandra followed?

How far? How far had she run?

Was the tarmeuth padding silently behind her? Was it crouched in the darkness, ready to spring? She could almost feel the impact of the sudden strike—the tearing claws. A violent shiver ran over her, causing her to lose her balance with its strength. As she pressed against the tree, she searched wildly but found nothing.

Delayed reaction finally crashed in on her. Hredroth! She had messed up everything! When she reacted to save Seuliac, she had used power. She had given away their position like a beacon on a hilltop, putting them all in even worse danger. How many Balandra were swarming toward this place right now?

A sob caught in her throat. Because of her lack of control, Seuliac had paid the ultimate price. She had carelessly used everything in one burst, saving nothing for a second, unforeseen attack—for the tarmeuth. She strained to hear any sound above the storm, knowing it was futile. She had run too far to hear anything taking place on the cliff top. Did she want to hear? The thought of the warlord screaming in death pains sent agony shooting through her heart.

She could not turn back. It would only diminish his sacrifice.

And now she was here, alone in the Grimmenwood. She shivered, feeling the cold, rain-soaked clothes on her skin for the first time as her situation penetrated her reality.

She was alone in the Grimmenwood.

She straightened, the stitch in her side forgotten, the horror and fear of what had taken place on the cliff top supplanted by a new fear.

Of course, there was no path on which to claim safety.

She searched out for the presence that had hung over them since their arrival at Cadarn.

It was gone.

That did not surprise her: the Grimmenwood was not her ally. She would find no refuge in this place. She must locate Frax and the others as quickly as possible.

Perhaps Seuliac would be with them. Perhaps. A fleeting, unlikely thought. As powerful a warrior as the warlord was, he wouldn't survive the dual onslaught of the Balandra and tarmeuth on his own.

Another sob wrenched her. If only she had waited just one more moment before reacting with that bolt of power. She might have directed her attack at the tarmeuth, the real threat, instead of the Balandran. Seuliac would have triumphed against the Balandra...

If she'd been better schooled. Better prepared. If she knew more about her own legacy. Regrets swirled in her head. With a shaking hand, she wiped away the rain, mixed with tears, running down her cheeks.

And what would the warlord say if he knew what she was doing right now? He would be furious and disgusted. He would say there was no room for the sorrow of emotional attachments. That she must move on and not waste his efforts. He had acted to ensure her escape, and all her doubts were doing were working against his sacrifice.

Straightening away from the tree, she gave herself a mental shake. She would not waste his sacrifice. She must focus on her own situation.

Could the Balandra pursue her into the woods? They managed the thicket at the edge of Omurda well enough when they captured her the first time. But would they dare brave the Grimmenwood after their deadly encounter on the trail days ago? And the tarmeuth was a creature of this place. Would it stalk her?

Encountering either of those pursuers was a secondary problem, however. She had to survive the Grimmenwood first. She must find a way down the escarpment without drawing its creatures' attention. Meanwhile, she stood in the Grimmen's realm, inviting trouble.

Which direction led back to the cliff? Briefly, she wished the geas still gripped her: it would have shown her east immediately. On the other hand, it might have stopped her from running into the woods, and she would be dead right now.

She had run up to the tree on this side. That must make east back the opposite way. But she couldn't walk directly back the way she'd come, back into disaster. She made a quarter turn to face what should be south, then sought out, searching the darkness.

Life in the Grimmenwood had withdrawn for the night, sheltering against the storm. The wood was still noisy, however. The pounding rain was a remote drone on the forest canopy, broken by the sound of steady drips where it fell to the ground. Occasionally streams of rainwater, pooled in the leaves high overhead, would break their surface tension and come crashing down through the branches in unexpected, icy, and loud deluges. The thunder was a muted, near-constant rumble. Despite all of that, there seemed to be a strange air of expectation about the place, as if it held its breath, waiting.

Which was reason enough to start moving again.

She thought to move south for a distance to skirt the area around the escarpment where... She bit her lip to silence the thought. She mustfind a new point where she could descend and locate the others.

A sudden, prickling sense of warning brought her rigidly alert, her skin going cold even before her mind consciously recognized it.

Something had moved in the darkness to her left.

She sent out a swift, seeking probe, fearful of what she might touch but more fearful of not using what she had to protect herself.

Nothing.

Bitter experience had taught her that answer was not always reliable. She searched the woods around her with every sense she had.

Even in the near-total blackness, she thought she detected a slight movement in the direction that, moments before had lain behind her. Heart in mouth, she turned toward it, staring hard, searching out. She did not find anything.

Balandra?

Though she could not sense the mental presence of the gray creatures, she had been able to find the density of their physical existence, even through stone, once she was aware they were about. Here, she didn't pick up anything.

Perhaps a falling leaf...

More likely, some creature of the woods going about its nightly rounds was startled or made curious by her unexpected presence. She hoped it was wishing her away as desperately as she did it.

Again, standing here, staring into the blackness, did not improve her situation. Turning, she walked again, all her senses alert.

For several steps, everything remained still and silent, then she sensed movement again, this time from behind her and also to her left. Whatever was out there, now there were more.

She forced herself to continue forward without quickening her pace, her mind spinning to find something to help her.

She sensed the trunk of a large tree ahead. The thing was huge. It would give her solid protection for her back if she decided to turn and confront whatever followed her.

A sudden tingle of heat ran over her flesh at the thought of mounting a defense. Her heartbeat accelerated, and she began to flex her fingers, fanning and curling them before she was aware she'd begun to do it.

What was this reaction? Did the creatures stalking her stir the effect in her?

No. Her fear of manipulation evaporated in surprised realization. This was a response to danger her own body generated, reacting to the situation around her, unbidden.

Her right foot skidded on the wet leaves of the forest floor, throwing her off balance. She regained her footing, but in the same instant, she felt a flash of movement off to her left as if her pursuer started forward a quick step and stopped as she recovered.

The tightening sensation inside her heightened.

The ground in front of her sloped steeply downward, making her footing more treacherous. How far was the tree? She reached out mentally, only to discover that, because of the unseen slope, it was further away than she first judged. Its trunk must be immense!

Whatever moved in the darkness must have recognized her intentions. It surged, charging her. She would never reach the tree and position herself in time to defend.

Despite her attempts to remain calm, her panic fired, and she ran.

She managed the first several steps without a problem, but then the slope steepened, sending her flight into an uncontrolled plummet. She stayed upright for a few more steps, until her foot met a rock. Her cry caught in her throat as she stumbled and fell. She bounced once, hard, knocking the breath out of her, and began to roll downhill.

The tree that had been her goal flashed past and she kept rolling, uncontrolled, until her shoulder glanced off something. Agonizing pain shot through her, but the impact slowed her momentum. Her fall roughly broken, she slid for a length before she came to a stop, face down, in a deep pile of leaves, where she laid, stunned.

Oh, Hredroth and Kep! It took a few moments to catch her breath, then more for her to muster enough strength to move one finger. It would take a lot longer for her to sit up.

Not an option, her brain screamed. The reason she ran would not go away because she clumsily fell down the slope. More likely, it prepared to attack. This was no time for physical weakness: she must confront whatever pursued her.

Gathering her thoughts, she sensed out into the dark. Despite the distance of her tumble, she was not at the bottom of the incline. She heard rushing water below her and sensed the closeness of another hillside beyond that, rising upward.

She would not cross water again during a storm—not after her experience at the edge of Omurda, and especially not in the dark. That left her with a long, angling climb up the slippery slope.

Bracing mentally, she clenched her teeth against the myriad pains racking her body and rolled onto her back—to stare up at a mass of darkness hovering over her.

She felt, rather than saw, it move; heard its grunt of surprise. A shrill keening tore at her ears as the dark form loomed, abruptly rising up, over her.

Hredroth! She had seen this...

A sharp and deadly object cut the air close to her ear. It struck the ground beside her head with a heavy thud and was gone again, spattering her with bits of wet leaves and debris. There was screaming in her head, though whether it was the creature or herself, she could not tell. Lightning flickered, and the creature was rising above her again like a cloud of darkness. A glint of light caught on a sharp and slashing hoof before it descended. She rolled, throwing her arm up to protect her face, and knew she had experienced all this before.

This! This was an illusion! A nightmare!

No. This was real.

And she could die.

Something thudded heavily into the dirt and leaves where her head had just been.

"That's enough," a voice said sharply.

There was a loud animal snort above her, mixed with a blast of hot air on her skin, then a mental whine of protest cut into her mind.

"*She is the enemy....*"

"*There is warrior claim. Leave her alone.*"

Tobin?

Before she was able to react, another snort and blast of air pulled her attention back to the immediate danger that hovered above her. She looked up, her heart freezing in horror. A nightmare creature from the gates of Cadarn towered over her, its front feet planted on each side of her ribs. But this was no statue. It shook its head and bared its fang-like teeth at her.

A sizzle of telepathic anger flashed, and the Cyrwin reacted with a sharp snort, jerking its head higher, away from her.

Kaphri's eyes flicked to her right, frantically seeking for the source of the voice. In a flicker of lightning, Tobin Kitahn leaned forward over the neck of another of the nightmare creatures, staring down at her with cold indifference.

Seeing him was a shock, but the events that had driven her to this point were an even greater concern.

"*Tobin! Tobin, oh, thank the gods! A tarmeuth! It attacked! There were Balandra. Seul—!*"

"*It has been seen to,*" Tobin cut her off. He leaned back on the animal he sat astride. "*Get up.*"

"*But you must—*"

He turned his head to stare back up the hollow between the two hillsides toward the east. Her attention snapped to the stirring sounds in the shadows around her.

"*She cannot simply be allowed to 'get up,' Lord. She is a deathbringer. She stole the blood of our Geffitzi brothers from us.*" The protest was petulant. "*She must be punished. She must be made to suffer.*"

"*I told you,*" Tobin sounded bored as he continued to stare away into the blackness. "*She is necessary. You will not act against her.*"

"*A bite—*" The creature above her moved to make good on its protest by baring its teeth.

As it lowered its muzzle toward one of her arms, Kaphri's body reacted, tightening with the same sensation of drawing from earlier in the wood.

"*No bite. Nothing! It is forbidden.*" Tobin twisted around to glare. His attention snapped to her. "*That would be most unwise.*"

That. The reaction growing inside her.

Kaphri suspected the word "unwise" might be an understatement. Despite her confusion at what she was beginning to recognize as an automatic reaction of self-defense, she forced herself to relax, trying to ease away the charge of energy that filled her body.

It proved difficult. She wasn't quite sure what she dealt with—or how to dissipate it. How did one rid oneself of starpower?

Cautiously she tried to will it away by visualizing it evaporating into the air through her breath. It seemed to have limited success. The drawing sensation faded, but it left her muscles tingling.

When she pulled her focus back to her surroundings, she felt a strong sense of hostility emanating from several sources in the darkness around her. She snatched out mentally, counting the hulking forms that met her search... Five, six, seven Cyrwin, including Tobin's mount.

All radiating anger. All resentful.

The young Cadarnian seemed to have them under control. He returned his focus to the dark, his bearing alert, intent. The Cyrwins grudgingly followed suit.

With the creatures focused in another direction, Kaphri took the opportunity to slide out from beneath the beast that towered over her. She slid on her back, inching warily away. Away from them all, while keeping her attention fastened on the young Kitahni warrior, wondering what held him so absorbed up that draw.

In a flicker of lightning, she saw a terrible bruise on his cheek and his swollen eye. More marks and dirt covered his arms. The way he sat on the Cyrwin's back told her the rest of his body was equally battered.

Uri's words from the caer came back to her. What had the young warrior endured in the company of these brutish creatures? Was he even the same warrior she had known these past weeks or had his experience with these forest beasts changed him into something else? What could she expect from him?

Impatience swirled through her. They had no time for this delay. They needed to go back for Seuliac.

Tobin had cut her off before she could tell him what had happened to the warlord. What did his comment, "it has been seen to," mean? Was it possible Seuliac survived the attack on the cliff top? And where were Uri and Frax and Velacy? What about pursuit by the tarmeuth and the Balandra?

A drop of rain, concentrated from the branches far above, struck her on the forehead. She gasped at the cold shock and lifted a hand to wipe it away.

The Cyrwin that had attacked her snorted, throwing its head up and shifting its footing on the soft forest floor as it focused its attention back on her.

Tobin locked on her instantly. "*Don't make a sudden movement like that again.*"

Kaphri lowered her arm while silently vowing to ignore the next drip.

The Cyrwin snorted again uneasily.

The warrior nodded, satisfied. "*You're learning.*"

"*Tobin—*"

He lifted a hand to stop her again and went back to staring up the hollow toward the hill crest.

The silence grew long, punctuated only by the rumble of thunder and the drone of rain on leaves far above. Kaphri sensed he was waiting for something before he acted further. Panic gnawed at her. Why this delay? Was he even aware of what had occurred this night?

He had her at a disadvantage, surrounded by these creatures. Could she expect the same behavior from him as before his disappearance into the woods? Was this even the younger Kitahn she addressed? He did not seem disposed toward killing her, so she must assume he and the Grimmenwood were not intent on destroying her at this moment.

What else, however, was being destroyed while they stood here in the middle of the wet forest?

She had to do something.

"*Tobin, the others,*" she sent firmly, determined that he would not ignore her. "*What about them? There was a tarmeuth on the escarpment...*" instinct told her not to mention the warlord.

"*Don't you mean what happened to Seuliac Aedec?*" Tobin's head snapped around, his sending full of scathing scorn as he glared. "*What a waste of concern. One less of Rhynog is good riddance.*"

"*She worries over the fate of an Aedec!*" The hostility swirling around her became almost tangible.

"*He was trying to save me—*" A circle of angry hisses cut off her protest.

"*Stow it, Priestess.*" Tobin dismissed her again as he shifted his attention back up the hillside above them.

This time she could hear something making its way noisily down the slope.

She reached in the direction of Tobin's stare, touching on a close knot of five Cyrwins moving toward them. There was another presence with them. Something familiar... Was it possible? She got to her feet and started forward a step in disbelief before remembering her situation. She stopped.

A few paces before reaching them, the group of Cyrwins broke apart to expose the lone figure in their midst. Dark stains smeared his face and body and matted his hair. Was it mud? Kaphri paled in the darkness, knowing better. It was blood, and the warlord was covered in it.

"*Warlord...*" Oblivious to the threat of the Cyrwins now, she took a step toward him.

"*Compose yourself,*" he snapped. "*You will not show weakness here.*"

Stung by the harsh reprimand, she froze.

The warlord did not even look in her direction. He raised his eyes to glare at Tobin through a tangle of wet, dark hair that she knew he dared not raise a hand to brush back. She could feel the fierce challenge burning in him.

For the first time, she saw the heavy coil of Cyrwin tail that wrapped his neck. It tightened and flexed, thrusting him forward. He fell to his knees, catching himself with his arms to keep from falling face down into the wet leaves.

Tobin flicked a finger, and the tail loosened and slid so that its tip hovered near the warlord's shoulder. The younger Geffitz stared down impassively for a long moment; then a slow, mocking smile twisted his lips. "Seuliac Aedec. Walking the Grimmenwood alone. You are either very bold—or very foolish."

Seuliac gave a rasping cough before he spoke. "Why don't you just get on with it, Kitahn? Your Grimmenwood obviously spared us for some purpose."

"*You will address the Cyrwinmaster with respect.*" The Cyrwin that had bound the warlord with its tail flicked the end so it caught Seuliac's jaw with the razor edge. Blood welled darkly to run down his neck.

Kaphri choked back her protest.

"How much blood have you shed in this place, Warlord?" Tobin grinned. "Do you know the ancient blood rhyme?"

Seuliac wiped the back of his hand along his chin where the rain and blood mixed. With a disdainful glare, he flicked his wrist, spraying flecks of crimson across the forest floor. "Take it, and be damned. You've bled too, Kitahn. Does that child's rhyme hold true for you?" He cut her a quick look.

Blood? How much control did the Grimmenwood actually have over Tobin?

Tobin laughed. "Save your anxiety for yourself. As far as I'm concerned, you have no purpose here, or anywhere. What was Frax thinking, bringing you into the Grimmenwood?"

"The Grimmenwood allowed it, so maybe it doesn't share everything it knows with you," Seuliac growled.

"Perhaps. Or maybe it was waiting for you to make your play. Where were you two going? Are your ambitions so high you'd abandon your clansman?"

"You—" Seuliac bit back the rest of his comment, seemingly aware his words would be wasted.

Meanwhile, Tobin's tone took on an even darker anger. "Answer my question, Rhynog. Where were you going?"

A chill of foreboding ran over her: this ridiculous Geffitzi posturing would only end one way if it went on, unchecked.

"*Tobin, stop it*!" She made her sending hard and strong.

She had waited too long. Tobin's next words stunned her. "Chaos-stepper, slay this scum."

Everything that happened next moved as if time slowed to a crawl. Kaphri took a step forward. The Cyrwin nearest her snorted and lifted its head in alarm. The rest of the big bodies milled around her, churning dangerously but giving way so that she had a clear space to their center where Seuliac stood. In a flicker of lightning, she saw the vicious barbed tail of a Cyrwin poised in the air. It slowly began to swing in for its fatal strike...

"No!" This time she screamed aloud, the cry projecting into the surge of power welling up inside her.

Control! The word snapped in her mind. You must control this thing! The image of smoke rising from charred flesh in the pouring rain flashed in her head. That would be a deadly mistake. She caught herself, pulling back her attack even as the barbed tail descended on the warlord.

It made her reaction too slow. The tail swung forward, its deadly sting ready.

As it curled to make the killing strike, Seuliac's left forearm was suddenly there, blocking it. There was a dull, sickening thud of flesh and bone meeting flesh and bone, followed by the Cyrwin's cry of pain. The cry became shriller when Kaphri's blast of energy hit the creature, sending crackling blue lines of power dancing over its scaly flesh.

Time snapped back to normal. Seuliac bent with silent pain as Tobin sent his mount surging toward her. She tried to step back, to avoid being trampled, but her body felt drained. Before she could move, he caught her by the throat, lifting her off the ground with one hand.

"You little bitch! I ought to kill you!" he snarled. His fingers tightened, cutting off her air as he leaned forward to glare into her face.

Ought? Kaphri was surprised she was still alive.

Despite the thunder of blood in her ears, her mind was spinning at a tremendous rate. That would mean—

"*But you will not,*" she sent at him narrowly. She glared defiantly into his gray eyes. "*You have your orders, Tobin. If the Grimmen wants me, the others must go, too. All of them. Unharmed.*"

She took a terrible gamble: if he killed her in a fit of rage because of her insolence, the Aedecs, at the very least, would certainly die.

His eyes narrowed slightly with surprise. "*So,*" the nasty smile lifted his lips again. "*You've started to grow fangs. Don't get too bold yet, girl; they're only milk teeth.*" He released her, thrusting her backward so she fell hard on her backside in the mud and leaves. The impact went unfelt as she sucked in a huge gulp of air.

He stared down at her. "*And don't be too sure of what I will or won't do.*" He twisted to look at Seuliac again. Between the columns of the Cyrwins legs, Kaphri saw the warlord slowly and painfully climbing to his feet. He held his left arm tucked close against his chest. The Cyrwin that had attacked him stood nearby, head lowered, its shoulder muscles quivering.

A stunned silence hung over the rest of the beasts.

Tobin gave a snort of irritation. "He is spared for now."

Kaphri snatched the opportunity to press her case. "*Then let us move, Tobin. The others may be under attack.*"

His attention came back to her, his mind shielded, his expression cold and calculating. Then he shrugged. "*True. We waste time on small pleasures we can delay. Get up.*"

As she stood, a Cyrwin stepped between her and Tobin's mount. Tobin leaned across the beast's back, his fingers reaching for her arm.

When she looked at him in confusion, he scowled. "*I thought you were in a hurry. You will ride Demon's Tongue.*"

Ride? One of these creatures? She took a step backward.

"You can't put her on that animal, Kitahn," Seuliac said sharply. "She doesn't know how to ride."

She looked up at Tobin, ignoring his outstretched hand. She would never dare the back of one of these huge, foul-tempered animals. But Seuliac—Seuliac looked barely able to stand. He needed to ride. He would never ask, and Tobin would never offer, even if it meant critical time lost. "*What about the warlord?*"

Tobin gave a hiss of impatience. "*He can walk.*"

"*No, he can't. He is injured. Let him ride. I will walk.*" She evaded Tobin's hand and walked around in front of the animal called Demon's Tongue with a bold defiance she did not feel, to take up a position beside the wearily sagging warlord.

Tobin glared. "*Don't push me, girl. You can't expect a Cyrwin to carry an Aedec.*"

A wall of outrage seethed in the creatures encircling them.

"*Then we'll both walk.*" She shot Seuliac a sideways glance.

"*It's too far and would take too long,*" Tobin said.

"*No longer for one than two.*" There was a compromise, if she could swallow her fear and suggest it. She looked at the younger Kitahn, still maintaining the boldness she did not feel. "*This creature you name Demon's Tongue can carry us both.*"

The vicious humor returned to Tobin's face. "*Yes. Why not? This could be an exquisite pairing.*"

The Cyrwin, Demon's Tongue, threw up its head, nostrils flaring. "*It is an Aedec!*"

Seuliac looked at the Cyrwin, an expression of arrogant distaste settling on his features as his eyes traveled over the animal appraisingly. "You could," he sneered, "carry a much less worthy warrior."

"*Just get on with it before I change my mind,*" Tobin snapped.

The creature looked as big as a mountain to Kaphri, but Seuliac seemed unperturbed as he stepped up to its side. "You have a wounded rider," he said. "Are you so ignorant of a war mount's training that you do not recognize that?"

Demon's Tongue bared teeth like serpent's fangs in displeasure but extended its nearest foreleg and bent in a half-kneel. The warlord managed an awkward but successful mount in one try. Finding his seat, he leaned down and put out his right hand to pull her up.

He smiled without humor when she hesitated. "*You can't stop now,*" he sent to her. "*You'll lose whatever face you gained here.*"

He didn't have to explain: hostile, wary expectation burned in the air around her. Stiffening mentally, she extended her hand, and he swung her up in front of him onto Demon's Tongue's back. Images of flailing hooves and screaming fury played through her mind briefly. These creatures did not want her here, and she did not want to be here.

"*Hang on.*" Seuliac slid his right arm around her stomach. There was a rocking sensation as the Cyrwin climbed back on its feet. Kaphri closed her eyes, her fingers tightening convulsively on the Warlord's forearm. "*And relax. I won't let you fall.*"

They moved forward with a lurch that made her heart race in terror. There was nothing for her to hold onto except Seuliac.

After a few moments of holding her ramrod-stiff body, he tried again. "*If you settle back and let your body move with the animal's motion, you'll be more comfortable. We actually enjoy riding, most days.*

"*Horses,*" he added as an afterthought.

Horses, Kaphri thought, not demon creatures with a deadly stinger and a vicious inclination toward biting.

Demon's Tongue, however, seemed to have taken the warlord's admonition on a warhorse's behavior to heart. Despite his demeaning load, the Cyrwin moved smoothly, and she gradually accepted the idea that she would not tumble off with the slightest jerk of movement. Her overtaxed muscles began to relax, ignoring her best efforts to fight them. Even the distance to the ground became less threatening while she sat, secure in the circle of Seuliac's arm.

Surely, she might even learn to enjoy this riding thing—if it were with the right person. An image of another warrior holding her close as they rode across a grassy plain like the ones around Windmer passed through her mind.

She pushed the thought away.

When they came up out of the shelter of the hollow, the wind and rain pounded them brutally. Kaphri looked down once to see dark stains running off her white breeches. She drew a startled breath, wondering if she'd been injured and not been aware of it; then she realized it was blood and mud washing off the Geffitz behind her. She stiffened, made aware of his presence again. She had never been comfortable around Seuliac, and now she was pressed against him with his blood washing onto her.

Seuliac shifted position behind her. "*Are you all right?*"

It wasn't that he asked the question; it was his tone, that said he was asking about her with the concern of a fellow warrior, the way Uri would have done, that brought an unexpected rush of warmth to her.

"*Bumps and bruises,*" she answered. "*I ran until I had to stop for breath. When I sensed the Cyrwins stalking me, I tried to defend, but I miscalculated and fell down the hill. They caught me at the bottom.*"

"*Defend. What were you going to do?*"

For a moment, she feared there might be an edge of sarcasm in his question, but she only found interest. And why not, she asked herself. He was supposed to be teaching her.

"*I tried to get my back against a large tree. But I stumbled and fell before I got there.*"

"*If you had succeeded, what would you have done?*"

"*I felt something building in me like the surge of power on the cliff top, but I didn't know what to do with it. I just hoped I could do something if I got the chance.*"

"*That blast of power—having used it twice now, can you control it better?*"

"*I'm beginning to learn.*"

"*Good,*" he observed wryly, "*because it feels like hot coals pouring over your body when it hits you.*"

"*Oh.*" She knew she had at least brushed him when she struck out at the Balandra. "*I'm sorry! I didn't—I tried... Were you hurt?*"

"*Not as badly as the Balandran.*" Did she detect a hint of dry amusement? "*My nerve endings still burn a bit, but I'm no worse than I was on the cliff. Let's just say that you still have a little—well, a lot!—of work to do on your targeting the next time you do whatever it is you do.*"

"*I did manage to control the second one better than the first,*" she ventured.

"*I should be grateful I wasn't cindered like that Balandran, then.*"

"*Oh, Hredroth!*" Now she had time to think; horror at what she'd done on the cliff top squeezed her. But she had been trying to protect Seuliac, and she'd no choice.

She twisted her head to look at him, "*What happened up there? How did you...?*"

"*A dubious, none-too-gentle rescue by our friends here. They drove the tarmeuth away. None of the Balandra survived them.*" An image of the Cyrwins crushing the winged creatures beneath their hooves made her shudder. "*That could have been me a few moments ago. Thanks.*"

"*What Tobin did is horrible,*" Anger burned in her.

She felt him shrug. "*A word of warning, Priestess: judging by his physical condition, Tobin Kitahn has bled several times over the last few days. I'm not offering excuses for the damned bastard, but if what Caspani said is true, we can't trust that he's acting completely as himself. We have to be very careful.*"

Blood twice shed. Not all the blood on the warlord might be his, but some of what oozed onto her was. He must realize it cast doubts on his future actions, too.

"*How seriously are you injured?*"

"*Did I bleed all over the ground, do you mean? No. I did not bleed until that damn thing cut my face. Am I myself? As far as I know. I don't feel a compulsion to embrace Tobin Kitahn and call him brother.*" She choked back a laugh at that comment. "*I can't say what will happen before this is done, but you did well to bring up the possibility. At least you're aware there could be a problem.*"

"*What should we do?*"

"*Nothing we can do except wait and see how this all plays out. We'll join up with the others: it's not smart to divide our forces right now. Stay alert and take note of everything that happens. And don't trust anything around you.*"

"Cut the chatter," Tobin ordered.

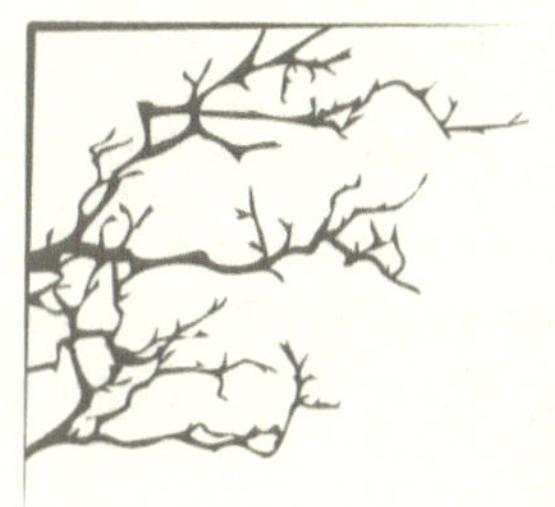

Chapter 78
Convergence

"*Why hasn't he come to?*" Velacy glared at Frax's unconscious body.

"*I don't know.*" The Cyrwins refused to let Uri treat Frax's wound.

"*They're Cadarn's demons.*" Uri had heard the observation several times in the last hour. "*You've got some Cadarnian blood. Why won't they listen to you?*"

"*I don't know,*" Uri repeated. Apparently, it hadn't occurred to the younger Aedec that Frax was an heir of Cadarn, and he certainly wasn't doing well at the moment. As for the rest of their group, Uri despaired to think about it.

"*If they're communicating with you—*"

Idiot Aedec. "*They're not.*"

The warning sweep of a barbed tail reduced them to mental silence.

The Cyrwins swung their heads southward and stood still as stone, focused on whatever had drawn their attention in the darkness.

"*Something's happening,*" Uri cautiously shifted to peer that direction. A flicker of lightning allowed him a brief glimpse of rain streaming over rocks and mud before a barb forced him to rock back into his original position.

The animals moved, spreading wider around them, leaving a narrow avenue open to whatever approached.

"*Stay where you are.*" The husky voice of the Cyrwin Uri had decided was the leader snapped in his head. "*Make no sudden or extreme moves.*"

Uri put a restraining hand on Velacy's knee in case the creature had not seen fit to include him in the warning. They were not above such treachery.

Rain ran off them in rivulets as they shivered on the ground, waiting.

"*What's going on?*" Uri asked, his heart pounding.

"*Silence! The Cyrwinmaster approaches.*"

Cyrwinmaster? What the hell? There would not have been a Cyrwinmaster in the Grimmenwood since the Geffitzi abandoned Caer Cadarn, along with the rest of the south. He doubted someone had survived here for twenty-odd years.

Could it be Tobin? The younger Kitahn might be able to reason with these stubborn beasts. He squinted, straining to see through the downpour and wondering where the lightning was when he needed it.

He caught movement out in the darkness. Willow? He'd seen a blur of white that could be her clothing, and, from the fleeting impression, she sat astride one of the Cyrwin.

But she was not a horsewoman. Only in recent weeks had she learned the role the animals similar to the Cyrwin played in Geffitzi life.

A flicker of lightning revealed a cluster of dark forms.

At the same moment, a mental presence burst inside his head. "*Uri! Velacy! Where is Frax? What has happened—?*" Kaphri's sending carried a shot of fear before it was abruptly curtailed.

He recognized the rider beside her. Tobin. The Cyrwinmaster? Relief, tempered with wariness, rushed through him. He had feared that was the purpose behind the younger Kitahn's abduction from Cadarn. Now the question was, how did it affect him? And, how would it affect the balance of other things, with Tobin having the backing of these creatures, which no Geffitzi, Cadarnian, or otherwise rightly considered sane or rational? The Cyrwins' violent temperament fit too easily with the younger warrior's fiery disposition.

Many times over the past weeks Frax and Tobin had disagreed on their plan of action. What would happen now?

Eldren interference, he thought bitterly. Again.

"Let me go!" Kaphri fought to slide from the Cyrwin's back. Uri watched with a knot of dread in his stomach as she tumbled from her mount to land on her hands and knees in the mud. Kep knew what a Cyrwin strike would do to her small, alien physiology. But the beasts did not react when she struggled back to her feet. Smearing muddy hands on her thighs, she waded forward. Amazingly, the Cyrwins around them widened their circle to allow her passage.

Seuliac slipped down more gracefully to follow. Uri noted he held one arm bent close to his chest.

"*Uri, Velacy,*" she brushed them mentally to confirm they were unharmed, but she moved past them to squat beside Frax. She looked up at Uri. "*What's wrong with him?*"

"*Cyrwin sting.*"

She twisted to look back at Tobin. "*Was all this necessary?*"

Tobin dismounted and strode forward to fill the gap behind her. "*To stop them doing something stupid, yes.*"

A chill ran down Uri's spine at the emotional detachment in the sending. No greeting. No expression or sense of concern. Was this his cousin, or was it some strange, possessed creature of the wood?

The younger Kitahn was only a black silhouette in the darkness.

Uri stood. "*Tobin. You are well?*"

The shadowy form gave a short nod in his direction.

No mindtouch in response. Uri's uneasiness heightened. "*What's going on here?*"

"*Now we're all together again—and intact, we can move on.*"

The ugly edge to the sending dismayed Uri. "*Move on to where?*"

"*Where are you going?*"

The younger warrior knew as much about their destination as they did, maybe more. "*Why are the Cyrwins here, Tobin?*"

"*The Grimmen has decided to extend its assistance.*"

"*Assistance.*" Not good, Uri thought, recalling Wyxan interference.

"*Your enemies have found you. The Cyrwins will escort and defend you.*"

"*And we can go where we need to, unchallenged?*" Uri demanded. The Grimmen would not step up to selflessly aid them. More likely, it was because they were moving beyond its realm of direct influence and it wanted to establish a stronger hold over the situation.

"*You may go where this one,*" there was a shadowed nod at Kaphri, "*is required.*"

Uri scowled. "*Help, with stipulations? No, thank you.*"

Tobin's indifferent mental shrug relayed a clear message: they had no choice. The Grimmen offered, and they could not refuse.

Kaphri stood. Soaked with rain, her clothes plastered to her body, she looked like a child among all the larger creatures, Geffitzi and Cyrwin, that surrounded her. Still, something in her movements radiated an air that would not be ignored.

It was something, Uri thought, that had not been there before.

What happened up on the cliff top, he wondered.

"*Can youwake Frax?*" Kaphri asked.

"*He'll come around eventually.*"

"*We make no plans without him, Tobin,*" she said.

Tobin glanced left, toward the escarpment towering over them. "*A tarmeuth is stalking the ridge above us. Even a Cyrwin risks injury or death in an encounter with it. We are moving across the river.*"

Only a large body of water would stop the tarmeuth's pursuit, Velacy had told them. If the Cyrwins offered a safe passage over the storm-swollen river, they should not refuse.

A rush of relief ran through him when she answered. "*We will go that far. No further.*"

"*You will ride with me. Uri can tend to Frax.*"

"*But—Seuliac and Velacy...*" The omission was glaringly obvious.

"*The Aedecs remain here.*"

A jolt of dismay ran through Uri. The younger Cadarnian's words were not unexpected. Considering Rhynog's history with Caer Cadarn, he was surprised Seuliac had made it alive this far in the company of these deadly creatures. Still, the action seemed unnecessarily harsh.

And Frax would not allow it.

But Frax was not awake.

Sensing Velacy's outrage rising. Uri flashed the younger Rhynogian a furious warning. If ever there was a time to remain silent, this was it. These creatures were looking for a reason to strike him down. The Priestess seemed to have things in hand. Let these two of their companions, who suddenly and strangely appeared to be on somewhat equal footing, settle this matter.

Seuliac's silence reinforced his reasoning.

Kaphri did not miss a heartbeat in her response. "*We all go together, Tobin.*"

"*The Grimmen does not include them in its offer of assistance.*"

"*Are you suggesting we leave them here?*"

"*Dead or alive. The Grimmen doesn't specify.*" Tobin shrugged.

TOBIN WANTED TO ABANDON Velacy and Seuliac on this side of a rising river, with an angry tarmeuth stalking them.

Anger overpowered her wash of horror. First the Wyxa, and now this Grimmen and its minions, with their ruthless resolutions! Frax had warned her that the Eldren did not think the same as Geffitzi. Well, think the same or not, they were dealing with the current denizens of this world, including her, and this was not how she chose to handle things.

"*I told you, they are part of this group,*" she said. "*They go with us. Unharmed.*"

"*That's not for you to say,*" Tobin snapped.

With Frax down and Uri sidelined by the Grimmen as irrelevant to the situation, Kaphri was on her own. She must persuade Tobin to let the Aedec warriors live—or be prepared to back up her position some other way. "*It is for me to say, Tobin, if the Grimmen wants me to go with you.*"

What had this Grimmen-being done to Tobin's mind? She refused to believe he was acting totally under his own volition. The scout had always been confrontational, yes, but never this coldly bloody-handed.

Then, she remembered that he sometimes argued for killing her, too.

She realized the Cyrwins were subtly shifting, concentrating their positions around the two Rhynogians. The threat to the Aedec warriors' lives appeared to be even more immediate than the tarmeuth.

Instinct flared a sudden warning. Where were all the beasts positioned? Her mind swept out.

One of them had maneuvered directly at her back. She could feel the slow rise of its tail, the positioning of the venomous tip. Movement flashed—the same sensation as one of Seuliac's cursed clods of dirt flying at her back.

The creatures leveled the same attack at Seuliac and Velacy.

Her brain reacted automatically. Everything in that ring of massive Cyrwin flesh must lose the ability to move!

All the Cyrwins around them froze.

"You bitch!" The younger Kitahn took a step toward her, hand on the knife at his belt.

"*Do not!*" She snapped a mental warning. He stopped of his own accord, but his eyes glittered rage.

"*Seuliac, Velacy! Come here.*" She sensed out behind her, a chill running down her spine when she touched on the barb within arm's length of striking distance behind her. She took a step closer to Tobin, away from it. "*Uri, you too. We must come to an understanding right now.*"

The three warriors remained mentally guarded as they gathered around her to face Tobin.

"The Cyrwins can't breathe," he snarled furiously. "You're killing them."

Of course! She had simply frozen all movement indiscriminately. "*Tell them to gather into one group, six times striking distance away from us. Tell them if any of them makes a move to attack any of us, ever again, I will strike them all, and the next time, I won't release them. Tell them!*"

Tobin spat a few words in Geffitzi—words she did not catch the meaning of. She glanced at Uri, and he nodded.

As she removed the power that held them in stasis, the creatures staggered and sagged, their ribcages billowing as they sucked air.

"*Get them away from us.*" She surprised herself with her lack of sympathy. They would have killed or immobilized her and the others in a heartbeat. They deserved whatever it took to control them.

"*Uri, please make sure nothing else approaches us.*" The Cyrwins weren't the only dangerous animals in the area.

"*Done,*" he sent back with a sense of approval.

"*Seuliac, if Tobin does something that makes you uneasy, disable him. Disable. Not kill.*"

"*Understood,*" Seuliac answered sardonically. "*Kitahn, lower your hands to your sides. Slowly.*" He was enjoying this sudden shift in their situations. But then, he was responsible for it, wasn't he—him and his clod-throwing tactics.

"*Frax,*" she had been aware of his growing mental presence for a few minutes now. Was the Commander of the Edge coherent enough to understand what was happening around him? Where did his allegiances lie? Would he side with her against his brother, against his family's ancient ally? "*You are still in command here. You should know: I do not intend to go anywhere that we all do not go freely and without a threat of danger beyond what we already face from Araxis. Please make Tobin understand that.*" Frax could phrase it more effectively, without stirring so much ill feeling.

"*You heard her, brother,*" the sending was weak but clear. "*Give her assurances for the safety of us all, and you might get the results you want.*"

Tobin's eyes never left her face. "*You are choosing them over family alliances?*"

"*No, Tobin,*" there was a slight cough and a mental wince of pain. "*I'm choosing to keep my word. They are allies, and allies are remarkably scarce right now; we need all we can get.*"

Scowling, the younger Kitahn looked away, staring off into the stormy darkness as if he were listening for something. "*The Grimmen agrees,*" he said, shifting his attention back to them. "*The Rhynogians will come with us. But there will be a reckoning on this.*"

Kaphri was sure there would be.

His word given, however, Tobin moved on with swift efficiency. He summoned the Cyrwins back, ordering them without elaboration to cooperate, then assigned mounts, putting Uri and

Frax both on a creature named Dervish so the now-conscious commander would have assistance if he became dizzy or ill.

Again, the animals resisted carrying the Aedecs. When Seuliac approached his mount, Demon's Tongue, it flattened its ears and stared back at him with eyes that glinted redly in the darkness.

"*Down, creature! Do you need another lesson in manners?*" The Cyrwin bared its fangs again, but it was already lowering its big body. Its back was still awkwardly high for Kaphri, so the warlord clasped her about the waist and set her firmly on it, then climbed on behind her. "Up."

The lurch of the animal gaining its feet sent her sharply back against him. She pulled upright, her back rigid, her face burning. Now that the immediate crisis was over, all her senses felt magnified by the release of tension. Close contact with Seuliac's body made her too aware of her own flesh.

Speaking of which—Hredroth! What had she just done? She had confronted Tobin and his Grimmen-backed forces and forced them to submit to her demands. Was she insane, challenging a Geffitz warrior like that? Delayed reaction caused her to begin to shake uncontrollably.

Seuliac had warned her earlier: she would lose everything she gained in this encounter if she exhibited weakness. Tobin and the Cyrwins would be waiting for that. From now on, she must think through every action she made carefully. One misstep and she could destroy the Aedec warriors as well as herself.

The nausea faded, but it left a terrible, cold place in the pit of her stomach. Damn Tobin! Damn these Cyrwin and damn Frax! She didn't need them. She didn't need this.

And she didn't want to be here on this creature's back with the warlord's body pressing against hers and adding more confusing thoughts and reactions to the long list of things that terrified her.

Velacy's Cyrwin was still adamantly resisting the warrior's attempts to mount.

Seuliac looked over at Tobin. "Are we in a hurry?" he asked pointedly.

"Firevenom! Cooperate!" Tobin cast a dark glare at Seuliac, but the warlord had shifted his attention to Kaphri.

"*Easy on the wiggling,*" he sent wryly when she tried to lessen the amount of contact between them.

She froze, her cheeks instantly coloring. She did not fully understand the impact of her movements, but she understood the spirit of the comment. Still, her wet clothing was twisted and knotted uncomfortably under her.

With an exaggerated sigh, the warlord tugged the bunched tunic from beneath her bottom, then, unceremoniously grasping her buttocks, he situated her in front of him.

She did not see the mocking smile he shot Uri over her head as he slid an arm about her waist and pulled her back against him.

Uri's expression went thunderous. "Now what?" he snarled at Tobin.

Velacy finally managed to get astride Firevenom.

"We cross the river. Then we shall see."

Yes, Kaphri thought unhappily, then we shall see.

End Part 3
THE STORY CONTINUES in Part 4, Taking It All

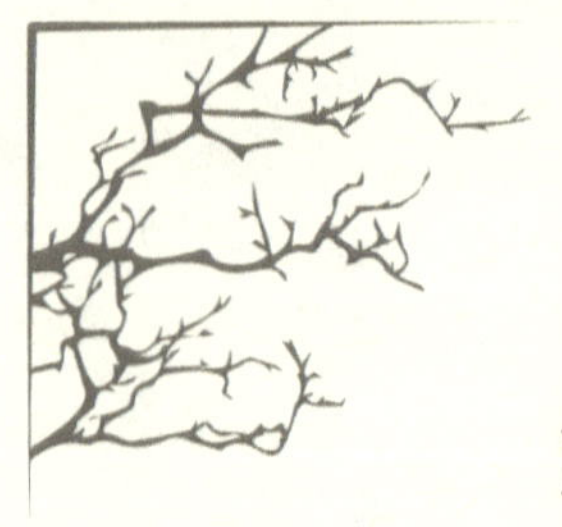

Taking It All
First Chapter
Chapter 79
Razek

Razek's metal spur-caps clicked against stone he as made his way along the veranda. Normally, the crisp staccato pleased him greatly. Today, outrage occupied the whole of his attention.

Six more lost and a new threat emerged—all because the fool would not take his counsel. Fury boiled inside him. Did the imbecile think their forces were unlimited?

Since his predecessor, Clackamas, had made that ill-conceived drive into the swamp on a mission of revenge two thousand years too late and lost half their force, their numbers were severely curtailed and dwindling with every failed attempt—their worst defeat brought about by, of all things, a forest! Imminent disaster hung over them.

He would have begged the right to kill the Ly Kai, to remove a major obstacle to their success, but the Master made it very clear: the small, pale one must believe he was in charge at all times. Razek could only bow, put on a respectful face and mask his frustration while he wondered what his Master planned.

Hopefully, it would be a long, excruciating end for the hated Ly Kai vermin.

Let me have my vengeance when the time comes, he pled fervently in his mind. *Reward me with some time to avenge the insults and humiliation your forces have endured daily.*

But even in his weakened state, the arrogant creature who thought it gave him orders could burn them all to a crisp with just a simple flick of desire. Curse his power! Araxis was an inferior physical and mental specimen. The tiny dart the Geffitz warrior delivered back at the Black Tower had left him more fragile. Razek did concede the poison might have been more potent than the Geffitzi used on the female as Araxis still languished while the girl moved on with annoyingly healthy speed. Razek knew that firsthand: he'd witnessed the whole attack last night.

They'd appeared on the brink of success. The Geffitzi had come out of the shadows of that cursed woods and down an open cliff face into an area of ordinary forest. With no silent, unseen deadly ally to protect them, it was only a matter of time before the Balandra struck and seized the girl.

Then things fell apart.

A flicker of movement along the top of the cliff had drawn them in to investigate. Now, bitterly, Razek realized it had been an overwhelmingly vicious beast stalking their same prey.

His troop was examining the area where their elusive targets had left the forest and descended the rock face while Razek, testing the treacherous air currents of the escarpment for a safe descent, flew out past the boulder.

He'd seen the Ly Kai female and one of the Geffitzi appear out of nowhere, startling his troop. The girl had run for the shelter of the forest while the Geffitz stayed to defend her escape. Before slipping into the shadows, however, she had turned and ruthlessly burned one of the Balandra to a char with that cursed power.

Then, the beast struck.

The attack was magnificent—Razek grudgingly had to admit that. The creature arrived so swiftly and unexpectedly that all the Balandran captain could do was watch it destroy his men with awesome, ruthless efficiency.

Then, on the cusp of that destruction, the cursed animals from the woods emerged to chase the beast away. They took the Geffitz warrior captive and—the ultimate humiliation—ground the remains of his troop into the mud of the cliff top.

Razek was not sentimental. He would have left the bodies of his fallen troops without a thought. But the action of those four-legged vipers, desecrating them, had been an insult he'd been forced to endure, unanswered, so he could bring news of another failure back to the despicable creature who thought it commanded him. News which, in further insult, had been put on hold until the Ly Kai considered the time convenient to hear it.

Convenient! There was nothing convenient about dealing with Araxis! It was only a long stream of bad temper, poor judgment, and sulks. Razek expected nothing useful from the upcoming encounter—just more rage and threats—which made him angrier. Balandra did not live under threat. Other creatures lived in fear of them! That was the order of the world. His world.

But this was not his world. Razek slapped at a buzzing insect—the biting, bloodsucking things were a plague in this bog of a place—and looked about. He hated the lush green of the living forest that pressed in around the stone structures Araxis had chosen for their refuge. He hated the sentient threat of it. Immobile things that grew from the ground should not have a presence. They were for shelter and burning, or fodder for the meat he hunted. Plants definitely should not act with considered thought.

The woods here was not the same as the thing that lay further south—the thing that had taken his forces in silent, stealthy ways over the past days—but he knew it also listened and watched.

Razek reached the end of the wide stone veranda and stopped, facing a huge set of double doors heavily carved with bas relief images. Metal warriors hunted strange creatures and fought horrific battles across the bronze surface. Obviously, this place once served as some sort of temple for the savage creatures that called themselves Geffitzi. It was surprising they managed such an intricate piece of artwork, Razek thought critically as he raised a hand to strike the ornate surface. Inferior creatures that they were, the door showed they at least respected the art of death.

But then, they had learned all the requisite skills for art and death as slaves under a very discerning, demanding master, hadn't they?

The doors swung open at the hands of two of his troops stationed inside the building. Araxis insisted on having an armed guard within his sight at all times. Razek considered it a senseless waste of resources for a creature who could slay anything around it with a blink of an eye, but it also, diabolically, worked in his favor. Feeding the Ly Kai's paranoia, making him feel under threat, made him less likely to strike out in the heat of passion against the diminishing number of Balandran warriors around him, a further deterioration in self-control he was lately exhibiting.

Could the Ly Kai worm ever appreciate the symbolic honor a Balandran armed guard represented? Razek doubted it. What sort of honor did the wretched, fragile creature command with its endless whining, petty demands, and foul temper? Given free rein, Razek would have snapped his thin neck and gone after the cursed Geffitzi warriors in an all-out attack. That plan of action more suited his tastes. Kill them all, take the girl, and start a long-delayed campaign of revenge and retribution on this world.

He looked forward to that. A simple strategy: make these creatures suffer. Make them all suffer for what their ancestors had dared do to the great Balandran race two thousand years ago. It would be slow and it would be agonizing. It would be pure pleasure for him.

The doors softly thudded behind him and Razek paused, allowing his eyes to adjust to the darkness of the chamber. He ran a narrow gray tongue over his thin lips to dampen them. He hated to speak the bastard language that strained his upper throat with its awkward sounds, but he had no choice. It was the only way to communicate with the Ly Kai.

Araxis was sitting at the far end of the shadowy room, next to a window. Irritation curled in Razek. The miserable little beast was killing whatever living creatures ventured into the area around that end of the building.

Razek did not care whether the creatures of this world lived or died, but the forest around them, though not as sentient as the vicious woods in the south, was still awake. It might have the capacity to retaliate if it suffered damage beyond what it considered tolerable, which was why Razek's troops took the time and effort to hunt over a wide range of territory and to kill sparingly.

While this miserable creature sat and picked at the same scab repeatedly.

As Razek stopped a discreet distance from the Ly Kai, he saw a flutter of movement outside as yet another small animal fell victim to Araxis' whim. There were charred scrub trees and undergrowth visible beyond the veranda wall where his forces had stomped out a fire the Ly Kai started the previous day in a fit of pique. Several of his men still limped from minor burns suffered in the incident.

"The forest is alive in this area," he observed stiffly. "We should avoid drawing its attention." He would have rather grabbed the Ly Kai and cuffed it up beside the head, calling it the fool it was. Instead, he made a slight, conciliatory bow.

Araxis twisted to scowl at him and Razek had the satisfaction of seeing his face was spotted with the welts of insect bites, too. "If your forces did what they were ordered to do, we would not be here and I would not have to resort to crushing vermin for entertainment."

Indeed. Did the worm think he would be crushing Balandra instead? Or perhaps he harbored thoughts of running away from certain obligations. The Ly Kai was not nearly as clever or subtle as he thought. Razek lowered his head, as much to hide a sly smile as to feign respect. At the end of this wretched endeavor, he would give this creature a lesson or two in inflicting pain for entertainment.

The Ly Kai swatted at an insect on its arm. "Well, what do you want?" The question rang out querulously in the high, hollow space of the stone chamber.

Araxis was on edge. Razek's mood elevated slightly. Perhaps he was feeling the pressure of the situation. It also meant Razek should exercise extra caution in their encounter: it would not be good for this creature to kill him out of sheer spite.

"Lord," he bobbed his head deeper to indicate greater humility and respect. "I bring news."

"But not the thing that I asked you to bring." Fabric rustled as the Ly Kai adjusted his position forward to glare at him.

"No, Lord. New foes have entered the battle. Our forces were attacked and ripped to shreds—"

"What?" Now the creature surged to its feet, its pale face even whiter than usual. "What attacked them? Not her—"

Razek looked back up. "No, Lord," he said. He wanted to lie and say she had struck out at them, just to see what reaction it drew. For him to insist they pursue his quarry so relentlessly, the Ly Kai behaved as if he were terrified of it. Razek often wondered how Araxis would react if forced to confront the girl face-to-face, the way he demanded of the Balandra.

It didn't matter: Razek received his orders from a higher source, and he acted on them for the Master, not for this fool. "A large animal, stalking our target, fell upon our forces. It moved with swift and deadly precision, pulling them out of the air—"

"What animal? Tell me what happened, you stupid fool!" Light reflected dully off the tarnished stars of the Ly Kai's robes as he quivered in a sudden fit of rage.

And fear. The Ly Kai stank of it. Razek drank it up, relishing the other's distress. "Some new, extremely dangerous creatures suddenly emerged from the cursed woods. I fear the force that reigns there has its own agenda."

"First you said the forest protected them. Now you say something else has come to interfere. I am tired of excuses. I want her brought to me!"

Razek did not bother to mask the anger on his gray, wrinkled features now. "We lost more resources! This cannot continue. We must use more caution. We must plan better."

"You must plan better, Razek! I want that girl. Bring her. How difficult can that be?"

More difficult than the Ly Kai thought. "The situation is changing. She acted to defend last night."

"Liar! I would have felt it."

Razek paused for a moment to fight the dizzying rush of fury that rolled over him.

"She burned one of my men to a cinder," he said. If Araxis did not understand what they were up against, he was of no use to the Master. He should be listening and suggesting strategies, the fool!

"It was not starpower! One of those other vile creatures you speak of must have acted." Araxis did not look as confident as he sounded.

The Balandran gritted his sharp teeth. "I cannot say. Before my forces could react, the creatures from the forest emerged to drive the animal off. Then they attacked and ripped my warriors to shreds."

"They did not harm her—"

"She fled. They took her companion, a Geffitz, prisoner and returned to the forest."

"You are sure she came to no harm?" The Ly Kai persisted, his whole body rigid with tension.

Razek ducked his head again to hide his fury. The vile creature did not even bother to ask after the loss of his own forces. "I can only say they returned to the forest." Razek knew about the four-legged, poison-tailed creatures from ancient times. They were deadly, cold killers, just like Balandra: which was why he felt such dismay at their sudden appearance. The Geffitz warriors, away from the protection of their cursed forest, he could handle. This new development complicated things.

"Where is she now?"

"The storm, coupled with these new threats... I lost them in the darkness."

"I want her brought here, Captain. No more delays! Your master promised me." Araxis settled back on his stone seat, scratched at a red welt, and glared.

Yes, the Master had promised him. But the Ly Kai seemed to forget his own half of the agreement.

"She appears to be going to the city. We can lay a trap there—"

"Captain, I want her here! Bring her to me. I do not care what it costs you. Bring her here!"

"Of course, milord." Razek bowed again in the face of that fury and turned to leave.

"It is impossible to get anything done with such incompetent fools," he heard the Ly Kai mutter behind him.

Razek's mouth tightened. They could not afford another quick, ill-conceived strike. The girl was growing in confidence and ability, pushed by their repeated, ineffectual tactics. The Master had warned: if things continued, she could become stronger than the physical form Araxis currently occupied. It might have already happened since the Ly Kai didn't appear to have noticed her deadly action last night. If so, all might be lost to them.

Whatever he did, he must do it fast, before this Ly Kai fool grew totally impatient and destroyed everything. Turning back, he made another effort to guide Araxis onto a more desirable, less obstructive path. "This place is unfit for habitation, milord. Let us carry you to your city. You would be more comfortable there while you wait." If the Ly Kai was ensconced in his mysterious city, perhaps he would find distractions that would allow Razek to do what needed to be done without the pressure of reporting his every move.

"What do you know of the city?" Araxis bristled.

It was interesting how defensive he became at any mention of the place. "I sent scouts to investigate it—"

"I gave no order!'

"No, Lord, you did not." Razek managed to maintain a patient tone. "It is a necessary precaution. We must know the state of the place, so that we do not walk into something, unprepared. The Geffitzi will move toward the city quickly if these new creatures join forces with them. We should secure the place before they arrive."

"You are not to go there unless I order it! I want her captured before she gets that far. How difficult is that? I will not walk into that place with less than my rightful Power."

"We are trying, Lord."

"Well, try harder. Your incompetence is astounding. And stay away from the city! It belongs to me." Araxis appeared to be working himself into a fit of hysterics.

"Of course, milord." Razek lowered his head in a conciliatory gesture to hide his pleasure at the other's obvious distress. "However," he continued, "you should know, everything appears intact and in working order." He peered from under spiky eyebrows to savor the reaction.

"You went inside?" The Ly Kai went so pale Razek thought he might pass out.

"Our Master would not be pleased if we allow you to walk into a trap." He wondered if Araxis even noted his use of the word 'our.'

He doubted the arrogant creature ever applied the term to include himself. He should.

"You fool; you do not do anything without my order! Do you understand?" the Ly Kai shouted in rage. "I wish Clackamas was still here. He knew how to take orders."

Razek felt a curl of scornful amusement: Araxis interacted with the demoted Balandran captain every day and did not recognize him now that he had stepped back into the ranks. Hatred burned inside the Balandran captain. When the day finally came... "If you will excuse me?"

Araxis glared at him. "Where are you going?"

"To collect reports. We have observers out, assessing this change in our situation." Again, he put a slight emphasis on 'our.'

"Stop observing and get the girl." The Ly Kai turned his back, refocusing his attention on the dreary landscape outside the window in a rude gesture of dismissal.

"By your leave." Razek did not wait for a response.

The guards opened the doors on the gray light of day. It was still raining, but the deadly lightning storm of the previous night had ended.

As soon as the captain cleared the portico he loosed his wings and took two running steps into the yard. His leathery extensions billowed, and he caught the air in a huge down flap that lifted him speedily. He had no reason to mask his fury now as he flew over several buildings in the ancient Geffitzi complex to the structure the Balandran troops were using as living quarters.

Several of his men tended their weaponry under the shelter of the porch. They scrambled to their feet and stood at stiff attention when he lighted in the yard. He flicked his wings, scattering a spray of water over them as he walked past, then re-tightened the appendages onto his back. None of the Balandra made a sound or changed expression.

The rest of his steadily dwindling force slept in the front two rooms of the building. He stalked through and shoved the door to his own quarters so hard it rebounded off the wall with a satisfying boom.

"Is that necessary?" a voice asked peevishly from the shadows on the far side of the chamber.

"Apologies, Master." Razek dropped comfortably into his mother tongue.

"Well?"

"He did not acknowledge noticing any use of her power last night. He will not change."

There was the sound of soft, dry laughter. Balandran laughter. "That is the beauty of it, my Captain. His arrogance will not allow him to consider that his choices might be in error." The other Balandra limped forward, into the light. He was older than Razek and shorter, his body bent from a past injury. Deep scars crosshatched his sinewy body. In form, it was the very Clackamas whose loss Araxis lamented so vocally moments before. In reality, however, he was something far more sinister.

Razek's companion was already aware of the previous night's events, having been apprised of them far sooner than Araxis.

"Send a few of your force out to monitor our targets, Captain, but warn them, they must not be seen. That fool of a Ly Kai need not know about it. We will soon defang this little serpent of ours and finish this..."

The story continues in Taking It All

ACKNOWLEDGEMENTS

My writing journey began a long time ago, and though there were times when I could not devote time to the process, it was always present at the edge of my mind, like puzzle pieces turning to fit the whole. There are people that kept me moving forward along the way, from my high school friend, Brenda Kirk, to Joan Summers, to the members of our local writing critique group, past and present, the SKY Writers—especially Noel Barton, Gerry Harlan Brown, Kimberly Bartley, and John Bowers—all published authors. I would not have been so bold as to believe I could do this without your inspiration. And then there's Sam, my loving husband who has always been here to support me with anything I needed to get the job done.

I sincerely thank you all.

Cover art by Tudor Popa

Photo by Will McCloud Photo

Don't miss out!

Visit the website below and you can sign up to receive emails whenever Bobbie Falin publishes a new book. There's no charge and no obligation.

https://books2read.com/r/B-A-JJHN-VEVJB

Also by Bobbie Falin

The Starchild Series

Taking the Stars

Taking Control

Taking the World

Taking It All

Standalone

Flashing Dark

Watch for more at https://www.bobbiefalin.com.

About the Author

Bobbie Falin wields magic, thwarts evil forces, pilots sleek ships through space, drinks and carouses with aliens in shabby station bars, and wanders the worlds of other writers with wide-eyed wonder—in her head. Here on Earth, well that's different. Here, she records Kaphri's adventures in the Starchild Series, stows away on the *Thief's Hand*, and complicates Gideon Rhue and Mei's life in Deformation. She still feeds the local stray cats who show up for breakfast and dinner every day, and, yes, it's unreservedly true; if there were a space program to explore the stars, She'd be first in line.

Read more at https://www.bobbiefalin.com.

www.ingramcontent.com/pod-product-compliance
Lightning Source LLC
LaVergne TN
LVHW050929080826
845145LV00001B/268

* 9 7 8 1 7 3 6 6 4 2 2 5 2 *